Knot Your Possession
Pack Origins – Book 3
L.A. Clyne

Copyright © 2023 L.A. Clyne

All rights reserved.

No portion of this book may be reproduced in any form without written permission from the publisher or author, except as permitted by copyright law.

All characters in this publication are fictitious and any resemblance to real persons, living or dead, is purely coincidental.

ISBN: 978-0-6456117-6-2

Cover art: L.A. Clyne

Reach me at: www.laclyne.com

Join me at: L.A. Clyne's Tribe (private Facebook group)

Follow me on:

Facebook www.facebook.com/l.a.clyne.author

Instagram www.instagram.com/laclyne_author

Pinterest www.pinterest.com.au/laclyneauthor

Dedication

I couldn't have gotten this book written without the wonderful readers who have sought me out to tell me how much they love this world and these characters.
Especially the kind, supportive members of my reading tribe.
When I lost my way a little, your encouragement got me back on the right path again, and reminded me why I started writing. For the stories, and the lives we live within them.
It may have been just a comment to you, a passing moment in your life. But to me, it meant the world.
So thank you. This one's for you.
xxx

Content advice

This is a reverse harem, omegaverse romance written with multiple points of view. It features a feral alpha, mysterious twin alphas, a sweet beta, a rare male omega, and a quiet female omega with a hidden strength that unites them all.

Each book in the Pack Origins series has a new pack with a happily ever after, while continuing the apocalyptic background story of the Crash. While they can be read as standalones, it's highly recommended to read in order, so you get the most out of the storyline.

If it's been a while since you read Knot Your Princess, or Knot Your Problem, check out the catch-up chapter. The characters from both feature heavily in this book. So, the family dynamics may get confusing if you've forgotten the earlier packs going into this story.

The story contains MF, MFMMMM, and MMMFMM spicy scenes, and the heroine doesn't have to choose between her men.

While this is not a dark romance, there are references to past institutional abuse and forced matings previously condoned by society. However, there is no abuse within the packs or the community they have built.

If any of the above makes you uncomfortable, it's okay if this isn't the book for you. Take care of yourself and enjoy your day. Otherwise, happy reading.

Need a catch-up?

Has it been a while since you read either Knot Your Princess or Knot Your Problem? If so, here's a quick re-cap of how this omegaverse world works. I've also included details of the Crash, the Omega Palace, and what went down with Maia and Lexie's packs that apply to this story.

If not, skip this part. You're good. I won't tell anyone. If you're still with me, here goes.

In the **Pack Origins** world, people once prized omegas but now treated them as chattel for breeding. They couldn't own property or live independently. Forced matings had resulted in omega fertility rates falling, as omegas no longer had heats. Omegas were more likely to have an omega or an alpha child. Betas still could, but it's always been rare. Betas now far outnumbered alphas and omegas.

An alpha's dominance bark could make a beta, omega, and even a weaker alpha submit to them. They expressed their bark through a growl, a word, or a sound. Beta society frowned upon alphas using their dominance bark, so an alpha had to be stealthy about doing it. Regardless, betas revered alphas. They usually ended up in the military, as CEOs, or in the upper echelons of society.

The Omega Palace promoted themselves publicly as an elite finishing school. In reality, it was a mandatory boot camp that brainwashed omegas into believing they were submissive. Secret, forced submissions were common for any omegas who didn't comply with their teachings. As soon as an omega presented during puberty, the Palace took them from their families, sometimes forcefully. Then confined them away from society and, as they grew older, taught them how to please an alpha.

After an omega turned twenty-one, the Palace presented them to society at a series of glamorous balls and parties to help them find a mate. It was a barbaric free-for-all where invited alphas picked their favorite scented omega and barked them into submission. Usually after money had changed hands. To the outside world, omegas appeared to live like princes and princesses at the Palace. Yet, they had no freedom or choice.

Alphas historically lived together as a pack with an omega. Until the Palace deemed them too dangerous, and the government outlawed them.

In **Knot Your Princess**, the electricity went out in a world-wide event people called the Crash. The government and military were nowhere to be seen, and anarchy descended. Maia was a captive at the Palace. They studied, and at times tortured her, because she was unique. The only omega who could deny an alpha's bark. She escaped during the Crash and found refuge on a sustainable, off-grid farm. While there, she met her mates, Damon, Leif, Hunter, and Max.

Damon was initially fearful of them all pursuing Maia because of the danger it would bring. However, the guys talked him round and Maia eventually broke through his defenses. Maia had an ancient book she'd stolen from the Palace, that helped them understand pack dynamics and what it meant when Maia went into heat. It also revealed that Damon was a prime alpha. A rare type of alpha that had long died out and was now legend. Prime alphas were highly dominant and could bark multiple other alphas into submission at once.

Ronan ran the secret labs at the Palace and had become obsessed with Maia. He was unwilling to let her go when she escaped, so he tracked her down. He stormed the farm with a rogue military unit to steal her back. His sister, Sirena, was a secret spy at the farm, but turned on her brother to help save Maia. The guys reluctantly agreed to allow Maia to act as bait to draw the soldiers out and reveal valuable intel. When Ronan threatened her life, Damon barked the entire group of soldiers into submission and killed him.

In **Knot Your Problem**, Lexie is Leif's sister and lives on the farm. She met Maia's long-lost brother Sam, and his best friend Dio, when they turned up unexpectedly at the farm to rescue Maia just before the attack. Sam and Dio discovered the farm was also a secret haven for abused women Lexie had rescued. While attempting a rescue in the nearby town, Lexie came across Pala. He'd been working undercover at the Palace and was the childhood friend of Sam and Dio. All three men felt an immediate true mate bond with Lexie. They also drew in Dave, a retired military beta who had watched over Lexie for years, and they formed a pack.

Sam, Dio, and Pala all worked undercover for the Network. An underground group of ex-military betas that had been operating secretly for decades. They had been trying to uncover and expose the secret group they suspected controlled the Palace, and had been manipulating the government. They wanted to shut them down. Sam salvaged a Network communication device from his gramps' farm to make contact after the Crash. But they couldn't work out the advanced technology.

Max's research and a letter Sam found from his gramps' revealed the secret group was called Maven. They were a mix of influential CEOs and wealthy aristocrats. Maven knew the Crash was coming, and let it happen to reduce the number of betas in the population and stabilize control for alphas. They also intended to make a fortune selling stockpiled solar energy equipment when they swept in to save the world. Only the Crash happened earlier than expected and they were unprepared.

Sam's letter also revealed he and Maia were adopted and had been rescued from Maven. Maven was a pack in secret and their omega was Sam and Maia's mother, but she died young after Maven experimented on them all. They were trying to breed stronger alphas and omegas. Their gramps was the pack's beta, and a famous tech entrepreneur. He stole Sam and Maia, then faked their deaths to hide them. They also found out that Hunter is Sam's half brother and Sirena is Maia's half sister.

Lexie discovered that the rogue military team from the Palace had infiltrated the nearby town and were mistreating locals. Many of them were her friends. So the two packs and their allies undertook a mission to free the townspeople.

If the first chapter in Knot Your Possession feels familiar, it's because Ava's story overlaps Lexie's during the battle to save the town. It's the same scene, now from Ava's perspective, and starts her story. Enjoy!

One

I crouched in the shadows as I hugged the aged stone wall next to me and tried to blend into the darkness. The cold leached from the stonework into my bones and added to the chilled fingers of fear running down my spine.

The town had been spookily quiet on the outskirts, as we'd stepped out of the forest and crossed the firebreak to the first houses. Moving as stealthily as we could through the moonlight and overgrown grass, there'd been no TVs or moving vehicles to mar the stillness. Even the buzz of the streetlights was gone. I'd almost forgotten how silent the world could be without the hum of technology intruding.

The eerie vibe had increased when we'd knocked on doors and the townsfolk had answered in hushed voices. As if nobody wanted to break the spell that had slipped over the town. Or maybe they just had reasons to be afraid of strangers at their door. The Crash had brought fear and desperation to too many, along with its ominous silence.

Yet here, in the center of town. Noises rose like lost memories, piercing the silence. Music, raucous laughter, glass clinking. The decadent light spilling into the dark street seemed almost obscene.

I shouldn't be here. It was insanity, and I knew it. I had no training and no idea how to defend myself, let alone help someone else. Especially considering the scattered scents of alphas from around the town mingled and concentrated here, at the pub. It made heavy alarms sound in my head and my senses spin. None of their individual scents were appealing or drew me in. Combined, they were overwhelming and made me want to flee. Yet my friends were here and I'd had too few of those in my life to walk away from one in danger.

Our only job tonight had been to help get the residents to safety in the museum. The experienced members of our group would then attack the pub and neutralize the threat of the rogue alphas inside. But we'd heard an owl hoot a few minutes ago, the signal to retreat and find a safe place to hide.

We'd been doing just that, Cary close by my side, when I'd spied Lexie heading in the opposite direction. Slinking through the darkness towards the pub and danger. Cary had sworn under his breath, and I knew he'd seen her too. Our eyes had met briefly, and he'd nodded, knowing I'd follow Lexie.

I'd made an art form out of going where I wasn't supposed to, and not getting caught. I'd always followed my friend Maia, even before she'd known it. From the first day she'd arrived at the Palace, kicking and screaming, trying to claw her way back out the doors, I'd been awed and fascinated by her. She was innately kind, but she also had a fierce, uncompromising spirit.

When I'd met her friend Lexie, I'd been equally awed. She had the same fight as Maia, but she wore it proudly, like armor. Yet the loneliness that bled from her eyes made her seem achingly vulnerable.

My life, my path, had been so different from both Maia's and Lexie's, but their inner strength drew me to them both. I'd admired them as I watched them stand up for themselves and then fight for the people they loved. I'd fought my battles differently, learning to camouflage myself and blend in. I'd stepped unwillingly, yet intentionally, on the difficult path life had thrust upon me and I hadn't strayed. Yet, we had something in common. We each hid in plain sight, holding fast to our secrets until they were torn from us.

I'd lived a sheltered life at the Omega Palace since my early teens. I'd sometimes wondered how I would react in the real world when confronted with a difficult situation. If, one day, pretending to be the perfect omega was no longer an option, and blending in wouldn't save me. I'd learned a lot about myself since the Crash had turned our world upside down. It seemed I was more like Lexie and Maia than I'd thought. I'd taken to running at danger, even though my heart pounded and I shook with nerves.

Nerves were drumming a heavy beat in my veins at this very moment, but I wouldn't let that stop me. We'd quickly lost Lexie and her mate, Pala, in the darkness between the buildings. The moon was bright tonight, but they both knew how to blend into the shadows and disappear. From the determined look on Lexie's face, there was only one place they could have been headed. The pub, where everything was about to go down.

I knew Pala was a highly trained undercover operative. He'd keep Lexie safe, and we'd only be a hindrance to them. Yet I'd felt a draw to the pub at the center of town that I couldn't shake, even beyond Lexie being here. A feeling of imminence, an awareness of something not here yet, that teased my senses.

I'd always had a strong sense of intuition, and I'd learned to heed it early in life. It hadn't surprised me when I'd presented as an omega, even though it had taken those around me unawares. I'd always felt a level of instinct drawing me towards or away from people that others around me didn't seem to feel.

Cary's dark, determined presence appeared above me as he leaned over to peek around the corner of the alleyway at the dim street beyond. I could feel his worry, yet also his resolve. I looked up at him, his savage beauty highlighted in the waning light of the moon, washing his ebony skin in silver so that he seemed to glow from within. His sharp cheekbones and full lips caught the shadows, giving him an otherworldly beauty that was hard to look at. For me, anyway.

I did what I usually did. I glanced away before I became hypnotized by the spell he wove over me every time I looked at him. Instead, I forced myself to watch the street again, feeling something was coming. We were on the precipice of something, as if the world was holding its breath. I could feel it. My heart trembled with it.

We'd arrived in time to see Lexie and Pala duck into the back door of the pub. Two unconscious, or maybe dead, alphas lay slumped beside it. Cary and I weren't stealthy enough to sneak in that way. So we'd ducked around the side of the old building and inched our way to the front corner on the far side. The street appeared empty, but it sounded like they were having a party in there. Every other building was dark. A few appeared to be boarded up.

I knew more of our team had to be out there, though. Haunting the shadows, the same as Lexie and Pala had been. We were part of the Honey Badgers crew for the rescue mission tonight, made up of volunteers. Our job was to evacuate the town's residents to the safety of the museum, before the trained team took down the alphas commandeering the pub. Yet something had gone wrong if the retreat signal had already sounded. We hadn't been out here for long enough to have gotten all the residents to safety.

A bright red light in the sky to the north of the town pulled my attention away from the street. That was bad news. It meant something had definitely gone wrong, and the pub needed to be taken now. An answering green flare shot up from across the street, a few buildings down. My breath froze in my chest. That was the go signal, and we weren't where we were supposed to be. We should be tucked in somewhere safe, away from the action.

I could almost feel the tension radiating from Cary as he huddled down over me protectively. Moments later, our team emerged from the darkness, running towards the front of the pub on swift, silent feet. I knew more would come in through the rear and the fire exit on the other side.

A sudden, piercing bang from inside the pub made me flinch. Bright flashes followed it, reflecting out the front window. I stuck my hand into my jeans pocket to dig out the flashbang that Lexie had given me to use as a last resort. I'd forgotten about it until now. My heart sank as I realized Lexie had set hers off inside the pub. Was she in trouble, or was it a distraction?

I had no way of knowing. All I knew was that the streets behind us were quieter than we were expecting tonight, but the owners of all those alpha scents had to be somewhere. A loud roar and exploding glass had my head snapping to the front of the pub again. I looked just in time to see Sam, Lexie's mate, vault over the shattered frame, followed by the rest of his team.

Please be okay, please be okay. I wasn't sure who I was begging, but if anyone was listening, I'd take any help we could get. Lexie was feisty and fearless. She also knew how to handle herself. I'd heard she'd dropped Sam to the ground when he was being an ass, and he was one of the most dominant alphas I'd ever met. Yet, she was a newly presented omega which made her vulnerable with so many alphas around. She'd only just had her first heat and her scent was still potent, probably because she'd suppressed it for so long.

The music cut off abruptly and everything went quiet inside the pub. Before I could breathe a sigh of relief, movement up the street caught my eye. The door to one of the boarded-up stores burst open, wood splintering into the street in a spray of violent confetti. A stream of enemy alphas came barreling out, headed for the pub. My breathing sped up as everything else seemed to slow down. My friend was in there, and the alphas on the street were not on our side. If they caught her in there, they'd snatch her for sure. I couldn't stand the thought of Lexie being taken to the Palace and suffering the same treatment as Maia before she'd escaped.

Was this what I'd been sensing? A trap? No way in hell was I leaving my friends undefended. If I could buy them even a little time to regroup, I'd do it.

I was moving before I'd even made a conscious decision. I sensed Cary grab for me, but I was too quick and I think I'd taken us both by surprise. My feet carried me around the corner and directly into the path of the alphas, as I screamed desperately over my shoulder, "Take cover!"

My arm seemed to work of its own accord as I launched the flashbang directly at the alphas headed for us. I threw myself back into a crouch and covered my head as the bang reverberated along the street. I could feel it vibrate through my bones as white flashes appeared behind my closed eyes.

I looked up as soon as it was over to see the alphas shaking their heads briefly before focusing in on me. They'd skidded to a stop and were now glaring at me menacingly. Not the reaction I'd hoped for. I knew the flashbang would have a limited effect on alphas, but I was hoping for a little more than a headshake. I felt Cary appear at my side, and I forced myself not to reach for him as I straightened up.

We had nowhere to go. I'd run right out into the street. We were closer to the incoming alphas than we were to our friends in the pub. There was no way they could get to us in time.

Time seemed to slow down as if someone was pulling on it, trying to drag it back. One heartbeat passed, then two, as the lead alpha stepped towards us with a growl. I heard Lexie scream my name, but my attention was on the threat in front of me.

As the enemy alpha reached a hand out to me, a menacing roar washed over the street and shook the surrounding windows. It had my senses sharpening and focusing in on a giant alpha barreling into the group in front of me. He punched and fought his way through the alphas in the street, dropping them like discarded petals in a game of *he loves me, he loves me not*. He made the other alphas look like kids' toys. There was more fighting going on behind him, but I couldn't see beyond him.

He had long, shaggy brown hair and was wearing some kind of hospital scrubs that barely fit him. I watched, entranced, as one sleeve ripped apart and his massive bicep flexed in a wild punch. His movements weren't fluid or practised, they were erratic and savage. Rage fueled him. I could feel it pounding an echo through every blow, and the snarl on his face made him appear feral.

The giant alpha roared again as he ripped away the alpha reaching for me. One moment, the enemy alpha's fingertips were grazing my arm. The next, he was being picked up and thrown against a nearby tree with a comically surprised look on his face. The force of the hit knocked him unconscious.

I barely noticed Dio and Pala run past me and help take out the last of the alphas in the street. The giant, feral alpha, panting and staring at me with a darkly potent focus, had me fixated. His messy hair partially covered his face, and he had a shaggy beard, but I could see his eyes glittering darkly in the moonlight. His fierce gaze raked over me from head to toe, and I could feel hunger clawing at me. Heat flooded my body in a primal response to the need I could feel pummeling me. I just wasn't sure if it was mine or his.

A wild heartbeat overlaid my own as time reset itself and the world seemed to rush at me. A sudden sharp scent hit my nostrils, of uninhabited spaces where nature reigned supreme. It was laden with the bark, fern, and mossy scents of a tropical jungle at night, with sharp underlying notes of orchids and ginger. A complex, dark scent that smelled wild and dangerous. It suited the beast of an alpha standing planted in front of me, as if no force on earth could shift him.

He had me locked in his gaze, as if nothing else around us existed. A dark, seductive pull tried to draw me towards him. I only barely held myself in check. My body trembled with the need to go to him, to lay my hands on him and claim him as mine. He looked wild and unhinged, but I knew deep in my bones, this alpha would not hurt me.

Movement on either side, and slightly behind him, snapped me out of my daze. I wasn't sure whether days or heartbeats had passed while that possessive stare had pinned me. My eyes flicked to two identical looking alphas, clothed in black, and my heart suddenly seized in my chest. Those faces, achingly familiar and yet so changed, had my heart seizing as if I had dunked it in ice water. I gasped a shocked breath, and the added scents of dark chocolate and salted caramel hit me with a rush of memories. Memories I'd tried so hard to keep from shattering me.

My distraction seemed to snap the giant alpha out of his trance as well. My gaze snapped back to him as he snarled and lurched towards me suddenly. Fear slammed into me as someone stepped between us and I recognized Cary's silhouette. Cary had a habit of subtly putting himself between me and any perceived threat. It had only gotten worse since the Crash. He behaved as if he was my self-appointed bodyguard, even though we barely acknowledged each other. Couldn't even look each other in the eye.

I tried to reach for Cary's shirt to pull him aside. Fear for him making my heartbeat trip over itself. There was no way he could defend himself against the gigantic, feral alpha. Cary was a solid guy. He lifted a lot of weights, but he had no training in hand-to-hand combat and he'd already gotten badly hurt defending me. He was still recovering. I couldn't stand watching him get hurt again. Everything in me rebelled at the idea.

Before I could grab Cary, the feral alpha hauled him up over his shoulder. A shocked gasp escaped me before the alpha reached for me too, and hefted me easily over his other shoulder. I froze as light exploded through me. My senses whirled dizzily as the alpha's, and Cary's, mingled scents enveloped me. My body wanted to wrap itself around his and hold on tight, yet I didn't know this alpha. I didn't have time to adjust or even process a thought at the onslaught of sensation that slammed into me. I'd thrown my hands out to steady myself, and I could feel the powerful muscles in his back flexing as he twisted and took off down the road with both Cary and me.

He was taking us, and there didn't seem to be a damn thing anyone could do about it.

I could see the twins following behind me as I bounced on the alpha's shoulder. They were staying close, but not so near as to engage the giant alpha. I glanced at Cary next to me. He looked as dazed as I felt.

Another yell from Lexie snapped my attention back to the road, and I saw Damon, Leif, and Hunter come flying around the bend from the north, running hard. Lexie gestured frantically at Cary and me while she screamed at Damon. He nodded to her without stopping and charged towards us. The twins paid them no attention, their gazes firmly fixed on me, as they slipped towards the shadows at the edge of the road, while keeping alongside us.

My panic surged as I watched Damon, Leif, and Hunter follow us with furious, determined glares. My two worlds were colliding, and I was terrified someone was going to get hurt. The beast of an alpha carrying me felt as if he was operating on pure instinct, kind of like a wounded animal. I felt suddenly and intensely protective of him.

My body jolted, and my hips slammed against the alpha's shoulder almost painfully, as he skidded to a sudden halt. The powerful arm he had wrapped around my backside and the hand on my hip holding me firmly to him branded me, even through the fabric of my jeans. I had to grab a handful of his shirt to steady myself before I turned to look up over my shoulder.

My panic rose as I saw Nick standing in the middle of the path, looking pale and terrified. He was valiantly wielding a stun gun in our direction. The alpha holding us cocked his head at Nick, as if he was confused.

Nick couldn't actually use his weapon. If he stunned the alpha, the electrical current would pass to Cary and me. I could see that knowledge in Nick's wide eyes. He was desperately bluffing and my heart rate hammered with my fear for him. I didn't think the alpha would hurt Cary or me, or he would have done it already, but I didn't know what he would do to Nick.

The hand on my hip tightened, and I felt a faint feeling of reassurance pass through me. I didn't have time to react though, as the guy's PMV rounded the bend in the road, approaching loudly from the south. It was a hulking, menacing presence on the dark road. The sudden noise of the heavy military vehicle felt deafening. I felt the alpha tense beneath me and a furious growl reverberated through his chest as the person manning the gun turret spotted us. He swung the gun in our direction and yelled, "Stop or I'll shoot."

The feral alpha gently, almost reverently, slid Cary and me to the ground, but kept his eyes focused on the gun pointed at us. He paid Nick no attention at all, instantly dismissing him as a threat. I shot a glance at Cary, who seemed as if he was coming out of a trance. He looked around wildly.

We had buildings and the twins on both sides, Damon with his mates at our backs, and the PMV in front of us. They had us hemmed in. The alpha moved away from us, stepping around Nick, who turned and backed up towards us, still brandishing his stun gun out in front of him.

"I said STOP," the alpha on top of the PMV yelled again. He seemed slightly panicked though, as if this situation was way outside his orders and he didn't quite know what to do.

I heard Lexie's mate Dave yell from a distance, "Hold fast unless attacked."

The alpha with the gun nodded that he'd heard, but kept his wary eyes on the feral alpha approaching him. The alpha was moving sluggishly now, as if his movements were becoming difficult. Yet he still reached up and wrapped his enormous hands around the gun on top of the turret.

His muscles bulged, and his shirt ripped further, as he tore the gun clear off its mounting and threw it to the side. Rendering it useless in seconds.

The power in his body and his movements had heat pooling low in my belly. He was prowling in front of the PMV, growling and snarling at the frozen alpha at the top. Yet his movements were becoming even slower. His arms slumped down, slack at his sides, and I could see his body shake. He looked like a wild animal trapped in a snare and trying desperately to stay conscious.

I stepped towards the alpha, my instincts, and his need drawing me to him.

"Are you okay?" I asked, my voice so breathy and quiet I wasn't sure he'd hear me.

I gulped as he turned, as if he'd sensed more than heard me. His eyes flared, and a potent yearning crossed his features before he sniffed the air and a sudden wariness had him stilling. I could feel a rush of unease burst from him, where there had been nothing but possessive need and reassurance before. The note of ginger in his scent spiked, coating the air. I halted in place, his sudden fear freezing my limbs. He'd just faced down an armored PMV and a horde of alphas with no hesitation. Yet the sight of me had a fine sheen of sweat breaking out all over his body.

I felt sick, knowing intuitively that someone had tortured this man.

Cary shifted into my field of vision, moving slowly. I grabbed his shirt, but he gently shrugged me off. "He won't hurt me," he said, but I wasn't sure if he was directing his words to me or the alpha. Cary's eyes still looked slightly glazed. He took another slow step forward and reached out his hand, resting it lightly on the alpha's chest.

"It's okay. We've got you," he whispered so lightly I barely heard. The alpha's gaze focused in on Cary and his whole body relaxed into Cary's hand as he breathed out heavily. A heartbeat later, his eyes rolled back in his head, and Cary yelled for help as he dropped.

I felt Nick move alongside me, but we were both too far away. The twins spun out from the shadows of the PMV and grabbed the giant alpha as he fell. They cradled his head gently and lowered him to the ground.

Seeing the twins had been a shock I hadn't yet processed. I hadn't seen them in a decade, yet they'd dominated every waking moment of that time. Many of my dreams too. Watching them move like creatures of shadow in front of me made me question if I was awake.

I glanced behind me as I heard Dave call out to Damon. Damon shot me a look, and I nodded at him to let him know we were fine, before he and his mates spun and raced back towards Dave. We weren't out of danger. There was a pub full of hostile alphas and betas behind us and a lot of injured alphas lying in the street. I had no idea what was happening back there.

I shifted closer to the unconscious alpha on the ground. Nick moved with me. He seemed to have taken up Cary's place at my side, as Cary checked the alpha's pulse.

"Is he okay?" I asked Cary. I stared vaguely at the unconscious alpha's shoulder, not able to look anywhere else as I felt the twin's gazes focus back on me and Cary raised his head to join them. The world pressed in as the three men focused on me with weighted stares. My Palace training had me straightening my back and slipping on a serene, polite mask. I hated my ingrained reaction, but I felt overwhelmed. I couldn't untangle any of my complicated feelings for these three men while they watched me so closely.

"He's breathing, but I don't know what made him pass out."

"I'm pretty sure the Palace guys sedated him," one twin answered. The deep, rumbling voice sent shivers racing down the curve of my back. I forced myself not to react as my body tried to arch into the sound. It was so familiar, yet so different. We'd been teenagers when we'd last seen each other. Reckless, young and naïve. Determined to take on the world for each other. This voice belonged to a man, one I no longer knew.

The sound of a gunshot ringing out had both the twins spinning in place. I dove, without thought, to cover the alpha on the ground, needing to protect him from the threat while he was vulnerable. I jolted as Cary landed, sprawled over both of us, and I felt Nick crouch behind me with his hand on my back. It was the first time either man had touched me, but I had no time to dwell on the precious moment.

I closed my eyes and my breaths seized in my lungs as two more shots rang out in close succession. Cary slid over to cover more of my upper body, hugging my head to his chest. I didn't think we were the targets. I couldn't hear shots landing anywhere nearby. But Cary muffled everything as he lay heavily on top of me and his vanilla ice-cream scent surrounded me.

Dread ran its ice-cold fingers along my skin. Too many people I loved were exposed out here, and I couldn't do a single thing about it.

Two

I launched myself on top of Ava and the unconscious alpha below her as three shots fired in quick succession. I was desperately trying to cover as much of Ava as I could while holding myself up slightly so as not to crush either of them. This was as close as I'd ever been to Ava, and despite our desperate circumstances, her nearness was overwhelming my senses and making my heart skip a beat. Every breath the alpha took beneath us also had me on edge, waiting to see if it would be his last.

Not knowing what had made him pass out, or what they may have done to him at the Palace, was messing with my head. I'd fought hard to keep my autonomy in a world filled with alphas who wanted to turn me into their toy. Yet this giant alpha's lush tropical forest scent, mixed with Ava's sweetness, pulled at me in a way that was primal and instinctive. The look of relief he'd given me, when I'd placed my hand on his chest, had momentarily stripped me bare. It made me feel exposed, shaken, and really fucking confused.

So I did what I always did. I shut it down. My senses narrowed as I ignored the chaos and danger around us for a moment, something I'd learned to do at the Palace. My focus was only on Ava and the alpha lying vulnerable beneath us. I trusted Nick to keep watch and warn me if anyone approached, as I slipped my hand closer to the alpha to check his pulse. It beat steadfastly against my fingers. Its rhythm was a siren call.

When he'd run at us, I'd stepped in front of Ava instinctively because I hadn't known him. Yet, for some inexplicable reason, I hadn't thought he'd hurt her. It had just become a habit.

Protecting Ava had been my life's purpose since the day I'd first seen her at the Palace, so naïve and innocent, and her scent had marked me as hers. Yet I'd protected her from the shadows, never getting close. Now, despite the Crash and our time on the farm, the barrier I created between us felt impossible to overcome. Yet I knew I now had to figure it out, fast. This alpha changed everything. She'd flung herself over him protectively, without a thought. She clearly felt the same pull to him as he did to her. *To us*, my mind tried to yell. I shut that down, though.

I felt our fate rushing towards us, as if I'd only been able to hold it at bay for so long, and now it had broken free in a torrent. If I didn't hold on to her, I feared Ava was going to get swept away in the flood.

A distant yell and a shot rang out from the direction of the pub, followed by one of the nearby twins firing at a building across the street. The echoing cracks startled me back into the moment and the incredible danger we were in, exposed on the street. I could almost feel the bullseye painted on us. I faintly heard Damon yell at Hunter to go, and the same twin took off after him. They both disappeared into the dim depths of the building.

Suddenly, the PMV behind us rumbled back to life from where it had been idling. It maneuvered around between us and the building. It hindered my view, yet gave us some protection. I reluctantly slid off Ava. She shifted off the alpha, too, and glanced up at me briefly, yet searchingly. Her eyes held mine for a haunting moment, that briefly calmed the turmoil within me, before she turned her attention back to the alpha.

"Hey, kid," the remaining twin, who was hovering near us, whispered. I looked up, startled, but he wasn't talking to me. He was talking over his shoulder to Nick while he shifted silently to peer around the front of the PMV. "Watch our back and call out anything suspicious you see to me."

Nick looked startled, too. Yet he still brandished his stun gun while crouched next to us. He peeked at me, and I nodded to reassure him I had eyes on Ava before he turned his back and focused on the dark street beyond us. Nick and I had become fast friends the day Ava and I had arrived at the farm. He'd surprised me tonight, though. He came across as a bit of a tech geek. Yet he'd enthusiastically signed up to become a Honey Badger alongside us, and hadn't baulked at running into danger to help.

"Are you okay?" I whispered to Ava. She glanced back up at me and those big green eyes pulled me into their depths the way they always seemed to do. They were a deep, cool lake I wanted to dive into. I always felt as if I was falling if I looked into them too long. I'd rarely let myself do it before now.

"Yes, you?" She asked, seeming a little hesitant. We rarely spoke directly to each other, even since we'd found the relative safety of the farm. We'd spent most of our time hiding out together at the Palace in fearful silence. Yet, we'd orbited each other for so long. Two planets caught in each other's pull but never touching.

I nodded at her as my breath caught in my chest. It was so strange. She felt so integral to my life and yet I knew so little about her. I didn't know her favorite color or what filled her dreams. She was a mystery and a necessity, bundled up in one gorgeous package.

We sat in awkward silence for a few minutes until a noise behind us had my head whipping around. Hunter appeared, shadowed by the other twin. Hunter slid gracefully to his knees next to me.

"Is everyone okay?" Ava asked, with more than a hint of anxiety. I'd been trying not to think about Lexie and everyone cornered inside the pub.

"Yeah," Hunter nodded as he checked the unconscious alpha's pulse. "Damon signaled on my way back. Three down, but none of ours. Whoever the shooter was, they're in the wind, but we weren't their target."

I relaxed slightly. From what I knew of Hunter, he wouldn't be here with us if he thought the shooter was still in the area or a danger to us. He'd be on the hunt. I had a lot of respect for Hunter. He put everyone at ease with his friendly humor, but it hid a deadly side. I'd seen it the night we'd met, when he and his mates had rescued Ava and me from the Palace.

"Do we know what's wrong with this guy?" Hunter asked. "He appeared to pass out from where we were watching, but it was hard to see in the darkness."

"We think they sedated him at the Palace, but didn't give it enough time to fully take effect before they hauled him into the humvee," the twin who had stayed replied.

"Fucking incompetent assholes," Hunter grunted in reply. He smoothed the shaggy hair off the alpha's face in a surprisingly tender gesture that was at odds with the confused frown on his face.

I whipped my head around as I sensed Ava move away from me. She'd taken a few steps back and was standing alone with her arms wrapped around her waist. She looked up the street, and I turned slightly as I stood up to see Lexie and Pala headed our way. I shot another look at Ava as I tried to figure out what had made her tense up, before I scanned the alphas surrounding us.

Pala was relaxed as he arrived, holding hands with Lexie. He introduced her to the twins, River and Ryder. Lexie only gave them a brief wave before she zeroed in on Ava. She gave her a hug that Ava melted into while Pala was busy getting his hug fest on with the mysterious twins. There was a lot of backslapping between the three men, as if they were old mates.

When Lexie quietly asked if Ava needed to get away, the twins instantly turned and zeroed in on her. The way they moved in unison in that moment was uncanny, and they both let out a possessive growl. Ava shot them a dark glare in response, and both of their mouths fell open as their growls cut off.

What the hell was going on? My protective instincts fired, and I took a longer look at the twins. I hadn't really paid them much attention earlier, even though they were hard to miss when they suddenly popped out in front of you.

They both had gorgeous blonde hair in a light silvery shade that seemed to catch the moonlight. But River had shorter hair swept back from his face, while Ryder had long shoulder length hair with a deep undercut. They were both incredibly tall and well built, with bodies that looked honed through a lot of martial arts. Both held themselves loosely, primed for rapid movement. I'd seen them move through the shadows earlier, as if they were born to them. They'd flowed into the light, rather than stepped into it. Like deadly predators that hunted in the darkness.

These men could protect Ava in a way that I could only dream about, and they felt connected to her somehow. There was a weird energy flowing between them that was making the hairs stand up on my arms. I belatedly realized the feeling of rushing fate wasn't just because of the unconscious alpha. These two deadly twins were a part of it, too.

"I hoped she was your Ava when I found her hiding at the Palace," Pala said lightly, as his eyes bounced between the twins. Memories drowned out the rest of his words, as I recalled how Pala had brought us food, and diverted attention away from us when we hid out in the library. I'd wondered at the time why he was helping us. He'd asked for nothing in return. I would have been more suspicious, only I'd seen him helping the other omegas at the Palace too. Standing guard while the other alphas were partying.

"Thank you, my friend," River said, as he gripped Pala's neck firmly and tipped his head forward until it rested gently against Pala's temple. It was a move that conveyed respect and deep friendship. Meanwhile, Ryder went rigid as he watched Ava closely. I could see his jaw working as he clenched his teeth and crossed his arms over his chest. He seemed conflicted, as if he felt pulled towards her, but she burned him at the same time. It was the first time I'd seen the twins not moving in sync and it felt wrong, somehow.

I noticed Ava stiffened as well, and she took a sharp breath. Her shocked expression appeared almost betrayed. "You knew who I was?" she asked Pala.

I felt like I was playing catch-up with missing puzzle pieces.

"No, not for sure," Pala replied. "I suspected you were their Ava, though. They'd said you were at the Palace." I saw Ava tense up even further. One of her arms cradled around herself before her hand slid down her arm to fiddle with the bluebird bracelet she always wore on her wrist. The movement drew the eyes of the twins. Both of their eyes widened at the sight of the bracelet, before Ryder quickly looked away.

"Their Ava?" I asked, breaking the sudden silence, not able to hold back any longer. I needed to know what was between them.

It was Ava who spoke up and answered, though. Not Pala or the twins, who were strangely silent.

"Lexie, I'd like you to meet my mates, River and Ryder," Ava said. Her arm moved stiffly as she pointed first to River, then to Ryder. She wasn't looking at the twins as she spoke. Or me. She fixed her gaze firmly on Lexie. Her eyes were wide, and she looked as if she was silently begging Lexie for something. I wasn't sure what, though.

"Holy shit. The twins are your mates?" Hunter asked from his position on the ground.

"Mates?" I echoed. I blinked rapidly and determination settled deep within me. I'd seen enough over the last week or so to know mates were real, and not always the forced kind. There was also the rare, legendary kind. True mates.

Knowing she'd end up mated to someone eventually, potentially forcibly, had driven my need to get her out of the Palace. It was why I had obsessively worked out and ran the perimeter of the Palace grounds, hoping I'd be strong enough to seize any chance I could find of escape. The alternative was a nightmare I refused to see brought to life.

Yet now that we were finally out, she was publicly claiming two mysterious alphas, ones she clearly knew and had some kind of history with, as her mates. While another alpha, who acted like her mate, was lying unconscious at her feet. It felt as if fate was taking a sledgehammer to my carefully erected walls.

A hand squeezed my shoulder, and I knew instinctively it was Nick. The gesture eased the bands that had tightened around my chest enough that I could breathe. Yet every breath brought the scents that had suddenly saturated the air into my lungs. A redolent haze of dark chocolate and salted caramel mingling with Ava's cherries that almost made me groan. Fate, or some other prescient being, had made their scents perfect for each other.

"For what it's worth," Ava said quietly, still not looking at anyone, as Lexie grabbed her hand. "We're unbonded."

Whatever was between the three was clearly unresolved. Ava's delectable cherry scent turned tart, and her distress hit me like a sudden cold shower. I felt as if she'd aimed those last words at me, but I knew with a sudden clarity that this wasn't about me. The last thing I ever wanted to do was cause her distress. I stepped in closer to Ava, giving her my unspoken support, as I glared at the twins. I didn't care what happened to me as long as I could be near her. Whatever she needed, I would get for her. Whatever stood in her way, I would remove. Or I'd die trying.

The twins didn't appear to appreciate my glare, as a dark look swept over both their faces. It wasn't menacing, though, more possessive, with a hint of obsessive. They didn't say a word, though. Not even to defend themselves. I could almost feel the unspoken accusations brimming from me, Lexie, and the others, as if the air had suddenly turned icy.

"And the big guy out cold on the ground?" Lexie asked Ava, expertly diverting attention away from the explosion about to happen.

Ava shrugged and furrowed her brow as she twisted to look at the hulking alpha lying alongside her on the ground. "I don't know who he is. I've never seen him before. He came out of nowhere tonight."

"He seemed to zero in on you and Cary, from where I was standing," Lexie said. Neither Ava nor I responded. I had no idea how to even start.

"He's a prisoner from the Palace," Hunter said as he looked down at the alpha with that confused frown back on his face. He reached out a hand, as if to touch the alpha's face, then pulled it back. "They were transporting him somewhere in a humvee, moving fast. We intercepted them north of the town. They had him heavily sedated when we got him out, but he was moving. He caught a scent in the air and took off. For a big dude, he's damn fast. We had to secure the Palace guards that were with him before we could chase him down after the humvee crashed."

"Do you know who he is?" Pala asked the twins. He'd been quietly watching everything unfold.

The twins finally shifted their gazes from Ava to the alpha. "No," Ryder replied.

"We infiltrated the Palace," River said, as he shot a glance back at Pala. "We were tracking Ava, but the scent in her room had faded, as if she hadn't been in there for days. We found a faint trace in the library. When we reached their underground labs, we found his cell, and her faded scent was there too. Someone had stuffed Ava's old blankets and clothes into his air vents."

Ava gasped, and her hand went over her heart, as she shot a confused look at the unconscious alpha.

Shit. What the hell had been happening at the Palace that I didn't see? I didn't like any of the answers that were running through my head.

"It looked like they were tormenting him, or maybe torturing him, with her scent," River added. "We tried to get him out so we could figure out why, but we tripped some kind of silent alarm. We had to fight our way out and they tried to move him while they had us pinned down below ground. As soon as we got free, we tracked him here."

Before anyone could say anything, Dave came running over and slid to a stop between Lexie and Pala. He was holding his satellite phone. "Sam's surveillance team at the Palace just made contact again. The military and lab techs are abandoning the Palace. They're bugging out right now."

"What about the omegas?" Ava asked, a hair's breadth before the words left my own lips. Knowing what was happening to the omegas every debut season had tested the limits of my control. Being forced to take part, wander and entertain, while knowing what was happening in dark corners, had been agonising. Only knowing I had Ava to protect had stopped me from tearing into alphas, and probably getting myself killed. My guilt weighed heavily on me, though. Taking care of Ava was my first priority, but helping the other omegas still at the Palace was my second.

The things I dreamed about in the dark of night, the ones that had me waking in a sweat, needed to stay there.

"They've turned off the security feeds, so we can't tell for sure, but they don't appear to be taking them. Now that we've cut off their supply of food from town, I don't think they have enough left to feed everyone." I growled low, a sound I didn't even know I could make. I'd warned them not to cut off the omegas food supply. Dave nodded in silent acknowledgement as he glanced at me. He was a good guy. I knew he'd be all in helping the rest of the omegas at the Palace if needed.

"Plus, their lab just got breached, so they're probably spooked," Hunter said, almost casually.

"Who breached their lab?" Sam asked as he strode over and wrapped his arms around Lexie. Her other mate, Dio, followed close behind. Damon and Leif were hot on their heels, their eyes on their pack mate, Hunter. Those guys were always more comfortable when they were within arm's reach of each other.

Hunter just pointed to the twins, who looked unconcerned at the sudden spotlight as everyone looked at them.

Dave shook his head. "That's a story for another day. We need to break up into groups. One questioning the people in the pub. A second letting town residents out of the museum and making sure everyone gets home okay. Then a third group to head to the Palace in the PMV right now and check on the omegas."

"We also need to figure out what Winston was trying to blow up and where those explosives are. We don't want local kids finding them," Hunter said. Dave just nodded. He looked weary of the constant conflicts the world was throwing at us, but there was still a determined set to his shoulders.

"What about tracking the unit fleeing the Palace with the lab techs? We need to know where they're planning to regroup," River asked. He seemed to be the chattier twin.

"We have a man tracking satellite feeds. He also has a long range drone. Max will follow them as best as he can," Damon answered.

River glanced at Ryder, doing some kind of twin communication thing, but they didn't object.

There was a lot of chatter and negotiation about who was joining which group, but I wasn't paying a lot of attention. I only had eyes for Ava right now, waiting to see what she would do.

"I'm going to the Palace," Ava announced, her quiet, but determined, voice cutting through the noise. "I want to check on the omegas and I'm the only one who knows where the secret passages are. We'll need to make sure they're all checked and there's nothing and nobody left behind that can surprise us."

What secret passages and how the hell does Ava know about them? I shook off my questions, but I wasn't letting them go. Not anymore. Clearly, I didn't know as much about Ava's movements as I thought I did.

That was going to change if she'd been putting herself in danger on my watch.

"Me too," I added. Dave smirked at me as if that was a given, and I narrowed my eyes at him. We'd gotten friendly while I was at the farm, so I knew he wouldn't take it the wrong way. He was a good guy.

"We'll go with them," River said without hesitation, staring intently at Ava, daring her to object. He straightened his shoulders as if he was considering picking her up and carrying her there if she denied him.

"I think we should take this alpha back there, too," I said, gesturing to the still unconscious alpha. "If he's feral, we can't risk taking him to the farm, or having him in town here. The Palace is the only place with secure facilities if we need it, and they should have more medical supplies too. I don't think they would have had time to strip it on the way out."

Damon, Sam, and their mates were glancing at each other, as if they were uncomfortable letting us go. Especially Lexie. Her eyes were wide, and she bit her lip nervously as she shot a worried look at her mates.

"I can come with you, Ava. Someone else can take the museum," Lexie said.

Ava's face lit up as she smiled at her friend and I desperately wanted her to look at me like that one day. "That's sweet, Lexie. But I'll be okay. You need to be at the museum. People there are going to be frightened. You'll be able to reassure them and figure out what they need. You're good at that."

Lexie nodded, but she was still biting her lip and looking unsure.

"I think I should go to the Palace, too," Nick blurted suddenly. He'd been quietly standing on the edges of our group while we talked, shifting on his feet nervously. "If their security cameras have been switched off, I can get them back online and see if I can find any tech they've overlooked in their rush to leave. Then I can let Max know what we need and can borrow from the farm to get them secure."

Dave patted Nick on the shoulder and dragged him closer into our circle. "Good man. I agree, they'll need your tech skills at the Palace if you're willing to go. You can coordinate with Max and get the two sites linked up."

Nick looked embarrassed at the praise, and flicked his eyes towards Ava. She gave him a soft smile that didn't make me feel jealous. It felt right, and something settled in my chest. Nick felt familiar, and necessary, in a lighter way than Ava.

Dave handed Ava his satellite phone. "Take this, and check in with us every day at 8am and 8pm until things calm down. If we don't hear from you, we'll head straight for the Palace. So if you forget, be prepared for a bunch of worried people to turn up and we'll probably come in hot. Outside of that, call us for any reason. There's a charger in the PMV. I'm sure Maia will call you when she wakes up, after she tears strips off us for letting you go without her."

Ava hugged the phone to her chest. "Thank you, Dave."

Lexie grabbed her and wrapped her arms around her, hugging her tightly. "I'm here if you need me, any time of the day or night. And I'll be on that call with Maia in the morning."

Ava nodded into her shoulder. "Honestly, I'll be fine Lex. I'm a big girl."

"No, you're a strong as fuck omega, Ava. Don't forget it."

Ava's eyes were wide and glassy as she stepped back. As were Lexie's. Maia and Lexie had been good for her. They'd cracked the shell Ava had built around herself, the one that was painted like a perfect omega. Watching Ava slowly peek out from behind it when they were around had brought me hope that maybe there was a place in the world where she could be safe.

"Okay," Lexie said, with only a little crack in her voice. "Let's get to work."

The others moved away until there was only Ava, Nick, River, Ryder, and me, standing over the unconscious alpha.

An echo of faint laughter drifted through the silence surrounding us. I'm pretty sure fate was laughing at me.

It was time to stake my claim.

Three

I stood on the front steps of the Palace, besieged by memories as I stared at the doorway in front of me. It was an impressive oak double-sided door with iron rivets surrounded by a stone archway. The doors curved and came to a point at the top that was more than twice my height. When the rogue military unit that had taken over the Palace left an hour ago, they hadn't bothered to close the doors behind them. They were wide open. I could see the marble floor beyond, as well as the lower steps of the elegant, sweeping staircase that led to the second level. Only it wasn't the doorway itself that had me halting, more the memories of the only other time I'd walked through it.

When walking the grounds of the Palace, the omegas usually went out through the atrium or the common room at the rear. I hadn't walked through these ornate entry doors since the day I arrived as a newly awakened teenage omega a decade ago. Back then, the sight of them had filled me with trepidation, adding to the heavy load of guilt and longing I'd been carrying. I was a much different woman now. Nerves didn't swirl in my belly at the sight. I'd grown beyond that. But the guilt and longing were even stronger.

I'd had no belongings back then. The Palace discouraged omegas from bringing anything of their old life with them. I still had no belongings beyond the cherished bluebird bracelet on my wrist. The one that suddenly felt like a heavy weight, where it had always brought comfort in the past. I'd hidden it the last time I walked through these doors, but I wouldn't hide it now.

I felt a solid presence at my right, slightly behind me, as I let out a deep sigh. Cary didn't say a word, just gave me his silent support. As he always did. I briefly wondered if he knew how much I depended on it, even through all the unspoken words that haunted the space between us. I realized the day he arrived was probably the last time he'd walked through these doors, too.

Before I could second-guess myself, I reached behind me and impulsively grasped his hand. Proving the barrier between us had been nothing but air all along. I didn't need to search around for his hand. I was always hyper aware of his body, almost as if it was an extension of my own.

I felt a flicker of wonder from him before he wrapped his fingers tightly around my own and stepped closer alongside me. The moment felt charged, yet laden with promise. An electric tingle ran up my arm and spread slowly over my body, making me feel warm and alive. I wanted to turn to him and bury myself in his warmth, but now was not the time. Not when River and Ryder were silent sentinels behind us, and I hadn't yet exchanged a word with either alpha. Even though my every breath felt choked with them. I could feel their eyes on me. Branding me, the same as the giant alpha's touch had earlier.

As if I'd called him to us, I felt River approach on my other side. He hung back slightly, though. Staying out of arm's reach. I wondered if it was me or himself he didn't trust right now. Neither was a good outcome. My two worlds were colliding, and I didn't know how to navigate the fallout without people getting hurt.

"Are you okay?" He asked in a low, rumbling voice that had me closing my eyes briefly so I could luxuriate in the sound. If only for a moment. They were the first words he'd spoken directly to me since he'd appeared out of the darkness and back into my life. The three simple words felt packed full of emotion. They had questions swirling within me, and I was suddenly sick of keeping them inside. Yet, now was not the time for them either.

"Yes," was all I said in reply. I was grateful when my training kicked in again and my voice came out clear and steady. My composure was a lie, though.

River hesitated a moment, and I hated it. We'd never hesitated around each other before. Our greetings had always been eager and joyous. All I really wanted to do was throw myself at him, but I wasn't sure if that would be welcome anymore. Or if my own feelings would allow it. A simmering anger and grief was tugging me away as fast as his dark chocolate scent was trying to pull me in. I realized for the first time that I may have irreparably broken something vital to me. The thought tore at me.

So many nights I'd dreamed about the twins breaking down these damn doors in dramatic fashion, coming to rescue me. Clearly, they were just girlish fantasies. I felt Cary's hold on my hand tighten as I mentally shook myself out of my reverie. I grasped it in return, a lifeline in a surging sea.

"I'd like to go in first, with Ryder, and check it out. Make sure there's no-one hiding in there, or any hidden traps," River finally announced. His voice had cooled and become impersonal, matching my own. I shook off my regrets and focused on the next steps as well.

River's plan sounded good in theory, only I already knew we weren't alone. The grand foyer behind the doors was mostly dark, the moonlight only filtered in so far. Yet there was a faint light coming from somewhere out of sight. It was enough for me to spot a small face surrounded by golden curls that had peeked around the corner, curiosity written all over it with an impish grin. The face had disappeared quickly, as if someone had yanked them back out of view. River must have been so focussed on me he'd missed it, which surprised me.

"Thank you, River," I replied as I stumbled slightly over his name, while avoiding looking directly at him. I hated how formal I sounded with him, but it was the only way I could get the words out without losing myself. "We have company, but I don't think there's any danger. Cary and I should go in first and talk to the omegas. Alphas going in hot may scare them. We don't know what they've been through lately. I promise we'll only go inside the entrance and stay in sight."

The cherubic face appeared again briefly, followed by a hissed admonishment. But that grin reappeared too quickly, and the young girl slipped away from whoever was trying to keep her back. I knew from experience how elusive she could be. She was a sweet, yet determined, little hellcat.

"Ava," she cried out as she launched herself through the ornate entryway, a determined missile heading directly for me. A dozen worried omegas appeared behind her, ranging from their late teens to early twenties. I recognized a few faces.

I sensed River relaxing slightly behind me. I dropped Cary's hand and rushed towards the young omega, dropping to my knees on the marble in front of her as she threw her arms around me.

"Angel," I admonished her with a grin as I shook my head. She was a mischievous spirit, and I'd come across her quite a few times over the last few months on my secret travels around the castle. She'd been hiding from her beta handler, the same as I was. We'd hidden behind the curtains in alcoves and giggled together. She was a shining light in the coldly elegant Palace, full of affection for anyone that would give her a moment's kindness. She'd once even covered for me. Stepping out and allowing her handler to find her before she could discover me, too.

Angel was young to be at the Palace, though. Far too young to have reached puberty and presented. I figured she was about five years old now. She'd been here for about a year, but we hadn't seen much of her at first. Her full name was Angelica, but everyone called her Angel.

I'd always wondered how they had found her. I knew now it was probably the same blood test they'd used on Maia. Back then, the fear of what the Palace was up to had kept me up at night. I'd grieved and despaired, thinking of all the ways they could break her infectious spirit. So far, they seemed to have left her alone. They had created a playroom for her, and they mostly confined her to it. It was a lonely existence for a child, though, hence the frequent escapes.

"You need to be more careful," I told her quietly, as I hugged her. "The world is changing, and it's not as friendly at the moment." Not that it had ever really been. Not to omegas, but she didn't know that.

She just shrugged with the carelessness of the young as I pulled back to look at her. "You're friendly."

I couldn't help but smile at the simplicity of her words and her world. Her appearance belied her words, though. She was wearing pajamas with a chocolate stain on the front and her hair was dirty, even though her grin was big.

"Hey, Squirrel," she said over my shoulder, as I felt Cary come up behind me.

"Hey, Chipmunk." I peeked over my shoulder and saw the answering grin on his face as he spoke, lighting it up and making my heart skip a little. He was usually so stern looking. It seemed I wasn't the only one who had come across her on my secret wanderings around the Palace.

"Let's go check on the others," I said as I stood up and held my hand out for her. I needed answers, but I wasn't about to question a child. She grabbed it and happily skipped alongside me, as if we weren't walking through the grand entrance to hell.

I glanced over my shoulder at River, and he nodded to me. I knew he'd stay put unless I signaled him, but he had his gun at the ready and he was standing more stiffly than he had earlier. A tense wariness had replaced the liquid grace, and his eyes never left me. I glanced further back and saw Ryder looking off into the surrounding forest, while standing next to Nick at the back of the PMV. Nick shot me a reassuring smile.

"Angel," one of the other girls admonished as we got closer. "You're going to be the death of me."

Cary shrugged and grinned down at the cutie pie by my side. "If her Palace handler couldn't keep her in line, we have little chance, Emma."

I felt a sudden burning in my chest when I heard Cary use Emma's name. It startled me.

Emma rolled her eyes at him and sighed. I knew her vaguely as our rooms were near each other, but we'd only exchanged basic pleasantries. She was one of the older omegas here and had been due to make her Palace debut with me, before the Crash had changed everything. She'd always appeared distant and aloof, yet perfectly put together. I suspected most of her attitude was armor, though. Most omegas developed some once they'd been here awhile and realized exactly what their future held. Emma had honed hers to perfection.

The Palace had liked to dress omegas nearing their debut in impeccable, beautiful dresses. Just in case an affluent alpha stopped in to peruse the delicacies before the main feast. Now, Emma's dark hair was messy, her wrinkled floral dress had a torn sleeve, and she winced slightly as if fatigue was riding her hard. It was a stark contrast. Yet she was still beautiful as she held her head high.

I couldn't help my eyes running over her as she did the same to me. I instantly felt guilty about the clean clothes, toiletries, and food my new friends had given me when I escaped to Damon's farm. Her gaze seemed to catalogue my dark jeans, sneakers, hoodie, and clean hair tied up in a neat ponytail. I must look a lot different to her, too.

"I'm sorry I couldn't get you all out," I suddenly blurted, startling her.

Emma shot me a tired smile. "None of us begrudged you your escape, Ava. We were happy for you. But why are you back now? Did you find Maia?"

Cary and I had sneaked to the kitchen doorway one night while we were hiding out. Hunger had made us risk coming out of the library to look for food. Emma had been washing dishes with a few other omegas. The others had distracted the guards while Emma smuggled us food. We'd had a few moments to whisper hurriedly, and I'd let her know Maia had already escaped.

"Yes, I found Maia. She came across a refuge. It's a farm, and she's there now. The guys that got me out are her true mates." Emma raised her eyebrows and I could see questions brimming behind her dark eyes, but I continued on before she could ask them. "Some alphas from here attacked the farm and tried to snatch us, then set up camp in the town between us. We have an ex-military unit with us now. Maia's brother, Sam, came looking for her and brought his whole team. We helped them clear out the town tonight and free the residents."

Emma nodded as if that made perfect sense, but her eyebrows were almost touching her hairline. I got it. Helping free captive towns wasn't exactly what the Palace had trained Cary and me to do.

I took a deep, shaky breath and asked the question I'd been dreading. "Are you and the other omegas alright?"

Emma tilted her head to the side and bit her lip, as if she was thinking about how to answer that question. After a pause, which felt agonizingly long, she answered in a quiet, hesitant voice. "We're alive and we're looking out for each other."

I felt relieved tears spring to my eyes, but I blinked rapidly. I refused to let them fall. Alive was good, happy and healthy would be better.

"So, why are you back here now?" Emma asked again, eyeing River further down the steps behind me. He held his gun aimed at the ground and watched us intently.

"We were told the military unit occupying the Palace left tonight, along with the last of the lab techs. Some of Sam's team had been keeping an eye on you all. We wanted to come and make sure you were alright. We thought new military guys turning up might freak you out. There's only a handful of us for now, but when we figure out what you need in the morning, we can organize more people and supplies if needed."

It was Emma's turn to hold back tears as she nodded rapidly. "Food. We need food. They took the mattresses from the bedrooms and put us in the ballroom together. When the shooting started, we barricaded the door. There was lots of yelling and people running, trucks leaving, but nobody came near us. We only came out because it's been quiet for a while. The first place I checked was the kitchen, and it looks like they took most of the food."

Of course, they took the food. Assholes.

Cary had been quiet since he'd greeted Emma, but he spoke up now. "The guys with us want to search the Palace, to make sure no-one left any surprises behind. Apart from Ava and me, there's a beta who's a friend of ours and six alphas. Plus the other two alphas who have been camped outside. There's another alpha in the PMV, but he's unconscious. Is it okay if they come in? Some of them were here before, but they defected. They're here to help, and we trust them."

"Okay, we need any help we can get," Emma said as she stepped further back from the doorway.

"I'll get them. Stay here," Cary said to me. He grabbed my hand and squeezed it briefly before he turned and hustled back out the door. The casual touch gave me a thrill. I hoped this would be our new normal. I wanted more.

When I looked back at Emma again, those questions in her eyes had doubled. I cut her off again. I felt bad, but I suddenly felt exhausted and my head was pounding. Explaining our confusing non-relationship was beyond me right now. "The unconscious alpha appears to have been a captive here. He's sedated. They were trying to take him with them, but we intervened. We thought it would be better to bring him back here until we could find out who he is."

Emma looked shocked and confused as she held a hand over her chest. "From here?"

I nodded. "There's a lot to tell, and it's one hell of a story, but we're all tired. The unconscious alpha was being kept in a cell under the Palace, but I don't want to put him back in there. He was alert for a while and he saved Cary and me from some of the Palace alphas. I was thinking we could put him in the VIP suite. It's away from everyone else in case he poses any problems, and we can stay in the other rooms to monitor him tonight. Do you think that would be okay?"

"Have at it," Emma shrugged, as if it didn't concern her. But I could tell she was curious from the way she leaned slightly forward to see out to the PMV better. Cary reached River, who turned and signaled in the moonlight. Two figures appeared out of the shadows beneath the treeline and headed towards Ryder at the rear of the PMV. They moved swiftly and silently, but were strangely misshapen. They brought to mind mythical yetis. But neither Ryder nor River appeared concerned. They had a brief conversation before heading up the steps. When they got closer, I could see the two newcomers were wearing camouflage suits covered in some kind of fabric that mimicked moss and leaves, which explained their strange shape in the shadows.

River's rigid posture relaxed as he got closer to me, coming up right alongside me as if he needed to be near me. "My name's River. This is Ryder, Nick, Miles, and Owen. We're going to sweep the Palace. Is there anyone else here that you know about?" He addressed all the girls to start, but turned to Emma as he finished talking. Her gaze flitted between the alphas and she stammered a little, appearing flustered as his gaze rested on her.

"Uh, huh. Yes. There are two dozen omegas in the ballroom. It's down the hallway behind us. They had the door barricaded with mattresses. It's another set of big double doors. You can't miss it."

"Okay. Thank you, Emma." Alphas had excellent hearing. In the night's stillness, River must have heard us address her from outside. That burning sensation in my chest came back full force, and I tried to swallow a growl. River shot me a dark look before he turned back to Emma again. "If you could come with Ryder and me, we'll get you to reassure the other girls that everything is fine, but they need to stay put for a little while."

"Oh, sure. I can do that." Emma brightened and looked entirely too eager to follow River and Ryder for my liking.

River didn't seem to notice as he turned away from her, but it had me on edge. "Cary, Nick, can you both stay here? I need you to guard the front door and watch the PMV and these omegas until we get back."

"Maybe you should take all the girls to the ballroom and keep them together? This place is enormous and it might take a while to search. They can get some sleep in there," I suggested, as I avoided eye contact by looking slightly over River's shoulder. Angel let out an enormous yawn as I spoke. "I'll stay here with Cary and Nick."

I really didn't want to examine my reluctance to have River, Ryder, and Emma alone together in a dark hallway. Besides, my explanation sounded entirely reasonable.

River tilted his head and shot me a look I couldn't decipher. "Sure, I was going to minimize movement by only taking Emma, but we can do that." I sensed there was more he wanted to say, but he pursed his lips and turned to the alphas hanging back. "We'll take this east wing, if you guys pair up and take the central common areas, the west wing, and the two wings upstairs."

"Roger," came the unified reply, as the alphas River had brought inside moved off in pairs. The two guys from Sam's team who had been watching the Palace had stripped off their camouflage suits while I wasn't paying attention. They now moved quickly into the large formal living room across from us. Their guns were raised and flashlights shined to illuminate the gilt furniture in their path. I watched, fascinated, for a moment as they moved through the room with controlled, precise movements, checking it thoroughly.

River hustled the huddled omegas in the other direction, as Ryder reached down to pick up a sleepy Angel. She wrapped her arms around his neck as if she trusted him implicitly and promptly fell asleep on his shoulder. River shot me a lingering look as he left, full of unspoken words, but the hot, angry gaze Ryder raked over me singed me in two. Despite the glare, the sight of a little blond girl being carried so carefully in Ryder's arms had me swallowing hard. I felt like someone had smacked me in the face with a future that no longer belonged to me. One I'd dreamed about so often. The ache that had tormented me for over a decade almost tore me in two now that the twins were in front of me, yet were still so far away.

I watched the twins until they were out of sight, unable to tear my eyes away as I shoved down a sudden panic that they might not come back. When they disappeared into the darkness, I turned back to Cary and Nick, who had taken up positions by the open front door.

"Are you okay?" Nick asked. His face had tightened with concern and he looked like he wanted to reach for me, as his hand twitched at his side. I'd thought I was, but the pounding in my head intensified as the adrenaline I'd been running on all night burned out.

"My head hurts a little," I said as I winced. The beam of the torches suddenly piercing my brain. The world tilted as I swayed on my feet and Cary was there in an instant.

"We've got you," he whispered as he pulled me close. I suddenly understood how Angel felt as I wrapped my arms around his neck and leaned into him. His body was warm and solid, and his hug was everything I'd been yearning for, for the longest time. I wanted to curl up and live right here, with his arms banded tightly around me and his vanilla ice cream scent filling my senses.

"Nick, can you grab one of the big armchairs and drag it so we can see it in the corner there, but it's out of the draft from the door?" He pointed, and I watched through half-lidded eyes as Nick darted into the room and spotted a massive arm chair sitting on a circular rug by itself. He yanked the rug and maneuvered the chair quietly into the corner, where they could see it easily from the front doors.

Cary picked me up briefly before he settled me down into it, as Nick reappeared with a cushion and a throw blanket he handed to Cary. I was immensely grateful, as my body suddenly felt too heavy to move.

Cary settled the cushion under my head before he tucked the blanket around me, while Nick carefully took off my shoes. It had been a long time since I'd felt as cared for as I did in that moment. My eyes slipped close, almost without my consent, as a hand gently slid a few loose strands of hair out of my face, brushing tender fingers across my chilled skin. I leaned my head into the feeling, letting the touch ease my headache, and I heard a soft sigh. I wasn't entirely sure if it was mine or someone else's.

I was back at the Palace, but everything had changed. I had a feeling things were going to change even more. And they were going to get messy.

Everything I wanted was within my reach, but I didn't know if any of it was mine anymore. Or if I deserved it.

Four

I woke slowly, snuggled into a comfy bed with a soft pillow under my head. The pine soap scent of the sheets was familiar, but there was an added hint of vanilla ice cream that had me licking my lips and moaning softly. I felt tempted to curl up further under the cozy weight of the comforter, but I was too hot. I kicked it off as I turned onto my back and stretched my arms up over my head while I yawned.

I blinked my eyes open slowly, but a feeling of being watched had me stilling mid stretch. I lifted my head slightly to see the giant alpha from last night curled uncomfortably into a high-backed chair in the corner. His eyes were closed, though, and he seemed to be asleep. A barrage of powerful emotions hit me. They had me shifting my eyes to the side to see Ryder sitting on the floor by my bed. The bare skin of my stomach had trapped his heated, conflicted gaze. Someone had removed my hoodie before they tucked me into bed in my black t-shirt and jeans, and my top had ridden up while I stretched.

I felt frozen in place, not knowing whether to cover myself or finish my stretch as he stared. A wave of need hit me that mirrored my own, making me arch my back slightly on a whimper. His gaze shot away before he got up hurriedly. Unfurling himself from the floor in one swift, fluid motion. I wanted to make him stay, but I didn't have the words. The unspoken ones that had been crowding me last night suddenly evaporated.

I hadn't told the whole truth when I'd said we were unbonded last night. Unclaimed would be more accurate. A fragile bond had sprung up between us when we were teenagers, that had fractured when I left for the Palace without them. It had been a raw wound I'd carried with me ever since. It had never healed, or even scabbed over, despite the decade we'd spent apart.

"If you're awake, I'll get River," Ryder said in a gruff voice that felt layered with even more emotion than his gaze.

I pulled my shirt back down and dropped my hands back to my sides, feeling that wound burn as if it was hot and fresh. A comforting hand grabbed mine, and I smiled as the subtle vanilla ice cream scent intensified. I glanced to my side and saw Cary, fully dressed, lying on top of the comforter, with a throw blanket twisted around his legs. He was watching me intently, and my heart skipped a beat. That bubble around us had well and truly popped last night, and I was thrilled. I was quickly becoming addicted to his bold touches.

Neither of us said a word about the hand holding. We both knew instinctively it had been a long time coming. I'd never doubted my connection to Cary, only the timing and the inherent danger in it while living at the Palace.

"No need, I'm right here," came a deep voice from the doorway. River was there, looking tired and rumpled in the same clothes from last night, too. His gaze locked to where Cary's hand had intertwined with mine, as Ryder slipped past him out of the room.

Christ on a cracker. It was too early for moody testosterone. Or maybe it wasn't. I had no idea what time it was, but if I could see people in my room, that meant daylight. I rubbed my face before I sat up and looked at the window. Someone had pulled the curtains closed haphazardly and a large slice of sky was visible. It was bright out, which meant it wasn't even early morning. I'd gotten used to waking up early during the last few days at the farm. I missed the sounds of animals demanding to be fed and people cheerfully calling hello to each other.

"Why is everyone in my room?" I asked suddenly. I didn't mean to sound cranky, but I wasn't used to having so many people watch me as I woke up, and I was suddenly a little flustered. Plus, I felt as if I'd barely slept.

Looking around, I quickly realized that we weren't even in my room. Nothing here was familiar. The room was dark and masculine, with an opulent gothic vibe. The curtains were heavy black velvet, while the dark comforter and sheets felt like silk. Gold embellished and outlined the black wood paneling on the walls and the dark timber bed frame. Plus, there were gold candelabras and candlesticks everywhere.

I knew I was at the Palace, but most of the common areas and the omegas' rooms were done in boring cream and gold. Then it suddenly clicked. This was the VIP suite. I'd snuck into the suite once before, and I'd peeked into the bedrooms out of curiosity.

River raised one eyebrow that seemed to say, *why do you think?* He just watched me for a beat, holding my attention, before he grudgingly answered.

"Cary insisted on staying in here with you. Your sudden headache and dizziness had us worried. You barely stirred when he carried you up here. The alpha woke up from the sedation a few hours ago, came straight in here and went back to sleep in the chair. He didn't seem inclined to move. Ryder and I have been taking turns to keep watch."

The alpha flicked one eye open and eyed River before closing it again. *Okay, not asleep.*

"Uh, maybe we should move this into the living room," I suggested. The bedroom was spacious, bigger than any bedroom I'd slept in before, but it still felt like too much with Cary and the two alphas in it. The only time I'd ever had a male in my bedroom before was the few times River and Ryder had snuck in when we were kids. We'd read comic books by torchlight when we were supposed to be asleep. This felt a lot different. I needed some air to get my composure back.

I let go of Cary's hand and slipped off the bed before heading for the door. River watched me intently as I approached him and his gaze felt loaded with as many questions as I had. At the last moment, he shifted slightly to block the door. I stopped right before him, closer than was socially acceptable. I had to tilt my head slightly to look him in the eye. His eyes roved over my face, as if he was mapping the changes since he'd seen me last. His bright blue eyes darkened as they settled on my mouth and he subtly leaned toward me.

I held my breath, waiting to see what he would do next. River had never been one to back down when he wanted something. The anticipation sent waves of heat racing through me and I felt my chest flush. The pull I'd always felt to River had intensified, rather than lessened with time. Despite our broken bond.

He'd been a boy the last time I saw him. He was all man now. The softness of youth was gone, replaced with blond scruff and lean planes. I could see his collarbone peeking out where his long-sleeved t-shirt had pulled to the side and revealed a slice of lightly tanned skin at his neck. My breathing sped up as I imagined licking him from his collarbone to the curve of his jaw, then kissing across to that delectable mouth. It was slightly parted, in invitation maybe?

River leaned even closer to me, while gripping the doorframe, almost as if he was falling towards me. He was so close I could feel the heat of his body. The pull I had always felt toward him had been innocent as kids. We'd been best friends. It felt entirely different now, as I felt a damp heat flood between my thighs at his proximity.

River stilled as a dark presence appeared at my back and the scent of a jungle surrounded me, a potent spike of ginger running through it. A low growl left goosebumps in its wake as it skated across my skin. River raised an eyebrow and looked over my shoulder.

"I'd suggest you let her past," Cary said from behind us both, with a studied, casual air that had a hint of steel running through it.

I couldn't see what passed between the two alphas, but River nodded slightly, surprising me, and stepped back. I was almost disappointed. Standing between them, with both alphas so close, had the building heat in my body surging almost painfully. Yet I also knew blocking me was a warning from River, even if his attentions had gone slightly astray. He'd always been a good guy, but determined to get his way once he'd fixated on something, and I could still sense that in him now.

He would never hurt me. But he wanted to talk and he wouldn't wait forever. If he had to get in my face to make me acknowledge him, he would.

As soon as I moved away from their combined heat and headed out to the living room, I shivered. I'd forgotten how draughty and cold the Palace could be, after being shacked up in a cozy wooden cabin at the farm. I crossed my arms over my chest and rubbed my hands up and down my arms. A tousled head peeked up over an ornate, gilt framed couch in front of me, startling me.

Nick rubbed at his face tiredly before stilling when he noticed me. He looked adorably rumpled, with a clump of hair sticking up at the back. I had the urge to run my hands through it to smooth it back into place. He couldn't have slept well. That couch looked beautiful, but incredibly uncomfortable.

Nick's eyes flicked down to my hands, still rubbing my arms, before he suddenly jumped up and held something out to me.

"Here's your hoodie." He looked embarrassed. *Had he been sleeping with it?* "I kept it in case you slept through the scheduled call with Maia and Lexie. The phone's in the pocket. You were pretty out of it last night. They should call soon." He was rambling, and his cheeks flushed red. It was cute as heck.

I moved over and thanked him as I took it from him. Ryder hopped up from the chair he'd flung himself into and opened the curtains to give us more light while I put the hoodie on. A brusque, pained noise had me spinning around. The alpha was standing in the middle of the room, staring out past the timber and glass French doors that had appeared from behind the curtain. They led out to a stone balcony and a view of the tops of trees and the sky outside. It was the VIP suite, after all. We were on the upper floor of the Palace, at the front of the building.

He drifted over to the window as if he was in a trance. I watched as he raised his shaking hand and placed it against the glass, almost reverently. Ryder moved closer on silent feet and opened the door for him, letting in a cool breeze. He gave Ryder the barest nod before he moved outside, almost hesitantly. I followed him, feeling pulled towards him as I sensed a hint of his wonder and agony. The moment seemed so personal, yet I couldn't look away.

My gaze wasn't on the view, even though it was gorgeous. The Palace was closer to the mountains than the farm, and they looked spectacular as they speared up from the surrounding forest. Yet this alpha was all I could see. He had appeared larger than life last night, but now he just looked broken. Almost fragile, despite his size. It was hard to see his features past the wild hair and the shaggy beard. In the sunlight, I could see how knotted and dirty it was, yet the light also brought out hints of auburn within the dark brown tones. It had looked much darker last night.

I wanted so desperately to go to him, but I had no idea what he had been through and what he could bear right now. I felt Cary come up behind me and wrap a throw blanket around me before he turned to the alpha and wrapped one around him, too. He was still barefoot and in his torn hospital scrubs, and the air was chilly. The alpha barely registered it, but the hand on his chest shifted to hold the blanket to him. He slowly closed his eyes and lifted his head up to the weak sun that was shining down, before he filled his lungs with a deep breath. My eyes traveled down from his face to where he was clutching the blanket, and I didn't miss the fine shake in his hands.

"How long were you in that cage?" Ryder asked him gently. Ryder had always been extremely empathetic to people and animals. This alpha felt like a bit of both. The softness in Ryder's voice now, compared to the harsh glares he had been sending me, made me want to cry. It took a lot to make Ryder mad, but hurting someone he cared about would do it. He didn't forgive easily.

The alpha didn't respond or even acknowledge the question. When he opened his eyes again, the distant mountains still held his gaze.

Ryder gave him a few moments before he tried again, as he asked gently, "What's your name?"

The alpha tilted his head, as if he was thinking. I didn't expect him to answer. His voice, when it came, was deep, yet rough and scratchy, as if he hadn't used it in a long time. "Wolf."

We all bounced our gazes to each other, trying to make sense of that one word. The first he had spoken. *Had he seen a wolf in the distance, and was trying out the word, or was that his name?*

My gaze snagged on Nick, who looked curious rather than puzzled. His gaze fixed on the giant alpha. I could almost see his brain mulling something over. In the short time I'd known Nick, it had become clear that he was incredibly smart and a quick thinker.

A sudden movement in my periphery had me turning back to the giant alpha. He was looking over his shoulder at me, before his gaze shifted to

Cary and a mix of emotions I couldn't decipher flashed through his eyes. He was trying to convey something to us, but didn't have the words. A heartbeat later, he dropped the blanket from around his shoulders and launched himself over the edge of the balcony.

I screamed, as Cary yelled, "No!" We both raced to the balustrade, but the twins beat us there. Their eyes met a moment before Ryder also launched himself over the edge. My heart seemed to plunge into the void with him.

I hit the stone edge of the balcony with a force that made me grunt and doubled me over. My upper body swung over way too far. I felt a flash of pure terror. The drop pulled at me for a moment before an arm banded around me and hauled me back against a solid chest. I could hear ripping noises as I looked down, and saw the giant alpha half climb, half fall, down a vine-covered trellis. He left large swathes of stone revealed in his wake, like scars. Ryder followed silently, rappelling down the trellis as if he was born to do it.

"Holy shit," I vaguely heard Nick mumble next to me, as the alpha turned while halfway down and threw himself to the ground. He rolled once before he sprang to his feet. His legs wobbled, and he stumbled for a moment before he took off across the lawn. I took in a sharp breath that hurt my lungs in the chill air, as Ryder pushed himself off the wall, somersaulted in midair and landed in a half crouch. He gave chase instantly.

Hunter had said last night the giant alpha was deceptively fast. He hadn't lied.

"Is Ryder trying to catch him?" Cary asked River, as he gripped the edge of the balcony so hard his knuckles turned white. He looked a heartbeat away from throwing himself over the edge as well. Nick had moved up alongside him and had his hand on Cary's shoulder, as if he was prepared to hold him back, much the same way River was for me.

I shot Cary a grateful look. I wanted to know, too, but it felt as if my throat had closed up. Trying to catch him didn't seem like an option that would end well. I didn't want to see either Ryder or the giant alpha get hurt, especially at each other's hands.

River still had his arms banded around me, and his dark chocolate scent blanketed me. The warmth and security of his body against mine seemed to strip me of the polite, demure act I'd defaulted to last night. The camouflage that had kept me alive. It bled away, leaving me raw and exposed. I didn't know the woman who lived underneath it, though. I'd rarely let her out. Maia and Lexie were the only other people who had ever gotten past it, and they'd barely peeled back the surface. Angel had too, but differently.

I felt River send me reassurance through the wisps of our bond that remained, confusing my heart. It made me wonder if maybe everything would be okay, if only we could hold each other. But it was a bittersweet fantasy. I swallowed hard as memories of the last time he wrapped his arms around me swamped me. The joy, chased by terror, of that night.

"No. He's following to make sure the alpha doesn't hurt himself," River said from behind me, startling me back to the problem at hand.

I nodded. That sounded like Ryder.

"If the alpha's going to come back, it has to be on his own terms. He's been in a cage too long. If he needs to be out there right now, then that's where he should be." River sighed suddenly, with a note of pain, before he squeezed me gently. "People need to have agency over their own lives. You can't cage people. Even if it's not with bars and you just want to keep them safe. You can cage people with your expectations and your actions, too. I learned that lesson the hard way and I'm not making the same mistake twice."

I pulled in a sharp lungful of cold air, as I got the feeling he wasn't just talking about the giant alpha. *Was he talking about me? Or was he talking about Ryder? Was he trying to tell me Ryder might not want to come back?*

Knowing Ryder didn't want me would be a lot worse than wondering if he did.

The sudden buzzing of a phone broke the tense silence, and my panic, as we watched the treeline Ryder and the alpha had disappeared into. River slowly let me go and it felt symbolic after his words. He slid his hands down my arms while I fumbled with my pocket and pulled the phone out.

I could barely meet River's eyes, feeling entirely too vulnerable, as I mumbled, "It's Maia and Lexie checking in. I'm going to take this inside."

Cary nodded, his eyes following me for a moment before darting back to the treeline. Nick shot me a grin. He knew those girls and what was about to go down.

Five

*F**uck, this guy was fast.*

I wasn't a slacker by any stretch. I could move swiftly when I needed to, and frequently did. Yet this guy, who was so huge he looked as if he should amble around like a bear, had me breathing hard trying to keep pace. There was a lot of power in that gigantic frame. I could feel a fine sweat break out between my shoulder blades, even though the air had turned cool in recent weeks. The beginning of winter had been an awful time for the Crash to happen, not that there could have ever been a good time.

I didn't begrudge Wolf his urge to run. I was happy to shadow him while he got it out of his system, but I was becoming a little worried he was going to run forever. Eventually, he slowed enough for me to look around and get my bearings. I recognized a marker on a tree and had an idea.

"Wolf," I called out, a slight bark to my voice, just enough to get his attention but not enough to be a threat.

He startled and skidded to a halt as he looked around wildly until he located me off to his left. I hadn't been sure if he knew I was following or not. If he had, he'd forgotten. Running had a way of doing that, clearing the mind of everything but what was in front of you. I put my hands up in a pacifying gesture.

"If you need a time-out, I have a hideout nearby."

Wolf regarded me with a fierce yet wild intelligence blazing in his eyes. For a moment, he didn't appear to know me. He growled low in his chest. I took in the way he was standing, slightly hunched and poised to attack. He looked more primitive than he had curled up in the chair in Ava and Cary's room this morning. His eyes glinted with danger as his lip curled. *Was it the forest surroundings playing a trick on me, or was he slipping into a more feral state?*

I wasn't sure, but either way, I didn't want to spook him right now. I crouched down onto my heels, to appear less of a threat. "You're free to do whatever you want. You're just not outfitted for a run in the forest. I'm worried about your feet. I have supplies in the hideout, and I have boots that should fit you."

Wolf looked at his bare feet, lifting each one slowly. He appeared surprised to see the blood on them. Adrenaline did that to people, blocked out pain receptors temporarily. He moved closer to me and I stayed still, while keeping my body relaxed. When he got close enough, he sniffed the air. As soon as he scented me, he seemed to relax slightly and his eyes lost some of their wild edge.

I stood up slowly. He waited until I was looking him in the eye before he nodded at me. I gestured for him to follow as I turned and took off, heading slightly east. It felt like I'd somehow tamed a wild beast. I didn't turn and make sure that he was following. I didn't need to. Every creature in the forest could hear him. He was fast, but no-one had trained him how to be stealthy. The forest had gone quiet around us, as the animals hid while the predators passed them by. Even the birds were quiet.

He stuck close to me as we ran. When we got closer to our destination, I scanned our surroundings to make sure no one else had followed. A few minutes later, I ducked down an overgrown ravine and stopped halfway to the bottom, scanning the trees. Wolf was watching me closely, but he was more curious now than anything else. He'd cocked his head sideways, and he looked intrigued as his gaze darted to our surroundings and back to me repeatedly.

"Can you help me with these?" I gestured to some overhanging vines and pulled them aside. Wolf stepped in closer and pulled a great armful to the side, being careful not to tug any free. He raised his eyebrows at the door made of cut tree trunks hidden behind the dense leaves. I flicked the hidden bolt on the door, pushing it open before I stepped into the darkness inside.

Wolf surprised me again when he followed me straight in. Showing a level of trust I wasn't sure I'd earned. I felt for the metal tin on the shelf inside the doorway, before pulling out a candle and a box of matches. I knew there were some solar powered lanterns in here, but we hadn't been back in a while, so they wouldn't have any charge left.

With careful movements, I put the candle on another shelf further in and moved over to a trunk. I crouched down to open the lid and started riffling through its contents before pulling out some socks and boots. I pulled out a black shirt, too. It was a stretchy fabric and might fit. I knew none of the jackets or pants would fit. We were almost the same height, but he was a lot broader in the chest and fuller in the thighs than River or me. I'd been keeping an eye on him as he moved about the dugout, touching things. A wild animal sniffing out a new environment. I kept my movements slow and methodical, so as not to spook him in this confined space.

River and I had worked painstakingly to dig out a section of the hillside, then compacted the dirt walls and put in timber supports. Our hard work had paid off. It was still intact. Memories rushed me. We'd been eighteen, on leave from the military, and had thrown ourselves into the manual labor. We still hadn't reconciled ourselves to Ava leaving us. Our bond had developed enough in our early teens, unnoticed by any of the adults in our lives, that her rejection when it came had caused physical pain. It had been almost three years since we'd seen her at that point, but the pain was just as intense as the day she'd left. There had been times I'd wondered if it would kill me. I didn't want to even think about how bad it would have hurt if we'd claimed her before she left. I'd been tempted, a feeling of impending doom riding me, but we'd been far too young.

River had focused on getting her back as his way of dealing with the pain. He made plans, built a network of hideouts like this one. All ready to help her escape and shelter her if she ever needed it. He still thought we'd end up running away together one day. I got it. The thought of her being barked into submission by a strange alpha, with the Palace's blessing, made me rage. Yet my anger at her betrayal flared just as deep. She had run from us instead of with us, and chosen to go to the Palace, of all places. To find a new mate.

My love for my brother had kept me going for the last ten years. I couldn't stand to feel his pain when, in the dark of night, he despaired of ever getting her back. He blamed himself and it tore at me. I blamed her. I was just grateful his plan gave us both a purpose. It kept us moving. Even if the things we'd had to do to keep her safe had changed us. So I went along with it and kept my thoughts to myself. We were twins, though. I knew he could feel my anger, but we never talked about it again after the day we realized there was no getting her out of the Palace. At least, not before she had her debut.

I snapped out of my reverie as I felt eyes watching me. It wasn't like me to zone out when someone else was around. It was weird how comfortable I felt around this strange giant of an alpha. I looked up to find Wolf watching me. I shook my head and jumped up from where I'd been sitting on the trunk. He'd settled on another one opposite me. I could hear the wind in the trees outside from the door we'd left open, and the birds that had started up their chirping again. It was quieter inside the dim dugout, with only the sound of our breathing.

"Swap," I said, more brusquely than I intended. I sounded more like my brother than myself. My emotions were still riding me. I'd never been good at concealing them. Wolf watched me closely as he stood up and shuffled over to my side. His feet seemed to cause him some pain as he moved. It seemed his adrenaline had finally worn off. I passed him the shirt, socks, and boots. He nodded in thanks as he sat down and examined them. The shirt was a performance style long sleeved tee, designed to keep you warm, but also wick sweat away from your body.

Wolf effortlessly tore the ripped hospital scrubs off his chest. He dropped the shreds to the ground carelessly before he wrestled himself into the shirt. I could see it stretched to capacity around his muscled chest and biceps as he flexed, testing it. By some miracle, it held. It would keep him warmer, at least. Even if it showcased every ripple of his muscles whenever he moved. He belonged on the cover of a steamy novel. Maybe a wolf shifter story, with that shaggy mane. They were my secret weakness. River teased me endlessly whenever he found me reading one. He didn't realize it was the packs in those taboo stories that drew me in, as much as reading the sexy scenes turned me on.

I glanced away from his chest when I noticed Wolf's narrowed eyes on me as he tried to puzzle me out. He followed my gaze down to his feet. I turned back to the trunk he'd been sitting on before and pulled out some bottles of water and long-life energy bars. I couldn't remember seeing him eat since we'd come across him last night. I threw a few at him and he caught them. His reflexes were good. I also pulled out a basic first aid kit. I approached him slowly and pointed to his feet. He nodded at me again, so I grabbed an empty crate, turned it upside down, and sat on it in front of him.

I gently picked up one of his legs so I could rest it across my lap and rolled his pant leg up as much as I could. I felt him tense briefly as I laid one hand carefully on his foot, before he relaxed and his leg sank heavier against my thigh. He closed his eyes and rested back against the wall of the dugout. I watched him the way he'd watched me earlier, and my curiosity piqued. It seemed my touch brought him comfort. I remembered how he'd relaxed when Cary had touched his chest last night, too. *Interesting.*

I filed my curious thoughts away to mull over later. With as much as this alpha had gone through, if touch soothed him, I wouldn't deny him. I carefully washed and dressed each foot as best as I could with the rudimentary supplies I had before I pulled the socks over his feet. The rocks and twigs of the forest floor had cut his feet up, but not as bad as I'd feared. He opened his eyes as I pulled the boots on and laced them up loosely. They were a little snug with the bandages on, but they fit. He winced as I worked, but his eyes seemed even clearer than they had before we'd entered the dugout.

"Thank you." He rumbled in that deep, scratchy voice. I wondered when the last time was someone had done something for him simply to care for him.

"Were you running, or running away?" I asked him. Hoping for any answer and an idea of what to do next. The idea of leaving him here didn't sit well with me, but I also didn't want to be gone from the Palace too long. I refused to examine why I didn't want to stay away, or the itchy feeling I had to go back.

"Running," he said simply. He was a man of few words. It was what I had suspected, though. I hadn't gotten the feeling he was fleeing when he leaped from the balcony. More running through the wild because he could, and he'd been denied so long.

"Do you want to go back now?"

A flash of fear crossed his face for the briefest moment, before a determined look replaced it. He looked at his feet and grimaced as he tested them on the ground before he nodded. It was clear he'd walk over hot coals to get back if he had to. I felt like a coward. This alpha had no reason to return to a place where he had obviously been tortured. Yet he'd not only stayed when he first woke up, he'd sought Ava and Cary out and slept in an uncomfortable chair in their room, despite only knowing them for hours. I'd known Ava almost my whole life, and I was avoiding her because I didn't want my worst fears confirmed. That she left because she didn't want us. Or maybe just didn't want me.

"Don't worry about your feet. I've got you." I said. My voice sounded suddenly rough. I jumped up, pushed the crate back out of the way, and moved to the dim rear of the dugout. Curious eyes followed me. I could feel them as I threw a tarp off two dirt bikes hidden in the back.

"I hope they still work," I said as I grabbed a gas can. I hoped the gas was still good, too. It looked sealed tight. I glanced up to find Wolf had gotten up and followed me over. He ran his hand over a handlebar almost reverently.

"Do you know how to ride?"

I only barely made out his nod in the dim light, and I let out a relieved breath. I wasn't sure one bike could take our combined weight.

"Okay, grab a duffle bag and start filling it with food, torches, anything that people might need back at the Palace. We'll take as much as we can now, and if needed, we'll come back for the rest later." Every resource was valuable now that we couldn't make more. Even the sturdy duffle bags.

We grabbed what we could fit, extinguished the candle and put the tin back in its place next to the door. Then we wheeled the bikes outside, and I slipped the hidden latch back into place as Wolf carefully rearranged the vines. He turned when he appeared satisfied and hopped on his bike eagerly. I thought I could see a grin through his shaggy hair. The suspension was straining, and the engine sputtered a little when he turned it on. But it ran. The smell of gasoline flooded the small ravine. He let out a wild whoop as the engine thrummed beneath him.

I turned my bike on and it reacted much the same, a few sputters before it settled down and ran smoothly. I angled my bike towards the bottom of the ravine and pointed towards the left, so Wolf would know which direction we would head. The ravine flattened out a few hundred metres around the bend and there was an old fire trail not far past it that led in the direction we needed to go.

I took a deep breath and steeled myself to go back to the Palace, and Ava, when a sudden realization hit me. All these years I'd stupidly thought that despite the pain, if I found her again, I could let her go this time. Let River have her and be done with it. I'd held onto my anger, hoping it would set me free, but I was a fool. I knew now, with absolute certainty, Ava had entwined herself so deep in my soul there was no escape.

Her scent and every stolen glance since I'd laid eyes on her again had yanked at me so hard I'd had to use all my strength to keep my feet firmly in place. And it wasn't only her now. Wolf, Cary, and even Nick were pulling at me in the strangest way. It was a different pull, but they were still drawing me in. As if I'd known them my whole life. Staying away was not an option. I needed to face this, whatever it was.

The thought scared the hell out of me.

I felt a tap on my arm and looked up to see the eyes of an old, wild soul staring back at me.

"Me too," he said, over the dull noise of the engines, and I knew exactly what he meant. My fear was reflected in his eyes, and he wasn't hiding it this time. I could have pretended I didn't hear him, or didn't understand, but I wouldn't do that to him. Wolf was baring his soul to me, and willing to lead with bravery. I could do no less.

"Why did you help us last night, and why did you stay this morning?" Wolf had not only rescued Ava and Cary last night, when we wouldn't have gotten to them in time. He'd stopped when Nick appeared, rather than barrel over him, which he could have done easily. There had been no such hesitation with the rogue alphas on the street. He also hadn't batted an eyelash when River and I had taken turns staying in Ava and Cary's room alongside him.

He shrugged, and his eyes were wide, as if the question surprised him. As if it should be obvious. His answer came out in a deep rumble. "You're pack."

All the breath left my lungs. *Was it that simple?*

I didn't know if I was ready to fight to win Ava back. I was still carrying a lot of hurt and I had questions, but I could acknowledge the truth. She was mine, and this strange medley of people was mine, too. As entwined as Ava, River, and I had been as kids, and as tightly meshed as I was with my twin, it had always felt like there was something more for us, too. Something bigger was out there. *Was this why Ava had felt driven to go to the Palace? Should we have listened to her?*

None of these questions were going to get answered sitting here. So, I sighed and eased down the ravine until we reached the bottom, then pointed our bikes toward our people.

Toward home.

Six

I dashed back across to the bedroom I'd woken up in and launched myself back onto the bed. I quickly crossed my legs and snuggled my feet down under the comforter. The chill of the stone balcony had seeped through my socks, and my feet felt frozen. I could only imagine how the giant alpha was doing, running through the forest with bare feet. At least Ryder had shoes on, he appeared to have slept in them. As if he hadn't yet decided if he was staying.

"Hello?" I asked, a little breathlessly, as I pressed the answer button.

A barrage of questions assaulted me, each one tumbling over the following one. Maia seemed both furious she'd slept through the raid on the town last night, and worried to find out I was gone when she woke up this morning. Lexie just yawned loudly as she tried to tell Maia to slow down.

"Okay, can we try that again? One question at a time?" I asked, a little sheepishly.

Maia huffed, sounding annoyed. She made me smile. She'd been so withdrawn during our time together at the Palace. I loved to hear her so animated now. Even if it was a lot to take in.

"Fine, are you okay?" she asked, as Lexie spoke over her to ask, "Why are you breathing so hard?"

"Maybe because there's a man between my thighs?" I answered Lexie's question first, trying to lighten their anxiety with an awkward joke. It didn't work.

I had to yank the phone away from my ear to avoid the screeching. I pulled it back hastily when I heard Lexie faintly yell, "Sam, get the chopper!"

"Stop! You don't need the chopper. I'm fine. Sorry, I was joking. I ran into my room to take your call in private, and I clearly have no stamina."

Maia let out a little kitten growl, but Lexie was laughing. "Don't worry us like that!" Maia said, letting out a deep breath.

"Why would you worry if I was having sex?" I asked. While I appreciated their concern, I wasn't exactly sure why they were concerned.

"Okay, truth bomb," Maia said. "We've never talked about it, but I always assumed you were a virgin. The same as the other omegas at the Palace. Despite how hot Cary is for you, you guys barely make eye contact. Now that you can finally choose a partner for yourself, I want you to know you have time. You don't need to rush anything."

"What if it doesn't feel as if I'm rushing anything? What if it feels like I've been waiting forever?" I'd never talked about this stuff to anyone before. Even with Maia. Before the Crash, it had seemed pointless. Our fates had felt so precarious. It felt nice to talk it out now with women I trusted.

"That's okay, too," Lexie said, as she jumped in before Maia could respond. "As long as it's your choice and you feel ready. But there are a few things you need to know that I only recently figured out. Being with a prime alpha changes things."

"A prime alpha?" Maia squeaked. "Are we talking about the giant, feral alpha you told me about just now?" They clearly hadn't had much time to catch-up with each other yet either.

"Yeah, he's definitely got that big-dick, prime energy. If he's been in a cage for who knows how long, it's no wonder he's feral. Could you imagine Damon if he hadn't found Hunter as a teenager, and no-one had touched him with affection or comfort in years? Or Sam without Dio? For both of them, touch from their pack mates calms their beasts."

Maia was quiet for a heartbeat. "I don't even want to imagine."

"Do you think that's why he relaxed when Cary touched his chest before he passed out?" I asked Lexie.

"Yeah. Uh, I do." She sounded distracted, as though she was thinking.

"You're both omegas. That sounds like it could get complicated," Maia said.

"Ava," Lexie said a little sharply, as if she had just thought of something, "the twins said they had your clothes and blankets stuffed into his air vents. I think the Palace believes you're his scent matched mate. It explains why they mostly left you alone. They had other plans for you. Your scent may have been the only thing keeping him somewhat sane. Or they could have been torturing him with it." Lexie's voice had softened while she spoke and she sounded near tears by the end. Her emotions had been erratic since her omega finally came out to play. I could picture Maia hugging her quietly.

The thought of the Palace lab techs torturing the giant alpha, who had been nothing but protective with me, made me feel nauseous. And now he was gone. His absence left a familiar ache in my heart that had me rubbing my chest. Even though I'd only known him hours, rather than years like the twins. There was no doubt in my mind he was my mate. Yet he also appeared to be Cary's, and I was surprisingly okay with that. I suddenly wanted him back with a ferocious need that scared me. Even if Cary was the one he needed right now.

I must have whimpered, because Maia asked, "Ava, are you okay there? What's going on? Dammit, I hate having these talks over the phone. We need to be there with you."

"The alpha ran just now, and it aches. I think Lexie's right."

"Shit. Do you guys need back-up?" Lexie's voice had firmed, and she sounded serious. As if she was about to marshall an army. I wouldn't put it past her. If we were staging a rebellion, she was clearly our general. Even Damon and Sam deferred to her. She had a unique ability to inspire people to act and make them feel empowered.

"No. Ryder went after him, but only to keep an eye on him. River wants to give him some space and see if he comes back on his own. He doesn't seem worried. I'll let you know if that changes."

"Okay. But if you need us, we're there. No questions asked. Got it?" Lexie said.

"I second what Lexie said, but also, I think River's right. Cages mess with your head. If he stays, it needs to be his decision." Maia sounded solemn. I figured she was thinking about her own history with the Palace's cages and how she escaped. If anyone could relate to him, it would be Maia.

"Got it. I hear you both. We won't force him back. For now, Lexie, I need you to tell me what you found out. What changes things with a prime alpha?" If Wolf came back, I wanted to know how to help him. I didn't know if that was truly his name, but I had decided to use it. I didn't want to keep referring to him as the giant alpha. He deserved to have a name.

"The most important thing is, if you're going to claim a prime alpha, you need to claim a beta first. Maia claimed Max with Leif, before any of the others, but Damon already had informal bonds with the guys, that were filtering his power. My pack came together so quickly and we claimed Dave last. It got hairy after I claimed Sam, and I don't mean chests. Sam's power spread through us when I claimed him, but it felt raw and unsettled. As if it was looking for an anchor and started to build towards something destructive when it couldn't find it."

"You didn't tell me that! What would have happened if Dave hadn't been willing?" Maia sounded outraged and worried.

"I don't know," Lexie said. Her voice sounded muffled. I think she was getting another hug. Or maybe Maia had her in a headlock. "I'm just glad we didn't have to find out. I'm going to read through some of the other books we stole from the Palace library. Until then, you need to be careful. He didn't seem like he would hurt you, but he also looked half wild and acting purely on instinct. I'm not sure how much humanity is left in him."

I bristled at that. If Wolf was truly wild, he would have bolted for his freedom the moment he was loose. He hadn't. He came to save Cary and me first. I got she was coming from a place of care, but anyone talking even slightly badly about him had me feeling riled up.

"His name's Wolf," I said, my voice going low and hard in a way that was unlike me.

"Wow, that's an unusual name." Maia sounded tentative, as if she didn't want to set me off. It was an unusual feeling. Nobody had ever worried about getting me riled up. I noticed my hands had clenched, and it freaked me out.

"Wolf suits him. The guy was never going to be a John or a George." Lexie said, her voice going soft, before she hesitated and I heard her take a deep breath. "I'm sorry if I upset you, Ava. I'm just worried about you. I know you're probably feeling protective of him right now. When I met Sam, I did too. Even though he pushed every one of my buttons and his anger issues felt insurmountable. For a while there, I wasn't sure we would ever bond. It scared me to think we might have to walk away from each other when I knew he was mine."

I forced myself to take a deep breath, shake out my fists, and calm down. "I already walked away from my mates once, when I was barely a teenager. Doing it again now would destroy me. I know my path ahead is rocky, but I've looked into his eyes and there's still humanity there. It's just underneath a lot of fear right now. I can already sense him and I know he's come close to going feral, but he hasn't tipped beyond a point he can't return from. I know you're both worried, but I'm a strong as fuck omega. Right, Lexie?"

I felt myself blushing, not used to cursing. I sometimes swore in my head, but never out loud.

Maia gasped. "Ava swore. What did you do to her, Lexie?"

Lexie just laughed, that deep husky laugh of hers, "Yeah, you are."

"What about Cary?" Maia asked. Neither of them were holding anything back right now, but I knew it was only out of concern and affection for me. I was used to hanging back in group conversations, letting more outgoing people take the lead. I preferred to watch their interactions and listen. Yet it seemed Maia and Lexie weren't going to let me get away with that around them.

"He held my hand when we got here last night, and it's become a thing." I could feel my blush deepening as heat raced down my neck and across my chest. To others, it may be a meaningless act. To me, it was a revelation. *Jeez, no wonder everyone knew I was a virgin.*

"Well, that's cute as heck," Maia said with a smile in her voice.

"If he's Wolf's mate, too, is that a problem?" Lexie, ever the practical one, asked.

"Not for me," I said, without a moment's hesitation. It gave me hope, for the first time, that we could be together. I'd always dreaded the day an alpha would take one of us away. Sharing an alpha with Cary would be no hardship. It would be a dream.

"You go, girl," came Lexie's quick response, my own personal cheerleader.

"Well, Wolf isn't there right now, so we have some time to find you a beta. If Lexie is right, you're going to need one in your pack if you plan to take on a prime alpha, an omega, and two alphas who sound more like ninjas," Maia said.

I didn't respond, not sure how much to admit to right now, but Maia broke the sudden silence when she yelped.

"Why are you poking me?" she hissed at Lexie. I grinned as I heard sheets rustling and light slapping. I imagined the hand gestures that Lexie was giving Maia right now, trying to explain silently. As if I didn't know what she was up to.

"Um, do you want to explain to the class, Ava?" Lexie finally asked. Clearly, whatever miming she'd been doing hadn't gotten through to Maia.

I rolled my eyes, even though they couldn't see. "I kinda have a thing for Nick."

"Oh my god, he's perfect!" Maia shrieked. "How did I not see that, though, when you clearly did, Lexie? And whatever you were trying to spell out looked nothing like Nick."

"I was pointing to my crotch and making the letter N. How could you not get that?"

"You don't have a dick, so I was trying to figure out what a vagina and an N together meant. You weirdo."

Before I could say anything, through my laughter, a sharp knock sounded at my door.

"Come in," I called out after asking the girls to hang on. The door swung open and Nick poked his head through with a small smile. I wanted to die. *How much had he heard?*

"Uh, hi, Nick," I squeaked out. I could hear Lexie and Maia laughing hysterically through the phone.

"I wanted to ask if I could talk to Max when you're done with Maia and Lexie. There's something I need to chat with him about."

"Yeah, sure. Of course. No problemo," I rambled. "Just give me a sec. We're wrapping things up. I'll come find you in a minute."

"No rush, thanks." He disappeared out of sight and closed the door behind him as I flopped onto my back on the bed with a groan.

"Do you think he heard?" Lexie asked through her laughter.

"Probably," I grumbled as I pulled the comforter over my head.

"Why is your voice muffled all of a sudden?" Maia asked through gasps of air.

"I'm hiding," I groaned from underneath the mound of fabric, as a fresh round of laughter assaulted my ears.

"At least you and Nick are the same age, and about as experienced as each other, from what I can gather," Maia said when she'd finally stopped laughing enough to talk properly.

"Uh, about that. I have to confess something." I fiddled with my charm bracelet nervously. When I was younger and the bracelet was looser, I'd been able to spin it around and make the enameled bluebirds fly. Now, it fit snugly to my wrist.

"Ava?" Lexie asked, her voice sharpened suddenly, and she sounded concerned. Her levity disappeared in a heartbeat.

"I'm twenty-three, not twenty-one."

"How is that possible? You would have had your debut. Unless the Palace didn't know. Oh my god, did they not know? You sneaky little squirrel. How did you get away with that?" Maia was floundering. I think I broke her brain.

"She might tell you if you stop asking her questions," Lexie said in a dry tone.

"They didn't know," I confirmed. "I looked young for my age. So my mom lied and said I'd hit puberty early when they came to take me in, and the Palace didn't question it. She figured it would give me more time."

"Time for what?" Lexie asked.

"That's a story for another day," I said. Thinking of my mother and the people who had disappeared from my life so long ago made me unbearably sad. I had no idea where any of them were now. I'd have to ask the twins, and that was going to be a tense conversation.

"So Nick will be your boy toy, because he's only twenty-one," Maia said, a note of glee filling her voice. She'd recovered quickly, and I was glad she didn't hold the lie against me.

"Sure, that sounds fun," I said, shaking off my momentary melancholy.

"Okay, moving on," Lexie said, taking charge as she tried to get serious. "We need to find out what the omegas at the Palace need. That was the point of the call, and apparently we're wrapping it up."

"Fine," I smiled to myself as I threw off the comforter again. I could do this.

I let Maia and Lexie know there was no food left at the Palace, but other than that, the omegas seemed okay. There were too many to bring to the farm. Maintaining them at the Palace long term was going to be tricky, though. There was a small kitchen garden with a chicken coop that was the pet project of the head chef, but other than that, it wasn't set up to be off grid. If Nick could sort out an alternate source of power, that would be a start. The Palace had relied on central heating and winter was starting to make its presence known. In a few weeks, this place would become a tomb without some big changes.

"I'm heading down to meet with Emma now. She seems to have taken charge of the omegas. I'll find out what else we need here."

"Okay, we can get some canned food from town brought up this morning, and we can send some fresh supplies this afternoon," Lexie said. She sounded confident, and I trusted she'd get it done.

"Thanks, Lexie. We'll talk again when I know more tonight. I'll grab Nick if you grab Max," I said as I peeked my head out my bedroom door, hoping and dreading to see Nick. He hopped up from the couch as soon as he spotted me, and came over with his usual long, loping stride. Nick was tall and a little lanky, with floppy brown hair and gorgeous light brown eyes that sparkled to match his infectious grin. He had light freckles smattered across his face that matched my own. He was all easy going, boyish charm.

His usual smile was missing though, as he stopped in front of me and searched my face. He opened his mouth as if he was going to say something, but stopped. I was staring at him, like an idiot, not sure what to say, when I heard a voice and realized I still had the phone against my ear.

"Hey, Ava." Max's friendly tone made me feel nostalgic for the farm. Everyone had been so open and welcoming when we'd arrived. The entire community had felt like a giant home.

"Hey, Max. Nick's here, I'll put him on, now." I passed the phone over hastily, but fumbled it as he reached out. We both grabbed for it at the same time and his warm fingers wrapped around mine, as well as the phone. He stared back at me as a blush spread over his cheeks that matched mine, and tingles ran up my arm. A slow, hesitant smile spread across his face, before someone coughed pointedly in the living room behind him.

Nick gently took the phone from me, then he raised my fingers to his lips and kissed them lightly before he let my hand go. It was an old school move, yet a sweet one. Full of intention. I hadn't expected Nick to be so bold, though. A storm of butterflies erupted in my stomach as I watched him casually saunter away into one of the other bedrooms, as if he hadn't just rocked my world.

I turned back to the living room when he was out of sight, only to find Cary and River standing awkwardly at opposite ends of the room. Both watching me. Cary had a small smile on his face, but River was scowling.

I'd told Lexie and Maia I knew my path was rocky. But I was fooling myself. There were avalanche warnings surrounding me. Like the ones on the windy, narrow roads through the mountains, that scream danger.

Except for the twins, the only common link between these men was me. Yet all five were mine. I wasn't some femme fatale or seductress, though. I also didn't have the innate confidence of Lexie, or even Maia. I didn't know how to bring these men together into a pack. *And if I managed it? How did I think I was going to handle five men when I'd never even handled one?*

I needed to ask Maia and Lexie way more questions. Or maybe find a book. With pictures.

Seven

Something wasn't right here.

I was standing, staring in frustration at a jagged hole in the wall, when a voice startled me.

"Let me guess, it was like this when you found it?"

I spun around to see River leaning casually in the open door. I figured he was trying to appear non-threatening, but it didn't work. He always looked a heartbeat away from catching a bullet with his bare hands. There was a coiled power within his body that he could never completely conceal. I'd spent a lot of time around Damon and his mates, but River and Ryder even had them spooked.

"No. I definitely did it." River's mouth curved slightly at my words, as if he was fighting a smile. I wasn't sure why, but he didn't intimidate me the way alphas typically did. I was usually a nervous wreck around Damon, my instincts telling me to run the other way.

"Why? Not that I'm complaining. If you want to tear this whole place down, I'll help you." There was an underlying darkness to his words, a promise, that had me stilling.

I watched River for a minute, not sure how much to say. I sensed I could trust him, but some of the secrets I carried weren't my own. He narrowed his eyes at me, then looked around the room.

"Okay, I'm assuming it wasn't for decorative reasons. Which means you're looking for something. Correct?" He wandered over next to me and crouched down to get a better look at the wall.

The guy could bark me into submission without even raising his voice, force me to tell him anything he wanted. Yet he was patiently waiting for me to answer. Even if he wasn't backing down. He seemed like he wouldn't let things go easily, if the answer wasn't what he wanted.

"What's the problem with the power?" He asked, point blank. He wasn't just a killing machine, he was perceptive and smart, too. Which made him even more deadly.

"There isn't any power," I answered, deciding to be honest. He'd done nothing so far to show he was untrustworthy. Even if there was something intense going on between him, his twin, and Ava.

"I know, it's called the Crash," he replied, with a raised eyebrow.

"No. I mean, I know that. But this building is running on something. The lights are on, and some of these computers are on. I assumed it was the generator, because there weren't any solar panels on the roof. I checked."

"Why are you worried about the power? Sam's team checked the generator. It's a big industrial one, and the gas canister attached is at least half full. If we're careful, we should be alright for at least a week."

"Yeah, I heard that. But I need to boot up some of these systems. The security here is shit. Everyone seems to have hacked it at some point, and I want to make sure people can't spy on us while we're here."

River chuckled. "I may have hacked it a time or two myself."

I rolled my eyes. It didn't surprise me. Ava had been here, and I didn't think a few flimsy firewalls on their security system would stop him from watching her, even from a distance. "Plus, I need to get into their deeper files so I can figure out what research they were doing on Wolf, and how it involved Ava. Each of these labs had its own secret server. Turning on these systems may suck a lot of juice though, so I wanted to confirm how much we have left. In a more scientific way than tapping on the canister. I don't want to leave these omegas in the dark."

River's head tilted at my mention of secret servers. So he hadn't found those. Neither had Max initially. The Palace had hidden them well. Pala had discovered them while undercover. It honestly surprised me the lab techs hadn't taken them or smashed them when they left. They must have been in a serious hurry to get out. Someone was going to be pissed if there was no back-up of this data. Which meant if whatever was in here was important enough, they could be back.

"Both tasks sound like a priority to me. If we have to find more gas, just let me know and I'll make it happen." The confidence of alphas always astounded me. It was usually justified, though. "What does that have to do with the power points or the cables in the walls?"

"I checked the generator. The gas cylinder is attached to it. But the actual generator isn't attached to anything at all. The power cord coming out of it goes behind a cabinet and is just laying on the ground. It's not on and it's not powering anything."

River stood up abruptly and spun to look around the room. Paying attention to the lights and the lone computer still turned on.

"The lab techs turned off almost everything before they left last night. Only this computer was left on, as well as one in the other lab. I want to know why, and what's powering them. If we don't figure it out, the power could go off at any second."

"The lights are working around the whole place. We checked when we did the sweep. We've just been keeping them off. Everything in the kitchen is working, too. Including the hot water. That means whatever is powering this place has to be big."

"Yeah." There wasn't much more I could say.

River motioned me out the door. "I'll help you, but we need to be discreet. I don't want to alarm the omegas."

He then opened the door to the next room, before gesturing me through, which was weird. "Is this a date?" I joked.

He looked bemused, but answered with a completely straight face. "No. If it was a date, I would have brought flowers."

"Good," I said, "because you're not my type."

"Noted," he answered. "Is Ava your type?" His voice hitched slightly on her name, betraying his emotions.

I stilled as I realized we were in the hidden lab area of the building and there was no-one else about. Even though he didn't generally intimidate me, he was an alpha, and her true mate. From what I'd heard, true mates could be incredibly territorial. *Shit*.

I chewed my lip as I looked over at him. I figured lying to this dangerous alpha wouldn't fly, but telling him the truth could end up with me in a bloodied mess on the floor.

"I consider Ava and Cary to be friends. I want to make sure they're both okay." It was a non-answer, and we both knew it.

"Good to know, but you didn't answer my question." He towered over me, even as he stood two paces away, hands in his pockets with a coiled danger wrapped tight around him. All traces of his smile were gone, and his eyes were those of a predator. I knew instinctively, running would do me no good right now.

"Yes," I answered, and held my breath as I awaited my fate.

That hint of a smile appeared again, and his body relaxed slightly. I felt like I'd passed some kind of test.

"This should help with the wall." He threw me a switchblade, and I tried not to fumble it as I caught it. I flicked it open. The blade was thick, but looked wickedly sharp.

"This will work better than throwing a chair at the wall, but it will probably dull the blade," I said.

He shrugged. "I have more."

I bet he did. He probably had a dozen on him right now. I knocked on the wall until I found a space between the studs, then stabbed the knife into the wall, at a high point to avoid the cables running along the base. As soon as I had a hole cut, River took over and ripped the sheeting off by hand, making quick work of it.

"Where were you half an hour ago?" I grumbled.

"Running the fence line, checking for weaknesses." I looked him over and he hadn't even broken a sweat. I didn't doubt him, though. He was in peak physical health, his body fat index had to be in the single digits. He was all long, lean muscle. I was a little envious. My appearance, and my physicality, weren't things I'd ever thought about. I kept fit helping around the farm, and it had always been enough. Now, facing down a raging alpha and the incursion at the farm had me rethinking things. I knew there were a lot of ways I could improve. Not for vanity. Now that I had someone I wanted to protect, I wanted the skills to do it.

I shook my head. That was a problem I couldn't do anything about right now, but I could help with the one in front of me. My mind shifted back to working on this puzzle again. "The fences are electric, but they've been out since the Crash. So I assume they're not connected to the same power source as everything inside."

River grunted at me as he effortlessly ripped off more sheeting. "Yeah, there's a power box next to the guardhouse that was connected to the main grid."

I guess it made sense to have the fence and the house on a separate power supply, in case of attack. We worked together and busted the rest of the wall, then followed the cords through two more rooms. Luckily we were in the secret labs, not in the main part of the Palace, so we managed it without anyone overhearing us. In the last room, we came across another secret door.

"Shit," River muttered. "This whole place is riddled with secret rooms. I need to get Ava to show me the tunnels she mentioned last night, make sure they're the same ones we've already found."

He pulled a compact, yet powerful, flashlight out of his pocket and waved it around inside the doorway.

"It's a stairwell," he called out. "I'm going down. Stay here and keep watch."

"Sure." I tried to sound confident, but I was groaning inside. I flicked the knife opening again, but I knew it was more likely to be used against me if it came to a fight. I had no idea what to do with it. *Why hadn't I joined in on the cadet training program Dave ran at the farm?*

Only a few seconds later, a light flicked on at the bottom of the stairs and River called out for me to come down. The walls were bare stone, and the air smelled stale. The temperature dropped slightly as soon as I started down the stairs, and the room below was chilly. We were deep underground now. He eyed the knife I still had held in front of me, and that tiny smile hovered again. I snapped it closed.

We were in a long room, with a giant metal container in the middle of it. It appeared to be sealed, with some kind of control panel in the middle.

The cables from the room above were leading down into it, as well as cables coming in from different directions.

"Do you know what this is? I've never seen anything like it," Ryder asked.

"No." I hadn't seen anything like it before, either. I walked around the entire container looking at every cable. "These cables are all drawing power, though. None are channeling it in. So unless there are underground cables, this is the source of the power."

"Can you see any way to open it?" He asked, as he circled it too.

I looked at the control panel, but nothing appeared to be labeled. I had a natural affinity for working with computers, and Max had been teaching me what he knew, but this was way beyond my expertise.

"No, and I don't want to risk setting off any alarms or accidentally shutting it down. That middle panel is showing output, and it seems to be consistent."

"I'm not exactly comfortable having a machine running underneath us when we don't know what it is. What if it's some kind of nuclear energy or something? Nothing would surprise me with these guys." He made a good point.

I tentatively reached out and put my hand on it. It felt only slightly warmer than the room. "Nuclear energy runs incredibly hot and is usually liquid cooled. So I don't think that's the answer. But it's too quiet for it to be any fuel based forms of power I know about. Those are usually the explosive types."

He nodded, but still looked wary. I looked up at the roof, as if I could see through it. "If we keep the omegas to the kitchen and the ballroom, where they've been sleeping anyway, they'll be at the opposite end of the building. We should be alright as long as we keep everyone away from the western residential wing above us."

"Good idea. Any others?" I looked at him in surprise. He wasn't trying to take over and solve this problem himself. He was looking at me for input. A rare thing for an alpha. I tried not to puff my chest out, but I did stand a little taller.

"Yeah, we need to get Max here. He's a tech genius. If anyone can figure this out, it'll be him."

"Can you make that happen?"

"Yeah. I still have Ava's satellite phone."

"Okay, I'll post a guard in here tonight. They can let us know if anything changes with it."

I put my ear up against it gingerly. There'd been the faintest vibration through it when I touched it, but it only made the barest whirring sound. When I looked up, I noticed River had moved closer and stood over me, as if he planned to yank me away at the slightest change in the machine. He didn't say anything when I straightened up, he just stepped back and gave me room to move.

"Anything concerning?" He asked. I shook my head. I wasn't even sure what I'd been listening for. "Good, I'm going to go find Ava and check out those other tunnels."

"Okay, she should be in the kitchen with Emma. I'm going to go back to the first lab and start going through their systems. Max will need as much info as he can get when he arrives."

River motioned for me to go up the stairs first, then handed me the flashlight and shut off the light after I'd passed. He seemed to be hyper aware of my movements and safety. It was strange coming from another guy, but felt comforting rather than creepy. As if he'd been watching over me my whole life. It was touching that he seemed to feel protective of me. I kinda liked it. It felt big brotherly in a way I'd never known before. I'd never been close to my own brothers. We didn't have the same interests or outlook. They were farmers by nature, engrossed in working the land, even as teenagers. I loved the farm, but farming had never been my calling. Still. I couldn't pass up the opportunity to mess with River.

"What's with the old school romance moves?"

River shrugged, with an actual grin this time. "Ava would kill me if anything happened to you on my watch, and I'm trying to get back into her good books."

That had me blushing furiously. I'd thought about little else but Ava since the day I'd met her. I'd assumed anything between us was an impossibility until I'd heard her mention she liked me to Maia and Lexie this morning. My heart had pounded so hard, and I hadn't been able to wipe the goofy smile off my face when I opened the door. *He knew Ava cared about me and he was okay with it?*

River smirked at me, relaxing more than I'd seen him do yet. "Plus, I like you, kid."

"Technically, I'm an adult. Have been for a few years now." I felt compelled to point that out. I figured there were about four or five years between us, but his experience and training gave him an air of being even older.

He just raised one eyebrow at me. *Was he messing with me, too?*

The idea that River felt comfortable enough with me to let his guard down and mess with me blew my mind. He'd been straight up intimidating with Sam's team and the other alphas who'd arrived with us. Glowering at them all.

I was good friends with Max, who was about the same age as River and Ryder. We'd clicked instantly when Max first arrived at the farm with his mates. I'd always gravitated to people who were older, even when I was young. My mother always told people I was born a few years too late. Yet I'd always watched the dynamic Max had with his mates with an intense longing. Growing up with my great grandmother, GG to everyone on the farm, as a major influence on my life, I'd learned a lot about the old ways. I'd known those guys were a pack before even they did.

Thinking of GG reminded me I needed to call her. She'd be worried that I hadn't returned from town, even though I was sure Maia would have told her where I was. I didn't need her turning up on our doorstep to check on me, and I knew she'd find a way to do it. We'd always had a strong connection.

"I'll leave you to it," River said when we got back to the first lab. "Let me know if you find anything worth noting. And if you hear any strange noises or vibrations coming from down below, I want you out of here."

"Yes, Sir." I saluted him and threw in a cocky wink. Sam had directed Owen and Miles to be in charge here, but even they deferred to River and Ryder.

He just shook his head before he turned and took off. I couldn't help but yell, "Thanks for the non-date, I'm keeping the knife as a courting gift," at his back. He waved over his shoulder and I imagined him grinning. I felt like my home had finally found me.

I rubbed my hands together as I turned to the wall of computers, humming one of my favorite songs. I may not be deadly, but I knew my way around computers. And those skills just might help the people I cared about.

The number of people on that list had recently gotten a little bigger.

Eight

Angel was gripping Cary's hand tightly as we pushed through the kitchen door into the dim hallway. We were being careful with our electricity usage and only putting lights on when we absolutely needed them. I think the dimly lit passages were scaring Angel a little, but she'd never say.

I sensed River hovering a few metres away. I snuck a glance, and the sight had me looking away just as quickly. He was leaning against the wall, with one foot propped up and his hands in his pants pockets. His head was bent slightly down, yet his hooded gaze tracked my every movement as he watched me through his lashes. He looked as if he belonged in a high end menswear commercial. That dark, gorgeous gaze intent on seducing me.

He wasn't the awkward, gangly teenage boy I'd known any longer. I missed that boy fiercely, but I also desperately wanted to get to know this man. This mesmerizing alpha with a powerful body that had my own igniting with just a look.

Before I could say anything, an omega sauntered around the corner and headed for the kitchen. I vaguely recognized her, but couldn't recall her name. She'd been due to attend her debut with Emma and me, along with one other girl. But she'd made no attempt to break the rules and befriend any of us, even though we had rooms in the same hallway. Never even attempting a hello. She'd always just lifted her chin and ignored us.

Right now, she couldn't look more different from us. Emma and I were both wearing leggings and tees while we worked to get everyone fed today and better set up in the ballroom. We'd decided to keep the omegas there to guard them better, but also reduce energy usage. Yet this omega had dressed in a low cut flowy dress, and was wearing gaudy jewelry, as if the apocalypse had never happened. If she'd found herself a tiara, I felt sure she would have put it on, too.

The hairs rose on my arms and I got a sense of danger from her I couldn't place. She barely looked at me, zeroing in on Emma. *Was ignoring me a ploy, or did she just think me insignificant?*

"Hey, so sorry. Did I miss lunch?" She asked. Her smile appeared pasted on like a fake tattoo. There was no sincerity behind it.

"Yeah. You missed clean-up too," Emma replied with a salty tone and a hand on her hip.

"Oh, shoot. Could you make me a quick sandwich, or something, then?" The omega flipped her hair over her shoulder with a dismissive arrogance as she spoke. I couldn't believe her nerve, but I didn't want to antagonize her and cause problems we didn't need right now.

"Did you miss the Crash as well, Nicole? What the hell makes you think we have fresh bread or sandwich meats?" Emma had no such reservations. She sounded incredulous, and at her wit's end. I figured she'd been dealing with a lot of drama from Nicole since the Crash.

Omegas from poor or unknown families, like Emma and me, were treated differently by the Palace compared to those from aristocratic families. Wealthy omegas still didn't get any choices, but the Palace usually paired them with an alpha their family approved. Instead of being thrown to the wolves. They were also discreetly sent a lot of presents by their families and chosen suitors while at the Palace. Despite the no contact rule. It was where the Palace princess misconception came from.

"Didn't they bring back food?" Nicole pointed at Cary and me, but didn't bother to look at us as she waved her finger vaguely in our direction. I wanted to slap her hand away, but I refrained. I didn't care about how she treated me, but Cary deserved better. Yet, I had no idea what life had been like for her lately, or what she had endured. I had no right to judge her. So I forced a smile back to my face.

"Some of our friends from town dropped off some tinned food this morning. We had soup and crackers for lunch but it's all gone, I'm sorry. There are some protein bars left, though. If you're hungry." Nicole just glanced at me before she turned up her nose dismissively.

"I'm not eating protein bars, and I'm sick of eating tinned shit. I want some proper food." She crossed her arms, but stopped short of stamping her foot. She was still acting less mature than the actual child with us, who was staring at her with her mouth hanging open in shock.

"We have some more food coming tonight and it's coming from the farm we've been staying at. So hopefully it will include some fresh food, as well as some provisions, so we can all make our own." I tried to placate the omega again, with no success.

"I'm not making food," Nicole said, as her mouth twisted into a sneer. She looked at me as if I was insane.

"I guess you're going to be hungry then," Cary said, as he picked Angel up and cuddled her against his chest. He took a step closer to me, while Angel buried her face in his shoulder, not liking the angry emotions suddenly swirling around the corridor.

"Yeah," Emma added, "because I'll be damned if I'm making anything for you with an attitude like that." Emma was feisty today. I hadn't known her before, but I'd spent the last few hours with her and she'd proven to be smart, capable and unafraid to speak her mind. I liked her.

"You can't talk to me that way. Especially you, Cary. You're just a freak. Do you know who my father is?" Oh no, she didn't. I rarely got angry, but talking trash about someone I cared about was a surefire way to get me there.

"Oh, I know who your father is," Cary retorted, not needing any help from me to defend himself, "and he doesn't treat all omegas like princesses. He likes to get his freak on."

I felt devastated at the reminder of what Cary had endured, as my anger dissipated and my focus turned to Cary. Guilt flooded me. While I'd been mostly left alone during my time at the Palace, Cary and Maia had needed to survive it.

"Maybe I can help this situation." River's voice behind me, had me stilling. I hadn't sensed him move closer.

Nicole and Emma's heads both swiveled toward River as he spoke, clearly taken by surprise. Yet Cary looked impassive, as if he'd also sensed River's presence. Which surprised me.

Nicole's face lit up as she saw River emerge from the gloom of the connecting hallway, and her entire demeanor changed. She arched her back slightly, pushed her boobs out, and took a deep breath of his scent as it spiked. She was delusional if she thought it was spiking for her, though. *Wasn't she?*

The thought that River might be attracted to her had my emotions spinning wildly in another direction. I was an overfilled water balloon about to pop. If someone pricked me, my emotions would spill out everywhere, splattering everyone around me.

"Mmmmm, dark chocolate. You smell divine," Nicole simpered as she sashayed over to him, "and you make those other alphas look like boys. I'm Nicole Arbutier. It's a pleasure to meet you."

Ugh. I wanted to vomit. *Could she be any more obvious?*

She'd confirmed my suspicions about where she'd just come from, though. She'd been sniffing out the alphas who had arrived with us last night.

My whole body stiffened as she reached River and moved to put her hand on his arm. I couldn't watch her touch him. I tried to glance away and caught the warning glare Cary shot at River. But looking away was useless. The slow motion movements drew my eyes back as if it was a car crash about to happen. I felt relief flood me as River brushed her hand away before she could touch him.

"Introductions aren't necessary," he said, with a cool chill to his voice I'd never heard him use before. "What's important is that you have a choice to make. Nobody is keeping anyone here anymore, and whoever was protecting you here is gone."

He glared at her as she sucked in a shocked breath. "So, either you stay, chip in and help figure out how to survive here, or you leave. If you have somewhere that's a better option, I suggest you go. We'll even pack you some supplies because it's likely to be a long walk."

He sounded harsh, but mollycoddling this omega would not help her anymore. Someone had clearly spoiled her enough. I wanted to tell her if her father hadn't come for her by now; he wasn't coming. But I figured she knew that, which was why she was so desperate to latch onto an alpha. She wanted a new daddy.

"How can you say that to me? You're an alpha. I'm an omega. Do you have any idea what my father's connections could do for you?"

"You might be an omega, but you're not *my* omega," River replied.

My heart soared as my emotions went haywire. Those words coming from River had my body hot and my spirit on fire. It took everything I had not to throw myself at him. I forced myself to calm my breathing and focus. We weren't alone right now.

Nicole huffed, turned on her high heels, and stormed to the kitchen door. She tried to push, rather than pull, the heavy door, though. Marring her dramatic exit. I probably should have helped her, but I didn't. The omega didn't need to be babied; she needed to figure things out for herself for once. She gave a frustrated little scream as she finally pushed through the door, and her dress caught on it as it closed.

Emma shot River a grin she couldn't seem to contain. "You're my hero. Just saying. Because that really needed to be said."

My friendly feelings towards Emma disappeared in a jealous puff, as River gave her a small smile. My emotions were giving me whiplash.

"You're welcome," he told her, a little gruffly. I imagined he wasn't exactly proud of talking harshly to an omega, even if it needed to be done.

Emma was still grinning as she turned to Cary and me. "I'm going to go watch Nicole. Make sure she doesn't steal the protein bars and try to stash them somewhere."

I nodded at her more stiffly than she deserved, as Cary added, "I'll take Angel outside to get some sunshine. I can grab some of the other younger omegas too, give the older ones a break. If I can find some rope, I might even rig up a tire swing for them."

"Sounds great, thank you." Emma waved her hand over her shoulder as she turned and disappeared through the kitchen door as well.

Yes, air and sunshine were exactly what I needed right now. "I'll come too," I said a little too quickly.

But River suddenly stepped up into my space before I could move away.

"Actually, Ava. I need you."

And there went my emotions again. Whoosh, they were up in flames, over three little words. I could almost feel myself burning.

Nine

River

The second the words crossed my lips, I realized how they sounded, but I refused to look embarrassed or take them back. I needed Ava desperately. I just hadn't meant in that way right now.

Ava was taking tiny, shallow breaths as she looked up at me through her lashes, and I had to lock my arms in place to stop myself from reaching for her. Finally, she was looking at me without her gaze instantly sliding away again, in that way that killed me.

"Why?" The word was so quiet I barely heard it, even with my alpha hearing and standing so close.

There were so many answers to that question, but it wasn't the right time for any of the ones I wanted to give. So I stuck to my plan. The one I'd devised to get her alone so we could talk. She was so poised and collected, so different from the farm girl we'd grown up with. She had walls built up around her. For years I'd assumed we just needed to find her. But when the shooting stopped and she'd stepped back from us, I'd known it was going to take more. We'd all changed, but I knew our Ava was in there somewhere. I had to believe we could find our way back to each other again. There was no other option for me. Keeping her safe was all I lived for.

I'd be with her, a part of her life, or I'd haunt her from the shadows.

She was watching me quietly, patiently waiting for my answer as I paused. "I need you to show me through the tunnels. We checked the ones Ryder and I found last night, but I want to make sure we didn't miss any. That is why you said you wanted to come to the Palace, because you knew where the tunnels were?" I knew I was pushing her outside her comfort zone right now, but if I let her avoid me forever, we'd never get past this awful tension between us.

I could almost see her mind working, trying to find a way out of this, but there was none. She searched my face, and it felt like a caress.

"Okay." One word, and hope speared through me. This was my chance. I worked to keep my breathing steady and my expression neutral. I didn't want to do anything to spook her now that I was about to get her alone.

She shot a glance at Cary, who was still hovering, and a frown marred her gorgeous face. I followed her gaze and noticed him wincing as he put Angel back down on the ground, straightening her tee for her as he went. She wore a matching outfit to Ava and Emma, little leggings, and a t-shirt, which was cute as hell.

"Sorry, chipmunk. I can't carry you right now. You got too big while I was gone." Angel straightened her shoulders and stretched her neck up, looking pleased as she tried to look even taller.

"Your ribs?" Ava asked him, as he shot us a wary glance. His eyes widened as he noticed us both watching him closely.

He looked at me for the briefest moment before directing his attention back at Ava again. He sighed as if he knew she'd persist if he didn't answer. "Yeah."

Ava walked up to him and hugged him gently. Making my jaw clench. Not in jealousy, though. If she was open to other people caring for her, I had no problem with it. I just wanted to hug her, too. "I'm okay, Ava," he whispered into her hair.

She didn't seem convinced, but I sensed this moment between them was about more than his ribs, as concerning as they were. Something else was going on with him. "I'll check the bruising when we get back, and we can call Luis if we need to."

He nodded, clearly not wanting to discuss anything in front of me. He gave me a hard, pointed look as Ava released him, before he took Angel's hand and turned her towards the door. His look was intentional. It was a warning and also a passing of the baton. He was letting me know I was responsible for watching Ava until he got back, and there would be hell to pay if I fucked up.

I gave him a quick, casual salute, and he rolled his eyes before he turned and left. His dedication to Ava was obvious, and I respected it. He'd barely left her side since we'd arrived. I wondered if he was also giving me some kind of permission, but that was ridiculous. I didn't need his permission for anything. *Or did I?*

I hadn't been around many female omegas, let alone male ones. They were so rare. Yet a male omega attached to a female omega was unheard of. He was almost more of an enigma than Wolf. I was going to need to talk to Ryder. He was better at figuring out people than I was. If he could get out of his own head for a moment.

"What's wrong with his ribs?" I asked, bluntly.

Ava narrowed her eyes slightly, as if she was trying to figure out what to tell me. "He got hurt badly about a week ago, when the Palace alphas attacked the farm and tried to snatch us back. We were with Lexie when it happened, and he tried to defend both of us."

The Palace alphas tried to snatch Ava back? Why was I only finding out about this now? Probably because nobody trusted us yet. I was going to have to ask Nick more questions. I needed to know who was gunning for her and why.

"Does he know how to fight?" I asked. Cary was clearly fit, but his movements didn't indicate any military or fight training. I couldn't imagine they would let a male omega in the military, or even in a boxing gym where he was likely to run into alphas. I knew the Palace would never let an omega learn any type of self defense.

Ava confirmed my suspicions. "No. He made himself an outdoor weights set-up here, using tyres and whatever he could find to stay in shape, but I don't think he's ever had any type of training. He still took on four alphas for us. They toyed with him for a while before they took him out."

"Shit, he's lucky to be alive." I glanced in the direction he'd gone and my respect grew even further. I felt protective of him, which confused the hell out of me because I didn't feel attracted to him. *Would he expect me to mate him too, if I mated Ava?*

I didn't feel as if I could do that. Yet, nobody messed with my omegas. *My omegas? Did I just think that?*

I shook off my confused thoughts and turned my attention back to Ava, who was also staring in the direction Cary had gone. I wanted to reach out and grab her hand so badly, the way I'd seen Cary do, and the way I'd often done when we were young. But we weren't there right now. I could feel the ghost of her hand in mine though, the feeling of that touch had never left me.

"After you," I said, as I gestured down the hallway. Ava startled slightly, but squared her shoulders the same way she used to do when she was determined. Even as a little kid. She'd always had a core of steel. Few people noticed it, though. They only saw the sweet girl. Even Ryder and I had forgotten when it counted most.

"Do you have a flashlight?" She asked.

"Yeah, up in our suite." I'd left mine with Nick earlier, along with my switchblade, but we had more in our go bags.

"Perfect, let's go."

Ava led me back up to the VIP suite, then moved to a section of wall in the living room and looked it over. It was one of only a handful of internal walls that were still bare stone as a feature. They had plastered most others over to help keep the chill at bay, especially in the bedrooms. She ran her hand over a section, then pushed on a broken corner. It depressed with the slightest click, and the wall cracked apart to reveal a doorway.

It was cool as hell.

"How did you ever find this?" I couldn't keep the awe out of my voice. We'd found other secret tunnels, but they weren't as cleverly concealed. They were mostly concealed doors leading to service type hallways. They were there to keep service activities out of the public view and kept the labs hidden. These looked ancient.

Ava's expression turned sad, and I instantly regretted my question. She shrugged and walked into the cold passageway. She didn't trust me anymore, and the realization was a stab to the heart.

"Hang on a second," I called out, as I ducked into the room Ryder and I were using. I grabbed a flashlight out of one of our go bags, then grabbed her hoodie off the couch on my way back. I strode into the tunnel and turned on the light, then held her hoodie up for her to slip into. She looked at me skeptically, but didn't challenge me. I knew I should have just handed it to her, but I was desperate to get as close to her as I could. The pull I'd felt toward her as a kid was nothing compared to the pull I felt to her now. It was all-consuming. She was all woman, and her curves were a siren song. Especially in those tight leggings.

She turned and slipped her arms into the sleeves. I reached over and swept her hair out of the way, so it didn't get caught on the zipper. I almost groaned as the long silky strands slipped through my fingers. I wanted to sniff them to see if they carried her scent, then bury my face in them, but I didn't dare. She'd worn it up in a bun last night, but she had it in a high ponytail today. It was much longer than it used to be. She'd worn her hair in a tomboy bob as a kid. It was halfway down her back now.

Ava pulled away suddenly, so I slipped the flashlight into lantern mode and handed it to her. I followed as she started walking, but I wasn't really seeing where we were going. She had me transfixed and suddenly terrified.

Seeing Ava last night had brought every nightmare I'd had over the last ten years to life. I'd come around the bend to see her standing reckless and vulnerable on the street while a horde of alphas ran at her. A scene from a horror movie playing on a giant cinema screen. Only it had been terrifyingly real. No matter how fast I'd ran, I'd realized with growing dread that Ryder and I would not reach her before the horde. Everything else had faded and the entire world had narrowed to her and the action playing out.

Panic had initially seized me when I'd noticed Wolf unexpectedly veer toward her as well. He'd zeroed in on the lead alpha gunning for her, barreling through everyone between them with a dropped shoulder and a well-thrown fist. Throwing the asshole completely across the road when he reached him. His actions had forced Ryder and me to cover his back, as he'd single-mindedly plowed his way through towards Ava. I owed Wolf, and it wasn't a debt I took lightly.

Yet the terror I felt now was completely different. I'd waited so long to make things right, but I knew I only had one shot. If I messed this up now,

I could lose her forever. And I wouldn't be the only one destroyed. Ryder thought he hated her, but he didn't. Deep down, he couldn't deal with the thought of a life without her knowing we were to blame. Neither could I. I just had different coping mechanisms.

She was walking quickly down the dark hallway when she suddenly screamed and leaped backwards. My heart in my throat, I grabbed her and pulled her into me, as my gaze swung around wildly, trying to find the threat in the spinning light of the dropped torch. A tiny, terrified creature caught my eye as it sprinted back into the darkness.

"Sorry," she whispered into my chest. "I forgot about the mice."

"Ava." The word fell out on a growl that sounded nothing like me. My arms banded around her as my alpha rode me hard. She was finally alone and in my arms, and I couldn't for the life of me let her go. I didn't want to move in case this moment shattered, the same as every dream I'd had of her on waking.

I hadn't been there when she left, so I'd never known if she'd gone willingly. Or if her decision had made her feel conflicted at all. The decision that took her away from us. The wondering had haunted me. But I could feel her now, faintly in our bond, and I felt how much pain she held tucked away inside herself. How much pain we had caused her. *Did she hate me? Would she ever forgive me?*

Suddenly, every word I had imagined saying to her in this moment fled. We'd never needed words before. Our closeness had always been instinctive and felt eternal. Until we'd broken it.

Her eyes were closed as I breathed in the delectable scent of cherries. The same scent that had haunted me. It caressed my own dark chocolate scent until the two combined turned into a heady mix of lust and need. I counted each heartbeat until she finally relaxed and melted into me. Her arms snaked around my waist and I pressed into her body as if I could mold her to me so closely, we'd become one and I wouldn't ever have to let her go.

Still, I waited, knowing the next move had to be hers. I couldn't decide for her what our fate would be. I'd made that mistake once before. Now I could only offer myself and beg for forgiveness. Moving slowly, so slowly, it felt as if time stood still. She tipped her head up towards me and opened her gorgeous green eyes. The shadows in them weren't only from the torchlight, they were from me, too.

Her eyes were deep pools in the dim light and mirrored everything I felt. The grief, sadness, and loss I'd known for a decade were right there, reflected at me painfully. But the need, desire, and love that spilled from me found a companion in her too. It was nestled within the bond that had always existed between us.

My heart pounded in my chest as the weight of my need to kiss her, claim her, forced me to my knees. I had to earn that right. My knees hit the uneven stone of the path, but I gritted my teeth and bore the sharp pain. My arms wrapped back around her waist and I rested my head under her chest. I had no problem prostrating myself in front of her. I would do a lot worse. Had done a lot worse. For her.

"I'm so sorry, Ava." The words ripped free in a burst of pain I could no longer contain. "The words are meaningless, I know, but they've been tearing me apart for ten years. I'm so sorry we failed you."

"River, no." She tried to lower herself to her knees in front of me, but I wouldn't let her kneel on the rough floor. Seeing her hurt in any way was too much right now. I wrapped her tighter and pulled her down into my lap. Holding her close and breathing her in. That wasn't what I had practised saying at all. *Shit, I'm messing this up.*

"I'm the one who has to apologize," she said, her voice cracking at the end.

I looked down at her in shock. "Why the hell would you need to apologize?"

She looked at me, confusion swimming in her shining eyes. "Because I...I left you both. Without a word, and I think it broke us."

She started sobbing, rivers of tears spilling over and tumbling down her face. The pain in her eyes was so real and jagged, it burned me to my core.

"No, no, Ava." I tried to brush her tears away, but there were too many of them. So I tucked her under my chin and rocked her as she cried. My heart tore in two as I felt her tremble against me while she sobbed out her pain.

I stroked her back gently until she quieted a few minutes later. Then I lifted her chin and looked deep into her tear streaked eyes. "Ava, you did the right thing. You weren't to blame."

"I should have talked to you."

"You tried, little bird. You insisted we'd never make it on our own. You begged us to hear your uncle out. We didn't listen to you. We tried to make the decision to run for you. But it wasn't our place. Ryder and I were young and stupid. We thought we could take on the entire world and win. Keep you safe from any threat. You knew better. So did your mother and your uncle."

"It still wasn't right, leaving and not saying goodbye."

"If you had tried to tell us goodbye, we would never have let you go. Your uncle knew that and I'm sure your mother suspected. Ryder would have picked you up and run away with you, and I would have been guarding his back. Being without you when you were at school in the city was hard enough. The thought of being without you for ten years was more than we thought we could bear."

We'd known Ava her whole life. We were inseparable whenever she was at the farm. Ava's dad passed away when she was young. Her mother worked as a lawyer for a non-profit legal aid center and they lived in a tiny apartment in the city, but she'd come stay with her uncle every school holidays. Our family owned the farm next door to his, and her uncle was best friends with our dad.

I sighed, thinking back to that terrible time. The dark despair I'd felt at the thought of her at the Palace without us to protect her. "We should have been stronger for you. Listened to you."

"You were only fifteen."

"And you were thirteen, but you were stronger than both of us." I smiled sadly down at her. She was even stronger now, even though I sensed she couldn't see it. She not only survived the Palace, but she convinced them for a decade she was the perfect omega princess. When I knew she was anything but, she was a free spirit, a wood sprite, who only adapted to her cage to keep us safe.

She shook her head, denying her strength, but it was the truth. She loved being outdoors growing up, always trying to climb as high as us, run as fast as us. Her pride and her huge smile when she pushed herself and reached us always made us grin. She never knew that we always slowed down so she could catch up, and picked trees we were sure she could climb. The only thing she loved more than running wild outdoors was the animals around the farm. Yet she'd put herself in a prison for us.

"Ryder and I always knew you were ours. Even in the innocent way of kids." I lifted my hand and gently dried the remaining tracks of tears from her cheeks, wanting to make them disappear. Her life should be full of laughter and smiles, not tears.

Everything we had done for the last ten years, what we had turned ourselves into, was to make sure we could keep her safe when we eventually got her back. Nothing else mattered to either of us.

"Ryder's so angry at me." She sounded resigned.

"Not really. Sometimes grief and fear can look like anger." Ava had snuggled into my chest, instinctively seeking my scent for comfort, but she gave me some side-eye now. Clearly, I hadn't convinced her. I needed to talk to Ryder. I'd wanted to talk to her alone this first time, and he knew that, but I wouldn't make another move without him. We were a package deal.

"If you don't believe me, ask to see his tattoo."

She shook her head before she took a deep breath, and her forehead furrowed. I knew whatever she asked next was going to be important.

"Is that why you and Ryder never contacted me?" She wasn't looking at me now. She'd focused her gaze squarely on her lap, but her voice trembled with suppressed emotion. "I hoped you'd get word to me somehow. Or my uncle would. But I never heard from anyone from the moment I crossed the Palace doors. Not even my mother. I knew we weren't supposed to see our families, but lots of other girls got snuck cards and letters, some even got presents. I kept wishing for something, anything, but eventually, I lost hope."

Fuck. Did she not know? How did she not know?

"Ava." I hesitated as I tried to gather my thoughts. "Didn't anyone at the Palace tell you about your mother and uncle?"

"What about them?"

My heart shattered. "Ava, have you spent the last ten years thinking we'd abandoned you?"

She gave me the tiniest, reluctant nod. Her teary eyes shining in the torchlight. They were begging me to give her some explanation she could understand. Something that would make it better. But I couldn't.

I didn't want to be the one to tell her this. I remembered the devastation when her father died, how broken she'd been and how helpless Ryder and I had felt.

"Ava, your uncle, and your mother both died ten years ago."

Her shocked gasp echoed in the tunnel around us as her pain speared me. My arms went slack around her as my guilt tore through me. I should have done more. I should have saved her from this.

She froze for a heartbeat, before a cry ripped from her throat and she launched herself out of my arms.

She was gone in the next heartbeat. Disappearing into the darkness of the tunnel as if she'd never existed.

Again.

Ten

I ran blindly, my tears silently running down my face, as I tried to escape his words. The darkness enveloped me in a tomb, the cold seeping into my bones as my heartbeat pounded in my ears.

I was so tired of being alone, yet I hadn't even known how truly alone I was. Everyone in my family was gone, except me. I'd been an orphan for a decade, living on fairytales and lies.

I needed out, now. Out of this darkness, and away from these oppressive walls. They were closing in on me.

Light filtering in through the secret door to our suite appeared like an apparition. I was grateful we'd left it propped open as I burst through into the room, but it wasn't enough. This place felt cursed. Its walls steeped in pain.

I kept running, straight out the suite doors, and collided with someone. "What the hell?" Nicole screeched as she shoved me back roughly.

I couldn't stop, though. I could barely apologize. Grief had obliterated my polite princess act. My frenzied flight took me into the corridor and down the grand staircase, as my tears almost blinded me. I faintly heard Nick call my name, but I couldn't stop. If I stopped, I would break. I knew River was behind me, keeping pace, but not stopping me. He knew me, knew I needed to run. He barked something about sweeping the tunnel to someone, but I didn't catch it all. My focus was in front of me.

The sunlight blinded me as I burst through the main doors. I stumbled when I hit the front steps, but I grabbed onto the railing and kept going.

My breaths came in great gasping pants, the pain in my lungs almost a comfort. I'd rather that pain any day than the one in my heart.

The Palace gates were in front of me and two trail bikes were tearing down the main road beyond them, heading straight for me. I felt hunted, and haunted, so I headed for the only safe space I knew. The giant tree within the wooded area on the Palace grounds. The place I would escape to whenever I evaded my handler and couldn't find Maia in the library. Where I went to let my soul breathe, even for a little while. I'd climb the tree to let sunlight wash over me, and the breeze stir my hair. I'd sit and remember what it felt like to be loved and free.

Shouting in the distance chased me through the woods until I felt the branches of the giant tree spread out over me. I'd poured my troubles into this tree many times before. It could take one more. I dropped to my knees under its embrace and let loose the scream that had been building in my throat. It tore loose and all my pain came tumbling out until it left me with nothing but a numb emptiness.

Startled birds took flight around me and running footsteps came crashing through the undergrowth. Suddenly Cary was there, his arms and legs wrapped around me as he cradled me and surrounded me with his calm, steadfast presence.

"Ava, what's wrong?" He panted, out of breath. I had no words to answer him right now.

"What the hell happened?" came Ryder's angry voice behind me. I heard a crash and a roar as leaves came swirling down around me. I looked up, startled, to see Wolf had River pinned against the tree trunk. River barely registered him. We locked eyes as he answered his brother.

"She didn't know her mother and uncle were dead. No one had ever told her."

Ryder spun back toward me and his eyes burned into me, but I couldn't look at him right now.

Dead. That word reverberated through me as if someone had struck a gong. My mother. My uncle. Gone. All this time. In the dark of night I'd wondered, but in the light of day I'd never let myself believe it. I'd made up many scenarios over the years to explain their silence. They'd gone into the underground resistance. They were building an army, as my uncle had promised. My mother had remarried, and they were staying away to keep my baby brothers and sisters safe. They'd become pirates and were sailing the high seas. Anything was better than the obvious answer.

I closed my eyes to block the world out. A childish move, but I felt so brittle. As if the slightest poke would break me. Shatter me into a million pieces.

Suddenly Wolf was there, surrounding us both and offering us the protection of his giant body. He pulled both Cary and me into him. He felt solid, as if the world could break against him and he wouldn't shatter. His scent flooded me, the night orchids, ginger and mossy jungle scents fitted this space, and calmed me. I whimpered as the most delicious feeling, almost a vibration, passed through me and washed everything clean. It was intoxicating. I snuggled myself deeper into him and Cary moaned on my other side as he tried to get closer, too.

"What the hell is that?" Ryder asked.

"He's purring," Nick answered. "Damon does it for Maia, too. It's a prime alpha thing. It calms their omega."

I vaguely remembered Maia and Lexie giggling about it. Sam did it too. They were right. It was the bomb. My whole body felt like a marshmallow, soft and relaxed. It didn't take away the pain, but it softened its edges. Made everything feel dreamy, but more bearable. I took a deep breath, able to breathe freely again.

"You're a prime alpha?" Cary asked Wolf. Wolf just grunted, which I figured was a yes. I noticed River and Ryder exchanging glances.

As if we'd yanked insistently on a string and drawn them to us, River and Ryder both slid closer. River settled in alongside us, wrapping an arm around me. Ryder hesitated, but sat down as well and put a hand on the edge of my foot. It was the barest contact, but I'd take it. Something else niggled at me in my dreamy cloud. Someone was missing.

"Get over here." Wolf's gruff voice sounded rough, but the feeling behind it was friendly, if a little exasperated. A moment later, River and Ryder shifted and Nick settled down with us, too. He tentatively leaned against Cary and put his hand on my leg. I sighed and closed my eyes as I basked in the feeling of them all touching me in some way. These men, together, felt like home. Nick was an integral part of that. I'd seen enough with both Lexie and Maia not to question why. River and Ryder were a minefield of emotions right now, but we had too much history for them to ignore my grief.

We stayed that way for a long time. Maybe hours. The guys just sitting with me in my grief. I think I may have even napped a little as the guys talked quietly about dirt bikes and random guy stuff. Feeling each other out and getting to know each other. The shadows lengthened around us and I knew night was drawing near as the air turned colder.

"I need to go help Emma get something sorted for dinner, and make sure Angel is still with her," I finally said. Only I felt torn. I didn't really want to move. I wanted to stay right here, surrounded by these men. It felt selfish though, when the world was in turmoil, to only think of myself. Even for a little while.

"Emma's fine, and Angel is too, or someone would have let us know. The delivery of fresh food came from Lexie earlier. Emma's got dinner covered. Miles and Owen are with her. They're falling over themselves to help her," Nick said.

I shot him a warning look, and Nick chuckled. "Don't worry. Miles and Owen are good guys, and Sam trusts them. Besides, River already threatened the alphas this morning, and warned them not to touch the omegas."

Ryder leaned over and gave River a fist bump.

Wolf increased his purr, and my body relaxed back into his. I briefly wondered if I should be concerned about how comfortable I was with Wolf right now, but I decided I didn't care. River and Ryder wouldn't be so chill if there was anything to worry about. Besides, I felt nothing but care and protection coming from him, surrounding me in a cocoon.

I'd shouldered my fate by myself for so long, it felt decadent to have so many people surrounding me now. Comforting me. I knew it was going to take time to process this grief. But for now, I was going to embrace this feeling of being held.

Eventually, Wolf's purr softened and quietened down. I could still feel its faint vibration, but my head cleared a little of the fluffy cloud that had settled around it.

The birds chirping overhead, as they settled into the branches above us for the night, made me smile sadly. My mother had loved birds and always missed them in the city. She always fed them whenever she came to the farm. Ryder reached out and lightly caressed the bluebirds on my bracelet with a shaky hand.

"You still wear it. I didn't think they'd let you keep it." The Palace didn't allow us to bring any personal possessions, even the clothes we came in got taken away. It was a barbaric way to treat young kids who had just left their families. It stripped everything from them. But I guess that was the whole point. The Palace wanted us submissive and completely dependent on them.

"Nobody was taking it from me and I refused to leave it behind." I looked directly at him for the first time. He'd always worn his heart on his sleeve. Pain and fear were colliding as they flashed in his eyes. River was right. His anger was a flimsy mask. "I hid it when I arrived and didn't wear it until after they'd given me a new wardrobe, so it appeared new." I'd hidden it in my hair, twisted into the base of my bun, so they wouldn't take it away with my clothes.

"Why is it so special?" Cary asked gently. He'd seen me wearing it over the years and knew when I gave it to Maia before we sent her running towards my uncle's farm that it meant something. I was glad now that she'd never made it. He wouldn't have been there.

"River and Ryder gave it to me." It was more complicated than that, but also that simple.

It was a charm bracelet with enamel bluebirds hanging from it that were in various stages of flight. It was unique. The boys had it custom made for me. They'd saved up their pocket money and did extra chores to buy it for my birthday. I loved it. My wrist felt bare without it.

"Why bluebirds?" Nick asked, looking at Ryder with his head tilted. He was savvy, that one. I sensed he and Cary were tag teaming us, trying to get the twins and me to talk. They'd both disappeared on me this afternoon. *Had that been deliberate?*

"Ava was always rescuing animals when we were kids. But one time, she rescued a baby bluebird." Ryder's gaze remained fixated on the bracelet as he talked, and he swallowed hard. "She fed it and cared for it until it could fly on its own, but it never went far. It used to live in the tree outside her window and eventually had babies of its own. It would fly down to her windowsill in the morning whenever she was at the farm, and sing to her."

I smiled at the memory. The little bluebird singing at my window had always made me feel like a cartoon princess. The twins and I had so much history wrapped up in our childhoods.

River suddenly leaned back and pushed to his feet. "Ryder, help me grab some wood."

Ryder's face brightened before he jumped up eagerly, an echo of the boy I knew appearing like a ghost. "Great idea."

He turned to Nick and Cary, who looked puzzled. "Could you guys grab some blankets and pillows from our rooms? The thicker, the better. We're having a fire and a camp-out."

Nick just nodded at River, as they shared a loaded look. Which was perplexing. I was used to River doing that with Ryder.

"Is that safe? Won't it attract attention?" Cary asked as he glanced at the surrounding woods. Damon and the guys at the farm were so militant about not having lights at night. But they had a big farm, with a lot of resources and people to protect.

"Using electricity at night is a risk. But anyone can start a fire. Besides, the most dangerous predators are here already. Nobody will bother us tonight." River sounded cocky, but he was just being honest. He always told it straight.

Wolf sniffed the air. "Nobody but us around," he confirmed. Nobody commented on his animalistic behavior. The guys just seemed to accept him and let him be.

Nick grinned. "I'm in." He seemed excited, and didn't even wait for Cary to follow, just ran back through the trees.

Cary shot me a questioning look. He'd only ever known the demure version of me. Out here, though, with River and Ryder at my side, I couldn't seem to find her. So I squeezed his hand to reassure him and gave him a small smile. Marveling that I could, now. He matched it before he jumped up and took off after Nick.

River, Ryder and I used to have bonfires and sleep under the stars all the time as kids. Those nights were some of my happiest memories. My spirits lifted at the thought of having one now. It was exactly what I needed to help reclaim a part of myself I'd suppressed for so long.

My mother had been a determined woman, letting nothing keep her down. She faced life head on, but had done it with grace and dignity. Wanting to make her proud was what had kept me going whenever I'd despaired over the years. I knew in my heart she wouldn't want me to lose myself in grief for her now.

"Do you need help?" I asked, feeling weirdly shy suddenly. The two men carrying logs back to the clearing felt so familiar, yet so different, from the boys I knew.

"No. We're good," River said gruffly, as he started stacking bigger branches over the twigs and dried leaves Ryder had bundled in a cleared space on the ground. I'd watched them do this so many times. They had their own rhythm when they were working together. Moving without words in each other's space. Never bumping into each other or fumbling. As if they were one consciousness in two bodies, flowing together. Ryder started twisting a stick between his hands, rubbing it against another stick he had wedged between two rocks. It wasn't long before it started smoking.

I could sit and watch them for hours, entranced, still hardly believing they were actually here, and I wasn't dreaming. But I was hyperaware of Wolf gently cradling me in his lap right now. I looked up to see Wolf watching River and Ryder as well. He seemed intrigued by them, but he quickly dropped his gaze down at me, as if he could sense me watching him. His eyes were the deep brown of rich earth. He seemed about a thousand years old, as I looked into them.

His eyes had been different last night, more wild. There was still a predator lurking there, but they were a little clearer now.

"Thank you."

Wolf's brow furrowed, and he tilted his head at me.

"For saving us last night, and for calming me down just now."

He shrugged, as if it was no big deal. But his eyes seemed puzzled as they searched my face.

"You make me calmer, too. You and Cary. Can I keep holding you?"

It was the most I'd heard him say since we'd met, and his voice slid over my senses like honey. *Was it only last night we'd met?*

"Of course." If my being in his lap helped him too, I'd happily stay here all night.

It felt as if I'd known him an eternity, yet he was also a complete mystery. He pulled me in closer and subtly breathed me in. I didn't mind. It felt comforting to know he was craving my scent as much as I was his. Touching him, and breathing him in, brought me peace and an uncomplicated sense of connection I hadn't felt since I was a kid. I felt no boundaries with him. My instincts were telling me he was mine and that he would never hurt me, couldn't hurt me. I had questions that were tugging at me, though. Pushing their way through the cloud he had me wrapped in.

"Last night, you seemed afraid of me. What changed?" I kept my voice low and soft, not wanting to spook him out of this moment.

His dark eyes flared. "You screamed."

His answer took my breath away. He seemed to see the world in the simplest terms.

"Why were you afraid of me before that?"

"Your scent," he grunted, before he paused for a moment. "They used it to control me." Horror filled me, tightening my throat. I was speechless.

"To calm you or threaten you?" River asked without looking up from where he was still tending the fire.

"Both," Wolf growled, as darkness shadowed his eyes

"How did you end up here?" River asked.

"Can we not talk about that right now?" Wolf asked, as his gruff voice lowered and his brows pinched.

"Of course." I said, jumping in before anyone else could. I got the guys would be curious, and also concerned about my safety with him, but I didn't want to push him right now. We all had things that were painful to talk about. I was just relieved he was actually talking to us. My instincts were telling me the rest would come when he was ready, and it would be hard to hear. I wanted to stay in our comforting bubble a little while longer.

"Why did you break free and run when they tried to move you last night, and not before?" Ryder asked.

"Her scent had faded. She was gone. When I got outside, I tracked her." He kept his gaze firmly on me while he answered, as if he was afraid I'd suddenly disappear. The longer he held me, the clearer his eyes seemed to get, but there was a haunted look creeping in, too.

Even this tiny part of his story made me want to cry, but I didn't want to burden him with any more tears tonight. I reached up and twisted a strand of his shaggy hair around my finger. In the fading sunset filtering through the tree branches, the hint of deep red in the dark strands stood out even more. He shuddered lightly as I played with his hair.

"Is this okay?" I asked, suddenly unsure. I was luxuriating in every touch from him right now, but he might not feel the same.

"Yes," he groaned and closed his eyes. I wanted to explore him more. His reaction to my simple touch was thrilling. After being denied touch for so long, I knew the feeling. So I ran my hand through his beard, then traced the line of his cheek as he leaned into my caress.

Every omega at the Palace had a handler, but the Palace forbid them from touching us. It was another way of breaking us. Taking away something an omega needed to flourish. We naturally craved touch. As did alphas.

A twig snapped nearby, and I stiffened, but Wolf just tightened his arms around me. "It's Cary," he said.

A moment later, Cary appeared out of the descending darkness, laden down with giant laundry bags full of blankets and pillows. He started spreading them out next to us. Wolf effortlessly picked me up and plonked us both back down onto a soft comforter. As if it was his job to keep me in his arms. I wasn't complaining.

Nick appeared shortly after, with a mound of pillows, a picnic basket in his arms, and a guitar strapped to his back. I had no idea where he'd gotten it from or if he could play. He settled down next to the fire and pulled a large cast-iron pot out of the basket.

"Owen and Miles had already prepped a basic stew for dinner. They said we just needed to simmer it over the fire for a while longer." Nick looked from the pot to the fire, like he wasn't sure how to make that happen. River and Ryder swung into action, showing off their outdoor skills, and expertly got the pot set up in the fire. Nick gave them an enthusiastic high five when they were done, which made me grin.

Everyone settled back down onto the comforter, but Ryder was restless. He fidgeted with a stick and shot a look at River, who frowned at him. My calm evaporated as my stomach sank. I didn't know how much more I could take today. Ryder, with his heart spilling out of his blue eyes, could easily break me.

He finally sighed and swiveled to look at me. "I have some questions."

Eleven

I looked at Ava snuggled up in Wolf's brawny arms. The young girl I knew was gone, and I couldn't get her back. She was all woman now. We'd missed so much. The Palace had robbed us of those years with her. I knew I was older too, and different from the boy she knew. Yet part of me had always expected thirteen-year-old Ava to come running out those doors towards us when we could finally come for her.

It was almost a shock seeing her again. Especially the way she'd appeared when we'd arrived here last night. The poised omega princess that had walked back through those ornate doors had felt foreign and untouchable. Seeing her out here, amongst the trees, was better. She felt more like my Ava, even if she looked different.

I searched her face, and her huge green eyes begged me for something I couldn't define. I used to know every expression in them.

"Okay," she finally said, with that same quiet, softness in her voice that I remembered. It stirred so many emotions in me. I'd always felt fiercely protective of her, so had River. Even before we presented as alphas. It had been an instinctive, yet innocent, feeling, though. She'd been our best friend, a partner in our adventures. I felt the same protectiveness now, but stained by my anger and fear.

How had Wolf let his fear go? The second we'd heard her scream, he'd been off his bike and running. Yet, so had I. I looked at him now, unsure what to do. My emotions were veering around wildly. He gave me an encouraging nod.

My obvious torment must have been too much for Ava, because she slipped off Wolf's lap and crawled on her knees toward me. She'd never been able to see us in pain without trying to fix it. I don't think she meant to, but she looked sexy as hell. Her t-shirt gaped loose around her chest and I tried not to look at the swell of lush cleavage it exposed. It had never felt like that between us before, but we'd been so young. I had to fight the possessive growl that tried to force its way out of my chest.

She stopped right in front of me and sat on her knees, looking at her hands folded primly in front of her. She suddenly went from sex kitten to pure virgin sacrifice, accepting her fate from a wrathful god. My alpha was clawing at my chest, wanting to pin her down and claim her. Needing her in a carnal way I'd never felt for her before. My head had other ideas, though. It had my body at war.

"What do you need to know, Ry?"

I hesitated. So much was running through my mind. A swirling mess of accusations and fear that had me on edge. But there was one question raging through it all. "I need to know why."

"Why?" she asked, confusion clouding her gorgeous eyes.

"Why did you leave without a word? Was it us? Was it me? Did you so desperately want to be a princess you'd give up your freedom for it?" I knew my words were harsh and unfair, my tone far too rough, but the fear we hadn't been enough for her had been burning a hole in me for a decade.

Her eyes widened as she gasped. "No, Ry. Leaving you and River was the hardest thing I've ever done."

"Then why? We would have died to keep you safe." They weren't words I spoke lightly. I meant them. If it came down to me or her, it would be her I'd save. Even now. Even if she didn't want me.

"Exactly. You both would have died, Ry. And I would have ended up here anyway, having to live the rest of my life without you. At least this way there was a chance."

"A chance for what?" A part of my brain was screaming for me to stop, but my heart felt twisted. I had to let it all out. I had to know. "A chance for you to find another alpha?"

"Is that what you think?" She seemed shocked. I noticed movement behind her, as if the others were getting up to leave, but River motioned for them to stay still as he glared at me. So be it. We were having this out now, no matter who was here.

"Ava, everyone thought you were a beta, and we didn't care. But that night at the barn dance changed everything. Your scent came in so suddenly while you and I were dancing, as if lightning struck us. You'd always been our best friend, but suddenly you were so much more. River felt it too. We both knew instantly you were ours. Our true scent matched mate. Happy is too small a word for everything I felt at that moment. I could see the entirety of our future reflected in your eyes, and it was perfect."

"I felt it too, Ry. That moment, when River joined us and you both held me in your arms, the world made sense in a way I'd never known before. You'd always felt like my home, but suddenly it was my every heartbeat belonged to you," she whispered. "I've always held that memory in my heart. But everyone at the dance freaked out. Then, when we got home, my uncle was frantic. He said the Palace would come for me, and if you stood in their way, you'd die."

I clenched my jaw as her words tried to pull my world apart even more. "I know. That's why we decided to run. We only left you to go pack some survival gear and food. When we got back, you were gone."

That moment felt etched in my brain forever. Every second apart from her had filled me with a rushing sense of fear. Running back to her house loaded down with gear, but ready to swoop her up in my arms and carry her to safety, only to find her gone. It had shattered me. Parts of me still lay scattered over the floor of her uncle's house, where I'd left them.

She dropped her head. "And all this time you thought it was because I rejected you? That I wanted a different life?"

I couldn't swallow suddenly, my throat was so dry. This was my truth. "I was still going to come for you, get you out, the way River planned. But that future I pictured for us, only hours before. It felt gone too, and it fucking hurt. You tore a piece of me out I couldn't get back."

The last rays of the sun had finally disappeared into the twilight while we were talking. Only the dancing flames of the fire illuminated us now.

It was enough for me to see the silent tears as they fell from her cheeks. Her eyes, when she finally looked up at me, were distraught. Each tear, a bucket of ice, dousing the fire inside me.

"I never, ever imagined you would have thought that of me, Ry. That I would cast you aside so callously. Did you know me at all? You and Riv were my world. My foundations felt built on yours."

"There was no note, nothing. You were just gone." I realized suddenly how childish and defensive I sounded. All my long-held rage crumbled into ash in my arms.

She looked over her shoulder at River. "Did you feel like this too?"

He shook his head, sadness etched in every line of his face. "No. I was angry at first too. But I knew you would never do that. I knew there had to be another reason."

I felt suddenly ashamed. In my panic and confusion, with our bond tearing out of my chest, the idea had taken hold and seemed to grow. A poisonous vine within me. It had choked me for a decade.

"We were kids, Ry," she pleaded with me. "We couldn't fight the Palace and the whole of society on our own. There was nowhere for us to go. My uncle told me how he had been working to smuggle out omegas before the Palace found them. So I knew what this place was. I knew it wasn't a princess school."

"Yet you still went. We agreed to run. Then you changed your mind," I insisted, struggling to let go of the arguments that had swirled in my head for so long.

"No, you and Riv decided to run. You tried to decide for me, but it wasn't your decision to make. I wasn't your possession to bundle up and carry away. I had to make my own choice."

"You made the decision to leave without us. You took away our choice to protect you." I was shouting now, and she flinched, but my pain was ugly and I couldn't reel it back in now that ash was spilling everywhere. I could feel River's frustration with me in our bond. He wanted to step in and put a stop to this. But he also knew I needed to purge my emotions, or they became pressurized and eventually exploded. And I'd been holding onto these for a decade.

"No, Ry. I made the hardest decision of my life, and it was mine to make. There was no note, because I didn't have the words for one. I couldn't say goodbye to you. Not ever. I only went because my uncle convinced me it was the only way to keep you both alive."

"Keep us alive?" Now it was my turn to be shocked. "We knew your uncle sheltered and hid omegas escaping the Palace. We overheard our dad and your uncle talking about it. He could have at least gotten you away someplace safe, even if you didn't want to be with us, but you came to this place, anyway."

My bitterness bled into my voice. I just didn't get why she'd come here. It was the question that had turned everything black inside me. It didn't make sense when there was an option to run. Even if it hadn't been with us. It was the splinter that had festered in my heart every time I tried to move past that night.

"No, he couldn't," she insisted. Her brow furrowed, and she looked completely confused. "The Palace knew about me already. Somebody from the dance contacted them. The Palace called while you were gone. My uncle told them I'd already left for my mother's in the city, because he couldn't risk having them turn up at the farm and discovering his operation. He said anytime an omega presented in an unexpected family, or in an unusual way, it alerted the attention of the Palace. They would immediately investigate everyone connected to the omega. I had to go straight away or risk everybody, and my uncle had to temporarily shut everything down. It wasn't just you, me, and Riv. Every omega he would save in the future was at risk. Didn't he explain this to you when he got back?"

I went still and shot a look at my twin. She really hadn't known. I hadn't realized fully what that meant until this moment. A frozen wave of understanding crashed over me.

"He couldn't," River said. He sounded hesitant, not wanting to cause her more pain.

Ava looked between us at my sudden silence. I clenched my fists as I realized the depth of what they had done to her, to us all. The layers of lies and manipulation she had endured. *What had she thought all these years, at the silence of her family? Of us?*

"Tell me," she demanded, that inner strength of hers shining through.

"Ava, your uncle never made it back," I answered her. I'd started this. I couldn't leave it to River and shy away from the hard bits now. "He and your mother died in a car accident late that night while driving back to the farm from the city. We only ever got a rushed message from him, saying you had gone to the Palace, but not telling us why or how. How did you not know that?"

Her lip trembled as she tried to hold it together, and the sight damn near killed me. "They died that night?"

I nodded. River shifted to sit behind her and wrapped his arms around her, unable to hold back any longer. She leaned into him and my decade of pent-up anger crumbled to nothing, not even leaving ash behind. It had only ever been a mirage. This was my Ava. *What the hell was I doing yelling at her right now?*

I suddenly felt sick. All I'd really wanted to do since the moment she'd left was hold her in my arms again. Now I had the chance, and I was blowing it because I was holding onto my fear and confusion more than I was holding onto her. "Ava, I'm so sorry."

The words felt cheap and empty the moment they left my lips. They weren't enough. Not for what I had just done.

Her eyes seemed suddenly far away, and I wasn't sure she even heard me. "Nobody told me. My uncle said he'd get me out. I just had to hide in plain sight, be patient, and play their game. That you would come for me at my debut if you couldn't get me out before then. I waited for years for any kind of message, but all I got was silence. Then the Crash came, and you still didn't come."

My heart clenched, as if it might actually stop beating altogether. She'd been alone in hell all these years, waiting for us to rescue her, and I couldn't even have faith in who I knew she was as a person.

"Is that why you insisted we wait for days, hiding in the library, even though you told Maia we'd follow her?" Cary asked when I couldn't seem to find any words. I'd flung so many at her moments ago. But the words I needed to fix the mess I'd made wouldn't seem to come. I felt frozen.

Ava just nodded, still with that faraway look in her eyes.

"So that's why you looked so mad at us when you introduced us as your mates to Lexie last night?" River asked, as he tightened his arms around her. "You thought we'd abandoned you?"

She nodded again, almost absentmindedly. I suddenly worried we'd pushed her too far tonight. Or I'd pushed her too far. Omegas were emotional creatures by nature, and we'd exposed her to too much, too quickly.

"Ava?" She looked at me slowly and a boulder settled in my lungs. She looked so beautiful, yet delicate. Her skin looked like porcelain in the moonlight, but her eyes showed how shattered she felt. I'd never meant to hurt her. I should have had more faith in her. As River had. *I'm an asshole.*

"Why didn't you come?" She asked, so softly I had to strain to hear her, even though the only competition was the crickets sending their mating calls into the night. The guys around us were quiet, but I could feel the weight of their angry stares.

"We were coming, we just weren't nearby or prepared when the Crash happened. Our years of planning went to shit. It's a war zone out there. We got here as fast as we could." It wasn't good enough, but it was the truth.

"Why didn't you get me a message before that?"

I sighed. "When your mom and uncle died, our parents knew it wasn't an accident. One of your uncle's colleagues got them a message before dawn warning we could be targets too. They shipped us off to military school first thing in the morning, trying to show we were part of the establishment and were willing to play by the rules. We couldn't get a message to you without putting you at risk. There were too many eyes on us all. We figured you'd know that when you heard about your family. We never imagined they wouldn't tell you."

"They had lots of sneaky ways of breaking us," she replied in a dull tone that had me worried. River glanced over at me. He looked helpless for the first time in his life. River was a fixer. He'd spent a lifetime fixing my messes when my emotions got the better of me. But he couldn't fix this one. Only I could.

"Over the last decade, we learned every skill we could to make sure when the time came to get you out, we'd be ready. We set up hideouts around the country, and networks with anyone we thought could help. We went AWOL from the military when we realized they were never going to let us anywhere near your debut to claim you," I said, my voice almost matching her dull tone. I felt suddenly lost and empty. I needed her in my arms, but I'd destroyed that possibility.

"He's telling the truth about the hideouts. He took me to one today. It's where we got the dirt bikes from. It was full of supplies and looked like it had been there for a long time," Wolf said.

I shot him a grateful glance, but he just raised a stern eyebrow at me in return.

"Yet the whole time, you were so mad at me." Her voice sounded so small. She always hated when people were mad at her.

I couldn't deny it, not when I had just vented that anger on her. So I just nodded. I was going to have to make it up to her and prove myself to her.

"I'm sorry." The words felt even more painfully inadequate the second time, but they were true. She just nodded absently back at me, and my heart ached.

"Ryder, can you give me a hand with the stew?" Nick asked. River nodded at me, so I shifted back and got up reluctantly.

Nick's jaw was tight, and he looked frustrated, so I avoided making eye contact. He helped me get the pot off the fire, then handed me a bowl and some fresh bread. "Give this to her."

Before I could move away, he grabbed my wrist and yanked me closer. "She needs you," he hissed into my ear. "Do better."

It was a bold move from the seemingly easy going beta. He knew I could put him on his ass in a heartbeat, yet he'd stepped up to try to get her what she needed. He was a solid guy. I couldn't fault him, because he was right.

All I could do was nod. Again. I passed her the food, then went back for more and handed it around. It was simple yet delicious. River and I had been living on protein bars and MREs for weeks. They were nourishing, but empty. The hot food warmed me up inside and melted some of the ice that seemed to have settled in my chest.

As soon as she finished eating, Ava moved back over to Wolf's lap and snuggled in as if she belonged there. His whole body relaxed into her, and he wrapped his arms protectively around her.

"Could you…?" He was purring before she even asked. She closed her eyes and was out before Cary got a blanket settled around her.

We waited for a few minutes until we were sure she was completely asleep.

"Hit me with it," I said, knowing I deserved whatever was going to happen next.

Twelve

Wolf

"Nobody here has led a charmed life. We're not judging you. We're just worried about her," Cary said. He reached over and brushed some hair out of Ava's face. He didn't seem jealous over her, or possessive of her around us, which surprised me. Omegas were supposed to be jealous of other omegas. Probably another Palace lie. He'd actually relaxed a little since hearing the twins' story. He hadn't been this welcoming towards them last night.

Even if Cary was understanding of Ryder's situation with Ava, I wasn't so forgiving of anyone messing with her. "Hurt her again. I'll hurt you," I growled.

I glared at Ryder. He nodded, taking me at my word. I noticed the way he'd slumped forward, and I figured he was beating himself up enough for both of us right now.

"You'll have to get in line behind Nick. He already gave me a warning," Ryder said. I leaned forward slightly and held up my fist to bump into Nick's. He looked surprised, but gave me the fist bump. He'd settled in close beside me, next to Ava. Nick kept glancing from me to her legs, as if he wanted to pull her feet into his lap, but was unsure what my reaction would be.

"Should we take her shoes off, make her more comfortable if we're sleeping out here?" Nick asked. He didn't seem to be asking anyone in particular. So I just grunted at him.

"I think that means 'tag, you're it,'" Cary replied, and his lips curved up in a small, affectionate smile aimed at the beta. Nick just shrugged. He shot me another quick look before he gently unlaced her boots and slipped them off her feet. He worked slowly, as if I really was a wild creature and might take a bite out of him if he startled me. I noticed he propped her feet up on his lap when he was done, under the pretense of moving them closer to the fire. I tried not to smile. He had a calm, yet protective, energy I liked. He was going to be good for our pack.

"I thought you'd be the one mad at me," Ryder said to Cary. He seemed surprised we weren't kicking his ass more. "Or maybe a little jealous of us suddenly wanting to claim her, seeing as you're together."

Cary's eyebrows hit his hairline. "We're not together. Not in that way. Not yet."

Ryder's mouth opened, but no words came out. It surprised me too. I assumed they were a couple, given the way they gravitated toward each other.

"Last night was the first time I've even seen him hold her hand," Nick said with a cheeky grin, teasing Cary. "Cary's usually standing silent and stoic at her side, like some kind of stone gargoyle."

Cary laughed and threw a twig at Nick, and the sound was a fresh vanilla ice cream scented breeze through my soul. I liked that Nick could bring out Cary's smile and that gorgeous laugh. Cary seemed aloof most of the time.

"Why?" Ryder asked quietly. Cary glanced at him, and I hated the wary look that stole back into his eyes. He seemed okay about Ava being mated to the twins, but nervous of himself around them, which put me on edge. He'd approached me instinctively that first night. His need to help had overridden any thought for himself, but now he seemed to retreat from everyone except Ava and Nick.

"It's never been like that between us. It couldn't be. Not here." That got my attention. Cary was an omega, too, but his emotions were closed off. His entire demeanor shouted trauma. I forced down another growl, taking a deep breath of Cary and Ava's mingled scents instead. Trying to stay in the moment and not let my thoughts get too wild. The more time

I spent with them, the clearer I felt, but I could feel that wild, feral energy hovering. It felt ready to jump back the minute they disappeared.

"Ava's always been mine, but it was impossible. It would have put her in even more danger. I had to shut it down," Cary sighed and looked at the twins searchingly. "The whole time I've known her, she seemed almost haunted, as if something or someone was holding her back as well."

"Did they ever hurt her?" River asked bluntly. He winced and stiffened, as if he was bracing himself for Cary's answer. I did too. They said they'd leave her alone if I cooperated, but I'd had no proof they were keeping to their word. Apart from the new scent marked blankets appearing regularly.

"No. Not that I ever knew about, and I watched them closely." Cary's answer had us all letting out held breaths, but I couldn't help feeling there was more.

Cary looked up at the smoke disappearing into the branches above us and chewed his lip for a moment before he spoke again. "Look, this place wasn't a picnic for anyone. They tried to break us down and make us perfect, submissive omegas. Ava didn't escape that, but they never targeted her like some of the other omegas. There are no words for what they did to Maia. Ava was playing a part to slip under the radar, the way she said, and she did it well. I think there was more at play, though. They watched her too much, just from a distance. They had some plan for her and I can't help but think it involved you, Wolf."

I looked down at Ava curled up in my lap, her head tucked into my chest as that strange vibration I didn't even know was within me soothed her. Her distress had brought it out instinctively. I'd reached for her without even thinking as soon as I'd gotten near her. She looked so vulnerable, but was so trusting, asleep in my arms. I knew I would do terrible things to protect her. Yet, *had I brought danger to her, purely by existing?*

I knew Cary was right. But no matter what he thought he knew about the Palace, they were capable of so much worse.

"I was barely through the door when I scented her. They noticed," I grunted. I remembered that day so clearly, even when everything else became fuzzy. My initial elation at scenting my true mate, and the sickening horror as the lab tech's smiles grew. At that moment, they'd known they had my compliance.

"She would have suffered a worse fate if they forced her into a debut," Cary said, as if he could sense my distress.

"We would never have let that happen," River snarled as both twins tensed in sync, their bodies instantly on alert.

It was deceptive to watch them as they lounged around the fire. It was too easy to forget they were highly trained, and deadly, predators. Even I had heard whispers about them. The guards liked to gossip, especially when they assumed I was sleeping. The mysterious twins were hot topics of conversation amongst the ex-military guys. I met both their eyes and bowed my head to them, out of respect.

"I would have gotten her out if I could." I couldn't keep the growl out of my voice, thinking of anyone hurting my omega.

"I spent every day trying to figure out how to do that. If there was a way, I never found it," Cary said, as he shook his head. "You don't want to know the desperate shit I had planned if some asshole alpha tried to bark her into submission."

Cary's face had darkened, and his gaze seemed to go inward. I didn't want to think about what he might have resorted to, alone and trying to protect her against such overwhelming odds. It would have been an impossible, and probably suicidal, task. Just the thought made me feel ill. The others looked equally disturbed, but nobody pushed Cary further on it.

"How long have you been here?" River asked me, as he stretched out his shoulders and changed the topic slightly. Although, not to an easier one. I noticed Nick watching me closely for my response. I wasn't sure why, but the kid was far too smart.

"Three years, I think. I was in another lab before that." It was hard to remember the details. The more I talked, the more things came back to me, though.

I stroked my thumb lightly over Ava's arm under the blanket covering her. Over the last few years, I'd slowly become a trapped, wild creature. I'd lost any appreciation for social norms, relying purely on my instincts and my senses. I'd learned to watch people, listened to them talk, and noted their body language, the way a caged animal watched its captors. Time had seemed unimportant.

I'd done whatever they wanted to keep her safe. To keep both my omegas safe. Yet I'd been powerless. The longer they'd kept me in that damned cage, the more wild I'd become. They'd tried to use her scent to control me, without realizing it was helping me keep my grip on my humanity. Just barely. I'd been more animal than human when River and Ryder had appeared on the other side of my cage out of nowhere. Her scent had faded, and my control had gone with it.

Now, every moment I spent touching her, or breathing in her scent, brought me back to myself. I'd noticed it when I ran into the forest this morning. The wildness had crept back in the further I'd run. Yet being close to Ryder had seemed to help force it back. The effect wasn't as powerful as Ava and Cary, but he had helped. I'd known in that moment my first instincts had been correct. These people were pack. The realization that I was now tied to these strangers if I wanted to stay sane should freak me out, but it didn't. It soothed me. I didn't want to be alone anymore. I had no idea what having a family felt like, but it if was anything like this, I wanted more of it.

Everyone was quiet for a moment, letting my words sink in. But I could see River's mind working. He was strategizing and working his way through a problem. His eyes focused on me intently.

"Where was the lab?" He finally asked, when he figured I wasn't going to volunteer the location unprompted. He leaned forward as if he was readying to leap into action.

"That's not a story for tonight."

"I think it is," River countered. His twin backed him up as he lifted his head and hit me with a steely stare.

"Why?" I asked gruffly. I wouldn't change my mind, but I was interested in what his answer would be.

"Because knowledge is power, and if we're going to keep Ava safe, we need more," River said. "Ryder and I have been underground for years, trying to work out who was behind the Palace's operation. We figured they were the same people manipulating the government. Now we're guessing they're behind the Crash, because whatever caused it, it wasn't natural. But we've never been able to crack their inner circle. They protected themselves well. I have a feeling, though, that you know exactly who they are."

I considered him for a heartbeat. I instinctively trusted him, but I didn't know if he could be patient and we couldn't leave right now.

"I do. I also have a rough idea of where they may have gone." River's eyes instantly lit up. "I'm only going to tell that story once, though, and Ava will be awake for it."

River's eyes shifted to Ava, and he backed down. "Fair enough. But it needs to happen soon. I think we're safe here for the moment, but that won't last."

I nodded in agreement. Everything had felt disconnected this morning, as I'd struggled to come back to myself from the wild state I'd sunk into. Yet the longer I sat here cradling Ava, with Cary next to me, the clearer my mind had become. Feeling the connection of their pack bonds, as fragile as they were, was bringing me back to myself. I needed to bring this pack together, not only for Ava, but for me, too.

I hadn't felt this aware in years. Clarity brought with it a lot of memories of my early years, though. Ones I would rather forget, but knew I needed to remember if I was going to keep my pack safe.

The clearer I got, the easier it was to talk and communicate, too. I'd struggled this morning, just to get words out. They'd felt rusty and foreign. They were flowing easier now. I tried to put the thoughts that were swirling around my head into words.

"If you want to go after the people behind the Palace, we need allies." I knew it was the only way to truly keep Ava and Cary safe, but I also knew we couldn't do it alone.

"We have allies," Nick said, surprising me. I'd expected it from River and Ryder, but not Nick. I made a mental note not to underestimate the plucky beta. "The people we were with last night will help. They've figured out a lot of what is going on, even what caused the crash. I don't know the specifics, but they've gathered tons of intel."

My body suddenly tensed. The people behind the Palace were manipulative and had spies everywhere. *Were our enemies closer than I'd thought?*

"Could they be working undercover for the Palace?" I asked, my arms tightening around Ava.

"No way." Cary jumped in. He put his hand on my arm in an instinctive, conciliatory gesture, and my body responded instantly, relaxing into his touch. "Max and his pack left the military because they couldn't condone the corruption. They've been trying to figure this thing out to protect Maia. Lexie's mates, Sam, Dio, and Pala, are part of the Network. They're helping them now, too."

"Do you trust them?" If Nick and Cary trusted them, I'd trust them, too.

"Yes." Nick said, without hesitation. "I've known Damon my whole life, and his pack members for years. They're good men. I don't know Sam and his team well, but I know Lexie and she doesn't trust easily."

"Me too," Cary said. "Damon and his pack risked their lives and compromised the security of their safehold, just to get Ava and I out of the Palace when they'd never met us. They treated me with nothing but respect and consideration while I was at the farm. More than anyone ever had in my life, even my family. Nick is right, they're good guys."

That was more than enough for me, but River jumped in too.

"We're aware of Sam and his unit by reputation. We've known for a while he and his mates were undercover for the Network. Pala was in training with us when we first joined up, and we kept in touch. Pala is one of the best operatives we've ever worked with, and an amazing guy. We know Damon by reputation, too. He's formidable, but loyal and honorable."

"Are you part of the Network?" I asked River and Ryder. I'd heard of Damon and Sam from the guards' chatter, and made a note of them, but I'd never heard of Pala. He must be an exceptional undercover operative. I'd noted the guards gossiping about the Network, as well.

"No. We helped them smuggle an omega occasionally, in exchange for their help if we ever got Ava out. But we're not a part of them. We preferred to work alone. Our focus has always been on Ava."

"We need to arrange a meeting with Sam, Damon, and their packs as soon as possible. Can that be done?" I asked Nick. Hearing about these packs coming together had me feeling hopeful for the first time. I'd been trying to figure out our next move, fearing we wouldn't be able to stay here long.

"Lexie and Maia check in on Ava at eight every morning and night, through a satellite phone they gave her. I have it," he said as he pulled it out from his hoodie pocket. He tapped it and looked at the time on the display. "They should call in about half an hour. I'll talk to them instead of waking her up and organize a meeting. Their farm isn't a long drive from here, but if they can't get here, we can maybe do a video hook up if I can get the systems here sorted. They're still online at the farm."

"Okay. Thank you, Nick."

Everyone suddenly went quiet. Our conversation about the Palace felt done. For now. But Nick, River, Ryder and Cary seemed on edge suddenly. As if there was a question hanging over them all, and nobody wanted to ask it.

"What do you think this means?" Nick finally asked, proving he was the bravest of us all. "I don't mean about the Palace, I mean about the way we all gravitate to Ava?"

He was trying to get us to talk about something specific, but I wasn't sure what. I noticed River's eyes flick to Nick as he smirked at him.

"What do you think it means?" River asked him.

"It means you're her pack. In the same way we saw happen with Maia and Lexie," Cary answered for him. He'd pulled his legs up and was hugging his knees to his chest. His voice was even, but the way he was staring at the leaf he was fiddling with and not making eye contact with us betrayed his emotions.

"We're your pack too," I growled.

Cary stiffened, the leaf going still in his hands, and both Ryder and River tensed. The idea Cary may reject our pack had my stomach feeling twisted up. I didn't even question the idea we were a pack. It seemed instinctive and natural to me. I wanted this more than I could express. The idea of a pack had always filled me with a painful longing. Despite the twisted example I'd been shown as a child. I knew things could be different, would be different, with my pack.

"I've had enough alphas forced on me. I'm not your typical omega, and I don't need protecting," Cary countered. He seemed defiant, and a little resentful, yet the fine shake in his hands made him seem intensely vulnerable. I got the impression he hadn't reconciled himself to being an omega and if we pushed him, he would push back like a trapped creature.

"I would never force you into anything you're uncomfortable with, Cary." My growl tried to force its way through my words, and I tried to soften it, not wanting to intimidate him right now. "I will be your alpha in whatever way you need. If you need me to stand back and watch over you from a distance, I will do that. If you need me to stand with you and help fight your battles, I will have your back. If you decide you need me to fuck you so hard you scream my name as I knot you, I am more than happy to oblige. But make no mistake. I am your alpha and this is your pack, too."

If it took him time to find his truth, I would wait. The only thing I would never do now that I'd found him, found them both, was leave them.

I waited a heartbeat to let my words wash over him, as my dick throbbed painfully in my pants. He'd closed his eyes when I mentioned fucking him and he'd crushed the leaf in his hand as he'd started breathing hard. I waited until he opened his eyes and I saw the desire shining within them.

"I scented you, as well as Ava. Not at first, a few months later. I hid it better. They never knew. But I did. I knew you were *mine*."

Thirteen

I felt frozen in place as I stared at Wolf. Everything was changing so quickly. Yesterday it had just been Ava and me, navigating our way through the unexpected freedom of farm life and a tentative new friendship with Nick. Yet still keeping each other at arm's length. Now, barely a day later, we'd broken our barriers down and we were sitting with a group of people who felt like home, along with an alpha who wanted to claim us both.

I could feel wariness and hope warring within me. Each emotion battling to cancel the other out, and neither winning. Life had fed me too many barbed promises.

"Alphas don't have two omegas. It's never happened before." Denial was my only option right now.

"There's never been an alpha like me before," Wolf growled, putting a little bite into his words. It wasn't enough to dominate me, just enough to get my attention, as if he needed me to hear him. See him. It sent a zap of electricity through me, shocking my heart into beating faster.

"This morning, I may have run, but it wasn't away from you or Ava. I would have told you that if I'd had the words. I just needed to feel my freedom for a moment. I knew you were safe and your pack was watching you."

He didn't look slighted at my silence, or that he'd declared himself my alpha and I hadn't reciprocated. Maybe it was enough for him, for now, to just tell his truth and have me hear him. *Was that possible?*

The intensity in his eyes, though, had me shifting my attention to the rest of the group before he stripped me completely bare. I swept my gaze over them. Ryder was hardly breathing as he leaned in, his arms rested on his crossed legs. As if he was watching a cliffhanger episode of his favorite TV show. River had leaned back onto his hands. His expression shuttered, as he carefully watched us. While Nick had curled around Ava and now studied me with a wistful expression.

I'd watched them today, and my defensiveness of Ava from our first meeting last night had gradually dissipated. My senses had become sharply honed over the years at the Palace. I knew what ill intentions looked like, tasted like. Even the shadowed kind. I didn't sense it from any of these men, towards Ava or me. There were plenty of messy emotions, especially between Ava and Ryder, but I could tell both the twins loved Ava deeply. Wolf was an open book, despite his wildness. He had no artifice and his intentions were clear. Nick was as smitten with Ava as he had been from the moment he laid eyes on her. If he was a cartoon character, he'd have giant hearts for eyes. It was sweet.

Watching them now, sitting under the stars together, this moment felt momentous somehow. As if it was the start of something beautiful and powerful. The thought that they might be mine, too, was a world made of cotton candy clouds and chocolate waterfalls. A dream. If only I could let them in and see if I could live there. I wished it were as easy as it sounded.

Wolf noticed my change in focus towards the other guys.

"Does anyone have a problem with two omegas in this pack?" His low growl gave them no option to deny we were a pack.

Nobody said anything for a moment. Each waiting for the other to speak first.

"Nick? I assume you're okay with it. You seem friendly with both Cary and Ava," Wolf asked, seeming impatient when no-one responded.

"You're asking me first?" Nick's head jerked up quickly. He seemed surprised, and a little overwhelmed. It was at odds with his earlier confidence when he introduced this discussion. He suddenly looked young and unsure.

"Of course. Why wouldn't I ask you?" Wolf demanded. His brow furrowed, and he looked genuinely perplexed.

"Um, I'm a beta. I know Maia and Lexie's pack both have betas in them, but they were in established relationships with their betas long before they became a pack."

"What does being a beta have to do with anything? You feel like pack so you're pack and you get a say in pack business." Wolf huffed, as if it was obvious and shouldn't require an explanation. Then his face fell, and a hint of vulnerability crept into his voice. "Do you not want to be pack either?"

"No," Nick almost shouted. He put his hand up in front of Wolf, as if to stop his next words. "I mean yes, I want to be pack. Ava and Cary felt like home from the moment I met them, in different ways. If this feels like a pack to you all too, I want in."

Nick talking so easily about me being home had a glow settling in my chest. I envied how simple it was for Nick and Wolf. To just want something and decide they were all in. Ava had broken through the wall between us last night, but it turns out we'd made that one out of tissue paper. The rest of my walls felt bolted in place, and would tear something inside of me if I tried to rip them down. Nick had somehow slipped past, though, without even trying. *Had he found a secret door?*

Wolf just nodded at Nick once, indicating it was done, and turned to the twins. They were sitting side by side, looking completely at home in the shadows. River frowned and seemed to wrestle with himself. His focus turned inward as he mentally examined all his parts to see what would fit in this new dynamic. He turned to his twin and River's frown fell away as his face softened. It was clear he'd do anything for his twin.

An entire conversation seemed to happen without words between the two, before River turned back to us. "I don't know as much about packs as all of you seem to do. But I can't deny we both feel a draw to you all, too. If that's a pack, we have no problem with it or having two omegas in it. Ava is ours. If she's also yours, that just means more people to protect her."

He hesitated again before he turned to me and addressed me directly. I forced my eyes to stay on him and not shy away, but my breath was being dragged through a field of boulders. When he spoke again, his words came in a careful, considered tone. They held weight. "I'm just not attracted to you, Cary. You don't feel like mine, and I need to be upfront about that. Ava is it for me. She's my true mate. You feel like a pack brother, though, so I'm happy to be here for anything else you need."

I felt the tension in my body ease and I let out the breath I'd been holding. River, not being my alpha, was fine with me. I didn't feel like he was mine, either. I could work with pack brother. A faint hope glimmered within the void in my chest. That I might be a part of something in this world after all.

"I'm good with that," I told him honestly. He let out a breath too and looked relieved. He shot me a tiny, lopsided grin, and it was startling given how stern he'd been since I met him. It changed his entire face and made him seem more approachable. He must have been worrying about our dynamic, too.

His twin hadn't spoken yet, though. I flicked my eyes Ryder's way and met his curious stare.

"I agree with River. If the way we feel drawn to you all is pack, then you're a part of that, Cary. Even if you're not mine the way Ava is. Although, unlike my brother, I'm open to *anything* you need. That includes sharing, as long as Ava is okay with it."

I mulled over his words for a moment, feeling intrigued. Sharing Ava with one of them, or even being with one of her other mates for her pleasure, hadn't occurred to me. I don't know why. In my mind, it had been one or the other, and I would always choose Ava. What Ryder was suggesting would take a lot of trust and open communication. The idea hooked inside me and stirred up embers I didn't know existed. *Would she be into that, though?*

Ryder had one eyebrow cocked as he took me in. Almost in challenge. "Ava has been mine since the moment I scented her. I'll give her anything she wants," I told him honestly, but kept it deliberately vague. Ava would be my guide on this. I wouldn't let anything mess up my chance with her, or distract me from her.

I deliberately didn't look at Wolf. He was different. More than the other guys, in a way I couldn't examine right now. My heart shied away from poking that wound. I focused instead on what I needed to achieve my goal of protecting Ava and the other omegas.

If I was going to be a part of this pack, it couldn't be as the person my father and the Palace had forced me to become. I couldn't live that half life any longer, not if I was going to be who Ava needed now that she was free. I had to figure out a way to do it that let me finally drop the mask and breathe. That allowed me to get to know the man underneath.

"For me, right now, what I really need is training. I want to learn how to defend myself and protect her. I got my ass kicked the last time I tried. Learning to fight has never been an option for me. I need that to change." It was the only way forward for me. If they denied me, this would not work.

"Ava mentioned you're injured and I've noticed you wincing when you move. She said you took on four alphas to shield her and her friend," River said.

"You're injured? Who hurt you?" Wolf's purr cut off, replaced with an angry growl. Death suddenly stalked our cozy glade. Ava stirred in his arms and Nick reached out to soothe her by stroking her back.

"I'm healing. I wasn't going to let those Palace assholes take either of them, but with no training, I was more of an inconvenience than a threat. If Maia and Lexie's packs hadn't intervened, it would have ended badly. I never want to be in that position again." I clenched my jaw as I remembered the way those alphas had stalked towards Ava and Lexie.

The first time I'd seen Ava, she'd been innocently standing at a window overlooking the Palace garden. I'd barely been there a day when I'd come across her, lost in thought, a small frown on her face. The stone window arch had framed her as soft rays of the late afternoon sun had lit her up. She'd been radiant. A goddess among mortals. Her hair had been up in a bun, long wisps falling loose around her face. I could still see the flowy white dress she'd been wearing, turned almost translucent in the soft light. The one that haunted my dreams.

Ava had been oblivious to my presence, as I'd stood transfixed. Watching her for far too long. A soft breeze had wafted her scent over me and I'd had to stifle a gasp as my heart had instantly raced and the world had seemed to zero in on her even further. The need to go to her had grown until standing still had lodged barbed hooks under my skin. Yet, even then, I'd known I couldn't. The Palace had made it clear they didn't want omegas mingling, and at that moment, neither of us had been where we were supposed to be.

As if she'd felt me too, she'd turned in my direction, a soft, uncertain smile on her face. I'd nodded at her brusquely, like a savage, before I turned and fled. I'd torn something inside myself in the process. She hadn't been for me. Not then. Nothing good lasted long at the Palace. I'd known it the moment I'd crossed the threshold and the polite veneer had slipped away. They broke beautiful things. Yet I vowed, as I ran from her, that I'd do whatever it took to keep her safe. From a distance. Now the Crash had changed everything, except my feelings for her. The pull I felt to Wolf, and this pack, was strange. It had me twisted up. Yet, what I felt for Ava was a clear beam of sunlight in my soul.

The guys were quiet, respectful, as they let me work out my feelings and my sudden agitation at feeling so helpless to protect her. "I'd defend her again in a heartbeat if she ever needed it, and I'll gladly do the work to make sure I'm more effective. But she still needs people who can protect her better, and give her the love she deserves. She needs a pack. She needs all of you. What I need right now is her and pack mates to help defend her, if that makes sense."

It was a carefully worded distinction, but nobody argued about it. I couldn't help but notice the twins hadn't yet acknowledged my request for training. It had my gut twisting uneasily. *Was it too much to hope for, that I could be myself around alphas? Would any ever let me be strong in real life, not just in the bedroom?*

"They weren't trying to take you? You're an omega, too," Wolf asked. He looked confused, and still fixated on me being hurt.

"No, they don't value me as anything more than entertainment." I tried to sound flippant, but my tone was wrong and I'd felt myself stiffen up again. These guys were far too observant not to notice. Ava murmured in her sleep and I reached over to stroke her hair. Her arm snaked out from under the blankets as she shifted, and she grabbed my arm and snuggled it into herself. I shifted closer to them and leaned forward slightly to breathe her in, needing to know she was here and okay.

"You are so much more than entertainment. I've watched you with Ava. You have more to offer than you yet know," Wolf murmured to me, his tone much softer now. "I will be eternally grateful to you for having her back when I couldn't."

I finally met his eyes as we both held Ava in our arms. A spark flared between us, hot and bright, only this time I didn't shy away. He didn't push me for more. Yet the way he was so instinctively in tune with Ava had me yearning for what he was silently offering. *Would he be that way for me, too? Could I let him one day?*

The idea of having someone anticipate my needs and then meet them was intoxicating. It was what invaded my dreams. But I'd fought so hard to hold on to tiny pieces of myself when alphas had only ever wanted to make me their toy. The risk of losing myself to the thrall of an alpha, and my independence along with it, was too great. I wasn't ready to expose that much of myself to an alpha just yet. If ever.

"You have the spirit of a fighter, and nobody can teach that, Cary," Ryder said with a quiet respect that dragged my focus back to him.

"Luckily, we *can* teach you technique. And we'd be happy to do it," River added. "You're always at Ava's side, so you'll be our last line of defense if anything happens to us. It would put our mind at ease, too, if you had training."

I looked over my shoulder at the twins as relief flooded me. At their nods, determination took over, until it was a drumbeat in my veins. "Can we start tomorrow?"

Ryder smirked, and I had a feeling he wouldn't be going easy on me. "Yeah, sure."

"Can I join in?" Nick asked. "I ran into that battle with a broom. I want to have a few more options in my arsenal, too." He gave a self-deprecating chuckle, and I grinned at him as Nick grabbed a stick from the pile by the fire and started play fighting with it. Nick could coax a smile from me, no matter what I was feeling. He was a rare soul.

"That was epic." I said, as a grin I couldn't hold back stole across my face. "I can still picture you running around the corner with that broom, ready to take them all on. And you yelling 'biscuit' at Damon when he growled at you. You're telling me the story behind that later. The look on his face was priceless. But no brooms, or sticks, if you're going to be my sparring buddy."

A broom. I chuckled at the memory. Nick was more than plucky. He was fearlessly protective when it came to Ava. I liked his spirit, but he was kind of klutzy. He'd also led a sheltered life and was a few years younger than us. He was going to need watching, or he'd get himself hurt, too. Wolf seemed to have the same thoughts, as he shot a glance at River, and River nodded. He was on it.

"Of course, we'll train you both," River said, as Nick's face lit up.

The protectiveness between the two alphas for Nick had those bolts on my walls loosening just a little. They wouldn't stop him from helping, just safeguard him.

"Why don't you take a nap with Ava, Wolf? We'll take turns to keep watch and keep the fire going," River said. He nodded his head at the open space behind Wolf on the comforter.

Wolf just grunted and looked up at the trees arching over us. He seemed to relax as he looked up at the wide open space. I realized River had known exactly what he was doing, suggesting a sleepout. Exhaustion settled over Wolf as he closed his eyes and laid back. He pulled Ava down with him and inadvertently pulled Nick and me down, too. Nick passed him a pillow, and Wolf settled it under his head, before he pulled Ava half over himself so he could be hers. Nick rearranged a blanket over us and grabbed a pillow for himself, too. He had no intention of going anywhere right now, as he snuggled in alongside the giant alpha without hesitation.

I awkwardly lay on my elbow and settled behind Ava. She still had a hold of my arm as if it was her favorite teddy bear, but I wasn't complaining.

"What's a prime alpha? Ava asked Wolf if he was one earlier," River asked after a few moments. I could see Wolf's chest steadily rising and falling, and I guessed he was already asleep.

I explained it as best as I could, but I didn't fully understand it myself. Nick jumped in between sleepy yawns and filled a few holes in. He seemed to know more than any of us. I tuned out their conversation and listened to the sound of the leaves rustle above us and the way the fire crackled. Being out here made me realize we could go anywhere or do anything we wanted now, and these men would help keep Ava safe. It made me feel free in a way I'd never felt before. I could only imagine how being out here made Wolf feel.

A low ringing sound a little while later had Nick jumping up to answer the satellite phone. I assumed it was Maia and Lexie. He wandered away to talk to them quietly. Ryder started singing something soft that I couldn't make out, and River joined in. When Nick got back, he picked up the guitar and started strumming along lightly. The hushed, soothing tones had the same effect as a lullaby, making my head nod in my hand.

Without overthinking it too much, I rested my head tentatively on Wolf's chest and snuggled in closer to Ava. I told myself it was simply practical to lean on Wolf, with the way Ava was clinging to my arm. Yet I knew it was anything but, as his arm instinctively came around my back. I tensed as his beard twitched, as though he'd smiled briefly. But he just seemed to settle into a deeper sleep. I let myself have this moment, just one. A stolen comfort.

Because tomorrow, I'd finally learn to fight. And it was because of these men surrounding me.

I realized something that had those bolts loosening further, as sleep took me under. These alphas didn't make me feel weaker at all; they made me feel strong.

The only thing holding me back now was me.

Fourteen

"We're not in Kansas anymore, are we?" I muttered as I lay beside River. The world had woken up slowly as light streaked across the sky and pushed back the darkness. Birds were sharing their morning greetings in the tree behind us. We'd built the fire under its leafy branches last night to disperse the smoke, but hadn't made the rookie mistake of sleeping under them. Nobody wanted a branch falling on them during the night, or to wake up to bird shit on their face.

I didn't mean our surroundings, though. We'd spent a lot of nights sleeping outdoors over the years. I meant the new pack we'd suddenly landed in, the mess I'd made of reuniting with Ava, and the void between us. The last few days felt like a tornado had whipped through me. I missed the simplicity of our childhoods. I looked up at the open sky above me, waiting for him to speak. We'd held so much back from each other lately, each of us locked into our coping mechanisms. I wanted Ava back with a need that left me breathless, but I wanted my twin back, too.

River was sitting up next to me, scanning the trees. It was his watch, which meant I was supposed to be sleeping, but I couldn't. My mind was too awake, going over everything Ava had said last night and realizing all the ways I'd failed her.

"No," River said, simply, without elaborating, his eyes on the surrounding woods.

My words suddenly dried in my throat. I could feel River shift to watch me with concern, as if he didn't know what I was about to do or say. We'd always been completely in sync as kids, but I knew he had felt differently about Ava leaving and had dealt with it in a focused, determined way. It rattled me to be so out of step with the two people who had always been in sync with me. I had to find a way past the hurt and the fear that had consumed me for a decade before I lost her for good. Maybe lost them both. Especially now that I knew my fears and anger were unfounded.

"You're never going to lose me," River said quietly, as if he could tell exactly what I was thinking, "and we're going to make her ours."

There was a fierce determination in his voice. He let nothing get in his way once he'd set his mind to something. I admired that about him. He'd always been the steadiness I needed in my life. He'd been my rock the last decade, even if I'd broken myself upon it.

"I worried for years she didn't want us. Or maybe only wanted you, but didn't want to come between us. And it was pointless." I'd never told him that part of my fears, and I wasn't sure why I told him now. Maybe because keeping it bottled up had gotten me into this mess. If I was going to change the outcome, I needed to change how I reacted. Opening up more seemed a good place to start. *If I couldn't do it with my twin, how would I ever do it with Ava?*

"Hang on, how could you possibly think she only wanted me? You and Ava were always attached at the hip. If anyone was going to be left out, it would be me." River had shifted around to look at me, but I couldn't meet his eyes. It had always felt like looking into the mirror, but at a better version of me. An upgrade. He was the man I aspired to be.

I kept my voice low, so as not to wake the others sleeping on the blanket next to us. Ava was still sprawled out over Wolf. She'd barely moved all night. Cary and Nick were curled in around them.

"Fears aren't always rational, Riv. Besides, we were just more tactile. It's our natures. It didn't mean she cared for me more. You've always been the perfect twin. Your grades were perfect, you were the best at every sport you tried. You've always been a natural leader. All my fears rose up when she left and it seemed to make sense she'd want you. What woman wouldn't? You were always going places. I just trailed along in your wake."

Shit, that sounded petty, saying it out loud. I didn't mean it in that way. I loved my brother fiercely. Sibling relationships, even the best ones, were hard sometimes. I just couldn't seem to express myself well at the moment. Everything I said came out twisted and wrong. *Maybe that's because my thoughts have become twisted and wrong?*

"Are you serious? How the hell could you think that, Ry?" He looked hurt, and it made me feel even worse. *This wasn't working.*

I sighed. "Forget it, Riv, it's okay."

"No," he insisted. "We need to talk about this. I hate this distance between us. We ignored it for too long, too focused on surviving the pain of our torn mate bond, and a decade disappeared. It's not enough. How can we be strong for Ava if we can't be strong together?"

I hated that he was right. We'd focused on honing our skills, learning everything we could to give us an edge in protecting her. We'd become deadly and were completely in sync physically when danger threatened, always fighting as one. But we hadn't worked on our minds or our hearts. The stuff that filled the quiet spaces.

"Look, it doesn't mean I'm not proud of you. I am. I'm always going to be the one up front cheering you on. Sometimes, growing up, it just felt dark in your shadow." It was an awkward truth that I'd never wanted to bring into the light. It hadn't always felt like that, only occasionally when I doubted myself. But it was still there, a fault line that had fractured when Ava left.

Our parents had an entire room dedicated to River's trophies and awards growing up. They'd always been supportive of me, too. I just hadn't given them a lot to cheer on.

"That's utter bullshit," River said, too loudly. He didn't hold back, he never did, but I shushed him so he wouldn't wake Ava or the guys. He looked across to the others, making sure no-one was stirring, before continuing on more quietly. "If you think that, you couldn't be more wrong. You're the one everyone loves, Ry. Everyone has always gravitated to you. I'm the one who was always too serious, too focused. I'd lose myself in whatever my current obsession was. Nobody cared about a room full of awards. You were the most popular kid in high school before we got shipped off to the military."

"High school is long gone. Besides, being liked by people isn't a skill," I said.

"Yes, it is. One I've never mastered." River growled. I stared at him, finally meeting his gaze. His eyes were blazing. "Do you have any idea how much I rely on you? How much I need you? I'm never going to be enough for Ava on my own. I know that. It's too easy to lose myself when I focus on all my plans and I disappear emotionally. It doesn't mean I don't feel. I can't make someone feel loved the same way you do, and that scares me. Your emotions may run away with you sometimes, but you're passionate and sincere. You build people up and make them feel seen. Everyone followed you with stars in their eyes, even me. You were so bright, like the sun, you were hard to look at sometimes."

How the hell did we get so messed up when we were two opposite parts of a whole? We always had been. I swallowed hard. Facing his truth the same way he was trying to face mine. So we could move past it.

"All I ever wanted, my whole life, Riv, was to be wherever you were. With Ava at our side. You're enough. You always have been."

"Outside of Ava's summer visits, you were my only friend growing up, Ry. I never felt as if I needed anyone else. Yet you made sure people always included me and I remembered to have fun. I worshipped you growing up. It may have been a quiet worship, but it was there. How do you not know that?"

The pain when Ava left had twisted something inside me. Darkening everything. I'd gone to a bleak place, and I'd never really come back. River was right. We'd been surviving, and it was time to do more. My twin deserved more from me, and so did Ava. She was the only woman for us.

I'd been with women since coming of age, but I'd never been able to feel anything for them. Alphas were primal creatures, and sex was an instinctive drive for us. Yet, it had been pure sexual release that had always left me feeling empty. Just lying here near Ava, not even touching her, or even on the same blanket, merely getting to see her face. I already felt more than I had with any other woman.

It was our job to protect her, and all I'd done since finding her again was unload a heap of crap on her I should have dealt with a long time ago.

"I was so scared when she left," I finally admitted to my twin. "The thought that she might not accept us twisted me up inside. I can't live without her."

"I know. Neither can I," River said, a quiet reverence in his voice I only ever heard when he talked about Ava.

"So I'll fix this, starting now," I said, borrowing some of my twin's determination. I wasn't entirely sure how to do that, though. River reached across and messed up my hair.

"No. We'll fix this, Ry," he said. He paused for a minute before he glanced over at the other blanket. "Any advice, Nick? I get the impression you have a lot of brothers and sisters."

I smirked. I'd sensed Nick waking up a few minutes ago. He was playing possum, trying not to intrude on our conversation. But if we were going to be a pack, we couldn't hide things from each other.

He gently slipped out from under the shared blankets the others were still sleeping under, then grabbed another one to wrap around him as he came to sit next to us. I noticed he checked it gingerly first to make sure no critters had snuck in to keep warm. Proving he'd done this before, too. We really should camp out with sleeping bags rather than blankets and comforters. I should have grabbed the ones in our go-bags for Ava.

"Sorry," he said, keeping his voice low. "I got used to being an early riser living on the farm."

"Don't apologize," River said to him. "We have to figure out how being in a pack actually works. But I don't think having a lot of boundaries is part of it."

"Yeah," Nick agreed with a grin. "I get that from watching Maia and Lexie's packs come together. Those guys are all up in each other's business."

"So, advice?" I asked him, really needing it. I'd never had to work at a relationship, or fix one I'd broken, before now.

Nick looked flustered. His gaze darted between Ava and us. "Are you asking for advice about brothers, or about Ava?"

"Both. I'll take whatever you've got."

He shifted the blanket tighter around him to ward off the morning chill. "Sibling shit is hard. I have a big family that I always felt lost in. I love them, but it always seemed as if my pieces didn't fit theirs. It's weird, but this pack feels simpler for me. It's a no-brainer. Nobody has ever needed me for anything before. Or chosen me. I know it's not going to be easy, but I just get the feeling our pieces all fit. Does that make sense?"

"Yeah, it does," River said quietly. I agreed with a slow nod as I pulled one arm out of my blankets to rest under my head. These people should have felt like strangers, but they didn't. They felt like home. Almost as if we'd already lived another life together, at some other point in time.

"And for Ava?" I asked. I couldn't help but notice he'd dodged that question.

He blushed, which was adorable. "I don't know a lot about women, but Ava seems to be the simplest part. Not that she's simple, I just mean, she's not a choice. For me, anyway. She's it, the one. Any part of herself she shares with me I'm going to hold on to and cherish. The how we can work out, and I don't really care about the why."

"So you block the rest out, and that's it?" I asked. Surely it couldn't be that easy.

"Not block it out. It just doesn't matter. Everything else is noise. Hold on to Ava, keep her at the heart of everything you both do, and I think you'll be okay. She loves you both, has her whole life, as far as I can see. That's all I've got for you."

"Huh," I said. It seemed our little tech geek was also a Zen master. He had more in common with Wolf's view of the world than I would have thought. *Was I overcomplicating everything? Was he right? Did it even matter why she left, if she was here now and I had the chance to make her mine?*

"Look," Nick blurted with a frown, before I could add anything more. "I know we agreed to be part of this pack last night, and I meant every word I said. I'm all in. But Ava didn't get a vote. She may not feel the same way about me. If she chooses someone else as her beta, it will slay me, but I'll honor it."

"I don't think you have anything to worry about, kid," River said with a small smile at Nick's earnestness. He seemed to have a genuine affection for Nick already, which surprised me. River didn't connect with people easily.

A faint vibrating sound had us both narrowing our eyes as Nick pulled Ava's phone out of his hoodie pocket. "Oh shit, that's Lexie and Maia. They're calling early. That's not a good sign. I better take it."

He jumped up and took off into the forest, so as not to wake the others up. It was impossible to talk quietly on a phone.

"Are we good?" River asked me when Nick was gone. I wanted to banish his hesitation in asking that question, but it was going to take time. As much as what Nick had suggested made sense, one conversation wouldn't fix a decade's neglect of our relationship. Especially with everything changing so rapidly. It was a start, though. Neither of us were going anywhere without the other.

"Yeah, Riv. We're good." I sat up and gave him a hug that had been a long time coming. He squeezed me tight in return and I felt like I could breathe for the first time in years.

"I'll put some more wood on the fire for when the others wake up," he said as he pulled back. He shifted to get up, but we both froze as a low moan filled the clearing. It was coming from Ava.

River sprang into a crouch, but didn't move any closer. Another low moan followed the first one, and her hips shifted restlessly under the blankets. Her hand moved down onto Wolf's stomach and pulled the blankets back with it, before moving back up to his chest under his shirt. Her eyes were still closed, but her breathing had picked up rapidly.

"Holy shit, is she dreaming?" I whispered to River, as her hips shifted again in a rolling motion.

"Yeah," he said, his voice coming out rough, "and it looks like one hell of a dream."

Fifteen

A delicious, tingly heat spread through me as a slow burning pleasure built in a spiral within my core. I heard a moan that seemed to vibrate through my chest. *Was that me?*

Awareness crept in as I came awake slowly, and I realized my hips were moving roughly against something hard. It was causing an exquisite friction and stoking the building heat between my thighs. I wanted more of whatever it was. I stretched like a cat, and my breasts pushed into the same hard heat. My hips rolled again as I chased more of the feeling. I'd often had dreams of being touched intimately, but I'd always woken up feeling achy and alone. If I was dreaming now, I didn't want it to end.

I tried to burrow back into the dream. Until a rumbled groan vibrated underneath my cheek and my eyes flew open, to see a broad expanse of male flesh filling my vision. My fingers were underneath the edges of a black shirt that had been pushed up. By me, I think. It left my head lying on a naked chest and my hand resting on a rock hard pec. *Holy cannoli, was I groping someone in my sleep?*

I felt dazed as I looked up to see Wolf lying with his eyes tightly closed. He'd pinned one hand beneath his head, while the other was screwed up in the blanket underneath us. His eyes shot open as I watched, and he lifted his head to look down at me. The frisson of energy that passed between us was electric as his eyes blazed, searing me to the bone.

I gasped as I realized I was rubbing myself against his hard thigh as it flexed underneath me. It turned out I wasn't just groping him; I was dry humping him. I couldn't find it in me to stop, though. My hand seemed to move of its own volition as I tightened it on his pec, before I scratched my nails across his skin.

A snarl crossed his face as his eyes darkened. I stilled, but he released his hand from the blanket and grabbed mine. He held it tight against his skin, as he tensed his thigh underneath me, thrusting it hard against me.

I moaned again, louder, as I ground down on his thigh. Heat flared through me even hotter as another body shifted behind me. Cary's vanilla ice cream scent spiked and wrapped around me decadently, drawing out the dark orchid in Wolf's jungle scent.

"Having fun?" Cary whispered as his lips brushed my ear. He ran his hand slowly up my side and grazed the tips of his fingers against the curve of my breast before he gripped my chin and turned my head in his direction.

"Do you mind if I kiss her while she pleasures herself against you, Wolf?" Cary's voice was deeper than usual, with a guttural edge. But he sounded as if he was politely asking to borrow a book from his teacher. Except for the dirty words. They had me heating instantly. A delicious contrast to the chilly air hitting the exposed parts of my body.

"Hell, no," Wolf growled, causing his chest to vibrate underneath me again. It was an entirely different sensation to his purr. This one electrified me. "You can both use me any way you want."

Cary needed no further permission. Every inch of my body was begging him to kiss me right now. My whole body stilled as he leaned down slowly and traced his lips over mine. Tasting me more than kissing me. He groaned, as if my taste drove him wild, and I felt Wolf's breathing speed up even further under my hand.

Cary shifted his body to press up harder behind me, before he thrust us both against Wolf.

"Don't stop," he groaned against my mouth. I cried out, and he swallowed my cry, covering my mouth with his own and devouring me. The sultry heat of his mouth on mine contrasted with the softness of his lips. His lips had entranced me for years. They were so full and lush. I'd waited so long to be kissed by Cary, imagining it so many ways, but never like this. This was so much more. Every glance, every almost touch we'd shared over the last few years suddenly exploded in a shower of sparks and heat.

My entire body lit up as Cary's hard length pressed into my ass cheek, and Wolf's hot thigh pressed between my legs. My knee pulled up higher so I could get more friction. Until I felt Wolf's straining cock underneath my thigh as if it was trying to burst through the fabric of his pants. Wolf reached down and anchored my leg against him, grinding against my thigh.

My body moved in a rough rhythm, completely taken over as I thrust between the two men. My movements became rougher and more erratic the harder Cary kissed me, my chin still firmly in his grasp. It drove me wild. Nobody was touching me anywhere inappropriate, this was all me. I felt wanton and hedonistic. As if I'd woken into an erotic fantasy, and left the sweet, demure Ava in the wind.

Both men thrust against me simultaneously, pinning me between their hard bodies, and I exploded. Fireworks erupted within me as my body shook. I felt, more than heard, Wolf roar as he gripped my thigh harder and Cary released my mouth to bite his own hand on my chin. I trembled as the fireworks fizzled out slowly. Cary and Wolf were both panting hard. I felt exhilarated and boneless at the same time. It was a novel sensation.

"You've ruined me, little one," Wolf growled as he wrapped his free arm around me.

"Yeah, same," Cary said, as he grazed his lips across my neck. "That was a hell of a first kiss."

I felt him smile against my skin. He seemed more relaxed this morning, and I wondered what had gone down last night after I crashed.

"Considering that was my first ever kiss, I'd have to agree with you."

"You've never been kissed before today?" Wolf asked.

I glanced up at him and felt myself blush as I shook my head.

He frowned. "You should be kissed every minute of every day."

He looked incredibly serious, which was sweet. "I don't think I'd get a lot done, if that was the case."

Wolf just shrugged. I wanted to savor the feeling of being held by these two men, but a growing feeling of wetness between my thighs had me frozen. I pushed the comforter back further and looked down. To my horror, I saw a giant wet patch against Wolf's thigh.

"Don't sweat it, Ava. We both have matching ones," Cary said.

I looked up slightly and saw another wet patch where my thigh had been rubbing against Wolf's cock, over his pants. A glance over my shoulder showed a mirroring stain on Cary's pants.

"Sorry," I stammered, blushing.

Wolf moved so fast I barely saw him. In half a breath, he'd rolled me over and pinned me against Cary.

"Easy now," came a dark voice I knew from somewhere close by.

"I would never hurt them," Wolf snarled over his shoulder before he turned his attention back to me.

"Never apologize for your needs, Ava," Wolf growled, his eyes blazing. "Not to us. Not to anybody. We are yours, in every way. To use in any way you want."

His words had me gasping loudly, and he looked chastened as he glanced over his shoulder again.

"I'm sorry. Did I scare you?" He asked. He looked suddenly wretched as his head drooped.

I grabbed his face and brought it back up so he could see my eyes. "I know you would never hurt me, and no, you didn't scare me. Just, nobody's ever said anything like that to me before."

"Are you sure?" he asked, seeming hesitant as he searched my face. He shifted as if he would move away, but I gripped him harder. I didn't want this wild, yet gentle, man to feel a moment's doubt about himself.

"If I feared you, would I kiss you right now?" He shook his head tentatively, but his eyes flared with hope.

I pulled his head down towards me and ran my lips over his, mimicking the gentle action Cary had used to first taste me earlier. Wolf's scraggly beard tickled my skin, but I found I didn't mind. I liked the roughness of it.

"Is this okay?" I asked him.

"Yeah," he groaned. So I kissed him harder, sweeping my tongue against his. He kissed me back, so sweetly and so gently. He looked so feral, but held me so tenderly. It was a contradiction I wanted to explore further.

Cary's moan underneath me startled me out of the kiss.

"And now I'm hard again," he muttered. Wolf just grinned at him over my shoulder. The first genuine smile I'd seen from him.

"It's not funny. Do you know how uncomfortable a hard-on is with wet pants?" Cary grumbled, but when I looked over my shoulder, he was smiling and looked pleased with the situation. Although he seemed to avoid looking directly at Wolf.

A pointed cough had us shifting to sit up.

"Getting carried away in the moment is one thing," Ryder said, "but now you're just rubbing our faces in it."

My face fell as I realized they'd been watching the whole thing from a blanket next to us. I'd been waiting for a decade for them to find me, yet here they were and I was kissing two other men in front of them.

Ryder was lying on his side along the blanket, his head propped in one hand, but River had squatted on his heels, ready to intervene if Wolf got carried away. He smacked his twin on the shoulder now. Ryder looked confused as he rubbed his arm until he glanced back at my face. He sat up quickly.

"Shit, Ava. I didn't mean it like that. You did nothing wrong. I was just joking."

Our argument last night was too fresh for me to brush off his words, though. He hopped up and moved over to me. Wolf shifted back, so Ryder could pull me to my feet. My wet leggings had me feeling intensely embarrassed. I tried to snag a blanket to cover myself, but Ryder grabbed it and dropped it to the ground.

"I haven't earned your trust back yet. Or your affections. I know that. But I will. As soon as I pull my foot out of my mouth." Ryder's emotions had always ridden him hard, and he sometimes spoke without thinking. It had gotten him into trouble a few times over the years. Usually when he was defending someone he cared about, though.

"I trust you, Ryder. My leaving was never about that. You don't have to earn anything back. I was just upset last night that you thought I wouldn't want you in my life, in any way I could have you. You've always been mine."

His face brightened, as if a cloud had lifted and the sun had come out. It dazzled me. He reached out hesitantly, and I willingly let him pull me into his arms. A look of determination crossed his face as soon as he had me, chased by a shadow that I hated. Ryder had never been shadowed, he'd always been sunshine on a spring day. "I don't deserve that, but I'm going to. I swear. Because you've always been mine, too. And River's. I know I had a tantrum last night, and I've been a dick since we found you, and I'm so sorry. The fear I'd never see you again had me twisted up inside and it had nowhere to go. I've been stuck in a dark, frozen wasteland without you. Having you back means everything to us. I'm going to do better. You deserve better from me."

I wanted to kiss him so much right now, but I wasn't sure if kissing three men in the space of a few minutes was okay. Considering I'd never kissed a guy before a few minutes ago. *If I kissed him, would River feel left out? Was kissing four men okay?*

I must have looked conflicted, because Ryder caressed my face gently. "It's okay, Ava. We've got time. We're not going anywhere." Just having his hands on me after so long had sparks shooting through me again and my heart in a puddle at my feet. I'd long dreamed of him looking at me exactly the way he was now.

Footsteps through the leaf litter decided for me. I turned to see Nick coming out of the trees. He stopped short when he saw us all. "What did I miss?"

River just chuckled, which surprised the hell out of me. He could be aloof with strangers. Yet Nick seemed to have gotten into his inner circle with no effort. I didn't blame him. There was something special about Nick.

I was suddenly glad I was wearing dark leggings and my wet pants shouldn't be too obvious from a distance. Wolf had no such reservations. He was lying back with his arm under his head again, wet patches proudly on display, as if they were badges of honor.

"How did your call go?" River asked.

"Good. Max is coming and uh, he didn't say directly, but he'll probably have company."

I gasped. "Oh no. I missed the morning call to Maia and Lexie. Dave said if I missed a check-in, they were coming in, guns blazing. I missed last night's too."

"Yeah," Nick chuckled. "I told them you were fine, but they didn't sound convinced. They said they wanted to hear it from you themselves."

"How long do we have?" Cary asked. "Because we need to get cleaned up."

My face flamed with embarrassment, but Nick just grinned at us all.

"It's a few hours' drive. But you know Lexie, she doesn't hold back, and Sam has a chopper at his disposal."

I almost swore, remembering her calling out to him for the chopper yesterday morning, but I swallowed it down.

Cary had no such hesitation. "Fuck, I'd say we have half an hour at most. Lexie and Maia will definitely hijack that chopper if they think something is up with Ava."

Wolf jumped up and picked me up easily, before he started jogging back towards the Palace.

"I'll get Ava to the shower, if you guys can grab the supplies and make sure the fire's out."

"I can walk, you know."

"I know, but I've wanted to do this for years," Wolf said gruffly as he looked down at me. "Just find you, pick you up, and carry you off. It was my favorite daydream. Give me this, okay?"

I felt myself blushing again. *How could I refuse when he put it like that?*

Sixteen

The hot shower did wonders for my spirits. Not that I was sad or upset or anything. There was just something about being clean that always made me feel good.

Yet, the shower also made me determined. I'd taken being clean for granted before the Crash, like everybody. I hadn't really suffered since then, not compared to other people out there. The hot water was still working at the Palace, and at the farm. I'd only really missed showers when we were hiding out in the library. I knew I was far luckier than most.

I didn't intend to sit around and enjoy it without attempting to make life better for other people out there, too. There had to be some way. It was the reason I'd insisted on joining the Honey Badgers. I'd needed to help. But right now, what I really needed to do was get dressed, or I'd be no help to anybody.

I wrapped my towel around myself and peeked out into the bedroom I'd slept in the first night. I really didn't want to put the clothes I'd been wearing back on if I could help it. My eyes widened when I saw Cary by the ornate wardrobe. He jumped and fumbled something when he noticed me watching him.

"Sorry, I didn't think you'd be out so quick. These are some of your clothes from your old room. I was putting them away in here. I figured you'd prefer to sleep in here from now on."

"Thank you, Cary," I said as I tentatively stepped out into the room, wearing only my towel. His eyes strayed to my bare legs and darkened before shooting back up to my face again. I could feel myself blushing and inwardly cursed my pale skin.

I'd had one orgasm. One thrilling, intense orgasm. Yet Wolf and Cary had barely touched me. I wanted more, but I didn't know how to make it happen. I didn't think I could be as bold while I was awake as I appeared to be while sleeping. Plus, Cary seemed more tense now that we were back inside.

Cary stepped towards me and wrapped his arms around me. I sighed and leaned into him instinctively, and he relaxed at the contact, too. It felt like nothing could ever hurt me as long as I was in his arms. *How had I ever gone so long without this?*

"Are you okay?" he asked.

"Yes, of course," I answered automatically. The Palace had drilled the importance of being pleasant and obedient into me. I'd never bought their teachings, but I'd had to pretend. Apparently, the training was harder to shake than I'd anticipated when I'd arrived all doe eyed and innocent.

"Ava," he chastised me gently. "I can tell you want to say something, or ask for something."

"You can?" I looked into his eyes, something I'd denied myself for so long. They were a lighter shade of green than mine, and they seemed to hold the entire world within them. They looked intent and serious right now.

"I've been watching you for a long time. You were damn good at being their perfect student. But sometimes, when no-one was watching, I'd see you look out the window, yearning for something. Whatever it was, I want to give it to you."

I felt a rapid flutter in my chest, knowing he'd been paying such close attention. "I wanted to be outside, climbing trees, sleeping under the stars, free."

"That's why you were so comfortable last night, and this morning," he said with a slow smile. It was so rare to see him smile. I'd gone years never seeing it, just watching that stern, aloof glare from a distance. This one flowed out of him like warm chocolate sliding over strawberries. I wanted to taste it. "And why you came alive at the farm?"

"Yeah." I admitted, trying to focus on my thoughts and not on the way my body reacted to him. "I lived in the city with my mom, but I spent every school holiday at my uncle's farm and I loved it there."

I hesitated, and he held me while I gathered my thoughts. "More than that, though, I wanted to be able to touch the people I loved."

"Yeah," he murmured, his voice going hoarse as his arms tightened around me.

I sucked in a breath. We'd been holding hands, and he'd kissed me during an intensely erotic moment this morning, but we hadn't talked about what we meant to each other at all. Everything we had learned about the other had come from watching at a distance. We'd hardly even spoken until a day or two ago. Yet I knew he frequently protected not only me, but other omegas too, including Maia. He'd been our strong, silent sentinel.

Yet his aloof demeanor had always been just as much a facade as my own persona at the Palace. The Cary underneath, the one I could sense, was an entirely different person. I knew instinctively his heart beat for everyone that got through his walls, and he had an innate need to help those who couldn't help themselves.

"All those years, you were so close, yet so far. It was torture, Cary," I whispered. Whenever I'd felt him near, a vibration would start up within me, trying to pull me to him. It had grown almost painful to ignore of late. I needed us to acknowledge it openly, for the first time.

He lifted my chin from where I'd snuggled into his chest and looked me in the eye. It was such a simple thing, yet even that we had denied ourselves.

"I know. I had to see you every day, knowing you were mine, but someone else was likely going to claim you. And not someone you'd get to choose. I tried to stay away from you, knowing in this place it would only cause you trouble. But I couldn't completely. I became a ghost, shadowing you and tracking you whenever I could."

Hearing him use the word mine had butterflies fluttering through my chest. His expression was still serious, but more open than I'd ever seen it. The ever-present tension had dissipated. I stroked the lines of his face, easing out the last of the frown marks.

"I always felt when you were nearby, it made me feel safe, even though I knew there was nothing you could do to help me. And I couldn't help you."

"Help me?" He seemed confused.

I nodded and cupped his cheek, loving that I could touch him in this way, finally. "You always looked so haunted after the parties and balls."

I had never attended; the Palace made me wait for my debut. Yet guessing what the Palace was forcing on him whenever there was an event had been an ongoing torment.

"Oh Ava, it wasn't what you thought." He reached up and grabbed my hand, turning it so he could kiss my palm. "The Palace paraded me around as entertainment, but most of the alphas who sought me out didn't want to dominate me. They wanted to be dominated by an omega. The Palace trained you to be submissive, but they trained me to be dominant, at least in the bedroom. I was a circus trick, and I used it to my advantage."

His expression shuttered a little, and he looked suddenly wary.

"Oh," I whispered. I didn't entirely know what he meant by that, but I could guess. I still hated that for him. Even if he'd turned it to his advantage.

"I used my body as a weapon, Ava. I would distract them and subtly pump the alphas for information, try to turn them into allies. I was trying to figure out how to get you out and I took any opportunity I could to do that. And I'd do it again if I had to. I was so haunted afterward, because none of them were willing to help. They wanted to play the game, up to a point, but they were still alphas and I was an omega. I felt like I was failing you."

My heart hurt, knowing he'd done that for me. I wanted to go back in time and erase it, but I couldn't. I felt a silent tear drip down my cheek. He let my hand go to wipe it away.

"Don't cry for me, Ava. You were what got me through. I didn't know where my place was in this world until I met you. The moment I laid eyes on you, I knew it was with you. In whatever way you would have me."

I could feel another tear join the first one trailing down my cheek. It was everything I'd ever wanted to hear from him. "Mine's with you, too. But it's also with them." It was the first time I'd said it out loud. I didn't think I needed to explain who I meant by 'them.'

"I'm okay with that, Ava. We got that squared away last night." The sudden tension in his features disappeared as a small smile flitted across his face.

What the hecking heck? Were they all talking about me while I was sleeping? Like gossiping old women?

Cary smirked at me and gently wiped the rest of the tears from my cheek, but didn't answer my silent questions.

"What about you and Wolf?" I asked, needing to know. I could sense Wolf drew him in the same way he did me. There was a deep well of fear in Cary, though, despite his words just now. I wouldn't do anything that hurt Cary, and I needed to know if my being with Wolf would hurt him.

Cary huffed out a breath. "He says we're both his, but I need some time. The alphas at the Palace may have pretended to let me be in charge for a while, but I never really was. I have a complicated history with alphas and with my omega. I don't know if I can be what he needs. That doesn't mean you can't be what he needs. He needs you more than anyone else. You're the heart that's bringing these men together."

"I don't know how to be the heart, Cary. I need you to help me."

"Be yourself, Ava. That's what we need. Just you. You've got this."

"That goes for you, too, you know. Just being yourself," I said with an encouraging smile. "Try opening up to them a little. They don't bite if you don't want them to."

He smiled back at me tenderly as he nodded. "It's hard to be myself when I don't really know who that is, but I'm willing to figure it out. I'll try being more open with them. That's all I can promise right now."

I couldn't ask for more than that. I could get addicted to his smile. He'd seemed tense around Wolf, River, and Ryder yesterday. Yet he seemed a lot more relaxed today. Obviously, whatever they'd discussed last night had helped settle him. I was glad, and didn't push him about it any further. All of them were important to me. If they were getting along, getting us where I wanted was going to be a lot easier. And I knew exactly what I wanted. A pack. I'd dreamed of it ever since I first read Maia's book.

"What do you need now, Ava? Tell me what you were thinking a minute ago when you walked into the room?"

I remembered what I'd been thinking. "I was thinking about how much I wanted you to kiss me again."

I felt a tremor run through him. "You have no idea what you did to me this morning, Ava. You were intoxicating."

"Show me," I whispered.

He gripped the back of my head gently and pulled me closer towards him. His mouth was on mine instantly, hot and feverish, making me burn. He pulled away too quickly, stepping back from me and leaving me feeling bereft.

"We don't have time for all the things I want to do to you, and I don't think you're ready for them yet, anyway."

I felt like stamping my foot. *What was it with the men in my life trying to decide what I needed?*

"I'll decide what I'm ready for. Thank you very much."

A grin split his face as he pulled me back and kissed me again, hard and fast.

"You're killing me, temptress. If you say you're ready, I'm going to give you everything you want. But I will not take your virginity in some quick, hard fuck. Your first time's going to take all night and you're going to remember it forever. I suspect I'm also not the only one who's going to want to be there for that."

I was suddenly so wet, I could feel wetness soaking my thighs. The thought of them watching while one of them took my virginity had me almost panting. I was more than ready. Cary groaned, and his pupils blew out. His own scent spiked in response, the vanilla becoming more decadent and saturating the surrounding air.

A sudden knock at the door had us springing apart. "Sorry to interrupt," came Ryder's tight voice. "But we have incoming. I can see a chopper coming in fast over the trees."

Cary gave me another quick kiss before he turned and slid out the door. I heard Ryder sniff the air and groan as Cary walked past, before

I rushed back into the bathroom and cleaned myself up quickly. Cary's scent seemed to linger as I got dressed in a pair of jeans and pulled a t-shirt over my head. My wardrobe had been mostly pretty dresses, but they'd allowed us some casual clothes to wear in our rooms.

I pulled the tee up to my nose on impulse and sniffed it. Cary's scent was all over it, as though he'd rubbed my clothes on himself, marking them, and me. I grinned. Two could play that game. I pulled the t-shirt tight around my middle and knotted it underneath my breasts. I'd seen one of the Palace maids wear hers the same way. She must have been on her day off and had been flirting with one of the security guards. He'd pulled her into a storeroom and I'd quickly walked the other way.

I was showing a lot more skin than I usually did, and my jeans were old and tight, so they left little to the imagination. I didn't care. A new awareness of my body seemed to make every movement feel sensual. I could suddenly feel every curve, and I felt flushed and feverish. If Cary was going to leave me hanging, he could suffer, too. As soon as I stepped out into the room, I realized I may have taken a bigger bite of my cake than I'd intended. I was suddenly choking on the frosting.

Wolf, River, Ryder, Cary, and Nick stilled and turned their heads my way as I walked into the lounge area. Their eyes instantly fixed on my exposed midriff, and the way my tied t-shirt emphasized my breasts. The room exploded with scents and a series of growls punctuated the air.

I held my head high and refused to cower or cover myself. My attention snagged on the way River was kneeling at Wolf's feet, though. Wolf had showered too, and was wearing clean clothes as well. But his feet were bare and River was wrapping them in bandages.

I rushed over. "Wolf, why didn't you tell me you were hurt?"

He looked like he was struggling to get his brain back online as I knelt next to River. River was taking shallow breaths, trying not to breathe too deeply, as he re-started wrapping Wolf's feet after letting the gauze go slack. "It's not as bad as it looks. He banged his feet up running through the forest, but most of it was pretty shallow. It should be fine in a few days."

"I don't care," I cried as I threw my arms around Wolf. "You should have told me. I would have tended to you."

I'd all but climbed in his lap, and he pulled me in further. I'd never been so tactile with another person before. But something about Wolf lowered my inhibitions and overrode my training instinctively. As if someone had molded his lap as the perfect seat, just for me. He didn't seem to mind.

"You needed sleep last night, and we had other things going on this morning," he growled into my neck.

His warm hand on the naked skin of my waist fried my brain, and I had no response. Before anyone else could say anything, the sound of a chopper getting closer had me scrambling to stand up. Nick threw a pair of clean socks at Wolf and he put them on quickly before River helped him with his boots.

I looked out the window to see a helicopter landing on the lawn outside our verandah. "Hurry, we need to get down there before Lexi and Maia start shooting."

River chuckled, but he'd only met Lexie briefly, and hadn't met Maia at all. Alone, they were both capable women. Together, they were formidable.

I turned for the door, but Ryder had blocked my way. His eyes raked me over, and he cocked his eyebrow. He opened his mouth as if he was about to say something about my choice of clothes. I narrowed my eyes at him, and he hastily put up his hands. There was a small yellow flower in one of them. He swallowed with a visible gulp.

"You always used to wear a flower in your hair," he said. "May I?"

He sounded so nervous, which was unlike Ryder. I nodded at him as my throat thickened. He leaned closer and tucked it gently into the loose bun I'd quickly pulled my hair into.

"Thank you," I whispered, as I gave him a quick peck on the cheek before bolting for the stairs. I could hear the guys scrambling behind me.

I ran down the stairs and out the front doors, just as Lexie and Maia hopped out of the helicopter. Nick had been right. As soon as they saw me, they barreled for me too, with Damon and Sam hot on their heels, yelling at them to wait. Maia was wearing an oversized military jacket, rolled up at the arms, with a pair of jeans. While Lexie was wearing her favorite denim overalls with a crop top underneath and a long cardigan.

I collided with them in a mess of arms and hair, as we tried to hug each other at once. I accidentally bumped heads with Lexie and she laughed as she rubbed hers.

"Girl, you are going to be the death of us," Maia mumbled into the side of my face, where she had squished herself. One of the medals on her jacket felt like it was going to puncture my boob, but I didn't complain.

Lexie pulled back to look me over as she gave a short wolf whistle. "That's a good look on you, Ava. Is it working for you?"

"It might if you two weren't *cocktail* blocking me right now. You really shouldn't have wasted the fuel on a trip here. I'm perfectly fine."

"Oh, you are damn fine," Maia added. They both dissolved into fits of laughter, and Lexie gave me a high five. It had only been a day or two since I'd seen them, but I'd missed these women. They both stepped back as Damon and Sam reached us.

Damon stepped around Maia and put a hand out towards me, but a vicious roar vibrated the air around us and he stumbled backwards.

A darkly floral, jungle scent, spiced with ginger, overwhelmed my senses, as all hell broke loose around me.

Seventeen

I couldn't stop the roar from ripping free when the alpha dripping with dominance reached for Ava. The bark that came out with it had been purely instinctive and had pushed him back several steps until he planted his feet. The air pressure cranked to unbearable levels as it filled with growls and competing barks.

"Wolf," Ava's normally soft voice was sharp and slightly desperate. She jumped in front of me, and those green eyes, wide and anxious, had me stilling.

I breathed heavily and a low growl thrummed through my chest, but she reached up and brushed the hair out of my eyes so I could see her more clearly.

"It's okay. I'm here. These are my friends. Damon and his pack rescued Cary and me from the Palace, and they shared their home with us."

I grabbed her and pulled her into me, needing her close, as I buried my face in her hair and took a deep lungful of her scent. I kept my eyes on the alphas in front of me, though. There were now five alphas, and a beta with glasses and a gun, standing in front of me. I got that Ava thought of them as friends, and I would be eternally grateful they rescued her. Yet their scents were currently spiking aggressively, and I couldn't calm down until they did. It didn't help that Ava's scent had now also spiked with her distress, becoming tart and acidic.

"You need to pull Ava back, Cary," the big, long-haired blonde one in the middle, holding the two female omegas behind him, growled.

"Uh, no. That would not work out well for you, Leif. She's the only thing keeping him from throwing you all into the closest trees." Cary's voice was calm, lighthearted, but I could feel his tension.

"He could try," Leif taunted. My lip curled into a snarl in response, and I let slip a silent bark. I had the satisfaction of seeing his eyes widen as it hit him.

I felt a hand on my back and Cary's vanilla ice cream scent wafted over me, as it mixed with Ava's cherries. It toned down the tartness that singed my nose and kept my beast on edge.

"Deep breath, sugar," Cary said to Ava, as his other arm came around her. "You need to get your scent under control so Wolf can calm down."

I felt Ava nod her head, and she took in several deep breaths. As she calmed down, the wildness faded, and I felt my awareness come back. I noticed River, Ryder, and Nick standing close beside us in defensive positions. My pack had backed me up and the knowledge was like fresh air clearing out my head.

The only calm looking alpha opposite me, with long dark hair, took a step forward, holding his hands up where I could see them. "I'm Pala, one of Lexie's mates, and a friend of River and Ryder. We're all okay here. Can you lower your gun please, Max?"

He was a powerful alpha, but like me, he was more at one with his alpha nature. Just in a calmer way. He wasn't leaking dominance the way most of the others were right now.

Max looked at the original alpha I'd pushed back for confirmation, but he was too busy shooting me a dark glare to notice. His posture was rigid. I could feel his dominance trying to pound me and I didn't appreciate it being directed towards my omegas. I felt my hackles rise again.

"Easy," River said to me in a gentler voice than I'd heard him use, before he turned to Pala. "Wolf slipped into a near feral state while captive. Now he's newly found his mates and they're unclaimed. He's on edge and won't be able to calm down while he sees you as a threat."

"I get it," Pala said. "They only found out their omega, Maia, is pregnant this morning. Now she's out here in the open. They're feeling just as jumpy as you are right now. So let's just take a deep breath."

Maia peeked out from amongst her pack and put her hand on the dark and glary one's arm. She looked at Ava and me with concern. "Damon, I'm okay."

Damon grabbed his omega and pulled her into his arms, much the same way I was holding Ava.

Their omega was pregnant? I would never willingly cause a pregnant omega distress. I relaxed back into myself and nodded, letting my wildness fade as I pulled my dominance back in as well. It was easier to do with Ava in my arms.

"You can let me go now, too, big guy," the pink-haired omega said. She gently extracted herself from Leif and walked over to the other blonde alpha, with shorter hair, still throwing his dominance around. She reached up, cupped his face, and stroked it lightly. "Hey, Sam. Come back to me, okay? We're all good."

He shuddered under her touch as she slid her arms around his neck and hugged him tightly. Pala stepped back and surrounded them both in his embrace. It was intriguing to watch Sam close his eyes and breathe deeply, letting go of his dominance, too.

I looked over at the other group and noticed they were in a similar, bigger huddle. The red head alpha, Damon, Leif, and Max were breathing each other in and relaxing. They still seemed alert, though. The redhead was scanning the surrounding trees while the others were focused on me, keeping an eye on their surroundings and watching their backs more than what was going on in front of him.

I could feel eyes on me, and curiosity washed through me. I twisted slightly to see River and Ryder both eyeing the groups in front of us, and me.

"Do you guys always hug like this?" Ryder asked as he looked back over at them all.

"Yep," Maia answered with a smile. "We're going to talk them into one big group hug with both packs sometime soon. It's going to feel amazing."

Leif chuckled as he looked down at her, adoration clear on his face. "We can work up to that."

"It helps settle our prime alphas and disperse their energy," Lexie explained.

Maia tried to disentangle herself, but didn't get far. As soon as she removed one arm, another one snapped into place. So she just looked over her shoulder at me.

"Sorry about that. Ever since we found out I'm pregnant, these guys have been insufferable," she groused, as she poked one of them playfully in the side.

"Oh my god, Maia. You're actually pregnant? I thought Pala was joking. That's amazing. Is that why you've turned into a giant sleepyhead suddenly? Why didn't you tell me?" Ava cried, and pulled away from me.

I stiffened, but three sets of hands suddenly appeared on my body alongside Cary's, and my eyes closed of their own accord. They were right. It felt amazing to have so many of my pack touching me at once, and my wildness calmed instantly. I'd never felt anything like it. My purr tried to start up, and I had to fight to keep it down. I didn't want to weird them out.

"If you'd answered the phone this morning, I would have," Maia said, as she fake pouted. She tried to disentangle herself again, with no success. She tensed slightly, as if she was going to say something, then let out a deep breath. It seemed as if she was humoring her mates, for now, but her patience was wearing thin. "Could we maybe move inside for congratulations and proper introductions, so my guys can calm down a little?"

"Good idea," Nick said from my side, sounding relieved. "And I'd suggest nobody but Wolf, River, Ryder, or Cary touches Ava for a while. They're going to be a little on edge until they claim her."

"You can touch her, too, Nick," Ryder said, and everyone's eyes suddenly swiveled to Nick. Max had his mouth hanging open. Nick blushed furiously.

"Clearly we have a lot to share," Leif said, humor lighting up his face. He seemed much more gentle now.

We moved inside, and the girls took over introductions as we settled into couches in the formal living room opposite the foyer. I just grunted a lot, only taking in about half of them. My beast had calmed down, but words still weren't coming easily.

Until the blonde omega looked at me and smiled. *What had Ava said her name was again?*

"Sorry if I scared you," I said to her, trying to keep the gruffness out of my voice. There was something familiar about her. Not her face, though. I'd never seen her before.

"You didn't. I'm made of tougher stuff than that. Besides, alpha barks don't work on me. Even yours."

I felt the air freeze in my lungs. "Your name's Maia?" I croaked.

My whole body shook as memories assaulted me. That familiar voice in the dark, as she'd chanted "I will not break," repeatedly. Her tears, the way she had screamed her frustration at the walls. Her inner strength as they'd tried to bark her into submission, and she'd refused to break.

Ava was suddenly in my lap, stroking my face. "Wolf, what's wrong?"

My gaze had become fixed on Maia, though. Her brow wrinkled, and she looked confused, as she looked me over, trying to figure out if she knew me.

Down in the cells, I hadn't been able to stand hearing her pain. I hadn't known who she was, but knowing she was an omega and I couldn't help her had made me feel helpless. I couldn't risk trying to have a conversation with her, knowing we'd have to yell, and they monitored us. So I'd started singing one of my favorite songs in the darkness, after everyone left, and she'd quieted as if by some miracle she'd heard me.

It was an old rap song, but the words had always resonated with me. Music was one thing I'd been allowed free access to growing up. They didn't bring her down to the cells often, but when they left her down there overnight and everyone disappeared, I'd always sing and she'd calm down. I didn't know if you could really call it singing. My voice was rough. I'd more spoken them loudly as I'd tapped out a beat. She'd started tapping the beat out against the metal bars in time with me; the sound filtering through to me in the darkness. Then one night, she started singing it with me.

"I could hear you," I said gruffly, "in the dark, in the labs. You sang with me."

Maia gasped as she jumped up. Damon tried to grab for her, but she slipped past him and Leif pulled him back gently, wrapping his arms around him. She crossed the room to me and kneeled on the thick golden carpet.

"That was you? The whole time, you were real?"

"Real?" I asked.

"I heard you repeating that same song, over and over. I thought I dreamed it, or maybe hallucinated it. It kept me sane down there in the darkness. I felt so alone," her voice broke a little as she spoke, "but those words you spoke in that lilting harmony. They got me through. You helped me stand strong."

I murmured some of the chorus in my husky voice, about taking my hand and breaking out of a cage together. She sang it with me. Her voice was beautiful compared to my gruff rasp. She had me transfixed. A shaft of light from the window hit her and lit her up. She was a warrior queen. She shouldn't be on her knees for me. A tear tracked down her cheek as I ground to a halt, unable to finish it.

"It was dark for days there at the end, and it felt like it was just you and me left in the world," I admitted. "Then you went quiet, as if you'd vanished. I clung to the idea you'd found a way out."

"I'm so sorry I didn't get you out, too," Maia said.

I shook my head. It wasn't her job to rescue me. "You couldn't have. I had multiple reinforcements on my cage. If it had been possible to get out when the power went out, I would have."

"Holy shit, they were in different labs, but their cells backed onto each other," Nick said. His voice sounded strained.

Suddenly, Lexie was on the ground next to Maia. She hugged her fiercely, and it broke a stasis. Ava yanked both girls up onto the couch with us, as my arms went around them all, and everyone in the room suddenly had us circled, arms and bodies entwined. Maia's weren't the only tears. I could feel the interwoven connections between these people, built on pain, love, friendship, and shared strength. It was one giant, all-encompassing embrace, and I took a long, shuddering breath as Maia beamed at me.

The no touching Ava rule went out the window, as I realized these really were her people, and mine now too.

"You got me my giant hug," Maia whispered, and laughter broke out around us.

Eighteen

Holy shit. We knew we were facing formidable foes and needed allies, but this group was something else. I looked at my twin, and he subtly nodded. He felt it too. The power in this room. In these people. Not just their physical strength, but the energy their connection forged. We'd always been a perfect unit, Ryder, Ava and me. I'd worried briefly when I'd seen her with Wolf, Cary, and Nick, that we'd lost her. We hadn't. We'd just grown.

I was on board with that. Perhaps having had a twin bond our entire life had prepared both of us for a pack bond. We didn't question it. I also didn't need time to get to know who these people were. They were out here living their truths for everyone to see. I'd heard rumors of Damon, and Sam to a lesser degree, but nothing could compare to meeting them in person. Both were highly dominant alphas, in the same way as Wolf. Something beyond ordinary alphas. Even me, I could admit.

Despite accidentally setting off Wolf earlier, I could sense that these alphas were not driven by power. Or dangerous, unless you messed with their pack. Many less potent alphas seemed to flash their dominance around at will, beating people with it at any opportunity. These two highly dominant alphas toned theirs down as much as they could. They even appeared to share their energy between their pack. The power that rolled off them tasted more of protection and care than tyranny. They were a rarity in this world.

Footsteps approached, then stalled in the entryway. Neither Ryder nor I turned our heads. We'd already catalogued those light but surefooted steps. But most of the others turned theirs.

"Hey, uh...nevermind," came Emma's voice from the entryway, and her footsteps rapidly retreated. I got it. The primal power cycling through this room right now was potent. Yet, to me, it felt harmonized. As if these dangerous men and the people that loved them were balancing each other out.

We pulled away slowly, as if by some secret signal, to let the girls in the middle breathe. Ava had an angelic smile on her face, contentment shining through as she looked up at Wolf. I wanted to see more of that smile instead of the worried frown she'd worn far too often since we found her.

Wolf looked a little shell-shocked, but so much calmer and clearer. As if the group hug had been cathartic for him. I'd felt him relax instantly when we'd all touched him earlier. When Ava had stepped out of his arms and he'd tensed, we'd reached for him instinctively. It seemed he needed us just as much as Ava did. We had to step up. For them both.

The curtains parted abruptly behind us, and a quick movement had the guys tensing. But I'd spied the tiny foot poking out from underneath the curtains when we'd walked into the room. Ryder flashed me a grin as a tiny, cherubic face with a shock of blonde curls darted out and climbed Cary like a tree. She then launched herself onto the couch and wriggled herself into Wolf's lap alongside Ava.

Ava shook her head and tried to hide her grin. "Was Emma looking for you?"

"Yep," the cheeky imp stated, a proud grin on her face. "Hi, I'm Angel," she announced to the room. I tried to hide my own smile. Angel was precocious and completely adorable.

I'd already put her on the list of things I wanted to find out more about. It was usually hard to tell if a kid was going to present as an alpha, beta, or omega, yet Angel had a clear otherness about her. My alpha had recognized her as an omega instantly. *How the hell had they found her so young, and why was she so different?*

Wolf was sitting perfectly still and watched her with wide eyes. He looked spooked to suddenly have a child in his lap. "I'd heard people talking about an omega named Angel, but I hadn't realized you were so little," he said.

"I never realized you were so big," Angel shrugged, as she looked up at him.

"You knew about Wolf?" I asked her, intrigued.

"I heard them talking, and I thought they were hiding a real wolf here. I tried to find him to pet him. But I figured out he was just an alpha. So I lost interest." Wolf grinned at being called just an alpha. He looked highly amused by the little omega as his shock wore off.

"What else did you hear?" I asked her. Ava shot me a warning look. I knew better than to interrogate a child, so I raised my eyebrow at her in return. I was only curious about the girl.

"A lot. Adults are dumb sometimes. They think because I'm small, I can't hear them when they're talking right next to me. Or I won't understand. But it's not that hard." She was a sassy little thing.

"Did they sometimes not know you were there, too?" I asked dryly, trying for a stern glare. She just gave me another cheeky grin. She knew I had her number. But she also had mine. My protective instincts had flared the moment Ryder picked her up the other night, and she'd immediately snuggled into him.

She yawned, a big fake yawn and snuggled down into Wolf as she closed her eyes. "I'm sleepy. Can I nap here?"

I wondered how many times she'd used that trick on her handler. She peeked at me out of one eye and shut it again quickly when she saw I was still watching.

Wolf started purring, and both her eyes flew back open. "Oh, I like that."

"Yeah, it's nice, makes you feel like a marshmallow," Ava admitted, as she stroked Angel's hair. She didn't seem to mind Wolf purring for someone else. Seeing Ava with a child in her lap, while curled up in Wolf's arms, made something shift inside me. I wasn't sure why Wolf had purred for Angel. Maybe he sensed an anxiety in her we couldn't. It wouldn't surprise me. The world was in turmoil, and Angel was perceptive. She may act mature for her age, but she was still a kid.

I glanced at Ryder, feeling him so much clearer after airing our shit this morning. As if our blocked emotions had been blocking our bond, too. He felt pained. I remembered him talking last night about his vision of the future, the night Ava presented. The one he felt he'd lost. There was an ache in his eyes now that was hard to watch as he stared at the two of them snuggled up together. I'd had a different reaction that night. There'd been so many people around, my protective instincts had rushed me, and I'd focused solely on getting her somewhere less exposed, safer.

I could see it now, though. The dream Ryder had clung to so tightly, yet also mourned. I wanted it too, with a sudden yearning that took me by surprise.

Angel's eyes drooped and as much as she tried to fight it, she was out in seconds. I focused in on her and heard her heartbeat slow down and her breathing even out.

Emma stuck her head around the corner again. "Do you want me to take her?"

Ava wrapped an arm more securely around the little girl and shook her head. "No, she'll only come back. We'll take her for a while."

Emma scarpered, and I looked over to see the other packs watching us closely.

"So, who wants to start?" I asked. We needed to put our cards on the table so we could work together.

"Maybe we should give Wolf a minute and you guys start," Ava suggested to the other packs.

Damon nodded as Maia settled herself into his lap, and he closed his arms around her with a relieved sigh. "Max, why don't you update them on everything you found on the Palace servers?"

I listened intently, leaning slightly forward in my seat with an eagerness I couldn't hide, while Max told us everything he'd found out about the Palace. It sickened me that Ava had been here through it all. He also talked about the secret group, Maven, that was behind everything and what had caused the Crash. We'd known something was up with the military, but I'd never imagined they could be a part of something on this scale.

"But who is behind it all? Who are Maven?" I growled when he finished. It was the one thing Ryder and I had never uncovered.

"That's Sam's story." Max replied. Sam jumped in and told us about his gramps' old letter and how he'd revealed the names of the people who were behind it all.

"Frank Gascombe was yours and Maia's gramps?" Nick blurted out. It blew my mind, too. He had been the biggest tech entrepreneur in the world. His death with two unidentified children in the car was fodder for conspiracy theorists everywhere. I was speechless when Sam told me who the rest of the group were and how they were involved. They were well-known leaders of industry and public figures, which I guess made sense. They were powerful men in their own right. I didn't know how they had kept Maven a secret for so long, though.

"They were a pack?" Nick asked, as he ran a hand through his hair. He looked a little intimidated by the group, which I didn't like. It made me want to shift closer to him, but I didn't want to draw attention to it. "That makes so much sense. If they accidentally killed their omega with their tests, that would explain why they were so unstable. They broke their bond. Which one was the prime alpha?"

My ears pricked up at his last question. Finding out more about prime alphas was high on my list of priorities. I hated surprises and if I was going to be part of Wolf's pack; I wanted to know how to help him.

"The letter never said. It only told us we were adopted, and that our biological mother was their omega. As well as which alphas in Maven were our fathers and why gramps had taken us into hiding."

"They never had a prime alpha, which is what started all this," Wolf said with a quiet steadiness in his voice I hadn't heard before. He looked at me, and his eyes were the clearest I'd seen them yet. The wildness had completely receded, and he was fully here with us. For the moment. His jaw was tight, and he looked pained, though. "But Phillip Barclay, the CEO of Alpha Tech, was the head of Maven."

"How do you know?" I asked him, hoping it was time for him to tell his story. He nodded once, briskly, as if he knew what I was really asking. I needed answers. It made me itchy not knowing what was coming for us, or how we were going to fight it.

"Because Maven raised me."

The silence in the room was suddenly deafening. Wolf kept his eyes on me, as if looking at anyone else would be too much right now. I instinctively knew he needed me to be his strength right now. I nodded at him to keep going.

"Before they brought me here, they mostly kept me in a different facility. They would move me around, but that was their base. It was an entire wing in a manor house on an estate outside the city. My earliest memories are of there, so I don't know if I was born there or brought there. I never had parents, only a series of carers. There was one consistently, Nelly, when I was young. When I was about five, she disappeared and never came back. It was a rotating roster after that.

"I had no contact with the outside world other than music, not even television. There was a carefully selected library of movies and books, but that was it. I was a teenager when I finally realized I was a prisoner, and not everyone lived the way I did. They didn't mistreat me when I was young, though. They gave me every toy a kid could want, but they did a lot of tests on me, disguised as games. And cameras were everywhere, inside and out."

Wolf appeared detached as he talked, and I tried to match his expression, but emotions were roiling within me. I wasn't usually an emotional creature. Strategy and planning had always consumed me, but I could feel a vortex of emotion trying to pull me under. I forced my brain to focus on the facts, and the implications for us, rather than the image that pulled at me, of a lonely little boy with no-one to love him.

Were the tests he was talking about the same ones they must have given Angel as a child? I tried not to groan in frustration. Every question that got answered lately seemed to bring three more with it.

Wolf blew out a heavy breath as he paused for a moment. Ava snuggled into him tighter as she hugged Angel to them. Ryder reached out and wrapped his arms around them from behind. He looked a little startled, as if he'd been wanting to do it but had been holding back and now he'd moved without conscious thought. Ryder had always been highly empathetic with people, and a hugger. My chest tightened when Ava grabbed Ryder's hand and gripped it hard.

I felt the draw to move in closer too, but I didn't want to get distracted from what Wolf was saying right now. Nick had drawn closer, but he was swiveling his gaze between Wolf and me, watching to see where he was most needed.

A sudden realization hit me as I watched them, about the depth of dynamic within a pack, and its strength. It was so hard to be one person's everything. Even with my twin, I sometimes felt as if I'd failed him. But with a pack, there was always someone to step in, or step up. To help shoulder the load. Wolf needed their emotional support right now, but he needed something different from me. It was in his eyes and the careful way he looked at me. I just had to figure out what that was.

As if he sensed my focus on him, Wolf gazed across the couch at me, ignoring everyone else in the room.

"How do I know?" He asked my earlier question back to me and I sensed his story was far from over. "I know because they would come and stay at the manor. They wouldn't let me leave the house without supervision, and there was a lot of high-tech security. But as I got older, the carers were around less and Maven were around more. When I was a teenager, I would sometimes sneak out of my room and listen to them talking at night. Looking back, I think they knew I was listening. They were openly a pack at the house, but not like you all. They could barely tolerate each other and were angry that the time together was necessary to maintain their bonds. Their bonds felt forced. They would accuse each other of being the reason their omega died, and they lost their beta and their first experiments."

Wolf briefly shifted his gaze over to Sam and Maia. "I'm sorry, but that's what they called you. It was a long time before I figured out they were talking about the children they had with their omega."

"It's okay," Sam said. Lexie was on his lap, and I could see he was gripping her tightly, but his gaze flicked to Maia.

She nodded at him in reassurance. Even though her face had gone pale. "Keep going," she added.

Wolf nodded and focused back on me, tilting his head slightly as he watched my reactions. I kept my gaze even and my breathing steady. As hard as it was, we needed to hear this, and I wanted him to know I could take anything he needed to unload.

"You have to understand, Maven has controlled our country from the shadows for hundreds of years. They are the product of generations of breeding and their wealth is unfathomable. They always had families, for show, but came together as a pack secretly. Each pack would induct the strongest male in the next generation, the next prime alpha. He inherited everything. The rest of the children would be clueless, thinking they were wealthy getting the scraps.

"Maven were the driving force behind the evil that has corrupted our world. They started the shift to stamping out packs, because they wanted to be the only one. It helped consolidate their power. They drove the change to treating omegas as submissive chattel. Purely because omegas drew packs to them naturally, and they didn't want them influencing alphas. They also hunted and killed other prime alphas. They didn't want anyone challenging their line of primes, because they were getting weaker each generation until the current one. This generation of Maven was the first to have no prime alpha born into it."

My whole body locked up at hearing Wolf's story. The one he'd been so reluctant to tell. I knew why now. Even I wanted to go back to five minutes ago before he'd started. I'd known for a long time that there was something seriously wrong with our world and that there had to be some powerful people involved. The scale of what he was talking about was unnerving. They'd been manipulating the world for generations, unseen and unknown. *How the hell were we supposed to fight that? They had to have layers of security and protection.*

All I knew was that we needed to find a way. This was purely another puzzle to solve. And just maybe, this Crash they had caused, would be the key to do it. They were more exposed now than they'd ever been, with all their carefully guarded secrets spilling out. I straightened my spine and Wolf's eyes glinted in acknowledgment.

"To keep Maven in the family, they had to pass the mantle down to the most dominant alpha. They were so blinded by power, they didn't care they were harming themselves as well as the rest of the world. They were so used to manipulating everything around them, they figured they could do the same with this problem.

"When the current head of Maven came into power, he started researching prime alphas. He captured a couple when they were young. Then he tested them before he had them killed. He wanted to transform his genetics and make himself into a prime alpha. It never worked. When I was born, I became his backup plan, as well as his test subject. If he couldn't turn himself into one, he wanted to bite me into the pack, by manipulation or force, but either control me or keep me captive. He knew prime alphas shared their dominance with their packs, so he tried coercion first."

It suddenly became clear to me why Wolf had been so hesitant to tell this tale, beyond the obvious horror. They needed him to keep their power, the one thing they cared about, which meant they would never let him go. His eyes were almost apologetic now, as if he felt guilty for dragging us, his pack, into his world. It wasn't his fault, though. He wasn't the one who had broken our world, or dragged us into hell. We were his fate, and his fate was ours.

Wolf's eyes had remained locked on mine as he talked, not letting me shy away from this. I had the feeling he was testing me, somehow. I didn't blame him. He needed to know if his pack could handle what was coming for us. I only hoped I passed, because I didn't want to fail him. If he needed someone to be strong for him, I knew I could be that person. I'd been doing it gladly for my twin for a decade.

But now, his penetrating gaze slid across the room. Everyone followed it as he looked at first Damon, and then Sam.

"Phillip's change of tactic away from outright killing prime alphas is why Damon and Sam are alive, too. He started monitoring everyone he thought could be a prime. You had him convinced, Damon. He knew you through your father. Phillip tried to throw every obstacle at you he could, to keep you down. He wanted you manageable and compliant, but not dead. He wasn't as sure of you, Sam. Yet he still tried to make your life difficult in the military. He said you were his test subjects in the wild. He never planned to let you live forever, though. Phillip set you up as competition. He tried to manipulate me by offering to let me kill you both if I joined his pack. If I refused, he would make the offer to one of you. He assumed I would be as power hungry as he was."

The room went still at that. Damon, Sam, and their packs were tense. "I would never have accepted his offer. From the time I knew you existed, I hoped we could become friends. I didn't care for any of the wealth in the manor. I craved people, connections. In all Phillip's years of cruelty, he still hasn't figured out it doesn't create loyalty."

My heart bled for Wolf. His years of isolation, craving basic human contact. Growing up with my twin, I couldn't even imagine a life without him and the comfort he brought me. I glanced over at Ryder to see he was staring at Wolf, his eyes bleeding sorrow too.

"So you never knew who your parents were?" Hunter asked as he leaned forward in his seat. He'd been lounging next to Damon and Maia, but he'd fixed his eyes on Wolf as soon as we got into the house and his gaze had barely wavered. He watched Wolf with an almost rabid curiosity, and I could see his mind turning too.

I had a horrible feeling I knew where this was going. There was only one reason they would let Wolf live and keep him so close.

"Yes and no," Wolf said. "Not when I was young. My suspicions grew as I got older, though. I heard them say one night that every prime alpha in their family was born with a white birthmark. I have one on my hip. It seems it skipped their generation, but not mine. Only they didn't want to hand Maven down to me. They felt cheated that they hadn't had a prime and experienced that shared power. So they started letting me join them in controlled environments."

He glanced at Ryder, who gave him a sad smile. "One of the pack was an adrenaline junkie. He bought us dirt bikes and would ride around the estate with me. He took me to jump out of a plane at a private airstrip nearby, too. After so long in isolation, I craved the contact and the limited glimpses of the world. By the time I was eighteen, they let me go to small parties they held at the manor. It took far too long for me to figure out they were trying to bribe me with more freedom, and with women, so I would let them claim me as a pack mate."

His eyes shifted to Ava on his lap briefly, and he looked nervous when he mentioned the women, but she only hugged him tighter. "They never brought their wives to the manor, so I never met my mother. One of them slipped and called me son sometimes, but I still wasn't sure. Not until just before they brought me here, when I overheard my dad talking about me one night. He let it slip, but I don't think he meant to. He was drunk, which was rare. I'd thought Maven was the only chance at family I had. That night, I realized what they had done to me. They always said they were keeping me safe, but never told me from what. I thought they were my protectors until I realized they were the monsters."

I noticed a look pass between Nick and Max, and my gut dropped even further. They knew something. I'd suspected Nick was up to something when he kept jumping in on Ava's phone calls. He'd also been cagey when I first found him down in the labs, but I'd hoped he'd tell me himself. I'd wanted to earn his trust.

"Wolf isn't your full name, is it?" Nick asked.

Nineteen

Wolf tilted his head slightly as he shook it. "It took me a while to remember. A lot of things fade when I get wild. Nelly called me Wolf, and it was the only name that stuck living in that cage, but my full name is Wolfgang Kingsley."

Hunter's entire body spasmed as if something had electrocuted him. Max looked devastated. The rest of his pack mates looked appalled, and reached for Hunter, but Maia had her nose crinkled in confusion. "What is it, Hunt?"

"You can't be. You died," Hunter whispered hoarsely, his voice barely audible, even with the silence of the room. The hairs on my arm stood on end, reacting to the electric feeling of the air as Maia gasped. Damon's lightning scent was surging through the room.

"Hunter?" Wolf breathed out. He looked as shell-shocked as when Maia had first spoken to him earlier. I'd thought he'd zoned out a bit when everyone was getting introduced. He'd seemed overwhelmed. Now I was sure he had. "They told you I died?"

I couldn't hold back from reaching for Wolf any longer. The draw to him became an insistent beat in my blood as his emotions spiraled. I slid along the couch and put my hand on his arm. There was a fine tremor running through him. Nick had moved instinctively too, and was standing behind Wolf now, his hand on his shoulder.

"How long have you known about me?" Hunter asked him. His tone was harsh. He sounded almost angry.

Wolf's face crumpled, yet he looked conflicted. "I didn't know until the night I found out for sure about my dad. Our dad. He was actually talking about you. He complained that by taking me, they had forced him to have another son so he'd have a legal heir. But that something was wrong with you and he'd had to send you away to a school."

Hunter's jaw clenched, and his whole body looked drawn tight.

"I wanted to find you. I'd thought I was alone in the world," Wolf said, his eyes boring into Hunter. "Knowing that I had a brother out there, and you might need me, made me desperate enough to risk an escape. I was young and stupid, though. I knew nothing about the outside world. They caught me before I got far. I was so angry with them for keeping you from me. I told them I'd never join their pack. As punishment, they sent me here. To the labs and a cage. I've been here ever since. If I could have made it to you, I would."

Hunter went deathly pale. He started gasping for air, like he was going to hyperventilate, before he got up and bolted from the room. Maia jumped up to follow him, but Damon gently maneuvered her into Leif's lap and said, "I'll go. Stay here."

Maia opened her mouth as if she was about to argue, but Leif whispered in her ear and hugged her tightly before turning to Max.

"You don't look shocked, Max. Did you and Nick know about this and not say anything?" Leif asked him quietly.

"No, we didn't know. We were just suspicious," Max clarified. "When Nick found out Wolf's nickname, knowing every one of Maven's secrets so far seems to lead back to one of our packs, he was worried and told me. He knew the name of Hunter's brother from talking to us. We decided not to say anything until we could get them in a room together. It seemed like a lot to put on Hunter without knowing more. If that was wrong, I'll apologize to him."

"Sorry to spring that on you, too," Max said, turning to Wolf. "Hunter's reaction wasn't really about you. His childhood was awful and filled with trauma. He told us once you felt like a ghost that haunted him in that house. So he's feeling shocked and overwhelmed. He just found out Sam is his half brother, too, and neither of them ever knew. It's a lot for him. Just give him a minute."

"I've spent years feeling as if I failed him," Wolf said, a quiet sadness haunting his words. "I'll give him as long as he needs."

He shifted his attention to Sam after a moment. "You're his half brother?"

"Yeah," Sam looked uncomfortable. "It was in my gramps' letter. I only told him a few hours ago."

"So does that make you my half brother too, if we all have the same father, but you have a different mother?"

"Yeah, it does. Welcome to our fucked up family," Sam said with a grimace. Wolf smiled at Sam briefly before it flickered and died.

"Did Hunter run on you too?" Wolf asked, and his vulnerability almost broke me.

"No." Sam looked pained. He glanced at the entryway before he dragged his eyes back to Wolf. "He hugged me. But I'm a shiny extra present under the Christmas tree. From the little he said this morning, I figure they held your supposed death over him his whole life. Finding out you've been alive this whole time can't be easy for him."

Wolf looked at Max, his eyes full of unspoken questions. "It was a lot worse than that. Your parents are assholes. They almost broke him, but it's his story to tell. I will say, though, he rarely runs from things. Just let him get himself together. He'll be back."

I could feel sadness wash through me, but it felt disconcerting. As if it wasn't my sadness. I shot a look at Wolf. *All the emotions I'm feeling? Are they mine? Or Wolf's? Is that even possible?*

Ryder and I have always sensed each other in our twin bond, but we've never felt each other's emotions before. Not like this.

"You just said Hunter is feeling shocked and overwhelmed, as if you could feel him. Can you?" I asked Max, my eyes not leaving Wolf. It was a strange question to ask someone, but these were strange times.

"Yeah, it's a pack thing," he said with a knowing smile. "It gets stronger when you're bonding, or touching each other. After you claim your omega, you get a direct line to your pack mates' emotions."

"If you have a really deep connection, usually built over time or an extreme bonding event, the books say you can even hear each other," Maia added.

"The books?" I asked.

"Yeah, there were an old series of illegal books about alphas and omegas in the library here. Until I stole them. One is about packs. I'll lend it to you when Dave finishes reading it. I should probably return them. The omegas here are going to need all the help they can get now that they're free and finally able to follow their instincts."

I nodded. I definitely wanted to read those, so I knew what was coming at us. Ryder smirked at me, knowing my thought patterns and already being in tune with my emotions. I rolled my eyes at him.

"I've read the pack one already," Ava said softly. Silent tears ran down her cheeks and dampened Wolf's skin as she nuzzled into him. "I can help if you want to know more."

"So can I," Nick said. "My great grandma often told us stories about the old packs. I've picked up a lot over the years."

It had been a long time since I had felt so clueless about anything. I'd spent years learning about everything that could give us an advantage in rescuing Ava. Yet learning about packs had never crossed my mind. Alphas and omegas living in packs had been a fairytale, made up stories. Yet, being here, I could see them working. I could feel bonds growing within my pack, even though we hadn't claimed each other yet. It made me realize just how much we'd been missing out on as a society.

"Thank you," I said, a little roughly. I wasn't as open with my feelings as Ryder was. I'd always been a little more reserved. Nick winked at me, and Wolf patted my hand on his arm. I smiled at them both, feeling my tension ease.

I looked around the room, desperate to get the attention off me, when I noticed the box Maia's pack had brought in with them. It looked cumbersome. I couldn't imagine they were dragging it around without a good reason. A memory sparked, of my dad running to Ava's uncle's place after we told him what happened, and coming back with a similar-looking box. He'd buried it in the backyard.

"What's in the box?"

"It's how the Network contacts each other. We rescued it from my gramps' farm just before Maven burned it down," Sam said. "We really need to contact the Network, but we don't know how to open it. Max wanted to keep working on it while we were all here."

"Why are you *all* here?" Ava asked.

"Sam had to fly the chopper," Lexie said. "Dio, Pala, and Dave did some complicated male negotiation thing to decide who was coming with me and who was staying to keep the farm secure."

"I won," Pala said proudly. "It only cost me a month of laundry duty."

"None of my guys would let me go without them," Maia shrugged. "They went next level possessive when we discovered my bun in the oven this morning."

"We did not!" Leif exclaimed. "Our reactions were entirely normal."

"Not even close," Lexie scoffed.

I got the feeling Ava was trying to distract Wolf from his thoughts while we waited for Hunter and Damon. He gave Ava a small smile, but seemed to have zoned out a little again, as if his thoughts had gone inwards. He was absentmindedly stroking Ava's waist. I figured it was a hang up from being alone so much. He seemed to crave touch.

I kept one ear on the girls' chatter about Maia's pregnancy as I got up and wandered over to the box to inspect it. New things had always intrigued me.

Nick came over beside me and ran a hand over it. "Sam said he saw it working once, and it was open and had lights on. But there's no obvious power supply or on/off switch."

The comparison to the giant box generating energy underneath the Palace unsettled me. I unconsciously glanced down at the floor, as if I could see what was beneath us.

"I know," Nick said, picking up where my thoughts had gone with eerie accuracy. "I suspect that's why Max really brought it."

I walked around the box, conscious of Max watching us closely. It seemed to be sealed tight, but there was definitely a front. It had a strange circular pattern embedded in it, then a large slot with a weird shape bisecting the middle.

"It looks like it turns," Nick said, "but nothing we've tried will make it move. It needs some kind of unusual key. If they left it behind at their gramps' house, it's long-gone now. Maven burned it to the ground."

"I had a contact at the Network, but there's no way my method of contacting him would work now. It involved leaving a coded message at a hotel. I can't imagine it's still open, even if the phone lines worked," I said.

My thoughts weren't really on my words, though. Something was sitting at the edge of my mind. Niggling at me. I looked over at the people on the couches, trying to think of what I'd seen and what connection my brain was trying to make.

"What are you teasing out?" Ryder came over and asked me. He knew the way my mind worked, that it had snagged on something. Sometimes talking helped, but usually if I just let my mind drift where it wanted to go, without forcing it in a particular direction, the answer came to me.

"What…" Nick started to say until Ryder put his hand over Nick's mouth playfully.

"Be quiet for a second," Ryder stage whispered. "He's got this weird voodoo thing he does with a problem. Just let him do his thing."

Nick just reached up and twisted Ryder's nipple. "Ow," Ryder hissed, but he was laughing as he let Nick go.

"Go, Nick, with the purple nurple," Lexie called out. But my attention kept getting pulled back to the box.

I looked at the device again, then back to the couches, and let my mind drift. My eyes snagged on Maia in her ridiculously oversized military jacket. It had caught my eye earlier because it was an unusual thing for a woman to wear.

"Whose jacket is that?" I asked her when I noticed they'd stopped talking and were watching me. I knew it couldn't possibly be hers. It had medals on it that looked real, but I needed to know where she'd gotten it from. I knew the Network was mostly made up of retired military guys. It seemed too much of a coincidence.

"It was my gramps' jacket. Leif rescued it as a memento for me. I know it's too big, but after reading his letter this morning, it's making me feel better to wear it." She sounded a little defensive as she pulled the jacket tighter around her. I was about to reassure her I had meant no offense with my question when my eyes snagged on the medals pinned to it. The light had hit them as she'd pulled the jacket closed, making the metal glitter brightly.

I felt a cold sweat break out over my neck. I looked at the device and back at the medals again.

"Could I borrow your jacket?" I asked her. Maia looked at Leif and seemed unsure.

"He won't harm it, I promise," Ava said. "He used to do this when we were kids. His brain works at a problem until he solves it. He's good at seeing patterns."

Maia slipped off the jacket and handed it to Max, who cradled it protectively as he brought it over to me.

"This jacket means a lot to her," he murmured. I nodded, and he handed the jacket over.

I looked at the medals, then at the device again. I carefully unpinned one and held it up sideways against the lock. It slipped in easily, fitting snuggly as something within the mechanism clicked. The medal had been an ornate four-pointed star, and three points were within the lock. I was holding onto the last one, trying to keep it steady.

"Holy shit," Max gasped. "I've been trying to figure that out for days."

"What?" Maia cried out as she slipped off Leif's lap and dashed over. She was speechless when she saw what I had done.

"Do you want me to turn it?" I asked Max.

"Not yet," he answered. "Can someone grab Damon and Hunter? They can't have gone far."

"I'll go," Pala volunteered.

"Ryder, can you take the girls and Angel into another room?" I asked him. We knew nothing about how this machine worked and, from what I'd heard, it had hidden in a basement for years.

Ava immediately got up from Wolf's lap, cradling the still sleeping Angel to her. Lexie and Maia tried to protest until Max grabbed Maia and kissed her hard. "You're pregnant, Maia. We're not trying to exclude you, but your priority is the baby. The device has been off for a long time. What if it malfunctions and explodes when we turn it on?"

Maia paled, and Lexie grabbed her by the hand. "We've got her. Ava, you lead the way."

That baby was going to have some fiercely loving aunts.

"Okay, I'm going, but if you all die, I'm going to find you and kill you again," Maia warned, a fierce glare in her eyes as she looked at her mates. She came across as a soft omega when she was snuggled into her mates, but she had some backbone, that one. And claws. I liked her more for it. Especially with how protective she and Lexie seemed of Ava.

"I'll come. We need to make sure the other omegas are away from here as well," Cary said.

"Me too. I'll help," Leif said quickly, his eyes locked on Maia.

Ryder nodded at both of them distractedly as they left the room in pursuit of the three girls, who had already disappeared out of sight. None seemed inclined to wait for their self-appointed bodyguards.

A small part of my tension eased. I hadn't wanted to send Cary away. I knew he felt conflicted about being an omega and wanted to be treated as a pack mate instead. Yet it went against my alpha nature to have an omega in harm's way. It was something I was going to have to work on. I was just glad for now that wherever Ava went, Cary seemed to follow. It wouldn't keep him out of trouble, but it would make it easier for me to protect him without him noticing and fighting me on it.

"Good job, River," Wolf said from behind me. I wasn't sure if he was talking about the device or about getting Ava and Cary out of the room. I looked over my shoulder as Wolf gripped it firmly. His eyes seemed focused again, and I let out a relieved breath. I'd been a little worried about what Hunter running out on him would do to his emotional state.

Hunter, Damon, and Pala came barreling back into the room. Max explained to them what I had done.

"I don't think we should all be in here when I turn it. Max has a good point. We don't know what this will do," I said.

"River and I will stay. Everyone else, wait outside," Max demanded.

None of them looked happy. Yet, Damon shuffled them out of the room with a worried frown in Max's direction. They clearly had a lot of respect for Max.

He adjusted his glasses slightly and looked at me. "Ready?"

"No," I answered, as I turned the key.

Twenty

I stood quietly behind the stone wall leading to the great room with the rest of the guys. We'd gone when Max demanded, but none of us had moved far. We couldn't. Not when people we cared about were in that room taking a risk for us.

Max was a good friend, and I hated him being in there. Yet the thought of River being in danger had a cold sweat running down my spine. Nobody had mated me into this pack. I'd barely even acknowledged the connection. But the bond between us already felt like a physical thing.

I'd always longed for a version of the intense friendship between Max and his mates, yet I'd never really understood the flip side. Until now. Part of my heart was beating inside that room. I could hardly breathe, even though I'd only met River two days ago. *What would it be like if they bit me into the pack, and who would it be?*

A metallic clicking noise coming from the room had my heart pounding.

"What's going on?" Wolf called out gruffly from in front of me. He was standing with Damon just barely beyond the entrance. His leg was twitching as if he was trying to hold himself back from running in there. I put my hand on his back. He nodded, but didn't look back at me. He'd focused his complete attention on the slice of the formal living room we could see from this angle.

"You're supposed to be somewhere safe," River answered, sounding frustrated.

"Just tell us what's happening," Damon barked lightly from next to Wolf. "This is as far as anyone's going."

"There's a series of hidden lights on the outer edge of the lock design. Each time he turns the medal in a full circle, one lights up. The first one was green, this one just came up red and it keeps coming up red."

Wolf growled softly. The tension of River being in danger was making him slip back into his feral state. Cary and Ava being out of sight probably wasn't helping.

"Try speeding it up," I called out.

"It can't hurt," Max said quietly to River.

I didn't have an alpha's hearing, but even I heard River let out a tense breath. The clicking noise came more rapidly and Max called out, "It's working. It's come up green. Good job, Nick."

"How many lights?" Sam called out.

"They're hard to see when they're not on. From the spacing, I'd guess twelve."

A soft metallic screeching sound had us all pushing into the room. Wolf led the charge. He'd picked River up and was about to haul him away when I patted him on the arm. "It's okay, Wolf. It just opened."

"I'm fine, wild man," River said, his eyes wide. Being a tall guy that was solidly built, I don't think he was used to being suddenly yanked off his feet. Wolf put him down with a reluctant groan.

"Why is River freaking out?" Came Ryder's yell from the connecting hallway that led to the ballroom.

"A giant alpha just picked him up like he was a barbie doll," I called out while River rolled his eyes.

"I'm fine," he yelled back to his twin. "Stay with our girls."

"Our girls?" Damon growled.

River was unfazed, still staring at the device. "Yeah. Ours."

Damon glared darkly at River, and I could scent lightning sparking hotly within the room. Wolf was already on edge. We didn't need an alpha dominance clash to set him off right now.

"Uh, Damon," I jumped in, as I swallowed hard and tried not to stammer. Damon had always intimidated me, but it had gotten worse recently. "By ours, I'm pretty sure he meant all of ours. Not Ryder and his, ours."

River looked genuinely perplexed and raised his eyebrow at Damon. "Of course I did. For the same reason you guys flew here just because Ava missed a phone call this morning. If Lexie and Maia are important to Ava, then they're important to us. Besides, I owe your pack for rescuing Ava and Cary from the Palace."

Damon opened his mouth as if he was going to respond, but River cut him off, done with the conversation already. He turned back to me and asked, "Why are you so nervous around Damon, Nick?"

Freaking hell. River didn't pull any punches when he was feeling protective. I could feel every eye in the room staring at me.

"That would be Damon's fault," Hunter said, stepping in to rescue me from answering as he pulled Damon into him and ruffled his hair. "He got a little growly while he was holding back from claiming Maia. Nick copped a full Damon hissy fit when he approached our table one morning to talk to Max. It's fine now. We carry doggy biscuits so Nick can give them to Damon."

I groaned. The biscuit thing had been a joke. Hunter had told me to say it to Damon as a safe word if he was getting growly, because it worked to distract dogs. But I would never live down blurting it out to Damon when he'd growled at me during the battle at the farm. Not while Hunter was around, anyway. I didn't miss the subtle look River shot Wolf and the way Wolf shifted closer to me. Neither did Damon, as his eyes narrowed at us.

"Nick is also important to us," Damon said, with a not-so-subtle warning. "But I apologize for being on edge. As Max said earlier, we only found out about Maia's pregnancy hours ago. And now she's back at the Palace. It's riling our alphas."

This morning had been a whirlwind, and my head was spinning a little. With three packs and so many alphas in the same space, there was sure to be drama. Along with a lot of dominance and pheromones. But with so many interconnections between our packs, we were going to have to figure out how to trust each other. Despite the truce we had come to this morning, River, Ryder, and Wolf were the new guys, and everyone was still sniffing them out. I figured if we were going to work smoothly together, someone would need to un-ruffle feathers for a while. And that person was probably me. I took a deep breath, but before I could say anything, Max piped up.

"Uh, I hate to interrupt the alpha dick measuring, but the strange and concerning communication device is open," Max said with a grin. All the attention in the room abruptly spun back to him, and the lit-up device he was standing alongside.

Phew, saved by Max. I stepped between the alphas to stand next to him. Max had pulled the pieces open wider to reveal a monitor and a flip down keyboard on one side. He'd also somehow removed a back panel to reveal the inner workings of the device. Looking at it fried my brain.

Behind the locking mechanism there was a series of intricate, and interconnected, micro parts that were whirring with the faintest hum. They led to a smaller box that had a bar indicator on the front panel. The bar was steadily rising. The machine gave a faint buzz when it reached the top. *Holy crap.*

"Did the Network figure out how to both miniaturize and boost kinetic energy?" I asked Max. It was the only logical explanation for what was in front of me. It was so complex, yet seemed so stunningly simple at the same time.

"It sure looks that way. Which isn't surprising, if their gramps' was Frank Gascombe."

"Why wouldn't he have commercialized this technology?" River asked.

"He was in hiding for decades. Launching an invention that would revolutionize technology and power doesn't exactly scream lying low. Especially when you're supposed to be dead," Sam said as he moved forward to look at the device more closely.

"But if Maven were planning the Crash, this tech could have saved a lot of people," Hunter insisted.

"Gramps has been dead for years," Sam said, sadness creeping into his voice. "He wasn't one to sit out a fight, he was just fighting underground. If he'd known about the Crash, he would have done something. I'm sure of it."

"Sorry," Hunter said. "I didn't mean to imply he wouldn't. I'm just so frustrated that people are hurting out there."

"We all are," Damon said, as he patted the arm Hunter still had draped over his shoulder.

"Could your gramps have built a prototype of this, maybe on a larger scale? Possibly before he faked his death?" I blurted, thinking out loud.

It was Max, not Sam, that responded though. He knew how my mind worked, because his worked in a similar way. "Are you thinking about the device here, under the labs?"

I nodded, and Sam shrugged. "Anything is possible. I think we should go look at it now and find out."

"I agree," Max said, as he clapped me on the shoulder and grinned. Now that we knew it wasn't dangerous, he was practically vibrating with excitement. He loved figuring out how things worked. "Let's go."

"I, uh, don't think I'm ready to go down into the labs again, yet," Wolf mumbled. "I'll stay here."

Shit. I hadn't even thought about that.

"That's okay," Hunter said, his voice sounding rougher than usual, as he flicked his gaze to Wolf, then away again. "I'll stay with you. Maybe we could go outside and talk?"

Hunter was naturally cocky. But his levity had disappeared abruptly. He was standing with his arms crossed over his chest defensively, as if he expected Wolf to reject him when he'd been the one to run earlier.

"I'd really like that," Wolf said. The rest of us suddenly found interesting things to look at, as the two brothers walked out of the room together and out the front doors.

Damon, Max and I bolted for the window. River just watched us in bemusement. "Really? We're going to spy on them?"

"Hell yes," Damon growled.

Max just sighed. "We can't even blame it on the girls making us do it this time."

"It's not really spying, more observing their interaction, so we can monitor their health and wellbeing," I said. "They're both highly dominant alphas in a stressful situation. We're really providing a public service."

"Sure," River said, his tone sounding extra dry. Yet he still came over and joined us at the window.

Hunter and Wolf had stopped under the trees at the edge of the lawn.

"Can you guys hear what they're saying?" Max asked. "Hunter feels really nervous."

"No," Damon said. He turned his head, though, as if he was straining to hear. I knew alphas had advanced senses, including hearing, but if he could hear anything from here, I would have been amazed. I wished I was more in tune with Wolf's emotions right now, so I could make sure he was alright. There was something about Wolf that made him seem intensely vulnerable, despite his size and incredible strength.

Wolf was standing in a defensive posture, listening intently to whatever Hunter was saying to him. When he suddenly moved like lightning, lifting Hunter up in a bear hug and squeezing him hard. Max and Damon both tensed instantly.

"Relax," I said, before one of them could jump through the window. "Wolf hugs with his whole body and doesn't really know his own strength. They're good."

Hunter managed to wrangle his arms free and hugged his brother back just as hard.

Damon let out a relieved sigh as he stepped back from the window. "Okay, let's leave them to it now. Our job is to check out the device downstairs."

We backed away reluctantly and gave them some privacy.

As we walked through the labs, I looked at them with fresh eyes. I'd been so focused on the computers and the power when I was down here yesterday, I hadn't really noticed the locked cells at the back. Hearing Maia and Wolf talk about them gave me chills now. Picturing them in there, left alone in the dark, made me angrier than I ever remembered feeling before. I must have stopped walking without realizing until River squeezed my shoulder. He was standing behind me, staring at them, too.

I looked over to see everyone else had halted as well.

"Is this…?" Damon asked. He didn't seem able to finish, but I knew what he was asking.

"Yes, this is the lab they used for Maia, other omegas too, but mostly Maia," I answered.

Damon visibly shuddered. "We shouldn't have brought her back here."

"She insisted, and you have to respect her choices. She's earned it," Sam said. He looked just as shell-shocked as Damon, though.

"We saw it in the videos we got from their hidden lab server," Max added, "but it's different being here."

I didn't even want to think about what was on those videos.

Damon muttered something about burning the place down as he turned away abruptly. He headed for the doorway to the stairwell that I'd pointed out when we first entered the room. We'd left it ajar. River flicked the switch at the bottom and flooded the room with light once again.

"That's a lot bigger, if it's the same technology," Max said. The device down here took up half the long room.

"It doesn't have that lock opening anywhere that I could see," I told him.

"I'm pretty sure that would have been something the Network added. The military medals fit from what I know of their core members," River said. I was impressed with how he'd figured out the device's lock so easily. He seemed to make connections the rest of us couldn't see. He was walking around the device again, looking at it from every angle.

"It has to have an opening somewhere, but I can't see anything," Max groaned.

I took a step back and looked at it again, trying to look at the whole device at once. *Were we overthinking this if this wasn't the Network's device?*

A sudden idea had me stepping forward. I pushed on the edge of the middle panel, the one with the console. It popped open. It was a simple push mechanism, the same as in a lot of kitchen cupboards.

"The Palace techs have never been that creative," I said. I dragged the door further open, then folded back the panels in a concertina, exposing the inner workings of the device. "Or particularly tech savvy."

"How the hell did I not see that?" Max grumbled, as he squatted down in front of the device. The inside had nowhere near the elegance and simplicity of the smaller device; it was a mess of moving parts, wires, and cables. There was no doubt it was producing the same kinetic energy, though.

"This was definitely either a prototype or the Palace tried to replicate something they saw and did a shit job of it. It seems to be stable, though," Max said.

"It's concerning that they knew about this technology and didn't implement it," Damon growled. "I don't understand why they wouldn't. Surely they could have patented it and sold it the same way they did solar panels."

"Don't forget, one member of Maven is the CEO of Integral Mining. Solar panels contain expensive parts as well as mined resources like silicon, silver, aluminum, and copper," I answered. "Producing them requires a lot of mining and they're not sold cheaply. If this technology got out, and it's as simple as it looks, anyone could replicate it using repurposed materials, once they knew how. It would be impossible to contain. Unless there's something I'm missing."

"There has to be something complex about it, or someone else would have invented it as well by now," Max said, as he squatted and looked over the device's moving parts. "We know how kinetic energy works, but it's never been able to produce this much power before. Maybe he built a large-scale prototype before he faked his death and couldn't destroy it without it looking suspicious. After he was gone, they probably couldn't replicate it effectively. Or clearly miniaturize it the way he later did. Maybe he had to leave the machine but destroyed his notes. All I know is, it's not as simple as it looks."

"Makes sense," I muttered absently. The moving parts inside, despite being chaotic at this scale, were mesmerizing.

"Max, are you okay down here alone? It looks like it may take a while to figure it out," Damon asked. His affection shined through as he smiled down at his pack mate.

"Yeah, you guys go. There's no use in you standing around. Check on Maia." Max waved us away, his mind already whirring, and his eyes seeking answers.

As he shifted, Max's t-shirt stretched, and I noticed two new bite marks, one on his biceps and another on the back of his shoulder. He had four now, and each one looked different. I was insanely curious, but it was none of my business and not something I'd draw public attention to. I'd ask him about it privately, if I got up the nerve.

"I'm going to head up to the lab Wolf was in and keep working my way through their server files. See if I can find any kind of plans or instructions for this thing that will help us," I said as I forced my gaze away.

Max paid us no attention as we left, already engrossed in figuring out the device.

"I'll pop down and check in on him regularly," I told Damon when we got to the top of the stairs. I was the only person Max would tolerate interrupting him when he was working on a problem, outside of his pack.

"Thanks, I appreciate it, Nick," Damon replied as he patted me awkwardly on the shoulder. He seemed nervous about spooking me.

River gave me a nod as everyone dispersed, and I wandered over to the second lab. I figured he would head to check on either Ava or Wolf, maybe both. I peeked back down and looked in on Max a few times, but he didn't even notice. He got like that sometimes.

Time slipped away as I became engrossed in navigating through the servers' files. Desperately trying to find anything else that could help the pack I was so desperate to join. And to figure out more about Wolf. As much as he had revealed this morning, I sensed Wolf was still holding something back, and I wanted to know what it was.

If Maven came for Wolf, it would come to a fight. One I knew would get ugly. Unless we held the balance of power somehow.

The knowledge was a shadow hanging over us all.

Twenty-One

I think I'd startled Hunter with my giant hug, but he'd quickly recovered and hugged me back just as tightly. After wondering about him for so long, daydreaming about what it would have been like to grow up together, having him right in front of me had been too much. I'd needed the contact.

He'd apologized for running, but I didn't need his apology and brushed it off. I was just glad he was talking to me now. We'd been sitting and chatting for a while. I wasn't much of a talker. I'd already talked more today than I ever had in my life. So it had mostly been Hunter keeping the conversation going, while I decompressed for a bit, and he seemed comfortable with that. I sensed he was good at putting people at ease.

He'd touched on his childhood briefly, but I imagined he'd left out a lot. I hadn't pushed, content with whatever he was willing to tell me until we got to know each other better. He'd quickly moved on to telling me about meeting Damon at school, their time in the military, and how they'd met Leif and Max. His life fascinated me, as did their pack dynamics, and I was happy to sit and take it all in, only giving him an occasional grunt and laughing at some of his anecdotes. He was a funny guy. He didn't seem to mind that I didn't have as many words right now.

"Man, I went from no brothers to gaining both a brother and a half brother on the same day. It's a bit of a mind fuck," he blurted suddenly, completely changing direction from what he'd been talking about. "We already had Leif and Lexie, then Maia and Sam, as siblings between the packs. Now I have brothers in two of the packs. I can't help but think there's something bigger at work here.

"Yeah, Maven couldn't keep their dicks in their pants," I grunted.

Hunter laughed. "Yeah, that's probably it."

"So Sam seems like a good guy," I said, wanting to get Hunter talking again. "Does he have a little trouble with his dominance, though? He was leaking all over the place this morning."

"Yeah," Hunter muttered. "We were wary of him at first. He and Maia didn't have the best history, and he came in hot headed, wanting to take her away. His dominance had been an issue his entire life. Or the world made it an issue, anyway. He wasn't good at leashing it, but he's been getting better since he mated Lexie. He could still use some of your Zen. Damon, too. You seem really calm until you beast out. Then your bark hits everyone with a sucker punch out of nowhere. You don't even make a sound. It's kinda cool, but a little intimidating on the receiving end."

I shook my head, bemused. "I don't know about that, but if I can help either of them, I will. It seems to me they both need to get rid of their leashes entirely and trust their instincts."

"Trusting our instincts isn't something the world has ever encouraged us to do. But if it works for you, it's worth a shot. I think we need to be on top of our game if Maven comes for us."

How the hell was I the one giving advice on being a prime alpha when I'd been living in captivity? The world must be way more messed up than I'd thought. It made me wonder what my mates had faced that they hadn't told me about yet.

We were sitting shoulder to shoulder under a tree, and the small contact was comforting. But I could feel the absence of my pack. I'd need to find one of them soon. Hunter didn't have the same punch as my pack mates. It made me a little sad. I'd hoped a blood connection would feel the same as a pack one. Now knowing that it didn't, I was willing to put in time to build a relationship. I wanted him in my life. Sam too.

I kept glancing surreptitiously at Hunter, trying to trace any family resemblance. His bright red hair was very different from mine. I only had hints of red in a certain light. My face was also a lot more angular than his. He had our father's looks, and I assumed I had more of our mother's, or maybe someone else in her family. I'd never met her, though, or even seen a picture of her.

"Do I look more like our mother?" I blurted out suddenly. He looked up at me, his eyes wide. While he was a tall guy, I had another foot on him, at least. I think I startled him.

"Not really," he said, as he searched my face under all my hair. I felt suddenly self conscious about my wild appearance, which was a new feeling. I briefly wondered if it bothered Ava or Cary, but got distracted when Hunter started talking again. "You actually look a lot like her brother, our uncle Harry. I only met him a few times when I was young. They didn't get along. Harry actually seemed to be a nice guy. He tried to get to know me and brought me presents, but she banished him at our father's insistence. He was big and gruff, like you. Highly dominant, too. Lived in the mountains somewhere and dressed like a lumberjack. It's not hard to imagine why dear old dad didn't want him around."

Hunter ground to a halt and sat quietly for a moment. I had the feeling there was a serious question brewing, one he was unsure about asking. He was fidgeting with a twig, twisting it between his fingers in a repeating pattern.

"Just ask me," I said, trying not to sound too gruff.

He glanced at me quickly and fumbled the twig. It dropped to the ground, and he hurriedly picked it up again to re-start the pattern.

"It's kind of personal," he answered, and winced slightly.

"Don't care," I grunted.

"I worried for a long time that Damon would end up feral. Sam seemed on that path when we met him, too," he said. "That first night, I watched you rip a gun turret from a PMV. You seemed more beast than man."

It was more an observation than a question, but I answered anyway. "I was."

"A small part of me always worried it would mean Damon losing his humanity, that he'd attack anyone without provocation, potentially even us. That he'd lose himself. Yet the night we met, you still seemed highly protective and able to determine who was a threat and who wasn't. You didn't come after us when you broke free of the humvee. I guess my real question is, what does it feel like?"

I tilted my head back, resting it on the tree trunk behind us, as I looked up at the sky through the leaves. It wasn't a simple question to answer, yet if I wanted him to really see me, I needed to find a way. I wasn't interested in hiding who I had become.

"I don't know a lot about humanity. It feels like a made up word for a division I'm not sure exists. We had a lot of wildlife around the remote manor I grew up in, wolves, mountain lions, even the occasional bear. I used to watch them out the windows. We call them beasts, yet they only attack to protect their pack or to feed. They have their own rules. They just aren't the same as ours. At our core, I don't really think we're that different. I think the Crash has proved that. Strip away the modern conveniences everyone thinks make us so different, and we'll fight to survive, too. I get that scares people, and they need rules to function. Every creature or pack does, even the ones who hunt alone. But maybe, sometimes, we need to strip everything away in order to grow."

Hunter watched me carefully. I don't think that was the answer he was expecting.

"As for how it feels, I don't feel like my alpha is separate from me. It confuses me when people talk about their beasts as something different from them. I don't have an alpha within me. I am an alpha. Maybe I missed something growing up, not having to fit into society, but I always trust and follow my instincts. I knew you weren't a threat when I broke out of the humvee. It was in your body language, so why would I attack you? My memories got murky while I was in captivity, and I hadn't talked in a long time. It took a while for things to come back when I got out, but I think that was more to do with captivity. My world was so small in that cage, as my dominance grew. It had nowhere to go. I became hyper-focused on my environment, watching the people who came and went in the lab and their mannerisms. Always looking for a weakness I could exploit. I changed, but I don't think it was into a beast. It was just the most basic level of survival. I think my body switched off what it didn't need."

"Wow." Hunter breathed out heavily, his brow creased, deep in thought. "How did you come back?"

"Contact with my pack brings me back to myself. As if it shocks me back into remembering. I focus on them, rather than my survival, and the world opens back up. Until someone threatens one of them." I shrugged my shoulders ruefully, remembering this morning and the way I'd reacted when Damon had reached for Ava with all that coiled tension in his body. It was both as simple and as complicated as that. I wasn't overthinking why. I was just grateful it was true. With time, I was hoping it would get easier. That the damage caused by my captivity wasn't permanent. If not, I'd keep them close. It wouldn't be a hardship.

"Huh," was all he said for a moment, as he thought about my words. "I think Maven has spread a lot of lies over generations, far deeper than we know. I always knew Damon was different and my touch settled him. It worked when Leif and Max touched him, too. I worried for a long time that we wouldn't be enough. It got harder as he got older, but he fought his beast more to fit in, and maybe that was why. He needed more prolonged contact to calm him down, and it wasn't always enough. At least, not until we met Maia. Her touch can instantly pull him out of a spiral."

"Yeah," I grunted. "It works best with Ava and Cary, too."

"Ava and Cary?" he asked. "How's that going to work?"

He wasn't judging. He seemed genuinely curious.

I grinned and raised an eyebrow at him.

He laughed. "I don't mean the sex, man. I mean, omegas are territorial and emotional. How will having two in the pack work?"

I tilted my head and narrowed my eyes at him. "Are Maia, Lexie, and Ava territorial with each other? Are the omegas living in a ballroom together territorial? Or overly emotional?"

"More lies?" he asked as realization dawned. I nodded. "Shit, there's a lot we're going to have to undo, isn't there? They built our entire world on lies."

"I think omegas may get territorial when they meet their mates and aren't claimed yet, but alphas are the same. We just got to write the narrative." That was a whole bigger discussion, though. One we'd have to deal with, eventually. I wanted a different world for omegas, but change wouldn't come quickly, even with the Crash.

"I guess I'm more concerned about Ava and Cary specifically," Hunter said as he deliberately looked off into the distance. "I got to know them the few days they spent at the farm. You and Ava seem tight already, but Cary is a wild card. He keeps himself tightly wound and I suspect he has a lot of scars, the kind you can't see. He's also obsessed with Ava. I don't want to see either of them get hurt."

I felt myself tense at the thought of anyone hurting either of my omegas, and he gave me a quick sideways glance. "All I know is they're both mine, and I will protect them with everything I have. What kind of relationship we have is up to them. I'll be whatever they need."

He nodded and grinned at me as he relaxed. "Fair enough. You passed. But be warned, you won't get off so easy if you get an interrogation from Maia or Lexie. Or worse, both."

I had no problem with that, but my sudden agitation wouldn't settle. I looked up as movement at the front entrance grabbed my attention. Ryder strode purposefully down the front steps and headed straight for us. He eyed Hunter carefully as he approached, but also scanned our surroundings. As soon as he got to me, he crouched at my side and immediately put his hand on my shoulder. I felt my body relax and my tension drained away.

"Everything okay here?" he asked. He made no apology for intruding. I was glad it was Ryder and not River. He may have thrown knives and asked questions later.

"Yep," Hunter answered with a grin, completely unapologetic, too. "I was just asking my brother about his intentions towards two omegas we all seem to care about. You and your twin are scary as shit, by the way, did you know that?"

Ryder seemed surprised, before he burst out laughing. "Oh, you're going to be fun to have around."

Hunter puffed out his chest and tilted his chin back dramatically, like a lizard throwing out its frill to make itself seem larger and scare off a predator. He had an easy humor I liked, but I also sensed an underlying core of steel.

More movement at the entrance had me squinting. I could barely make out Ava hovering in the shadows, just inside. A sudden need to hold her almost took my breath away, and my vision tunneled in on her.

"Go," Hunter said. "We've got time. We don't need to fix everything today."

Ryder stood and pulled me to my feet while Hunter jumped lightly to his beside me. I couldn't pay attention to either of them right now, though. My focus was entirely on Ava. I left them in the dust as I ran towards her. I heard chuckles behind me, but I didn't care.

My omega was waiting for me.

Twenty-Two

I watched River and Cary circling each other warily on the patch of grass we'd chosen as a training field. It was at the back of the Palace, near an old shed, with a few old tyres and ropes stacked up that Cary had used for strength training in the past. The library was behind us, so there shouldn't be anyone watching us out the windows.

We'd found more equipment in a dank room the guards appeared to have used as a gym, including an old punching bag. We'd moved it all outside. The gym had no air circulation or natural light and had smelled of stale alpha sweat. Cary had walked in and instinctively backed straight out again. His eyes had flared wide in panic, putting River and I on guard as we'd swept the room for any danger. Cary was usually so reserved, so seeing his reaction and the raw emotion spilling from him had been startling. He'd shut it down quickly, though. Shook it off and pretended like it had never happened, so we didn't call him on it.

I hated it. Cary was a good guy. He cared about all the omegas at the Palace, not just Ava. I'd been watching him while he watched them all, trying to protect them with stealthy acts no-one else noticed. If any omegas looked uncomfortable with an alpha guard nearby, Cary would physically put himself between them. Even if it made him tense up himself.

I could see that same tension in him now. He'd put himself in this situation to learn how to protect Ava, but he was fighting his own body and instincts to do it. It shamed me he fought so hard for her and I'd spent a decade raging at her loss. Blinded by my pain and unable to see that she'd sacrificed herself for us. I needed to make that up to her, and getting Cary comfortable with us was something I could do to make her life easier. To help get her what she needed. As much as I wanted to do it for his own sake, too.

I knew he would probably be more comfortable with Nick here. But we needed Nick down in the labs right now and River had wanted to do the first session with each of them alone so he could assess their existing strengths. We had started Cary out with stretching exercises to see his range of motion and warm his muscles up. Then we'd moved to some simple boxing repetitions with the punching bag to work on his fist style and rhythm. River now had some sparring pads on his hands and was encouraging him to try what he'd learned on a moving target. He'd taped up Cary's hands, rather than put boxing gloves on him, wanting him to feel the punches and practice getting his fist aligned right. He wouldn't have gloves in a real world fight.

We'd only found one roll of tape, so we'd used it sparingly. It had struck me in the moment just how much the world had changed. Something as simple as sports tape was a finite resource now. We couldn't pop down to the shops for another roll and nobody was making it in factories anymore. We were going to have to improvise a lot of things we'd taken for granted.

I shook off my thoughts and focused on the duo sparring in front of me.

"Can you take your shirt off?" I asked Cary.

He paused with his fists in the air and glared at me suspiciously. "Why?"

I rolled my eyes at him. "Because you're wearing a baggy shirt and I can't see which muscles you're engaging when you punch, or your hip movement. It helps to correct your technique."

He shot a glance at River, who nodded at him. Cary pulled his shirt off in one smooth motion by grabbing it from behind his neck. It was sexy as hell. I was going to have to practice that one. River raised his eyebrow at me and I smirked back at him. He knew me too well.

"Happy?" Cary asked me, with more than a hint of sarcasm. His nerves had him barring his teeth. He'd been more relaxed this morning, after our campfire chat last night. But now he was retreating behind his wall again.

Getting him to knock it down for good was going to take work. I knew it would be worth it, though. Our pack needed him healthy and whole.

"No. I'll be happy when you trust us, but I know we need to earn that," I replied, keeping my voice calm and even, not reacting to his taunt.

He dropped his hands and seemed startled at my honesty.

"Cary, we all want the same thing here," I said. "Plus, you're going to give yourself an injury if you keep trying to spar while you're so tense."

Cary sighed. "Sorry, I get jumpy when alphas are behind me. I know you're here trying to help me, but it makes me feel like prey."

I shook out my fist when I instinctively clenched it, imagining alphas stalking him through the stone corridors of the Palace. "Did you always feel that way while living here?"

"Yeah," he said simply. "I learned to keep a wall at my back as much as possible. The assholes liked to ambush me and take me by surprise. Even if they weren't trying to hurt me, even a back slap would affect me. I could brace myself when I saw it coming, and dodged when I could. But when they took me by surprise, I froze. So they loved doing it. I guess it made them feel powerful or some shit."

"We can help you with that," River said, in a rough voice as he lowered the sparring pads. "When you've got this technique down, we'll work on your situational awareness and quick pivoting. When Nick joins us, we'll also teach you both to fight in formation, keeping each other at your backs."

I was grateful for River stepping in and taking over the conversation when I knew he wasn't great at dealing with people's emotions. He knew I needed a moment to pull myself together. I took a few deep breaths before shifting around to River's side so I wasn't at Cary's back anymore.

"You need to tell us this stuff so we're aware of it," I said. "We don't want to trigger you unintentionally."

"I've never had a team before. It's always been me against the wolves. I'm working on it," he replied with a too-casual shrug.

"You have one now," I added. "Any asshole comes at you, we'll have your back." River nodded in agreement.

Cary sighed and rolled his head on his shoulders, trying to loosen up. "You can stand back behind me, Ryder. Just maybe make some noise. You're too fucking quiet on your feet. I can't tell where you are."

I laughed as I moved around to his side, but stayed in his peripheral vision. River put his pads back up, and they started sparring again. Some of Cary's tension had eased, which was good. His moves were flowing easier.

"Watch your thumb," River warned him. "If it pops out, you're going to break it."

Cary grunted and punched again as River shifted his stance. Cary wasn't throwing a lot of power into his punches yet. We'd started just focusing on technique. Still, his muscles rippling along his sweaty back were distracting.

Neither Wolf or Nick did anything for me physically, but Cary had me intrigued. I didn't make a big deal of being bisexual. I'd never even really talked about it with River. He just knew. It wasn't even that Cary was an omega, and a gorgeous man. He wasn't mine, yet I could appreciate that his body and face were a work of art, with those chiseled planes and dark skin sliding over sleek muscles. I got why alphas at the Palace were fascinated by him. But it was more than that. It was something about Cary himself. His vulnerability and determination, maybe. Everything that shone through his eyes.

The thought of Cary going into heat alongside Ava stirred something in me. So, maybe being an omega was part of it. I couldn't be sure. Cary didn't seem to affect River, though. He'd been clear about how he felt last night.

"How's his form?" River asked suddenly and glanced at me pointedly. *Shit, had I been standing here drooling over Cary? That was not helpful right now.*

"Uh, good. Hit him harder for me on the next one," I mumbled.

Cary gave the pads a harder punch and looked over his taut shoulder at me.

"Can I correct your stance a little? I'm going to need to touch you," I asked.

He nodded, and I approached him slowly. I kicked at the inside of his foot gently. "You need to widen your stance slightly. You've got a wide upper body and a narrow waist, you don't want to overbalance yourself. Most of your power is going to come from your hips and your legs. Your arm is an extension of that."

I stepped back slightly. "Try it again."

He punched, and I watched his hips and legs closely. "Okay, you need to start the punch at your foot. Push off with your heel, then feel that power travel up to your thighs, then your hips as you swivel, until it finally runs up to your arm."

I ran my hand up the outside of his thigh after he pushed off and twisted his hips lightly. "It doesn't need to be a big movement or you'll unbalance yourself again. It's more about controlled power."

I glanced at his face, and his eyes were wide. I was suddenly intensely aware of how close we were standing and the ice-cream scent filling my senses. He was breathing hard, and I wasn't sure if it was the exertion or something else. I stepped away quickly before my body betrayed me, and to give him some room.

"Here, watch me." I demonstrated the motion slowly, starting with my heel. Then sped up and did it a few more times. He nodded at me, but his eyes seemed a little glazed as they traveled over my form.

"Okay, here, try again on the pads," River said, bringing our attention back to him. His face hadn't changed, but I could feel his mirth through our bond. I flipped him the bird behind Cary's back and his lip twitched.

"That's better," River said as Cary hit a punch with a lot more power.

"Yeah. Wow, that really works," Cary said, sounding amazed. He threw a few more, getting more confident with each one.

"Good job," I praised him. "Remember to keep your back straight and don't lean too far forward. You'll leave your chin open to an uppercut."

"You've got good upper body strength, but we need to work on your leg strength a bit more. It will help give you more power," River added.

"I never really thought about my legs," Cary admitted. "I figured it was all about my arms."

I chuckled. "Yeah, most people do. Take a look at Wolf's thighs. It's where a lot of his power comes from."

Cary had been mid-punch, but he faltered and almost missed. River grinned at him. "Asshole," Cary grumbled, but he didn't seem mad. He'd relaxed a lot.

I couldn't wait to get him started in martial arts. He had a natural grace to his body that would work well, but it took time to learn. These boxing lessons would help him immediately.

A movement in my periphery had me on alert. Someone was watching us. I shifted my body slightly, as if I was examining Cary from a different angle, and watched the building behind River. He glanced at me and narrowed his eyes, but kept sparring.

A moment later, I caught sight of the culprit. I subtly gestured to River to keep going and ran silently up to the corner of the building. As soon as the head peeked around again, I roared and grabbed at the little blonde escapee. Angel squealed in delight and threw her arms around me. We really needed to teach her about stranger danger.

"Got you," I said. "Who is supposed to be watching you right now?"

She just shrugged unconcerned, as if it wasn't her problem.

Cary came up behind me and tickled her. "Ew," she squealed in laughter. "You're sweaty."

"I think that's enough for now, anyway. We don't want to overdo it or you'll be too sore for more tomorrow," River said. "Let's head back up to the kitchen and figure out where this little ninja is supposed to be."

"Can I have a cookie?" She asked, all big pleading eyes.

"I don't know if we have any, but we'll figure something out," Cary said with a grin.

I tried to put her down, but she clung to my neck like a baby monkey. I guess I was carrying her. It didn't bother me. I'd never been around kids much, but I liked the feel of her snuggled into me. She was so trusting and sweet. The thought of her being raised at the Palace made me feel ill.

I looked across at River, and he nodded. We needed to figure out who Angel was, and why the Palace had her.

I almost ran into Ava as I rounded the corner of the building. She looked frantic.

"There you are," she cried in relief. "Emma lost you. We were worried, Angel."

"We found her spying on us," Cary told her.

Ava sighed in exasperation and reached for her, but Angel only clung to me tighter.

"It's okay, we're coming in. I'll bring her." The intense look of longing in Ava's eyes as she looked between Angel and me had my heart galloping wildly.

Did she want kids? It wasn't something we'd ever talked about growing up, but the look in her eyes reminded me of the vision I'd had the night she presented. The moment I'd known she was mine, beyond being my best friend, it had hit me. A vision of our future together, a family we made. I would do anything to see it come to life. When she'd disappeared, it had been the loss of our future, the one I could see so clearly, that wrecked me. Beyond even the pain of the fractured bond.

I could see it again now, the vision of our family, only it had gotten a little bigger. And that was okay with me.

I just needed to do everything in my power to make it happen.

Twenty-Three

Ava

I'd shooed the guys away to go have showers as soon as we got back to the kitchen. I didn't need sweaty, pheromone soaked alphas distracting everyone. River and Cary had complied, but Ryder had announced he was going to run the fence line first and Wolf had gone with him.

Wolf had stuck to me like glazing on a doughnut since he'd come back inside earlier, after his chat with Hunter. I hadn't minded. I'd sensed how much he'd needed the contact and the quiet after the revelations and emotions of the morning. So I'd sat cuddling with him while River, Ryder, and Cary had trained, relying on Maia and Lexie to take over in the kitchen for a while. A run with Ryder now would do him even more good.

Angel had demanded a hug from each of my guys before they left, and they'd complied with indulgent smiles, even River. She was a definite handful. I kept a close eye on her now while she sat propped on a counter, munching on one of the last protein bars and sipping on a glass of milk. It was the closest thing we could find to a cookie. Not being able to give her one broke my heart. I knew it was irrational given how much suffering there was in the world right now, but my instincts were screaming at me to provide for her, and I couldn't. Not in the way she deserved. She was a little kid; a cookie wasn't too much to ask for.

She'd looked at the protein bar with disappointment, but hadn't complained. She shouldn't know about rationing and food shortages, or sleeping on group beds in a room filled with women for safety. Yet her quick acceptance made me think of the kids out there right now who had nothing to eat at all.

"You okay?" Emma asked me.

"Yeah," I said, putting on my big girl pants as I turned to her. We had things to do. There were half a dozen omegas I'd gathered earlier, now standing awkwardly around the kitchen, looking lost. The Palace hadn't taught us how to cook, or do anything useful, and it made me angry. They'd deliberately kept us subservient and helpless. That changed now. I'd asked the older omegas if anyone wanted cooking lessons and I'd felt heartened, if not a little overwhelmed, when most of them had volunteered. I'd had to create groups to rotate through at each meal, because we could only fit so many people in the kitchen at once.

The others were going to start on learning other essential things, like how to do laundry. This was the first group coming through the kitchen and we were starting with the basics, considering most didn't even know how to boil water. Including me. I only knew scrambled eggs so far.

Emma had figured out a basic porridge this morning, with help from Miles and Owen. Then Lexie and Maia had taught us how to make our own bread. My friends had figured they may as well make themselves useful while keeping Maia at a safe distance until the guys worked out the devices. The bread had not long come out of the oven, and the kitchen smelled delicious. Lexie had brought several enormous jars of home-made jam with her, and I couldn't wait to taste it.

I divided up the omegas and got half working on making jam sandwiches to feed everyone for lunch. While the other half started chopping vegetables to get tonight's stew going. Lexie watched them carefully to make sure no-one hurt themselves.

"Teaching people how to cook from scratch and grow their own food is going to be important going forward, isn't it?" Emma asked me quietly. "We're lucky you and Maia found these guys, or we'd be starving right now." We both knew there were even worse things that could have happened to these omegas, but we chose not to talk about it with little ears so close.

"Yeah. I know Lexie's been thinking about it a lot, how to teach more people what they know. Freeing the town and rescuing us was just the first step. It's an enormous task to take on and there are so many people who need help."

"She doesn't have to do it all, though. It will have a ripple effect, surely, if she asks everyone she teaches to pass the knowledge on. She just needs a place to start." Emma seemed excited by the idea, and her cheeks flushed red at talking so boldly. She'd dressed down in leggings and a t-shirt again today, and she had flour in her hair. I thought she'd never looked so beautiful.

"That's an interesting idea. I'll talk to Lexie about it." Emma was really coming out of her shell and stepping up to take care of the other omegas, and I wanted to encourage her new confidence. It gave me hope that the Palace hadn't completely broken us all.

"Talk to me about what?" Lexie asked, from right behind me, making me jump. She chuckled darkly.

"Emma just made a good point," I said, before I explained Emma's idea.

"Yeah, I've been thinking about that, too," she said, as she picked up a knife and started spreading jam on the bread slices I had just cut. "I was hoping the farm would be our starting place. That we could have people come and stay in the unused guest cabins and teach them, then send them back out into the world to put it into practice. But inviting strangers into the same place where our major food supply is doesn't make good sense from a security perspective."

"Does it have to be the farm?" Emma asked, a little haltingly, when I nodded at her in encouragement.

"No. Why? What are you thinking?" Lexie replied, subtly prompting Emma to talk more. Emma seemed nervous around Lexie, which I understood. Lexie was feisty and fearless, everything we'd been taught not to be. She'd done the same thing with me when I'd met her, gently prompted me, and I adored her for it. Even with Lexie's encouragement, it had taken me a few days to get up the nerve to approach her and talk freely with her. I'd surprised myself the first time I'd done it.

"Well, uh, what about here?" Emma waved her hand in the air. "This place has power, yet it's mostly empty now. There were far more staff here than omegas, and there's a lot of land surrounding it. I don't know if it's suitable for farming, but if you could help us figure it out, we could set up something on a smaller scale than what you have at the farm. They built the Palace to be secure and withstand attack. If we asked the first students to help with the manual labor to set it up while learning, everyone would get something out of it."

Lexie tilted her head as she watched Emma closely. "It's a brilliant spot, because we're close enough to give you support, and the town would benefit too, from people traveling to the area. We could set up a trading post there. The biggest issue would be to figure out the water supply, because you're not on the river here. But would you be happy to stay here? Would the other omegas? Given what you've endured and survived here? That's the first thing we need to figure out."

Cary slid in behind me, freshly showered, and wrapped his arms around my waist. The temperature in the room instantly rose by five degrees. "Omegas need to take back their power. It's time for us to stop hiding in the shadows and step into the light. We just need a starting point, too," he said.

"I love that," Emma said as she beamed at him.

I tried really hard to tamp down my instant jealousy. Yet an itchy and uncomfortable feeling rose in its place. Emma must have seen the look on my face, because she quickly looked away. I felt bad because I didn't really think anything was happening between them. The surge of irrational emotion just had me rattled, and I couldn't figure out why it was happening. *Was it because I'd met my pack but we hadn't claimed each other yet?*

I'd embraced my omega a long time ago, but I'd never felt mood swings like this. Cary nuzzled his face in my hair before he kissed my cheek lightly, an attempt to ease my surging emotions by marking me with his scent. But it had the opposite effect. It heated me up even further.

"The other issue is security," he said smoothly. "They built this place strong, but you'd still need help to defend it. And with omegas inside, a power supply, and a food source, it will be an attractive target."

Emma frowned as she thought it through. "I know you're right, but nothing worth doing is ever easy, or so my mother used to say."

A quiet voice came from the other side of Emma, so soft I barely heard it. "There's an underground stream that runs through the conservatory pool. We could start by converting the conservatory gardens into edible foods. We had one at home, growing up. It would be more secure than starting outside." The voice came from an omega who was only slightly younger than Emma, but was currently half hiding beside her. She'd been determined to help when I'd asked earlier, even though her hand had trembled as she'd raised it.

"There is? That sounds perfect. What's your name, honey? I'm Lexie."

"Rose," she mumbled, keeping her eyes on the sandwich she was cutting, before flicking a quick, curious glance in Lexie's direction.

"You did great speaking up, Rose," Lexie told her encouragingly. "You both need to talk to the other omegas and see what they think. I suspect some will want to leave, maybe even try to find their families, and we may need to move the youngest omegas out, but I hope the others will want to stay. Your ideas are exactly what we need, and I'll back you if you decide you want to move forward with it."

It wasn't a small offer, Lexie could get the impossible done when she put her mind to it. She was so protective of other women, especially ones who had suffered abuse in any way. Her generous spirit and her kindness always leaked out past her tough exterior. Her brothers always paid attention and got involved in every scheme she thought up. I imagined her new pack would, too. Emma shot a sweet smile at Lexie, and I could almost see Lexie plotting out the ways she could help them both, not only to implement their ideas, but to stand strong.

"What about you, Ava? Would you want to stay here permanently?" Cary asked me quietly. I could see Lexie glance at me with worried eyes.

I focused on spreading jam for a moment as I thought it over. "No. Once we get the omegas safely set up, if I could choose to live anywhere, it would be closer to the farm. I want to be near my friends."

It was what I wanted, but I was also thinking about Wolf. I don't think staying here would be good for him. Lexie punched me lightly on the shoulder before giving me a bruising hug. Almost muscling Cary out of the way. He just nodded to me in agreement, with a small smile, and went to see if he could help with the vegetables. Rose followed him now that the sandwiches were almost done.

"You had me scared, you witch. And you won't be living near the farm. You'll be living on the farm if Maia and I have any say about it," Lexie said, sounding a little choked up. "If Hunter, Wolf, and Sam are brothers, and you're Wolf's mate, that makes you family. And I couldn't be happier about that. Maia feels the same. We've decided we're sisters now."

I nodded, feeling emotional myself. I'd never had sisters before. Nicole ruined the sweet moment, though, when she sauntered into the room.

"Is lunch not ready yet?" she asked, giving Lexie and me a quick once over, before dismissing us as unimportant. Lexie raised her eyebrow at me as she pulled back, and I subtly shook my head at her. We didn't need a scene right now. There had been a lot of quiet chatting in the room between the omegas as we worked, but everyone was silent now.

Emma just sighed, but didn't rise to the bait. "No."

It was actually almost ready, but Emma didn't seem inclined to tell her that. Nicole glanced around the room, looking for a reason not to help. "That's fine. I'll take Angel to the library for a little while, so she won't be in the way."

I was instantly suspicious. She'd shown no interest in Angel until now. Before I could say anything, Nicole marched over to Angel and picked her up off the bench. She grimaced as crumbs fell over her pale pink satin shift dress. "Do you want to come to the library with me and read some books?"

Angel shrugged. She was bored, and she loved to read, but she didn't like Nicole.

"Here, take this with you, Angel, for the road," Emma said as she winked at the little girl and put half a jam sandwich in each of her hands.

Nicole turned on her heel with a huff, but seemed to bite her tongue as she headed back out into the hallway.

"Are we really okay with Nicole watching Angel?" I asked Emma. She wasn't my daughter, but we didn't know who or where Angel's parents were. So we were all she had. A few of us had been taking turns watching her, but Nicole had never volunteered before. "I don't see that ending well. She'll probably dump her somewhere in five minutes."

Emma just smiled enigmatically. "It will be worth having to hunt Angel down again, just to see Nicole's dress covered in strawberry jam."

Lexie and I both burst out laughing. "I take it we hate her?" she asked.

Emma and I both nodded vigorously. I loved that Lexie used 'we' and was immediately in on our shenanigans. She was a loyal friend. Maia looked up from across the room at our laughter. I couldn't help but notice how tired she looked. Leif was hovering beside her anxiously.

"I think we've got this covered now," I said quietly to Lexie. "Do you think you could convince Maia to take a nap in one of the guest rooms? She looks beat."

Lexie sobered up quickly and squeezed my arm. "Yeah, I can do that. Leif and I are on it. Then I might grab Pala and see if he can give me a tour." She winked at me as she headed off, and I figured I knew what she would really get up to if she could get Pala into a dark, secluded space. It gave me an idea.

"Okay, make good choices." I called out to her. She waved at me over her shoulder.

"You're different. In a good way," Emma said, as she looked between Lexie's retreating back and me.

"Oh," I said, surprised.

Emma blushed, as if she hadn't meant to say that out loud. "Yeah, I just mean, you were this perfectly poised princess. Yet you always stayed in the background, never standing out. Until the Crash. Then you turned into a warrior princess, hiding out, escaping, then coming back here to save us all. It was like a mask slipped away. You're inspiring. You give me hope we can all be something different now."

I felt equally flattered and stunned at the way she saw me. I wasn't sure I'd earned it, or wanted it. Being seen at the forefront of anything didn't interest me. Even as a kid, I'd preferred to let other people stand out while I quietly worked in the background. That part of my Palace princess routine hadn't been an act. There just weren't many people stepping forward to help right now, outside of our friends, and they could only do so much.

Yet Emma was echoing my thoughts from earlier, at seeing her come out of her shell. Hope wasn't something I would begrudge anyone. I leaned over and hugged her impulsively. "I'm no warrior princess, that's Lexie and Maia. We all just did what we had to, to survive this place. Now we need to figure out who we are and how we're going to survive in this new world. Together."

"You may not think you're like Lexie and Maia, but you are. Or at least, you are to us. I'm not the only one who thinks it, or the only one you've inspired." Emma's eyes looked slightly glassy, but she gave me a determined smile before she focused back on the task at hand. "Let's get these sandwiches onto platters and into the dining room. It will keep the kitchen clear for everyone still prepping dinner."

"Great idea," I said, happy she'd changed the subject. I didn't know what to do with her praise, so I focused on what was in front of us, too. We'd deal with one thing at a time. That was all we could do right now.

I looked at the growing pile of delicious smelling sandwiches we piled onto the platters Emma grabbed. Feeling strangely content to be preparing food for people I cared about. It was such a simple thing, but something I'd longed to do. *Is it weird that I'm insanely proud of a pile of sandwiches?*

I watched as everyone made their way through the dining room. River was back and he and Cary grabbed a plate each, and an extra for Ryder and Wolf when they got back, then sat down to eat together. Watching them eat my sandwiches with gusto put a smile on my face. I waited until everyone had eaten enough, before I shoved a sandwich in my mouth and piled a few more on two plates. It wasn't polite, decorous, omega behavior, but I no longer cared. Not that I ever really had. I was a farm girl at heart and I couldn't wait to get to know that girl again. I was tired of waiting patiently for my life to start. So, I was going to own what I wanted. I'd just do it quietly. Maybe there was a little warrior princess in me, after all.

In the meantime, we were missing two betas holed up downstairs, and I had plans for one of them.

Twenty-Four

I didn't know how long I'd been down in the labs when the scent of cherries broke my concentration, and I startled. I spun around in my chair to see Ava leaning in the doorway, watching me.

"How long have you been there?"

"Not that long," she said with a small smile. She looked as if she wanted to come in but had suddenly lost her nerve.

"Where are the others?"

"Oh, Maia was tired, so she's having a nap. Lexie wanted to explore. She's never been here before, so Pala went with her. They're probably having a quickie somewhere."

I almost groaned. Ava was so innocent. She had no idea what her talking about a quickie did to me. I was uncomfortably hard instantly. Even if she was talking about someone else.

"I meant your shadows," I said, as I tried to shift and discreetly adjust myself.

"Oh. I might have given them the slip." Her blush was adorable. Everything about her was perfect. Her long dark hair was back up in a bun today, and I had the craziest urge to pull it apart and get her all messed up. This was the first time I'd ever been alone with her, without Cary or another omega with her. I suddenly felt flustered as we stared at each other. Neither one of us said anything more.

I was so ridiculously into her. It wouldn't have surprised me if I'd looked up to see a giant neon sign over my head that read, *I heart Ava*. Yet she'd seemed completely unaware until I'd heard her talking yesterday morning. I still wasn't sure if she knew I was into her, even though I'd heard her admit her feelings for me.

Watching her blindly run past me, with tears streaming down her face yesterday, had caused me physical pain. Like someone had yanked hard on something inside me. Getting to sleep with her last night, when she'd finally crashed, had helped ease it. I'd spent a long time just watching her breathe softly in the moonlight.

I finally noticed the tray with two plates and two glasses of juice in her hands. She seemed to startle as my eyes landed on it, almost as if she'd forgotten she was holding it.

"You missed lunch. So I brought you some down." She was still standing in the doorway, so I gestured for her to come in. She squared her shoulders as she came through, and her lips were moving slightly, as if she was giving herself a pep talk. *Was she nervous about being down here with me? Or was it this room?*

"If you're busy, I can just drop it and leave you alone. I have some for Max, too," she said, but her eyes seemed to beg me to let her stay.

"No, no, come in. Stay with me for a bit. Please." If she had sought me out, she had my complete attention. I wasn't passing up this opportunity. I jumped up and grabbed a chair, then dragged it over near mine. Like an eager puppy dragging over a toy just so their favorite person would play with them. I needed to find some chill before she realized what a ridiculous dork I was. "I meant to tell you earlier that I still have the satellite phone Dave gave you. Do you want it back?"

"No, it's okay," she said as she shifted some folders aside to put the tray on the desk. "We only have a few of them. The girls are here now, and if Dave calls and Max doesn't answer his pack's phone, he'll probably try to reach you."

"I think Damon took their phone when he saw Max getting hyper focused on the device downstairs. But Damon's not doing much better with how he's obsessively watching Maia. So your point stands. Talking of Max, pass me his lunch and I'll run it down to him. That way you can stay longer." She passed over a plate and a glass as I hopped back up, but I stopped halfway out the door.

"You're staying, right? You won't disappear on me?" She nodded. So I bolted out the door. I was back in minutes, panting slightly. I'd practically thrown the sandwich at Max. He'd hardly noticed.

As I collapsed in my chair, she passed over the other plate. I grabbed it and started munching on the sandwich. "This is so good, thank you."

"It's just a jam sandwich," she laughed.

I shrugged. "Yeah, but you brought it."

That brought a pleased little smile to her face. I wanted more of those. But there was something else on my mind, too.

"Have you seen Wolf? Do you know how he's doing after his conversation with Hunter earlier?"

"River told me about that. I went looking for Wolf as soon as I heard and cuddled with him for a while. He seemed introspective and quiet, but I think he's okay. He's gone to run the fence line with Ryder. Those two seem to have developed a bromance while they were gone yesterday."

"Yeah, I noticed that too. It's a good thing."

"I agree. It's just a little weird seeing River and Ryder not joined at the hip. It might seem as if they still are, but I can see a distance there. They were almost like one person growing up. They were never more than a few metres apart. I'm worried what I did has somehow come between them."

She gnawed on her lip and I had to fight not to reach out and pull her lip free, then kiss it better. I kept a firm grip on my plate instead. "Ava, don't take that on board. You can't be responsible for someone else's relationship. Especially a sibling one. I talked to them this morning and they're figuring it out. From what I heard, you did what you had to in order to keep you all alive. I think they both know that, even if they processed it differently."

"I know. It just feels like it broke something in each of us."

"I don't think anything got broken, just maybe a little bruised. It seems like they've been fighting to get back to you for a long time. It makes sense that a lot of stuff you've all pushed down is going to come up now. Just give it time and don't give up on them."

She puffed out a heavy breath, then smiled sweetly at me. She seemed suddenly lighter, and my chest swelled at the idea that maybe I'd helped her. Even just a little.

"Thanks, Nick. You're so easy to talk to. Are you sure me being here is okay? I don't want to bother you if you're busy."

"Are you kidding me? Come find me anytime you want to talk. You could never be a bother, Ava."

Her eyes widened, and I put the plate down. I gulped some juice, wishing it had a shot of tequila in it for liquid courage.

I was going to shoot my shot. Her pack was forming quickly around her. As much as I craved being a part of it, I needed her to know that who she included in her pack was her decision, and she had options. She hadn't had many in her life. At least, not since she'd presented as an omega. It was important to me she had one now.

"Ava," I swallowed hard. "I don't know if you've noticed, but I really like you. And I don't mean in a 'you're a cool chick' kind of way. I mean, I have deep feelings for you. I know it's fast, but this isn't complicated for me. What I feel for you, it's the simplest, most pure thing I've ever felt in my life. I've felt it since the first moment I saw you."

I remembered that night. She hadn't seen me. Lexie had been taking her and Cary to a cabin the night they'd arrived at the farm. I'd watched on the monitors with Maia and Max earlier as the guys had rescued them, but hadn't been able to see much. Standing in the shadows as she passed, seeing her in person had knocked the breath from my lungs.

She'd been dirty and looked exhausted, like a neglected ballerina doll someone had left at the playground. Yet she'd walked with her head high, with so much poise and dignity. Her pale skin had practically glowed in the moonlight. Cary had been a dark, wrathful, fallen angel at her side.

I'd wanted so badly to reach out to her, knowing instantly I wanted to be the one to look out for her, care for her. Make sure she had everything she needed. But she'd been there and gone again in a moment while I was still figuring out how to breathe again.

I reached out to her now, as I grabbed her hand and pulled it gently into mine. It felt so right to wrap my long fingers around her delicate ones. Even if mine were shaking a little.

"If you need time, though, if you need to work through things with the others. Even if you want to check out your options. That's okay. You're allowed to make choices and feel out what's right for you. There are a lot of really great guys living on the farm, and I know a few in town, too. Any of them would count themselves lucky to spend some time with you. I just want you to know I'm an option. One that's really, desperately, into you."

Ava moved swiftly and before I knew what was happening; she was sitting across my lap and her arms were around my neck. She was breathing hard and looked me directly in the eyes. I could get lost in that star flecked sea of green, as her cherry scent enveloped me.

"Nick," she breathed my name, as if it meant something to her. "I really like you, too. Everything else in my life is so complicated right now, but not you. You're the sweetest, most perfect gift."

I breathed out, heavily. But I couldn't wipe off the enormous grin that spread across my face.

"Can I take you on a date sometime soon?" I asked her. "On a picnic or something?"

"I've never been on a date. I'd love that." She squirmed on my lap until she stilled suddenly and a serious look crossed her face. "Are you going to wait for our date to kiss me, though? Because if you are, I'd like to have the date now, please."

She was so cute, asking politely for what she wanted. I gave her a grin I was sure looked goofy as hell, but on the inside I was jumping around and punching the air.

"I just have to do one thing first." She scrunched up her nose and looked adorably confused, as I reached up and tugged the scrunchie out of her hair. The long brown strands fell in waves over my hands and down her back. I almost shuddered at the silky feel of it. I leaned forward slightly and breathed deeply. Her scent didn't affect me the same way it did her alpha mates, but it still had me spinning. Her hair smelled of her natural cherry scent, with a layer of vanilla. Either she had a vanilla shampoo, or Cary had been nuzzling it. I figured it was probably the latter, and I found I didn't mind at all.

I glanced at her. She had one eyebrow raised and a small smile on her face. I swallowed hard and shifted back slightly so I could caress her face. Her skin was so soft as she leaned into my touch, rubbing her cheek on my hand like a cat. I ran my hand back up under her hair and pulled her slowly towards me. Savoring every moment of this, because I knew it would become branded on my brain forever.

She closed her eyes and sighed softly, as her mouth parted slightly. I couldn't hold back anymore. I lowered my head and kissed her tenderly. Her lips tasted the same as her scent. My groan echoed in my head as she opened her lips wider, and her tongue flicked out, licking over my lip. I lost it, as I pulled her harder into me and kissed her with abandon. Her hands ran through my hair before she tugged on it. I almost dragged her up onto the table as the sensation rocked me, but I held myself back.

I don't know how long we kissed for. It could have been minutes or days before we finally pulled apart, both of us struggling to draw a breath.

"Wow," she whispered in that soft voice that drove me wild. Her lips were plump and swollen, and her hair was gorgeously tousled from my hands. She had a satisfied smile and looked pleased with herself.

"Yeah," I mumbled, my brain offline for the moment. I reached up and smoothed down her hair for her.

"Don't worry, I can fix it," she said, a little breathlessly, as she grabbed the scrunchie off my desk where I'd dropped it and forgotten it instantly. I kinda didn't want her to.

"Can I do it?" I asked, trying not to sound too eager. The next best thing to leaving it down would be to fix it myself.

"Uh, sure," she said as she swiveled around on my lap.

Great, she probably thought I was some kind of weirdo now. I ran my fingers through it to get it back into some kind of order. Then I pulled it up high on her head and wove it around, before I twisted the large scrunchie in place to make a messy bun. I even put Ryder's slightly wilted flower back in. It wasn't as neat as it was earlier, without a brush, but it would do.

She leaned forward and looked at her reflection in a dark monitor. "You're good at that."

"I have nieces," I laughed. I also often volunteered at the informal childcare cabin at the farm to give the mums a break. So I was used to fixing ponytails and buns. I didn't tell her that, though.

"What other skills do you have that I don't know about?"

I just shrugged, feeling a little embarrassed. It wasn't a skill, but I loved to take care of people. I had a big extended family, and everyone was noisily up in each other's business. I loved them dearly, but I'd always felt a little lost amongst them. None of them needed me. Which is why I'd been so happy when Max had taken me under his wing and started teaching me what he knew about tech. It had felt like a way to help. To be a useful part of something.

Then Cary and Ava had come along. They had both looked so lost at the farm at first; it had been a pleasure to help settle them in. I think I'd gotten more out of showing them around, and getting them the things they'd needed, than they had. Now, meeting their alphas, it was clear they needed this pack. If I was honest, I did too.

I must have zoned out, because Ava gave me a quick kiss on the cheek before she hopped up off my lap. I missed the feel of her instantly. Now that I'd tasted her, I was a junkie. I wanted another hit.

"I'm going to let you get back to it. I know what you're doing here is important."

She had it wrong. She was the most important thing in the world to me. "I'd rather kiss you all afternoon," I blurted out, and that blush stole across her cheeks again. I wondered what she'd look like laid out naked on a bed, if she'd blush the same way while I ate her out. *Get a grip, man.*

I'd never felt so much overwhelming desire for another person before, as if someone had hijacked my brain. *Well, maybe not my brain.*

"Another day," she said, as she backed out of the room. She blew me a sweet kiss, and I caught it, before I pressed my hand against my chest and grinned like an idiot.

Only when she turned in the doorway and stepped out, she jumped and gave a startled scream.

I was out of my chair instantly and across the room in a heartbeat.

Twenty-Five

Before my startled scream had even faded into silence, there was a loud metallic screech and a crash behind me. Nick was suddenly pulling me back through the door and behind him, as he brandished a switchblade at the darkness shadowing the hallway. I had no idea where he'd gotten it from. It wasn't something I'd ever expected to see him holding. Although I already knew he was reckless about his own safety if he thought he could help someone.

"Glad to see you're putting my courting gift to good use," River said to Nick, in a voice as dry as the desert. He was crouched low against the wall opposite the door, in a patch of shadow between the lights from the doorways.

Courting gift? What the hell was he talking about? I breathed heavily as I tried to calm my nerves and make sense of what was going on in front of me.

"Was this a test?" Nick asked as he carefully closed the knife and slid it into his back pocket. I didn't know why that was so damn hot. Maybe because it drew my attention to the delectable curves of his butt. Nick could wear the hell out of a pair of jeans.

"No," River said, humor lacing his voice. My eyes slid back to him, and he shot me a wicked grin.

"Then what are you doing there?" I asked River, more than a little breathless as he rose from his crouch in one long, fluid movement and stepped towards us.

"I saw you try to sneak off and followed you." He was completely unapologetic. So much for giving them the slip. *Had he been here the whole time?* "Shall I walk you back?"

He held out his hand to me, a flicker of vulnerability sparking in his eyes. I recalled the last time we'd been in a darkened hallway together, less than a day ago. It had gone a different way than I'd hoped. My breath caught as I stepped around Nick and up to River, feeling his tension ease as I took his outstretched hand. I didn't blame him for being the bearer of bad news yesterday. I was glad it had come from him, and not from a stranger. Although, I suddenly felt bad for the way I had run from him. It hadn't been him I was running from, more the walls and the Palace itself.

"Bye, Nick," River said, his eyes still on me.

Shoot. I was completely ignoring the man I'd just been kissing because another one had dazzled me. I really needed to figure out this multiple men thing.

"Uh, bye, Nick," I said as I gave him a smile over my shoulder

"For now," he said as he winked at me and turned to walk back through the door. He didn't seem the slightest bit upset, which had me relaxing.

River was quiet as he pulled me closer to his side and led me toward the stairs leading up to the main level. He gestured me ahead of him when we reached the bottom, but kept hold of my hand. I got halfway up before I spun around and halted him in place with my free hand on his chest. His heart beat frantically beneath the fabric of his shirt, and the heat of his skin warmed my chilled hand. I wasn't sure what I wanted to say. Or if there even was anything to say. I just needed a moment with him. Needed to breathe him in after missing him for so long.

He was a step below me, but he was so tall, it put us almost at the same height. He searched my face silently, tracing my features, until his gaze landed on my lips.

"My little bird," he whispered, almost like a prayer. "Do you have any idea what it does to me to see you mussed up and your lips swollen from kissing?"

"Not so little anymore," I said, breathlessly, as I released his hand. I ran my fingers across his hip and up his stomach to join my other hand on his chest, before I traced a slow path up to his shoulders and wrapped my arms around his neck. It was a dream to be touching him so deliberately. Everything felt hazy as my movements pulled him closer to me. His hands instantly grabbed onto my waist, and the heat felt like a brand against my skin. Goosebumps rippled up my sides as he traced slow circles with his thumb. "Does it bother you? Knowing I was just kissing Nick?"

"No. I like you being ours. As long as you're mine, too. Are you mine, little bird?" he asked. The burning need in his voice almost had my knees buckling as heat raced through me.

"Always, River." His eyes darkened and his lips parted on a breath. His body may have changed since I knew him, but his eyes were the same. Unfamiliar emotions were reflected in them now, but it was still River looking back at me. He'd always had a determined glint, but now there was a new hardness. It slowly disappeared whenever he looked at me, though. The blazing desire was new too, but I didn't mind that at all.

He was too still, as if he was waiting for me to make a move. I swayed towards him, and my breath hitched in my chest as it grazed his.

"There you are," came Lexie's voice from the top of the stairs. "Why are you hiding out here…oh. Crap on a cracker."

A dark chuckle came from behind her that sounded like Sam, as River growled low in his chest.

"Sorry, we were looking for Angel. We'll go. Carry on," Lexie said in a rush. "Come on, you little sprite." I could hear muffled giggling.

"Actually, I was looking for you, too, River. Damon needs to talk to you about security," Sam called down. "I contacted the Network, and they asked us to send some men into the mountains to rescue their stranded leader. We're the closest unit, so we've already sent three of our alphas who were in town. It will leave the town, and possibly the farm, exposed though. We may need to pull some guys from here tonight."

I could see the frustration and conflict in River's eyes. He wanted to help sort out security, make sure we were safe. Yet he also wanted to stay with me.

"I'm not going anywhere," I whispered. "We can finish this later."

"I'm going to come for you, if you don't find me first," he said, on a low growl that skittered over my skin. It was pure, potent, alpha and had me shivering.

I had no words, as he leaned forward and grazed his lips over my cheek. His lips left a burning trail across my skin before he pulled away too quickly and led me up the stairs. His expression was murderous as he let me go and glared at Sam, getting up in his space and forcing him back slightly. "Let's go. If I have to, so do you."

Sam was undaunted, but he backed away from the top of the stairs with a confused frown on his face. "Will you two promise not to get up to too much mischief while we're gone?" he asked Lexie, who was just outside the door, with a firm grip on Angel.

"Nope. It would just be a lie," Lexie sassed, and he growled at her in exasperation, but he couldn't help his smile popping through either.

As soon as they were gone, Lexie whirled on me. "I'm so sorry."

I slapped her on the arm, harder than I meant to. "That's twice," I growled.

"Ow, okay. Manners," she sniffed and rubbed her arm as if she was some kind of delicate waif. Which she wasn't. She could take me down right now if she wanted. "Did you at least get to kiss him properly before we interrupted?"

"No. We didn't get that far," I huffed.

"Ew, kissing is gross," Angel said with a pout.

"Good, no kissing boys for you," Lexie said to Angel, before turning back to me, undaunted, and looking me over. I could see questions brimming in her eyes.

I crouched down to Angel's height, trying to fend off Lexie for the moment. "Who are you supposed to be with?"

"Nicole, but she dumped me straight in the library and took off. She's mean. She said she was going to get someone who wanted to meet me, but she never came back. So I came looking for you."

Who would want to meet Angel? Everyone here already knew her, as far as I was aware. I couldn't focus on that right now, though.

"Are you mad? You look flushed," Angel said, quieter than I'd ever heard her.

"Not with you, Angel," I said, as I pulled her into me and hugged her tightly. "I need to talk to Lexie right now, though, so is it okay if we find someone else to hang out with you? Who do you want to hang out with?"

She looked a little lost, and I suddenly felt bad that she was being shunted around between people. She needed some consistency. "Emma, or maybe Rose, she draws with me and lets me brush her hair."

As luck would have it, I spied Rose walking past the end of the corridor, headed towards the kitchens again. "Uh, Rose," I called out. She popped her head around the corner, looking nervous, but her polite smile softened when she saw Angel. "Could you look after Angel for a while?"

"Absolutely. Come on, sweetness. I was looking for you before. I found some paints. Want to paint on the walls with me? We're going to make a mural."

Angel's face lit up instantly. "Yeah. Yeah. I want to paint on the walls." She let go of my hand and ran to Rose. I mouthed thank you and she nodded at me.

As soon as I stood up. Lexie grinned wickedly at me with a glint in her eye.

"I wanted to know who's been kissing you. Angel was right. You're flushed."

"Nick." There was no point trying to hide anything from Lexie.

Lexie's eyes lit up brighter than a Christmas tree. "Now we're talking. I need details."

"Actually, I think we need Maia for this, too. I have questions."

"Questions? What about?"

"Uh, logistics?"

"As in catering? Or security?" Lexie had her pert nose scrunched up, but she grabbed my arm and pulled me through the short corridor, the same way the guys had just gone. "Because the guys will handle that for now, and they won't let anyone in here. I'll check in on them soon and get a debrief."

"No," I almost growled. My blood was boiling, and I didn't feel like myself. "As in sex with five men logistics, Lexie."

She whirled as we crossed the marbled entry foyer and slapped her hand over my mouth. Her laughter echoed in the open space. "Okay, you don't have to yell. I get it. I just wanted to hear you say it."

I rolled my eyes and mumbled profanities that I'd never, ever uttered before. But it didn't matter because her hand muffled the sound. She suddenly stilled, though, and her expression changed to one of concern. She moved her hand up to my forehead.

"Are you feeling okay? You're hot."

"No, Lexie. I don't feel okay," I hissed. My skin felt so itchy, and my calm was seeping out of my pores along with my sweat. I felt half wild.

"Okay, we don't have a doctor here, but if we call the farm, we can get Luis on the line. Do you have a sore throat, any pain anywhere?"

"I don't think it's the fever kind of hot, Lexie." I suspected what was wrong with me, but it was too soon. Far too soon.

"It's not...oh. OH. Shit. It can't be. It's too soon."

"I know," I growled, feeling like there was an echo in my head. I needed more time. To establish bonds, get my guys acquainted with each other better, and to figure out how to actually do this. I had the worst feeling of déjà vu from the night I presented, that the timing was terrible and everything was about to go horribly wrong. Again.

"That explains why River was so growly and practically shoving into Sam just now. He would have been reacting instinctively to your oncoming heat and another alpha getting too close." It probably explained why he'd tracked me to the lab as well.

"This isn't fair to Nick, Lexie. We only just met, and he's a beta. They're not driven by instincts the way alphas and omegas are. You'd known Dave a long time and Max was already part of Maia's pack through Leif. Until I know he's ready, I won't do to him what the Palace tried to do to us. Force us into something we weren't ready or prepared for. You said yourself, I have to claim a beta before a prime alpha. Well, this heat is going to set Wolf off. You know it will. And if that happens, Nick will have his choices taken away."

Lexie looked suddenly pale, but a cool breeze hit me through the open front door and I knew what I had to do. I had to slow it down. "You said you used to work yourself into exhaustion whenever your scent would peek through. I need to run, Lexie. I always ran it out as a kid when things got too much."

"I don't know if that's a good idea, Ava. There are too many alphas patrolling around. What if it doesn't work? I think we need to tell your guys."

"No. No, Lexie. I've barely kissed Cary and Nick. I haven't even kissed Wolf, River, or Ryder. This is too much, too soon. We're not ready. Trust me, please. I need to at least try to run it off. Please." I tried to keep my mounting panic out of my voice.

"Such a bad idea," Lexie muttered as she shook her head. But she seemed to understand why I was panicking as she straightened and pushed me toward the door. "Let's go, before I change my mind."

"You're coming?" Relief crashed through me. The building pull towards my guys was growing to an angry, incessant beat, and as much as I was trying to pull away from it right now. I didn't want to be alone.

"Of course I'm coming. I've got you. Let's do this."

I was out the door in a flash. Lexie hot on my heels. The cool air washed over me, but it wasn't enough. I pushed my body harder as we lapped the building, but the sun was high overhead, and the heat in my body was cycling up to a burn. Another lap and the burn was becoming painful. A whimper wrenched itself from me and I doubled over. We were at the back of the Palace, just past the kitchen.

"Shit, it's not working," Lexie panted as she felt my head. "You're burning now."

"Need to cool down. Need water," I moaned. It was the only other option that might help.

"If we try to get you to a cold shower, we're going to have to pass the guys. Is there anywhere else?"

I looked ahead and saw the glass conservatory emerging from the back of the stone building. "There, the conservatory pool Rose was talking about this morning. It's more decorative than for swimming, but it's fresh, flowing water. So it should be cool."

"Perfect," Lexie grunted, as she got her shoulder under me and half dragged me to the conservatory. She grabbed the ornate door handle roughly, but it someone had locked it. She reached into her back pocket and pulled out some kind of tool, then immediately picked the lock. The door swung open within seconds.

"You're kind of scary. Why do you even have that?" I groaned.

She shrugged like it was no big deal. "In case Pala and I came across any locked doors during our tour."

Tropical greenery assaulted my senses, and the scent, so similar to Wolf's, had me groaning. Plants were spilling from large garden beds over the cobblestone paths and trailing from clusters of hanging pots. Our footsteps seemed to echo in the silent space as we staggered along the path until we reached the pool in the center. I immediately started pulling off my clothes.

"Uh, do you really need to strip?" Lexie asked.

"Yes," I ground out. My clothes felt as if they were choking me. My scent had been growing stronger and in the more confined space, its syrupy sweetness suddenly seemed too much. Even for me.

"Ugh, I'm never eating cherries again. I think I have a lady boner," she muttered.

I pulled the last of my clothes off and climbed over the ornate stone railing that bordered three of the edges, before I jumped into the water. I didn't have the patience to walk around to the wide stone steps at the far end. The bottom was smooth rock, and the water level came up to about my neck in this spot. I dunked myself under the cool water.

"Better?" Lexie asked from where she was crouched at the edge, gnawing on her lip, as I emerged, gasping for air, in a shallower spot.

"No," I whimpered, as I doubled over. It wasn't working and my anxiety was rising. "Lexie, it hurts."

The more I tried to deny this heat, the fiercer it burned.

"Think, Lexie," she muttered to herself. An echoing bang drowned her words out as the large double doors to the conservatory flung open. Nick came running through and skidded to a halt on the wide stone path between the pool and the entryway.

"What's wrong?" He called out. His eyes shot to the roof when he noticed I was naked. I tried to back away, deeper into the water, but a painful cramp had me doubling over and my legs crumpled. I lost my footing and water rushed over my head again as I choked.

Someone yelled my name and the sound of splashing reached my ears as familiar arms hauled me above the water. I came up spluttering and crying, as something deep inside me twisted.

"She's in heat, Nick. And in pain. She's trying to hold it off, but she needs an alpha."

"Get the guys," he yelled frantically.

"Sorry, Ava." Lexie's yell echoed down the hallway. She was already gone.

Twenty-Six

"Ava," Nick pulled me to him, and as much as his nearness soothed my heart, it didn't stop the cramps that were splitting me in two. "Dammit, you're burning up."

He splashed water over my body while still holding me against him, but it did nothing to cool me down. The urge to rub myself all over him was driving me mad.

"Why the hell were you running, Ava? I came up for some water and saw you out the window."

I pulled back from him, not having the words to explain. But the sight of his soaked white t-shirt sticking to his skin and the droplets of water running down his neck had a burning hunger raging through me like a wildfire.

His brows furrowed. "If you don't want me here, I'll go. But I'm not leaving until either River or Ryder is with you." His voice was firm, as he pulled me back into him and placed a soft kiss on my wet hair that broke me.

Before I could try to form words, thundering footsteps rang down the internal hallway, and River came barreling through the doorway. The heavy oak door rebounded from the wall and swung shut behind him, but was half ripped off its hinges by Wolf, hot on his six. River didn't slow, throwing himself into the pool and wading across to me with his powerful legs pulling through the water.

"Thank fuck. She needs you. She's in pain and was half drowned when I got here." Nick nudged me gently towards River, who scooped me up with a furious growl. My legs went around his waist instinctively and I plastered myself to him. I sighed, half delirious as the pain receded slightly, but it still wasn't enough.

"Help Wolf," River growled at Nick.

"On it," Nick said, his voice already moving away.

"Skin," I begged. I needed to feel his skin against mine, or I was going to combust. My brain tried to tell me I should care about being naked right now, but it wasn't running the show anymore. I needed a reprieve from this agonizing heat. Just for a minute. Then I'd regroup and figure this out.

"I knew I shouldn't have left you before," he growled, his voice barely coherent. "I just couldn't figure out what was suddenly driving me to stick so close."

River didn't bother trying to pull his t-shirt over his head while I was clinging to him. He just grabbed it near the neck and ripped it clean off. I sighed as he pulled the fabric from underneath me and my breasts pushed against his naked chest. He pulled me more firmly to him, shifted to a deeper spot in the pool, and dunked us both up to our shoulders, covering me with the cool water. The longer I held him, the more the pain ebbed. His dark chocolate scent seemed to surround me and caress me in soothing strokes as I nuzzled into his neck. I could almost feel him vibrating against me.

Until I realized the growl was coming through the bond instead of from him. I looked up to see Nick planted in front of Wolf on the top step. Wolf had halted at the edge of the pool. He'd clenched his fists hard and every muscle in his body was bulging, as if he was pulling against an invisible enemy. He looked as wild as I'd felt a moment ago and his dark edged gaze fixed on me with an intensity that made me moan.

"Wolf." It was both a plea and a denial wrapped up in one desperate word. Yet his eyes only flared hotter at hearing his name fall from my lips.

"Can you hold back, or do we need to get you out of here?" Nick asked him, every muscle in his own body drawn tight with tension.

"Not. Leaving." Wolf's voice was deeper than I'd ever heard it, and his eyes never left me.

"I'm just trying to keep her safe, Wolf. Can you hold back? You can't claim her yet. Your power will hurt her if it's not anchored first."

Nick knew about that? Wolf's eyes flicked to Nick, a predatory, instinctive intelligence lurking there.

"Tie. Me. Down." His eyes flashed at Nick. An order and a warning. He held Nick's stare for another beat before his gaze fixed back on me, making my heated blood spike again.

"Where's Cary? We're going to need him to keep Wolf calm," Nick called over his shoulder to River.

"Ryder ran to get him. He looked agitated and said he was going for a run earlier," River ground out.

Like we'd called them into existence, more footsteps came pounding down the hallway. Cary pushed past the ruined door and tumbled into the room. Ryder quickly stepped through from the darkened hallway behind him, bringing up the rear. His eyes kept snagging on me as he tried to scan the room for threats. Cary gasped a pained breath, and Ryder moaned as my scent hit them. Both of their pupils blew wide, and Cary unconsciously grabbed his cock through his sweatpants. Nick sagged in relief in front of them all.

"Fuck me, that's potent," Cary said as he panted, hard. His eyes ran over every piece of me he could see. "She's definitely in heat. Maia's scent went syrupy when hers started, too."

"We need rope. You have to restrain Wolf," Nick said.

"Wait, just wait," I groaned and five sets of eyes fixated on me. It was too much. My back arched, pushing my chest into River and I ground against him shamelessly, as his wet jeans created a delicious friction against me. But I needed a minute to think. I shoved away from him insistently. He let me go to avoid hurting me and I pushed myself to the other side of the pool.

"What's going on, Ava?" River growled, haunting every step I tried to take away from him, but not touching me again. "We could feel your pain and your fear. We've been chasing you all over the damn place, but we couldn't find you. Why didn't you come to us?"

"I think it's me," Nick said quietly, his voice cracking. "I'll go now. I was just waiting for you guys to get here. If you tie Wolf up and Cary distracts him, River and Ryder should be able to ease her enough to get her through this heat."

"Pack. Stays." Wolf growled. He turned and stormed back to the door, causing Ryder and Cary to scramble out of his way. He shoved the ruined door back into place and picked up a heavy stone bench, shoving it in front of the door. Wolf roared his determination at Nick, his wildness taking over, but Nick stood his ground.

"That makes no sense. Why does Wolf need to be tied up, and why would you go, Nick?" Ryder asked, his head swinging between Wolf and Nick. His jaw worked and his eyes blazed as he planted his feet, ready to intervene if he needed, but not sure where.

"Ava," River growled. "Let us help you. We're all here for you."

I couldn't help it. My eyes flicked to Nick in my distress.

"Oh no, Ava," Cary cried, understanding lighting his face.

I tried to hold it in, but the pain was back and building too fast. It spiked quickly now that I'd had a taste of what my body craved. I whimpered as I propped myself up on the side of the pool, trying to keep my head out of the water as a violent shake traveled up my legs and through my whole body.

"Fuck this," Ryder yelled, running around to my side and throwing himself down into the water alongside me. He ripped off his shirt and pulled me into him. Wolf was snarling, eyes pinned on me.

"No, no, no," I sobbed into Ryder's neck, hating myself as I pressed into him and my hands stroked over his skin in contrast to my barely coherent cries. I sighed in relief as River pushed in behind me and they sandwiched me between them.

"Ava, we're here. You need to talk to us this time," Ryder begged, his voice breaking. "Please don't shut us out again."

My heart shattered, and my resolve wavered. I didn't want to hurt them again, but either way, I would hurt somebody.

"I don't think she can. She's in too much pain. Nick, Cary, somebody talk to us," River growled low from behind me.

"Wolf, get Nick in the water," Cary said as he stepped back. Wolf roared as he picked Nick up and hauled him over his shoulder to drag him into the pool.

"What the hell are you doing?" Nick yelled at them both. He didn't fight it, though. He knew he was no match for an enraged Wolf.

"She's trying to protect you," Cary answered, as he crouched at the top of the steps. "She's going to burn herself out rather than hurt you."

"What?" Nick asked, breathless, as he whipped around to face me.

"Is that true, Ava?" Ryder asked, tilting my head up to him as I groaned.

"Of course it is," River murmured in my ear. "It's what she does. Tears herself apart to protect the people she loves."

"Feel her in the bond," Cary said. "The more you touch her, the more you should be able to feel her."

Ryder closed his eyes. "Oh, little bird," he whispered. "You've been a bad girl."

Suddenly Nick was between them, crowding into my side. "Is that true? I can't feel you the way they can."

Having both River and Ryder touching me eased me enough that I could finally get words out.

"You asked me on a date. I want that date, Nick." It sounded stupid out loud, but it was so important to me. I wanted to start things with Nick right. The Palace had robbed me of time courting with the twins, and Cary. Wolf being a prime alpha made a heat complicated. Nick was simple. Pure. I wanted to keep him that way. I didn't want to force his hand with a heat that had come too soon, before we were ready.

"Ava," he said, exasperated. "No matter what happens now, I'm taking you on that date. Even if it's as my mate."

"She's worried you're not ready," Cary said to him, as if he was an Ava whisperer and knew my emotions without me having to explain. "She thinks she's forcing you into this."

Nick stroked my face gently as he pushed wet strands of hair out of my eyes until I could see him clearly.

"Why is being here forcing your hand, Nick? You said something before about Wolf's power. What don't we know?" River asked, his voice sounding strained, like he was trying to hold himself back.

"She can't mate a prime alpha without a beta in her pack, or his power will tear the bonds apart. Lexie's pack almost found that out the hard way. Dave told me," Nick answered, his gaze unwavering on me.

"Shit. Based on how the other packs interact, I suspected she needed a beta to balance Wolf somehow, but not that it was so serious," Ryder groaned.

"So she needs to mate you first?" River asked Nick.

"Not first, but before Wolf," he replied. "Are you only worried about me being ready, Ava? Or is there something else you're worried about?"

I tried to push past the haze of need descending over me, to make them understand why I felt I had to do this alone. But I couldn't think straight and I didn't want to make a choice that could break us. Maia and Lexie both told me the urge to claim a true mate during sex was overwhelming, and it was near impossible to hold back during a heat.

"I've seen too many forced claims at the Palace. I won't do that to any of you. Even if I'm not barking at you, this is forcing you all. If I can ride this out, it will give us time to develop our bonds naturally. To mate and claim each other when we're ready."

"You can't do this alone, Ava. Heats can be dangerous without an alpha's knot and pheromones to ease you." Nick shook his head, his forehead furrowing. "You said earlier that you liked me. Has that changed?"

"Like is too small a word, Nick. You're mine, in the same way my other mates are. I'm just not sure you feel the same, yet. Betas usually take time to make a commitment to each other. I want to give you that time, Nick. I won't have my heat force you into this."

He breathed out heavily, relief flooding his eyes, but my breath still hitched as my heart pounded, waiting for him to say something in return. He didn't keep me waiting. "You're mine too, Ava. I just didn't want to scare you by showing you so quickly how much I need you. My whole life I've known about packs and hoped mine was out there. I may not have alpha instincts, but I still knew you were mine the moment I saw you. Before you even knew I existed, I wanted this. I don't need time, not even another second. I just need you."

Satisfaction flooded me at knowing he was just as into me as I was with him. I needed him so badly.

"Nick," I whimpered, before he kissed me quick and hard. Gone was the gentle exploration he'd started with earlier today.

"You've always seemed so in touch with your omega, Ava. Even more so than Maia or Lexie. You've just been quieter about it," he said, capturing me with his earnest eyes, not letting me look away. "Now you're overthinking this, and trying to deny your instincts. You're in your head rather than feeling your bonds with your mates. Trust yourself, trust us. Let us show you how we feel."

"Mine," Wolf instantly growled, and I got a rush of love from him that lit me up inside. There wasn't a smidge of doubt in him about us, and I felt the same way. My giant, feral alpha had gripped me from the moment he charged through that throng of alphas to save me. Our bond was pure light and comfort. I'd claim him this very moment if I didn't know it would hurt us both.

"Mine," I whispered back to him. It was all he needed. Wolf growled low and long, making the water ripple around him, as his eyes roved over me possessively.

"Temptress," Cary murmured in a husky voice. "You have owned me body and soul since the first moment I laid eyes on you. If anyone thinks I'm going anywhere right now, they're going to have to shift me themselves." His dark eyes glittered dangerously, even as they burned with need.

"You've always been mine, Cary. Even when I couldn't look at you, you were mine."

"What about River and Ryder?" Nick asked. I dragged my focus back to the two men holding my naked body so tenderly between them. They were patiently keeping the worst of the pain at bay, even while I could feel their bodies almost vibrating with need. They were hot, glowing sparks in my chest that had never burned down, despite time and distance.

I looked between each of them as Nick released me and shifted backwards, giving us a moment.

"Don't start doubting us now, little bird," River whispered in my ear. His breath skittered shivers over my heated skin.

"You held faith in us for a decade, even when we let you down," Ryder added, as he kissed a line up my jaw, making me tremble. 'You've always been ours, and will always be ours. We're more than ready for this. Are you?

He pulled back a little to give me space to answer. There were so many powerful, confusing feelings attached to the twins. Yet my feelings for them were also the simplest of all. Love underpinned everything, even the pain and fear. A part of me was holding back from them because I'd followed my instincts before, and made a decision that had caused the three of us a decade of pain. I didn't want to hurt anyone I loved in that way again. It made me realize Nick was right. I'd gotten spooked by this sudden heat, and stopped following my instincts. That wasn't me. I didn't run from things or hide from them.

My eyes snagged on Ryder's chest, and the cherry blossom tree tattooed on it. The roots reached down and intertwined with a depiction of his beating heart, wrapping it in their embrace. The branches reached up to his collarbone. Cherry blossoms were blowing off it in a breeze that wrapped over his shoulder. There were tiny bluebirds flying amongst them. It was achingly beautiful. It was a representation of us, tattooed forever as a piece of art on his body.

"Ry," I whimpered. I remembered River telling me to seek out Ryder's tattoo. He'd promised me Ryder wasn't angry the way he thought he was. I hadn't imagined it would be anything like this. Someone who was truly angry could never ink this on themselves.

Ryder grabbed my chin and dragged my face up to meet his eyes as he pressed back into me. His pupils had blown wide and need etched his face with a ravenous hunger that bordered on agony. Yet he was frowning.

"Tell me we're good, Ava." Pain and remorse bled into his growl, and it tore me open. I'd done this to him.

I also realized with sudden clarity that the space between the three of us, filled with unspoken words, was of our own making. I pulled River and Ryder tighter to me in our bond, as well as with my arms, and they both groaned in relief as it felt like our souls finally crashed back into each other.

"In the dark of night, when I dared to dream of having a choice, it was always the two of you," I said, as my feelings overflowed the well I'd tried to contain them in. "From the day I left until now, that hasn't changed. You're both mine."

"Ours," River growled from behind me.

"Ours," Ryder repeated in a matching growl.

They both put their heads towards mine, as they kept me encircled in their arms. It felt as if we were right back on that dance floor with our bond newly springing to life. Only now, we were so much more. Now, arms wrapped around us from all sides as Wolf, Cary, and Nick shared this moment with us. Our pack bonds grew roots that entwined us as I yanked on each one and pulled them to me. My mates held me tightly in a moment that felt like it left ripples within time itself. As if every moment of joy we'd ever experienced together had been a ripple flowing from this perfect moment that hadn't yet happened. And all the ones to come would flow from it too.

I wanted to stay in this moment forever. Yet, with all of them touching me, the burn in my body built to a searing level. My heat rushed back into me, demanding more.

"So, how will this work?" I moaned, my voice sounding huskier than I'd ever heard it. Lexie had never gotten around to answering that question. As much as I wanted to know what would feel good for them, I wasn't sure I meant the mechanics anymore. It was more that I felt so much for each of them I didn't know who to touch first.

"It's okay, Ava," Cary said roughly, understanding flickering into his heated gaze. He always seemed to know what I was feeling almost before I did. "We all just want to be here for this. Do whatever feels right for you, and if anything makes you uncomfortable, you say stop and we stop."

"You're not responsible for all our feelings, Ava," Nick added. "That's too much for any one person. It's on us to make this work, not you. Trust us to take care of you and figure our own shit out, okay? Just like we did last night."

I glanced at Wolf. He'd calmed slightly with the pack contact, but I knew the feral wildness that plagued him was creeping back over his senses. I could feel it growing in the bond. Yet he wasn't fighting it, he was embracing it.

"You are yours, before you are anyone else's, Ava," he growled with surprising clarity. "You're not our possession and you have the control here, even as you give yourself to us."

It amazed me how connected I felt with Wolf, and I realized it was because he was completely open to me. He had no artifice, and he held nothing back. The growing wildness I felt within my heat was filtering through the bond from him. It wasn't scary though; it felt exhilarating as I opened myself up to him and his energy blasted the last of my inhibitions away. He smiled darkly at me.

I sighed and let my head fall back onto River's shoulder, as I trusted my instincts and let go completely. I gave myself up to my mates, trusting them to take care of me, but also to know their own needs. My syrupy heat scent swiftly turned intoxicating as it detonated around the room. Groans and growls sounded around me as River and Ryder pushed into me, thrusting their hips against me. I could feel their hardness straining against their jeans.

I realized, for the first time, the power in submission when there was trust. It was heady and intoxicating, knowing I would let my mates do anything they desired to me, but that it would stop instantly if I gave the world.

I may have started out the day as a sweet virgin, but I wouldn't end it that way. For years I'd had innocent, girlish fantasies of white lace lingerie and a worshipping alpha or two on a rose petal strewn bed. They'd gently and sweetly take my virginity.

This was definitely not that fantasy, which was fine by me. I felt powerful, and that was so much better. I wanted this to be raw, real, and wild.

"Clothes off," I demanded, as I let my omega out to play.

Twenty-Seven

River and Ryder both pulled back from me, letting me stand on my feet again, but moved only far enough to wrestle their wet pants down their legs. Nick untangled my wet hair, freeing me of the bun that was pulling at my head with its soaking weight.

"You, too, Nick." I urged. "I want to see you."

I wanted to see all of them. Feel all of them.

Nick reached behind him and pulled his wet t-shirt over his head, exposing acres of long, lean muscles. His pants came off next, and I finally got a view of that glorious ass, as he turned and threw his wet clothes to the other edge of the pool. Nick's natural complexion was a little paler than Wolf's, but not as pale as the twins. Working around the farm had tanned Nick's arms and legs, but I don't think his ass had ever seen the sun. It was still a work of art. The twins both sported the same uneven tans from spending so much time outdoors. *Maybe we could do more skinny dipping together, outside, to even out their tans?*

Ryder's hand landed back on my chin again, as he directed my wandering gaze back to him. The dominant touch had me panting.

I'd dreamed about his mouth on mine for years, wondering what he would taste like, how we would fit together. It was more than I could have possibly imagined as his lips met mine and he growled into me, his passion blazing through me. He was all teasing licks and nips, followed by hard thrusts of his tongue as he devoured me. The warmth, the salted caramel taste of him, the hot, hard feel of his strength underneath my hands as I clung to him. He was all man now, in a way that had my body responding instinctively. Waves of dark desire crashed into me and I moaned against his lips.

As soon as he released me, a firm grip clamped onto my hips, and River was there, pushing against me. As he turned me into him, he kissed a wet trail from my shoulder to my neck and across my jaw. He was the epitome of controlled seduction. By the time he reached my parted lips, I was aching for him.

"I need you, little bird," he whispered against my lips.

"You have me," I panted.

River's kiss was uncompromising and fiercely determined, filled with endless years of longing. He pressed my entire body into his and brooked no resistance as he completely dominated my senses. There was no room for thought or second guessing. I felt owned by him, in the best kind of way. All I could do was hang on.

Despite being identical, the twins had always felt different to me. Their personalities were so distinct, one was hot fiery passion and the other controlled dominance. It was clear to me in the way they talked and moved, even if others couldn't always see it. It was even more clear to me in the way they kissed. I reveled in the realization that I now knew that. Knew how each of them moved when they kissed me.

I felt River's body tense a moment before he spun my body, gripped my waist, and lifted me into his powerful arms. Ryder grabbed my legs and brought them up around his waist, anchoring me back between them. River's mouth never left mine, even as his hands slipped up from my waist to graze against my breasts. Ryder shifted his upper body back slightly to give him room. I heard him groan as if he was watching as River's hands finally closed around my heavy, aching breasts.

It was the first time another person had touched me so intimately and shivers wracked me. I arched into his touch and shifted slightly so I could grind myself against Ryder's hard length pressed between my thighs.

"Fuck, she's so responsive," Ryder groaned.

"Who do you want first, little bird?" River asked, as he finally ended his assault on my lips.

"I could never choose between you, even in this," I moaned. I'd given myself up to them and I trusted them to make this work.

They glanced at each other and did the silent twin communication thing before River nodded at Ryder. Ryder bent down and trailed wet kisses down my chest before planting one on my wet nipple. I gasped at the sensation of his mouth there. *If just a kiss felt that good, how would the rest feel?*

As his mouth worked me over, back to the alternating sucks, licks, and gentle bites that had me writhing, he trailed a hand down my stomach and between my legs.

"We need to shift her to shallower water. I can't tell if she's wet enough," Ryder groaned, as his fingers brushed against my pussy. As soon as his fingers left me, I whimpered.

"We've got you," River murmured in my ear. "This is going to hurt, but if we make sure you're relaxed and ready, it won't hurt as much. Okay?"

"I trust you," I moaned. I didn't care about positions, or even comfort, right now. My need overrode everything else. "Just touch me, please."

He growled, low and long, at my words, as they shifted me toward a spot that wasn't as deep, but also had a natural rock ledge just below the water. It was almost a long seat. They didn't sit me on it though, the way I was expecting. Ryder held me as River laid himself down on the ledge and got himself comfortable, then he gestured at us.

Ryder bent over and laid me down between River's legs, so my torso rested against him like a sexy pillow, but my lower body was in about an inch of water. I could feel my ass hanging half over the edge of the ledge and the gentle flow of the cool water over my skin here in the shallows. It flowed past through the rocks from the source of the underground stream just behind River. I could also feel River's hard length against my back and I whimpered, wanting more already.

"Careful with her. The rocks are smooth, but some are uneven. If anything is going to redden her ass, it will be me," River said. I gasped at his rough words as Ryder chuckled.

Ryder slid his hands under my ass to raise it out of the water even higher. He slowly spread the lips of my pussy apart with his thumbs, and held me there, as he devoured me with his gaze. His cock was hard and at the perfect height to enter me, teasing me with the possibility, but he held himself away from me. He kept me wide open and exposed to them all, as groans reverberated around the room.

I'd never really been shy. People just assumed I was because I preferred not to insert myself into situations. I liked to hang back and watch people. But this was different. His eyes on me made me feel empowered. I suddenly felt a slick wetness coating my thighs that was different from the water.

"You're gushing. It seems our Ava likes to be looked at," Ryder growled, as he rubbed his thumbs through the wetness. My nipples pebbled so hard at his words and his touch so close to where I wanted it they ached.

"Fuck, is that slick?" Cary asked from somewhere nearby. "I've wondered what that would feel like. It only happens when an omega gets incredibly turned on or is in heat. It's rare for most omegas."

I looked toward Cary's voice and gasped at the feel of all their eyes on me while Ryder spread me open so intimately. Cary was now hovering over the balustrade behind Wolf. He'd leaned so far over; he risked falling in. His gaze was hot against my skin as he ran his eyes over me. Wolf's hands were now tied to the stonework with rope. I had no idea where Cary had found it. Wolf had crouched down into the water until all I could see was his upper face. His eyes blazed with feral need, hovering just above the waterline, like two dark suns rising. The rope didn't seem to bother him, instead; it seemed to make him burn even more.

Nick had edged closer to Wolf to get a better view. He looked entranced as he watched us. He had one arm propped on the edge and the other below the water. There was a ripple spreading out from him, as if his arm was moving under the surface. *Was he touching himself while watching?*

The thought was insanely hot. Desire rammed into me, and I grit my teeth to avoid crying out as my back arched again. River suddenly gripped my chin and tilted it up, as he forced me to look up at him.

"Don't do that. We want to hear you. We need to learn your body together, figure out what you like and what you don't. Your moans and your cries help us do that. So we need you to let it out. Ask if you want us to do something, too. Okay, little bird?" His voice was smooth and seductive as it rumbled underneath me.

"Plus, it's hot as hell," Ryder added darkly.

"Tell me you understand," River demanded.

"Yes, I understand," I whimpered. I had the craziest urge to add a 'Sir' to the end. Maybe I'd work up to that. The idea of exploring my body together and trying new things with them had my blood boiling. Because I wanted to do the same with them. Learn what made them moan.

"If we do anything that makes you uncomfortable, promise me you'll tell us immediately. This is important, little bird."

"Yes, sir," slipped out before I could stop it. River's eyes darkened even further, and he growled deep in his chest. I could feel satisfaction pulsing through the bond from both twins. The more intimately they touched me, the more emotions I could feel coming from them.

"Good girl," River growled, and I felt my slick gush, right as a hot tongue ran through my pussy. I cried out as my hips tried to thrust into the sensation, but Ryder had me held firm. I moaned loudly as a finger joined the tongue, caressing me and stroking me gently, before it nudged inside me.

"Oh, fuck," I heard Cary mutter, along with the sound of clothing hitting the floor. "What does she taste like?"

"So delicious, like cherry jam," Ryder growled from between my legs. Hearing them talk to each other while Ryder touched me had me writhing against his mouth.

"You want to see Cary naked?" River asked as he raised one eyebrow in question.

I nodded eagerly. River instantly released my chin, and I shot a look at Cary. He'd finally stripped. His dark skin glowed in the afternoon light streaming through the ceiling-high windows behind the foliage. He was lithe and toned, with shadows chasing over his skin as he flexed slightly. His cock was hard and jutted out proudly in front of him. It was thick and long, and my eyes devoured him. He made no move to cover himself.

His recent smiles and relaxed posture had disappeared, and the stern Cary was back. He wasn't angry or withdrawn, though; he was just intensely focused on me and every movement I made.

Another finger joined the one in my pussy, though neither was penetrating deep. It caused a deliciously stretched feeling and a friction that had me moaning again. I tore my gaze away from Cary and looked down at Ryder. His tongue was teasingly licking over my clit while his heated gaze focused on me, watching my every reaction much the same way Cary was. He'd released his hold on my ass to better use his hand, and I thrust into him instinctively. A darkly wicked grin spread over his face, and he 'tsked' and shook his head slightly before he pulled his fingers free and scissored them at my entrance.

"Ryder," I begged. I knew he was trying to ease me into this, but the heated ache was building again, along with a fizzing, tingling sensation in my core.

"What do you need, little bird?" River asked in a voice gone rough and husky.

"More," I whimpered. "Now, please." My earlier demands had dissipated as waves of need wracked my body. I was close to begging.

River reached down and tweaked my nipples, as Ryder sped up the attention of his tongue on my clit. I thrust against his face harder, as he switched and thumbed my clit while plunging his rough tongue inside me. I exploded in a shower of sparks that flashed through me with the speed of a spreading wildfire.

Ryder growled and pounced. He covered my body with his own and thrust his hard cock inside me as the first wave of my orgasm swept through me, forever altering me. There was a sharp bite of pain that was quickly drowned out by wave after wave of pleasure. With each thrust, Ryder drove deeper inside me, filling me and owning me. His knot pressed up hard against me.

"Can you take all of me?" He asked as he panted.

I nodded. He'd almost fully sheathed himself inside me, as my body stretched tight around him, but I still felt empty. The heat was scraping at me, demanding more. The orgasm hadn't dulled it; it had woken it up and turned it into a furious beast. I needed his knot, but I needed River's too. Having skin contact with River wasn't enough. I wanted them both inside me.

"I need you both to knot me at the same time," I moaned, barely able to get the words out.

"No," River grunted. "It's too much for your first time."

"Riv, you told her to ask for what she wanted," Ryder ground out. His face was strained.

"Ry, no," River argued, he sounded agonized. I could feel how hard he was against me.

"Please," I begged. It had been the three of us at the start. I needed that again now. "I need you, too, Riv."

He growled in frustration, and I could feel him tense up behind me.

"She's not a beta, River. She's an omega. Her body is biologically designed to take multiple alphas. You're not going to hurt her," Cary said. I would have kissed him if he were any closer.

River grabbed my chin again and dragged my gaze up to his. "Are you sure about this?"

"Yes. Please, Riv," whatever he saw in my eyes seemed to ease his fears.

"Hurry up, Riv," Ryder groaned.

"You can change your mind at any time and we'll stop."

I nodded, and River sprung into action. They both wrapped me in their arms and managed to have me upright again before I'd even blinked. I'd forgotten how agile they were. Ryder was leaning against the ledge, with River at my back. I wrapped my legs around Ryder's waist and grinned at him.

"So you're secretly a brat, huh? I like it," Ryder whispered, but didn't let me respond as he kissed me. There was a syrupy taste on his tongue that I assumed was me.

"Pull out, Ry," River demanded. "I need her slick."

Ryder groaned, but did as his twin asked. River thrust himself into me and the quick switch between the two different cocks had my pussy fluttering with another impending orgasm. The heat had every part of my body feeling so sensitized a brush of warm air could probably set me off.

River was gone again just as quickly, and a keening cry ripped from my throat. A threatening growl from Wolf, followed by a splash, had both twins tensing.

"You guys better stop playing around and speed it up. He's at his limit and can feel the heat riding her," Cary said. Wolf had stood up and his arms were straining against the ropes. Cary had jumped in and pushed up Wolf's shirt to put his hands on his chest. While Nick had squeezed in behind Wolf and was hugging him from behind. Uncaring that he was naked.

"I'm okay, Wolf." I tried to send him reassurance through the bond, but my senses had become scattered. The wildness in his eyes receded slightly, but he was still far too close to the edge. I kept my eyes on him as Ryder thrust back into me and River pushed against me from behind. There was a brief feeling of pressure, an almost too much feeling of resistance. Then River was inside me, too.

I moaned and closed my eyes, unable to take so many sensations battering me simultaneously. A heated spiral started at my core, as they set a matching rhythm that destroyed any illusion that I was in control. River and Ryder dominated my body, pounding into me until the heated spiral erupted in a blast of lava. They both shoved against me, hard, and their knots slipped inside me at the same time. Two roars split the room and rattled the windows, drowning out my cry, as white light split me in two.

I shook as my second orgasm burst through me just as the roars cut off and two mouths latched onto my neck. I turned my neck and bit one shoulder, hearing a groan and feeling Ryder shudder against me, before I twisted and bit the other shoulder. River growled as he continued grinding into me while my orgasm was still crashing through me. The white light intensified until it was blinding and suddenly River and Ryder were there, within me, and we were whole. Finally.

The light crystallized into two pools of warmth anchored deep within my chest as our broken bonds healed and solidified. I sighed, feeling the heat release me momentarily from its grip and I slumped into waiting arms.

I let darkness overtake me, knowing it would never be completely dark, ever again.

Twenty-Eight

I watched as River shifted and snuggled closer to Ava while she lay across Wolf's chest in her favorite sleeping position. River had one arm wrapped around her and the other under his head. Ryder was on his other side, with an arm thrown over his twin so he could touch Ava, too.

Ryder had a contented smile on his face that made me envious. It left a hollow feeling in my gut. He'd been so angry and conflicted, but mating with Ava seemed to have washed it all away. Nick was on Wolf's other side, lying on his back with his eyes closed. They were each butt ass naked, but nobody seemed to care.

Except for me. I'd thrown some pants on when we'd gotten back and was now sprawled on the chair in the corner, even though there was room for me on the bed.

"Stop thinking so hard," Ryder grumbled at me. I noticed a smirk appear on River's face, and heard Nick chuckle.

"I thought you were all asleep," I said as I sat up slowly, tension I couldn't shake riding my movements.

"No. Just resting," Wolf answered.

"Is that why you're hiding over there?" Ryder asked as he stretched his legs out.

"I'm not hiding," I said, shooting him a frown. I didn't enjoy being called out so openly. Probably because I wasn't used to it. I'd never had siblings growing up.

"You're overthinking so hard you're going to pop something," River complained. "We can feel you."

"You can feel me?"

"Yes," River and Ryder answered in unison. *What the hell? How could they feel me if I hadn't bonded anyone?* I was about to hyperventilate.

"We can feel enough to sense you're conflicted, but not why," Wolf added, trying to reassure me.

"You have a bond with Ava," River said. "Even if you haven't claimed each other yet. We can feel you through her. It's faint, but it's there. The claim just opens up the bond more fully. Once an alpha claims you, you'll feel all of us, too."

My eyes roved over them before I dropped my gaze to the floor. I swallowed hard. This was exactly what I'd been thinking so hard about. I'd promised Ava I'd try to open up to them, so I figured it was time to practice doing that.

"How does the mate claim work, if it's not a sexual one? I know Maia and Lexie's packs did it for their betas, but not the specifics of how. Leif is with Max, so that makes sense, but Dave's not with anyone other than Lexie. Nick's not with anyone other than Ava, either. As far as I'm aware."

Nick blushed and looked up at the roof. "I'm pretty sure an alpha has to bite me at the same time Ava does. I don't think we need to be having sex. The endorphins during sex help ease the pain and boost the bond. It works as long as there's some emotional connection with the alpha. Even if it's just friendship."

"There's no such thing as *just* friendship," Wolf grumbled. "Friendship is a connection and an emotion as valid as any other. Often just as strong."

Everyone shot him puzzled looks, including me.

"What?" he growled, looking flustered.

"You're very perceptive about people for someone who has lived most of their life in captivity," River said, trying to be diplomatic.

He shrugged the shoulder Ava wasn't lying on. "I read a lot growing up. You can learn things about people from books, you know. Plus, I'm deeply connected to my alpha nature and that part of me sees things in simplistic terms. People complicate things too much."

Wolf shot a look at me, and I grimaced.

"The only thing I know for sure, and seems simple, is that Ava's mine," I said.

"Why don't you tell us a bit about yourself Cary, while we're waiting for Ava to wake up?" Ryder suggested. I wasn't used to talking about myself, and the idea sat uncomfortably in my gut. But I'd already started opening up to River and Ryder earlier and they'd shown empathy and understanding. They hadn't mocked me or yelled, or insinuated I was being overly dramatic. None of the things my father had done when I'd tried to explain myself to him.

"What do you want to know?" I asked. I slouched back down in the chair, trying to look unaffected, but I could feel my heart beating erratically in my chest.

"How did you end up at the Palace?" River asked. I almost groaned. River was so direct. I'd hoped to start off with something simpler, like my favorite food.

They were watching me curiously, but there was no judgement or animosity on their faces. Ava was right. They only wanted to know me. It had been a long time since anyone had cared enough to ask me about myself. If ever. *Here goes.*

"I came here willingly. I thought anything would be better than home. My dad was a highly dominant alpha and found it hard to conceal his disappointment that I wasn't one too. He didn't know what to do with a teenage male omega son after my mother passed away. He hid the truth for a while, but not because of the Palace. The asshole was embarrassed and didn't want people to know. It didn't last. We had a big house for the two of us, and he always seemed to have his alpha friends staying for some party or political fundraiser. I tried to appear dominant, but I couldn't always control my reactions when alphas approached me. Sometimes they caught me off guard and I'd freeze. I'm not as strong as Lexie or Maia."

"Hey, cut yourself some slack," Nick said, as he leaned up on an elbow to look at me. "Lexie and Maia were both hidden away from the world, living amongst betas. It sounds as if your dad expected you to hide, then surrounded you with alphas. That would never work, and it had nothing to do with strength. That's biology."

I shrugged, unconvinced. I appreciated him trying to make me feel better, though. He was a loyal, steady friend.

"High school was a nightmare," I pressed on, feeling awkward and wanting to get this done. "I craved touch, the same as any omega. I hooked up with a few curious beta girls, but it wasn't what I needed and left me feeling worse. The newly awakened alphas at the school would have an intense reaction if I touched any of them, or if they touched me. So, I learned to avoid touching or being touched by anyone at all. If I bumped into an alpha accidentally while walking around a corner, it became a big deal. It would set them off, and it was always my fault. I hid in the library most of the time. Eventually, I got homeschooled when the school complained I was distracting and confusing the alphas. After that, I couldn't go to university, or join the military. Even getting a job was impossible."

"No wonder you were so tense when I was behind you during training this morning," Ryder said. I'd told River and Ryder about my experiences with alphas jumping out at me this morning, but not how long I'd been avoiding touch.

"It is what it is." I sighed roughly while picking at a thread on my sweatpants before sneaking a look at the guys. They all looked tense and Ava stirred slightly in Wolf's arms.

"The Palace never pursued me when I presented because they didn't know what to do with a male omega. My father's alpha friends encouraged sending me here when I was in my early twenties, and one of them made the arrangements. The idea was that I could find a mate here, and then I would be someone else's problem. My dad was relieved to see me go."

My father's treatment was at the heart of a lot of my issues. My becoming an alpha's mate solved his problem. It meant he could rid himself of his burden and absolve himself of responsibility for his son. It was a part of the reason I was so conflicted about Wolf. I didn't want to be anyone's burden ever again. I glanced at Wolf and I could see understanding bloom in his eyes.

"When did you realize this place wasn't what was in the brochure?" River asked in a dry tone that I was coming to realize masked how deeply he cared for people.

"I figured out quickly that I'd voluntarily given away my freedom, that they would never let me leave," I answered. I tried for a playful smirk, but I could tell from the way River narrowed his eyes it hadn't had the effect I intended. He had the same look whenever he was analyzing something. Right now, that was me.

"A few of my father's friends turned up and sought me out immediately. They'd arranged with the Palace that I would be their toy in exchange for large charitable donations. A group of them had a particular kink, and I'd fallen right into their laps. They secretly liked to be dominated in bed by someone less powerful than they were. It seemed they found using betas distasteful, so I was their perfect prey.

"They taught me to do what they needed. I didn't hate it at first. I was so lost about where my place was in the world and felt conflicted about being an omega. Being a dom sounded like a better option, but I ended up feeling numb. Nobody cared about how I felt. It wasn't a relationship. It was one-sided, and I was only playing a role. I tried to avoid touch as much as possible during the sessions they set up, using whips and toys instead. I also tried to use it to my advantage, coerce them to help get Ava out, but that didn't work."

"Cary," Nick said as he sat up. He looked pale, as if he was going to vomit, but didn't finish whatever he was going to say.

"It's okay, Nick. Plenty of people here had it worse." I looked out the window as I spoke, not quite meeting his eyes.

"It's not okay," Wolf growled. He'd clenched his fists and his face had twisted in a snarl. He looked like he wanted to maim something. It amazed me how he could switch from looking so wild, to being so gentle with Ava. It made me yearn for something I couldn't clearly define. *Was River right? Was I overthinking everything?*

"Not even close," River seconded. He looked at me pointedly when I glanced at him.

"I don't know how we can let this place stay standing. Every stone in it seems saturated in pain," Ryder said quietly. He was watching me with a fierce gravity. As if he would help me tear it down brick by brick if it was what I wanted.

I couldn't agree more. I was itching to leave this place and go somewhere else. Anywhere else. But none of us wanted to leave the omegas here vulnerable.

"I get why you're wary of us, Cary, given your past," Wolf mumbled haltingly. "If it takes time to earn your trust, we'll put in the work. I meant it when I said I would be anything you needed, even a friend."

I groaned. "You've got it wrong. It's not that I don't trust any of you. I do. I just don't know who I am within myself, let alone in this pack. And I need some time to figure it out. Does that make sense?"

It was the truth, but not all of it. I could see River's eyes widen as if he'd figured something out. "You were much more relaxed this morning. You even let Ryder touch you during training. What about Ava's heat tonight spooked you?" he asked.

I felt myself stiffen. For someone who supposedly wasn't great with people, he was remarkably insightful. "I was with you all right until the point you and Ryder claimed Ava. There was nothing wrong with what you did, and it was hot as fuck. I just realized if I let one of you claim me, I could end up having a heat too. If that happens, Ava won't be enough to ease me. I'm going to need an alpha. Maybe more than one. I'm not sure I'm ready for that. Or we're ready for that. I've had enough empty sex in my life."

"I will destroy anyone who tries to force you into something you're not ready for, Cary," Wolf said simply. "Even if it's one of us." Ryder reached over absentmindedly and put his hand on Wolf's arm in reassurance. His eyes never left me, though.

"Take any time you need. Sit this one out, or don't. That decision is up to you and there's no right or wrong," Ryder said. "But if a heat happens, we'll figure it out. As Wolf said, friendship can be just as powerful as attraction. Nothing between any of us is going to be empty."

"Ryder's right. This won't be her only heat. There's no pressure," River said. "Besides, this pack bond feels more like a net than a straight line, Cary. I never thought such a thing was possible, but I can almost see the interwoven strands running between us already. It's not designed to trap you, it's here to catch you."

"You've felt like a brother since the first day I met you, Cary," Nick added. "I don't care if you're a beta, an alpha, or an omega. Or even some mix of the three. Be whoever or whatever feels right to you. It makes zero difference. You're just Cary to me."

I could feel my eyes dampen at the support these four men were showing me. More than anyone had in my life, even my biological family. I gave one abrupt nod before I changed the subject. It was all I could manage right now.

"So who's going to bite Nick? Because I'm pretty sure Ava's heat isn't over and it will wake her up again soon."

"I'll bite him," River and Ryder said simultaneously.

"No, I'll bite him," Wolf growled.

"I'm definitely going to bite him," Ava said sleepily. She stretched her body along Wolf and a growl forced its way out of his chest.

She looked so beautiful lying naked between her men. I figured my resolve to stay back for the rest of her heat was about to be sorely tested. Especially when my emotions were riding me so hard.

One crook of her finger would be all it took.

Twenty-Nine

I shifted my hand across a broad chest, feeling a smattering of wiry hairs and hard muscles flex underneath my touch. The faint vibration of a growl caused a trail of sparks to run along my skin everywhere we were touching. And there was a lot of skin. A leg shifted deeper between mine, much as it had the other day waking up in the forest, only now I could feel hairs tickling my thighs. I could get used to waking up this way.

A deep breath of the leafy jungle and orchid laden scent surrounding me told me it was Wolf beneath me. A sudden tension in the bond and in the body behind me had me opening my eyes and looking up into Wolf's heated gaze. It seared into me, making heat simmer deep in my belly.

I ran my hand down Wolf's chest and watched the way his eyes darkened as my fingers trailed over his stomach. I felt bold as I let them linger for a moment, before I ran them across to my hip and down onto the leg draped over my thigh, squeezing it in reassurance. I could feel that River was on alert, and watching Wolf and I closely, making sure neither of us got carried away just yet. "Nobody here is going to harm me, River."

I knew that deep in my soul. Wolf's fierce desire hadn't worried me earlier, and it didn't now. I'd briefly worried when he'd first demanded Nick tie him up, given his history in captivity. But I trusted Wolf to know himself, and I'd sensed his flare of pleasure when Cary had wrapped the ropes around his wrist. It had intrigued me.

"Nobody is harming you ever again, mate," came River's growl from behind me. It came with a wash of possessiveness through the bond from both River and Ryder. Wolf's smile was almost predatory, as if he was the big bad wolf and he was about to eat me. The growls and possessiveness, while they sandwiched me between them, had me melting in a pool of heat. Like butter on popcorn. A flare of River's dark chocolate scent, mixed with Ryder's salted caramel, had me whimpering and my mouth watering.

"Nick, I think you're up," Ryder said from behind River, as his hand ran slowly up my side and his thumb caressed the side of my breast.

Nick rolled onto his side and popped into view on the far side of Wolf with a soft smile. His hair was tousled, and he had acres of gorgeously toned skin on display. I swallowed hard.

Were they all naked in bed with me? I liked that they were comfortable enough with each other to lie around naked while I was sleeping. I'd worried that being bared to them and seeing them all naked might have been awkward, but it felt natural. In life, I'd been happy to stand back and watch the world go by, but with these men, I wanted to be seen. I remembered watching Cary standing proudly naked earlier, while he'd watched me with River and Ryder. I wanted more of that.

Where was he now? I sat up as River moved off me. Cary wasn't behind Nick.

"Cary?" I asked, as I blinked my eyes, still coming awake.

"Over here," he called out, his voice husky.

"Are you okay?" I asked him. He was sitting in the chair, apart from us all, with a pair of light gray sweatpants on.

"Of course," he said, but there was a weird vibe coming from him. I shifted towards him but became distracted by the mounds of pillows and blankets between us, circling the bed. Beyond them, someone had covered every surface with candles and vases of flowers. They also strung fairy lights around the room, giving it a warm glow. "What...?" I mumbled.

"You can thank Wolf for the decorating," Ryder said. He moved to snag a pillow from the wall of them alongside him, but hesitated when Wolf growled at him. "He put a lot of work into it this morning. Stripped half the Palace bare of bedding to build it."

I looked at the wall of bedding surrounding us and noticed he had woven clothing into it. I leaned towards the closest pillows to take a deep breath, and each of the guys scents hit me. It wasn't coming from just them. Wolf had saturated the bedding with their scents. I looked at him over my shoulder with a raised eyebrow and he looked embarrassed.

"It's a nest for your heat," Nick explained quietly. "I think he sensed it was coming. He's uniquely in tune with his alpha."

"Do you like it?" Wolf asked. That note of vulnerability that tore at me crept back into his voice.

"I love it, Wolf. Thank you." I truly did. It was cozy, warm and smelled like heaven. It made me feel safe. I leaned down and swept the shaggy hair off his face so I could look into his eyes. Before I gently pressed my lips to his. He groaned against my mouth as he let me roam my hands over him again. I gasped as he tore my hands off him suddenly, before he rolled me onto my back and trapped them above my head. The heat in my veins built quickly, and an ache in my core tore at me. Wolf rolled away again just as quickly, with a growl, as I whimpered.

"Nick," Wolf begged.

Nick sat up and climbed over Wolf, his eyes focused on me. "Shit, sorry," he mumbled, as he accidentally poked Wolf in the hip with his hard dick.

River burst out laughing, surprising me. He'd been so intense around me since he'd shown up. Finally, being mated seemed to have relaxed him. I could see the River of old peeking through along with his smile. He shot me a wink.

"There's five of us. Shit's gonna get poked," Wolf said with a shrug as he moved further out of the way, but Nick blushed anyway. I noticed nobody insisted on tying him up again. The contact with me seemed to have taken the edge off his wildness. It was still there, just lurking at the edges of his eyes.

Nick settled in alongside me. I opened my mouth to talk to him, but he leaned in and kissed me, as he picked right up where Wolf left off.

"Don't ask me again if this is okay," he whispered against my lips, as if he could read my thoughts. He shifted to nuzzle my neck, then kissed just below my ear, making embers spark to life. "Do you trust me?"

I nodded instantly. Whatever he was planning needed to happen quickly, though. My heat was building again, fast. "Good, because we need to get Cary out of his head. Okay?"

"Okay," I whispered, not entirely sure, but sensing what he meant. Nick was so generous and kind. This would be our first time together, but he was worried about his pack mate and willing to include him if it would help him. He was the perfect beta for us. He was already our center.

I dragged his face back up for another scorching kiss. I could kiss Nick all day. He took his time with it, like it was his sole purpose in life to kiss me. He turned it into an art form and had me drowning without touching any other part of my body. But my heat was building towards pain again. He pulled back as I whimpered.

"We've got you," he said, as he shifted back and drew me up to a sitting position. "Crawl to the edge of the nest, then stay there on all fours."

I was instantly an inferno as my slick wet my thighs. I angled forward and dropped to my knees, then crawled slowly to the end of the bed. A symphony of growls and groans flared behind me, but I kept my focus on Cary. I felt Nick settle in behind me. He put his hands on my waist to steady me as I held my hand out to Cary. Cary ground his jaw, but stood up slowly. I wasn't complaining about the sweat pants anymore. They hugged him tight around his thighs and my eyes were instantly drawn to the bulge highlighted beautifully below a happy trail of dark hair that disappeared into the waistband. They were gift wrapping. My body burned as he stalked towards me.

"Do you have any idea how long I've wanted you to look at me this way? You're so fucking beautiful, Ava," Cary said as he reached the end of the bed. He reached out and stroked my hair back from my face. I didn't want to even think about what a mess it probably was.

"About as long as I've wanted to look at you," I said, more brazen than I thought possible, as I reached forward and yanked his pants down over his hips. His cock sprung free and bobbed in front of me. It was dripping from the tip like a melting ice cream cone. I hadn't gotten a good look at River or Ryder earlier. Too consumed by the heat. While it was building again now, it wasn't choking me the way it had been earlier. I'd only ever seen pictures of men's cocks in educational books before. The Palace hadn't allowed omegas to have internet access, unless supervised, so I hadn't even had porn.

Movement alongside me had my gaze flicking away to meet Ryder's. He'd laid down at our end, but at the far edge of the nest, out of reach. I sensed he wanted to help Nick and I draw Cary back in, but in a casual, non-threatening way. I guessed Cary's problem wasn't with me, but that he was worried about his relationship with the alphas. Ryder was a good option to ease him into it, if that was the case. He'd always had a lot of empathy and compassion. He probably wanted to help me through this too, knowing I had no experience. Ryder just nodded at the question in my eyes, and I turned back to Cary.

"Touch him, Ava. He wants you to," Ryder said. I reached up and stroked the length of Cary with a finger. He felt silky smooth, yet so rigid. "You can be rougher than that, Ava. You won't hurt him. Circle him with your hand, then lick the tip."

Cary swallowed hard as I did what Ryder instructed. "He tastes like ice cream," I moaned. I could feel Wolf's growl as it vibrated through the bed.

"Suck just the tip and lick it with your tongue," Ryder said next, as I felt one of Nick's fingers slip through my own wet heat. Ryder's instructions were getting me as hot as the feel of Cary and Nick. Nick's tongue licked through my pussy, mimicking what I was doing to Cary's cock, and it had me moaning. Heat was spreading through my limbs again, and a low fluttery feeling was already building inside me.

"Now lick it all the way down, get his dick nice and wet before you suck it again." When I complied, Ryder hit me with a "Good girl," and I almost came on the spot.

Cary was rigid, every muscle in his body flexed hard, and he almost looked in pain. But his moan told me it was a good kind. Nick groaned behind me as my pussy flooded with slick.

"I need you, Nick," I panted. My core was aching and burning. I felt right on the edge of a cramp. I felt Nick move back slightly, then a hard length pushed through my slick. Nick nudged my legs apart and did it again, coating himself in it.

I took as much as I could of Cary into my mouth, loving the feel of the hard length against my tongue. I let out a moan as Nick finally pushed inside me, filling me, and I felt Cary pulse in my mouth.

"How does her mouth feel, Cary?" Ryder asked.

"Like heaven," Cary gasped.

"Can you hold still? And not fuck her face. We don't want her gagging her first time."

"Yes," Cary ground out through gritted teeth.

"Pull her hair into your fist, Nick, then tug it gently. See if she enjoys it," Ryder suggested.

Nick groaned as he wrapped my hair in his fist and tugged gently. He pulled me slightly off Cary's cock, then pushed me back on as he thrust into me again. His grip on my hair forced my back to arch, and I moaned again.

"Fuck," Cary yelled as his dick jerked in my mouth.

"You look like a wet dream right now, Ava," Ryder growled. "With your mates filling you up."

Nick started pumping into me harder and Cary stepped back, pulling his dick out of my mouth with a pop. He grabbed himself around the base and started pumping the length of his shaft, then twisted his fist around the end.

"Pull her up, Nick. Let Cary see all of her, so he can paint her in his cum for Wolf," Ryder hissed.

They both complied, and Cary instinctively climbed into the nest, chasing me as Nick pulled me up against his chest. I almost lost my mind, thrashing and whimpering on Nick, as I watched Cary pleasure himself while his cock glistened from the attention of my mouth. Cary came hard and quick, splashing cum over my stomach and up onto my breasts. He slumped onto the bed, panting when he finished.

"Now, was that so hard?" Ryder asked Cary with a chuckle. Cary reached over and slapped him on the abs with the back of his other hand, and Ryder groaned.

"Nick, I want to see you," I begged.

He instantly let go of my hair and pulled out so I could turn around. He landed on his knees and lent back slightly before he pulled me forward. "Ride me, Ava. Make me yours," he pleaded.

Oh, hell yeah. I felt like a queen as I straddled his lap and lowered myself onto his dick. I started thrusting myself up and down him, and he gripped my waist to help me.

"You're mine, Nick," I growled lightly. He gasped as I increased my pace and three alphas appeared behind him, their eyes blazing. The friction of him so deep inside me, rubbing a spot that sent pleasure spiraling through me, had my thrusts growing more and more erratic. The heat pushed me to abandon all restraint and give all of myself, to it and my mates. I was so oversensitised every tiny movement lit my body on fire.

I cried out as I tipped over the edge, and intense pleasure slammed into me. Nick jerked, and I felt hot cum spurt deep inside me, as the three alphas bit along his shoulders and biceps. He bared his neck to me and I bit him hard, too. The feel of his skin between my teeth had my orgasm imploding, then white light flooded me. Nick was suddenly there, a solid presence inside me and surrounding me. Centering me.

Nick and I both sagged, and River braced us. "That's incredible. I can feel you all," Nick mumbled. He sounded dazed, but I could feel his awe through the bond as he reached out and connected with me, sending me affection and reassurance. His love was so pure and uncomplicated, it made me want to cry.

Yet his bond ramped up my heat, as if my body knew there was nothing holding me back from Wolf now. Need slammed into me. I didn't have time to do more than kiss Nick quickly, as Wolf picked me up off his lap and bounced me down onto the nest. He licked some of Cary's cum off my body, as he rubbed other splashes into my skin, and I heard Cary groan. There was so much desperate need rolling off him as he watched us, he looked almost delirious. Yet he clenched his fists and held himself still.

My attention shifted back to Wolf as I felt him pull my legs apart. He stared at the mix of cum and slick that dripped down my thighs. His gaze went from hot to feral as he gathered it up with his fingers and pushed it back inside me. A roar ripped itself free from his throat and suddenly he was on top of me. He thrust deep inside me before I'd even gasped out a breath. He was huge everywhere, but my body was more than ready for him. It burned for him.

"Mine," he growled as he set a punishing pace.

"I'm here. I'm yours," I gasped. My omega instincts pushed me to reassure him, to please him. He'd been so patient, with so much wild energy riding him. But that time had passed.

"Theirs too," he ground out between desperate thrusts, his voice so rough he was barely coherent. "Want to breed you. Need to fill you up with our cum over and over. Brand you with it until you're swollen and full with our baby."

"Oh god, yes! Please. I want that too," I sobbed. His words undid me. The thought of them breeding me until I was pregnant drove me wild. It was everything I'd ever wanted and secretly feared may never happen. He growled and snarled as my ready compliance sent him into a frenzy. But rather than scare me, it lit me up. I thrust up into him and clawed my nails down his back. Feeling his wild energy pounding into me, making me into something new.

"Take it all, like a good omega," he growled.

"Yes, Wolf. More," I needed to be his so badly. It felt essential to my very existence. I could feel how much he needed it too, the wildness was demanding it with an insistent drumbeat and my heat had cycled up to a frenzy. He grabbed my face and forced my eyes to his. Owning me completely while he slammed into me so hard I saw stars as his knot forced its way into me. I exploded around him, coming so hard I almost blacked out as he bit into my neck. I blindly searched for any skin I could find, tears streaming down my face, as I latched onto him and bit him just as hard, feeling a tinge of blood in my mouth.

I felt River and Ryder join us as they bit Wolf on his shoulders. Nick joined in, too. Driven by our wild need pulsing through the pack bond, he reached out and latched onto Wolf's wrist.

My world exploded into vivid light and colors whirled around me as Wolf's wild energy pulsed through us all. It felt animalistic, hedonistic, and perfect. As if a wild piece of myself I hadn't known I needed settled into place. I didn't know how I had ever lived without these bonds. I could almost see them, the way Wolf had described. As if my senses had sharpened and I had a whole new view of the world.

Only Cary was missing. He was an aching space in my chest that needed to be filled. But he'd come closer, and that was a start.

"Mine," Wolf growled, again, as his heavy weight pushed me into the mattress briefly, before his arms wrapped around me and he rolled us onto his back. He stilled as he noticed the tears on my cheeks.

"Happy tears, Wolf. You all make me so happy. I feel so full, after feeling lonely for so long."

"You'll never be alone again, little bird. You have us now," Ryder said, as he hovered over us and kissed my wet cheek.

They let me cry as they stroked me. Even Cary shifted over and ran long strokes down my leg. He looked so conflicted, yet watched us longingly.

All the touching had my body instantly heating again. I ground down on Wolf's knot, still stretching me deliciously and stoking the embers, while I licked over my bite mark on his neck possessively. "Mine," I growled at him, feeling the heat haze settling over me, and he moaned as he shuddered underneath me.

I may have been a sticky, sweaty, emotional mess. But this heat wasn't done with us yet. Our nest was about to get a lot messier.

Thirty

I stood and looked at myself in the mirror, running a critical eye over my body. I'd woken while the others were sleeping and went to have a shower in the main bathroom so I wouldn't wake everyone else. Ava's heat had lasted for almost three days. Three incredible fucking days. I felt at peace for the first time in a decade.

River had looked up at me sleepily as I'd gotten up, nodded to me and fallen back asleep. Something he rarely did. He was more relaxed than I'd seen him in years. He trusted our friends to have us covered while we were vulnerable, and he didn't trust easily.

I'd always cherished my connection with my twin. I'd worried at first that Ava finding her pack may have damaged our bond further, knowing it was already strained by my behavior. That I'd maybe lose River in the process of getting Ava back. But I hadn't. Our twin bond was stronger than ever. It was just enhanced by the pack bond. The bonds grounded me in a way I'd never felt. It went beyond our own pack, too. I don't know what we would have done without Ava's friend Lexie. She'd delivered meals to our door, along with notes about security and movements around the Palace. The last few days had given me a greater appreciation for being part of a village.

The hot shower had been wonderful, but now I'd gotten lost in my thoughts. Movement in the doorway had my gaze skating away from my reflection. I already knew it was Cary, though. I'd already catalogued the way each of my mates moved and their heartbeats, as well as their scents. Cary's vanilla scent and his heavy footsteps had preceded him.

He startled when he noticed me in here. We really needed to work on his awareness of his surroundings, as well as his physical training. Maybe we could start on that later today. I was looking forward to working out with both Cary and Nick together. I genuinely liked them.

"Sorry, I'll use the other bathroom."

"No, come in. I'm glad you're here. I'm hoping you can help me with something."

He raised a suspicious eyebrow, but came into the room. He'd thrown his sweats back on, but I was naked, having dropped my towel to the floor. "Let me just pee, first," he said.

I nodded at him as he headed into the toilet cubicle. Ava was the heart of our new pack, and Nick was our much needed center. That didn't mean it was on them to develop our pack bonds. I wanted to do my part, too. I wanted to get Ava everything she needed, and she needed Cary to be comfortable with us.

"You too, Nick. Get your ass in here." I called out, being careful not to be too loud. I'd heard his distinctive shuffling footsteps pause in the hallway, just outside the door. We'd need to teach him to lift his feet while he trained with us.

"I was going to have a shower," he said as he popped his head around the door, "but I can use the other one."

"No. Get in here. Shower's free."

"Uh, okay." He walked in, still naked as well. I didn't know where to even look for any clothes right now. Especially considering Wolf had stuffed most of my dirty ones in Ava's nest.

Cary came out of the bathroom and headed to the sink to wash his hands, passing Nick on his way into the shower.

"I'm glad you're both here," Cary said in a rush before I could start talking. "I wanted to thank you for helping get me out of my head that first night of her heat. You both helped without being dicks or pushy about it."

Cary had joined in after we'd gotten him into the nest, but focused only on Ava for the rest of her heat. He'd been with no one but her, and their bites on each other hadn't solidified into a claim. I'd hoped they would. He felt right in our pack. It seemed they were going to need the help of an alpha. It had made some things a little awkward during the heat, which was a shame. Yet I figured with six of us in this pack, there were going to be times we weren't in sync.

Cary didn't feel like mine the way Ava did, but I definitely found him attractive. Especially watching him with Ava. It had been no hardship to step in and direct them. Initially, I'd done it for Ava, but I was hoping we could have something fun and light together if he could relax enough. I had an inkling it would drive Ava wild. I'd also happily step in if he ended up having a heat. The idea of him potentially suffering alone through it didn't sit well with me. He was pack, and I wanted him happy, healthy and safe. So I needed him to be comfortable and trust me well before anything like that happened.

I shrugged, "That was mostly Nick."

"No, it was both of you," he answered, as he looked directly at me in the mirror, "and it helped."

"You're welcome," Nick said from inside the shower as he turned the water on. "Fucking hell, that feels good."

Nick had such an easy way of being gracious and utterly charming, yet not making a big deal out of things. I had a tendency to overthink everything, but I was trying to change that. Maybe Nick would rub off on me a little.

Cary jumped up onto the counter and narrowed his eyes at me. "I brought up some of my clothes and put them in Ava's closet. You're welcome to help yourself to them if clean clothes are your problem. We're about the same size and I can get more from my room downstairs."

I was a little leaner than Cary, and slightly taller, but he was right. We were close enough that his clothes should fit okay. "Thanks, I'll take you up on that until we can figure out how to get some washing done. But that's not the problem."

"Okay," he shrugged as he tried to keep his eyes on my face. "So, what is the problem?"

"This," I said as I pointed at my junk.

"Uh, you didn't seem to have any problem using your equipment over the last few days."

I rolled my eyes. "It's not the way it works, Cary. It's the way it looks."

Cary finally edged his eyes down, and I tried to stay calm and not react to his gaze. It was hard, which was what I was trying to avoid. "I don't see the problem."

"I've been living rough for years, in hiding, since we went AWOL from the military. Then living on the road the last few weeks since the Crash. Keeping up appearances hasn't exactly been a priority. You're groomed to perfection. I look like a cave dweller who's never seen a razor," I said as I lifted my arm up and showed him my underarms. "I'm not just talking about my junk."

"Yeah, well, the Palace required I stay groomed. It's become a habit that's hard to break," Cary huffed.

"I get that, but Ava couldn't keep her eyes off you. Nick either, and you're both groomed."

Cary's eyes flared wide open. "Let me get this straight. You're seriously feeling insecure about your body right now?"

I just nodded, and a solemn look passed over his face when he realized I was serious.

"Ryder, you have the body of a god. Ava won't care about a little hair here and there." He gestured to my junk and my arms.

"I know, but I want to make an effort to look nice for her." My arms came up and crossed over my chest self-consciously. I hadn't thought it would be such a big deal, but now I was feeling a little embarrassed.

"Okay, that's fair. But why do you need me?" Cary asked, wariness creasing the corners of his eyes.

"I'm scared of cutting off my junk. I've never shaved anything but my face and my hair before. Guys in the military weren't into this kind of stuff."

Cary fought his smile, but I didn't care, because his whole body finally softened as he released that tension that had been riding him for days.

"Okay. I'm not shaving your junk for you, but I can talk you through it. Deal," he said as he hopped down from the counter.

"Deal," I agreed. Fighting my own smile.

"Me too," came a dark voice from the doorway. Cary stilled, half bent towards the bathroom cabinet with his hand outstretched. "I want to look nice for Ava, too. The Palace wouldn't give me a razor or scissors."

Wolf came and stood next to me in front of the mirror, looking over himself with a critical eye. He pulled some of his shaggy hair away from his face. Cary looked suddenly unsure, and I held my breath.

"Nice robe," Nick said as he stepped out of the shower and walked over to a shelf to grab a towel. "It looks comfy."

Wolf was wearing a pale pink silk robe. He was lucky it was a kimono style, with deep sleeves and designed to be wrapped around a woman's body and tied in the back. It only just covered him. I figured he'd been trying not to spook Cary now that Ava's heat was over, but wanted to join in whatever we were doing in here.

"Thanks," Wolf said. "It was in the wardrobe, but I like it. It feels nice on my skin."

I shrugged. He looked entirely comfortable in it and I had no problem with a guy wearing pink or silk. "Whatever works for you."

"I was thinking we could look for more and get matching ones. Put our pack name on the back," Wolf said. His expression hadn't changed and I couldn't tell if he was joking or not until his lip twitched. I punched him on the arm, and his smile grew.

I shook out my hand. "How the hell did you get so jacked while living in a cell?"

"They had a home gym type thing in a sealed room next to my cage. The type that uses your body weight. A treadmill too. I had nothing else to do, so I spent a lot of time on them." He shrugged as if it was no big deal, but it was. Nobody deserved to live in a cage.

"The cage was shitty, but I'm kinda jealous of the gym," Cary said as he straightened suddenly and shook his head. He seemed to forget for a moment that he was avoiding looking at Wolf. "I begged them for any kind of gym, but they refused. I had to make an outdoor one out of old tyres and a pillow taped to a tree as a punching bag."

"Whatever you did worked," Wolf blurted. Then his eyes went wide as he realized what he'd just implied. That Cary was hot. Which he was, and I was man enough to admit it. His dark, chiseled good looks almost seemed too perfect to be real.

"Uh, thanks?" Cary mumbled and ducked his head. "Maybe we could steal some of the equipment out of your lab gym and put it somewhere more useful. The equipment we took from the guard's gym was crap."

"Yeah, sure," Wolf replied. Their conversation was stilted, but it was a start. Wolf looked grateful Cary was talking to him at all, after Cary's freakout the first night of Ava's heat and the way he'd been avoiding him since. Wolf subtly tracked every one of Cary's movements.

"You guys are lucky they seemed to keep this suite well stocked," Nick said, ignoring the awkward sexual tension and swooping in like the superhero he was. The guy needed a cape. "There's a few electric razors in the bottom drawer and a hair trimming kit. I noticed them the other day when I was looking for a toothbrush. I came straight here from town and didn't bring anything with me except the clothes I was wearing."

"Cary said I can borrow some of his clothes," I said, helping Nick out with the subject change. "Is it okay if Nick borrows some, too?"

"Of course," Cary said as he seemed to shake himself and bent to open the bottom drawer. He pulled out a bunch of grooming appliances.

"Wow, the Palace really was big on grooming," I said, as I rifled through it all.

"You have no idea," Cary chuckled. It sounded as if there was a story there, and I hoped one day I'd get to hear it. For now, he was slowly loosening back up around Wolf, and that was enough. "Wolf, can you please grab that stool and drag it over here next to the power outlet so you can sit on it? This thing doesn't have a long cord."

I felt River's presence a moment before he stepped through the doorway, although he hadn't made a sound. I knew he'd woken up just before Nick arrived. It was a twin thing. He strolled in and hopped up on the counter without saying a word. His hair was damp, and he had a towel wrapped around his waist. The five of us hanging out together felt right.

"Morning," Nick said cheerfully from where he was still drying himself off while standing on the bathmat. River just winked at him. Nick had a way of making River lighten up and focus on what was in front of him that made me happy to see. Ordinarily, River barely acknowledged people around him. It wasn't on purpose, his mind was usually just elsewhere. Working out a problem five steps ahead of where we were at.

"Can I join in?" River asked Cary. I tried to keep my happy smile to myself and not make him self-conscious. I often had to drag him to interact with people, but he genuinely seemed to want to be in here with us.

Cary rolled his eyes, completely resigned to his fate at this point. "Sure, why not?"

"So, what are we doing?" River asked, and to my surprise, Cary laughed.

"Manscaping," he replied.

"Man, what?" River asked. He looked at me, confused. He'd never been one to follow trends or worry about his appearance. What you saw was what you got with River.

"Shaving our junk," I answered. "Oh, and giving Wolf a haircut."

"Oh, okay. That sounds fun," he said, dryly, and I laughed, knowing it wouldn't interest him in the slightest.

"Trust me, you don't want to be the only one with hairy balls, Riv." I looked at the different options on the bench, glad the splinter that had festered between us for so long was finally gone. "Which one should I use around my junk, Cary?"

"The bigger hand-held electric trimmer is good for trimming your pubes. You can set it to a higher length, so it's neat but not bare. Just let me use it on Wolf's head first. The slim one with the flat head is better for your balls. It won't pull the skin or accidentally cut you. It works off a fast vibration more than a sharp edge. You'll want to rub a little oil on them first, though."

He chucked me a tiny bottle, before he turned back to Wolf, who was sitting patiently waiting for him. A giant on a toadstool. His eyes were wide amongst all the hair. For such a big guy, it floored me how vulnerable Wolf could seem when interacting with us.

"What do you want done with your hair?" Cary asked him softly.

"I've never really thought about it," Wolf said, quietly. He looked at me and I smiled gently in encouragement. It broke my heart he'd been so neglected. That was going to change. As a pack, we'd make sure of it. "I like Ryder's, but I don't think I want it that short all the way up the sides. I'm used to it long."

"Okay," Cary said, as he lifted some of Wolf's hair and focused on it. "What if we do a small undercut to neaten it up, then just trim the length? I should be able to handle that. It feels really dry, though. I'm not sure what to do about that. Any ideas, Ryder? You have long hair."

Cary kept his dark hair buzzed short, and he looked genuinely perplexed. I dropped the razors I was holding and moved over to feel Wolf's hair. "I'm not an expert. As I said, I've been in the military or on the run. Mine's probably dry as shit too. Some basic conditioner is probably a good start."

"Any ideas, Nick? You've lived in society more than any of us have."

"You make me sound worldly," he laughed. "I grew up on the farm and I haven't traveled far. Conditioner sounds good. I've always had shorter hair. Maybe we could ask Ava?"

"Yeah. Small undercut, trim the ends, conditioner, then we'll ask Ava later," Cary agreed.

Wolf closed his eyes as Cary started piling sections of hair up on his head and securing them with some hair ties. The moment felt strangely intimate, much more than me standing here with my dick out. I picked the bottle of oil up again and started putting some on my balls as River chuckled.

"Shut up, Riv. I'm nervous about this." I chucked the bottle at him. "You're next."

"I'm going to watch you do it first," River said, as he caught it.

"Pull your dick up. You don't want that monster in the way," Cary said, keeping one eye on me as I nervously switched on the razor and held it near my balls. My hand froze a few centimeters away.

"You can take out a room full of alphas, but you can't shave your balls?" River teased.

"This is way harder," I grumbled, and Nick laughed. He'd finished drying himself off and had moved over to lean against River and watch the show. I loved how comfortable they were becoming in each other's space.

"Oh, give me that," Cary huffed, as he moved over and grabbed the razor out of my hand, where it was still hovering an inch off my balls. He kneeled down in front of me. "You hold your dick and I'll shave."

"I'm trusting you here, Cary," I warned him.

"Yeah, yeah. I won't cut off your precious balls. I promise. This thing tickles more than anything."

"I might have to try that later," came a sweet voice from the doorway. Cary and I both froze.

Thirty-One

Ryder shot a glare at River, who was chuckling. "Oh yeah, Ava's awake. She just had a quick shower. Did I not mention that?"

Ryder huffed, but I could see the smile he was trying to hide and feel his affection for his twin in our bond. It made my heart happy to see them back in sync with each other.

I looked over at Wolf and smiled when I noticed him wearing my robe. He seemed completely at home in it. He clearly didn't care what anyone else thought. "Can you keep the beard? Maybe just tidy it up? I kinda like it. The robe, too. I might have to steal it back later, now that it smells of you."

"Whatever you want," Wolf growled. The sound, and the way his eyes burned through me, sent a shiver up my spine. *No, down omega.*

I looked at Cary and River. "Can I watch, too?" Cary had frozen with one hand on Ryder's balls and the razor in the other. He looked up at Ryder, then back at me.

"No. Sorry. You need to go, Ava. I am not shaving Ryder's balls while he has a hard-on."

A laugh burst from me that felt good. I was floating on air today. The only jeans and leggings I had here were dirty, so I'd put on a chunky cream cable-knit sweater, paired with a short, pleated tartan skirt. The kind that was perfect for flipping up and taking me against a wall, or so my romance books liked to imply. Five sets of eyes currently fixed on my legs seemed to have the same idea. The thigh high socks and chunky boots I was wearing didn't seem to be any deterrent.

"Okay, let's take you to get some breakfast," River said, breaking the spell. He slipped off the bench, picked me up, and walked away as I wrapped my legs around him. "I just need to find some clothes first."

"Right side drawers in Ava's wardrobe. Grab whatever fits," Cary yelled.

"Thank you," River called over his shoulder.

"So you're getting dressed?" I asked, as I bit my lip and pressed myself closer to him.

River groaned. "Yes, or we're never leaving this suite today." I knew we had to. Our friends had been covering our absence for days and we'd stretched our security team thin, covering so many bases.

"I'll turn around then," I said as he dragged me down his body. I spun towards the wall and he pushed me into it with his heavy weight. His hands were instantly up under my skirt. I liked this version of River. He was all alpha, and it had me captivated.

"You're addictive, little bird," he whispered in my ear, before he kissed his bite mark on my neck, making me gasp. It felt like he'd just kissed my clit. As if the two had become intimately connected. He ran his finger over the wisps of lace I was wearing under my skirt.

"What are these?" he growled.

"A surprise for later. Something I've never worn before." The Palace had provided me with lingerie to wear during my debut season. I'd looked at the sheer panels and lace, and thought they were impractical. So I'd put them aside. Now, they fit the mood I found myself in this morning. Curious, alive. Every movement of my body was new and exciting.

He pulled back and smacked me lightly on the ass, making me gasp.

"Wait in the living room, but don't leave without me. You're not going anywhere alone today when you smell like that and are wearing those," he growled.

My heat may have ebbed, but my scent was spiking at the slightest provocation and I only had to look at one of my mates to feel horny. It was a novel sensation. I smiled sweetly at him over my shoulder. "Have fun getting some pants on," I said as I eyed the bulge in his towel. "I'd be happy to help, but apparently we're in a hurry."

"Oh, little bird. You're playing a dangerous game."

I was. I planned to explore every aspect of this new dynamic between us.

I put a little extra sway into my step to make my skirt swish. I'd seen it in a movie once. He groaned loudly as I left the room, and I fought the urge to laugh. I hadn't known having a mate, or mates, could be so fun.

He was back out with me before I'd barely sat down, wearing some worn dark jeans that fit him like a glove and a dark t-shirt. He pulled on a warm jacket before he yanked me up off the couch roughly and kissed me thoroughly.

"Whatever you guys are doing out there, cut it out," Ryder called from the bathroom. "I'm about to poke Cary's eye out."

My laughter finally burst free, and River smiled at me. "We could be evil, but I don't want to freak Cary out too much."

I nodded, "Let's go."

He grabbed my hand, and we made our way down to breakfast. It was such a little thing, but something I had desperately longed to feel again. The simple comfort and companionship whenever the twins held my hand. Mixed with the new desire sparking between us, I felt giddy. We found Emma, Lexie, Angel, and a bunch of omegas in the kitchen, with a few alphas hovering, too. As soon as Angel saw me, she jumped down from the chair she'd been standing on, darted over and wrapped her arms around my legs, trapping me in place.

"Where have you been?" she demanded to know.

"Uhhh," I said awkwardly, lost for words.

How do you explain heats to a little kid? It was something she'd need to know eventually, but explaining it to her too soon could cause anxiety. They were so rare; it wasn't even something the Palace taught omegas about.

Emma approached us quickly. "She was a little worried you'd left without saying goodbye again, even though we told her you were still here."

My heart broke. My heat had been so all-consuming, I hadn't thought about what she might think when I essentially disappeared. I hadn't realized it had affected her the first time, either. She'd been popping up more frequently during my secret travels around the Palace, but I'd figured she'd just been getting older and more mischievous. *Had she been following me?*

"I'm so sorry, sweetie," I mumbled. Suddenly near tears at the thought I might mean something vital to her, even though we'd only ever had stolen moments together before now. I'd hated leaving her behind the first time, when Damon, Hunter, and Leif had rescued us, yet Emma had assured me she was fine while I was hiding in the library. I'd briefly considered trying to smuggle her in there. But keeping her quiet would have been impossible and they would have noticed her missing, being the only child at the Palace. I'd figured finding Maia and getting more help had been our best chance for freeing them all. And it had. It didn't mean Angel understood that, though. Or hadn't been scared.

River dropped to his knees beside me and stroked her hair. "Hey, munchkin, I'm sorry we kept Ava away for a few days. But we'd never take her away from you, without at least telling you we were going and why. I promise. Okay?"

Angel nodded against my leg, but she still didn't seem happy, so I disentangled her from my legs and crouched down to give her a big hug. "You're my girl, Angel. I know the world is a little scary right now, and I've disappeared a couple of times, but I'm never going away for good. You're important to me, okay?"

"Okay," she said in a hesitant whisper.

"Why don't you show me what you were cooking, so I can taste it?" River asked her and she perked up. She was wearing an apron someone had made out of a dish towel and had been stirring a pot with Emma's help when we came in.

"I helped make oats," she said proudly. She tugged on River's hand, so he hopped up and let her drag him over to the pot as he sent me a wink over his shoulder. If I thought seeing her snuggle into Ryder was bad, watching the usually stern River let her lead him around had me melting.

Lexie suddenly pulled me into a giant hug that rivaled Angel's.

"Are you okay?" She whispered in my ear, before she pulled back and searched my face.

"Yeah. Thanks, Lexie. You're a good friend."

"Anytime you need someone to help outrun your demons, I'll be there. Okay?"

I nodded at her, feeling tears well in my eyes. After being so lonely, it was overwhelming how many people I had who cared about me now. In the space of weeks, my family had grown out of nowhere. She squeezed me tight.

"Your emotions are going to be all over the place after your heat. Fair warning. You're probably going to cry at the slightest thing," she said, as she grinned at me and wiped away the tear that spilled over my lashes.

"You think?" I asked, mimicking River's dry tone. A pair of muscular arms wrapped around me from behind as River's dark chocolate scent enveloped me. Drawn back by my emotions. Lexie instantly stepped back.

"Where are the rest of your guys?" Lexie asked as she looked past us out the doorway.

"They're, uh, um…"

"Manscaping together," River finished for me. Lexie burst out laughing as I elbowed River.

"Where's Maia?" I asked, changing the subject before anyone else could jump in.

Lexie immediately sobered. "She wanted to stay, but she was finding it hard being here and the pregnancy hormones were making it worse. Her guys were picking up on it and losing the plot, so I sent them back to the farm. It didn't make sense for us all to stay, anyway. It left the farm too exposed."

"You must be missing Dave and Dio, too," I said, guilt swamping me. I didn't want to be here either, but I felt as if I owed the omegas for leaving them behind when we were rescued. That didn't mean Lexie had to be here, too. "Thank you for staying and looking out for us, but if you want to get back, we'll make it work."

"Actually, we have to stay," Sam said. "At least another day. My guys are bringing in the head of the Network. She's been living in the mountains, but she wants to come and check on the omegas here. Help figure out how we can best protect them. She should be here in a couple of hours."

"She?" I asked.

"Oh yeah," Lexie said, as she shrugged off her longing and got back on task. "Let us catch you up while we get breakfast going. It's just oatmeal with honey and some toast with jam, but it will fill everyone up."

Everyone pitched in and we got breakfast cooking in no time. Sam got us up to speed. It seemed he'd been busy collaborating with the Network while we'd been otherwise engaged. He relayed what his team had told him on a phone call earlier this morning. A beta woman called Constance started the Network decades ago and ran it from a safe house she set up in the mountains. Constance built it to everything it was today, but she died the night before the Crash. She'd had an omega, who was about our age, living with her. Her name was Sadie. She'd rescued Sadie and taken her in when she first presented in her early teens. It turned out Sadie had been on her own up in the mountains for weeks, and had been secretly running the Network while Constance had been ill.

Matt and Anders from Sam's team and Oliver, an alpha who defected from the Palace, volunteered to rescue Constance and Sadie. They left just before I went into heat, not knowing Constance had passed away. They got stuck in a snowstorm and were only just making their way down from the mountain with Sadie this morning. A frown marred Lexie's face as Sam talked.

"Did you know Constance, Lexie?" I asked.

"I think I might have," she answered. Sam looked shocked.

"Why didn't you say anything when I told you this earlier?" he looked a little hurt. She turned around and grabbed his face to kiss him.

"It didn't click when you were talking to me earlier. All the problems here had me distracted, but hearing you tell it again, something clicked. I had a contact who would sometimes help me get an abused woman out of the safe house and into another one in the mountains. I never asked where, exactly, because I trusted her implicitly and it was better if I didn't know. It was often an older beta guy who would come, but sometimes it was a young woman. I suspected she was an omega. She wore a lot of perfume, but I never asked and she never talked much. It never occurred to me they could have been with the Network, because it wasn't omegas I was sending them. It just fits that it was Constance and Sadie. We used code names, so I can't be sure."

"She'll be here soon, but if she's a contact of yours, I trust her already," Sam said sweetly. Lexie just smiled up at him.

I was just untying my apron when I heard hurried footsteps coming down the main stairs. I rushed out and was instantly swallowed up in a giant hug by Ryder, Cary, and Nick. They squeezed the breath out of me. I was a little disconcerted at how much I had missed them. They stepped away, and I saw Wolf hanging back. He rubbed the back of his neck self consciously as I swept my gaze over him.

He was wearing clothing similar to River. Tight dark jeans that looked criminally good on his thick thighs, and a black long sleeve t-shirt that was stretched to capacity. He'd pulled his hair back from his face, in a bun, and he had a short, neat undercut. His beard was shorter, too. Trimmed of its wildness, but still sexy.

With that straggly hair out of the way, his face was more visible. I'd thought his eyes were intense before, when they were all I could really see. I'd been mistaken. Now that sharp cheekbones and a heavy brow framed them, there was no escaping them when he looked at me.

"Wow," I whispered, as I reached up to trace his cheekbones. "You're a work of art."

He was gorgeous in a rough hewn kind of way. As if someone had carved him out of the earth. He had the spirit to match. That wildness was still there. The make-over hadn't tamed it; it was just camouflage.

He relaxed into my touch. "Only you could see beauty in me."

"Beauty is too small a word for you," I replied. There was something about Wolf that seemed barely contained. He'd let some of it out that first night we'd met, but it had only been a whisper of his power. I don't think we'd seen the depths of Wolf yet. He was a prime alpha. I knew that intimately. But where Damon and Sam spilled their dominance everywhere, Wolf's was a part of him. Only a hint escaped. He was no less deadly for it.

"Where did you get the clothes?" I asked, changing the subject. There was no way Cary's clothes would have fit him.

"Lexie had them dropped off. She said Leif left them behind for me. The jacket didn't fit, but the rest does. Kind of."

I'd have to thank Lexie and Leif later.

"Okay," Lexie said, coming out of the kitchen as she clapped her hands loudly, startling me. "We have a million things we need help with, so stop hogging the big, strong men and let them get to work."

I grinned at her as I gave my guys another hug, then let them go. The next couple of hours passed in a blur. Lexie was right. There was a lot to do. If the Palace had permanent power, it made the building a valuable base, even if the omegas chose not to stay here.

Lexie gathered the omegas together, then pushed me forward to talk to them about Emma and Rose's ideas for the future of the Palace. I frowned at her, but she insisted they trusted me and didn't know her. So I took a nervous breath and jumped in. It went better than I would have thought, even if I stammered a bit at having so many people listening to me talk.

A surprising number of the omegas were on board with turning it into a place of refuge and training, run by omegas. Some were fearful of repercussions after everything the Palace had put us through. Which was exactly why we needed to do it. To show them what omegas could do, and that we weren't weak, the way the Palace wanted us to think. That we were stronger than even we knew.

So we divvied up jobs to any omega willing to pitch in. Things like figuring out laundry and compiling a list of useful resources we could find throughout the Palace. Then Lexie, Angel, Rose and I headed to the conservatory to see if Rose's ideas for it were workable. Although, Rose found somewhere else to be when some of our guys came to help. They couldn't seem to stay away, and I couldn't find it in me to mind. I didn't want to overwhelm Rose, though, sensing she was naturally timid and a little wary of alphas. So we let her flee back to the kitchen, where she seemed more comfortable. She took Angel with her, at Angel's insistence. I was quickly working out, food highly motivated Angel.

Nick gave us advice about what kind of plants might grow well in the conservatory. He'd picked up a lot helping around the farm over the years. Then we got some of Lexi's farming team on the phone to find out what we needed to do to prepare the soil better. They gave us detailed instructions we wrote down, then they offered to send us some young plants and some seeds they had stored. So, we put Wolf and Sam to work, pulling out the existing plants and piling them up. While Lexie and I mapped the garden beds and figured out a new layout.

We were all focused on our work when I got the feeling I was being watched while I bent over a garden bed. I looked up to find River leaning against the pool railing, his gaze running hotly over me. It seemed to be his new favorite pastime.

"Do you need help with something?" I asked him as I straightened. Maybe he was hot and needed help to undress. A girl could hope.

"No. I just came in to tell you we have visitors," he replied. "Sadie's here."

"And when was that?" Lexie asked with a smirk.

"About five minutes ago," he replied darkly, eyeing my skirt.

Thirty-Two

Sam was up and moving instantly, shooting me a glare on his way, until Lexie stopped him with a hand on his bare chest.

"Hold up. Clean off, then get dressed first. You're not meeting another omega in your trunks." Sam looked down at himself and then grinned at Lexie.

"Are you feeling territorial?" he asked her.

"Hell yes," she answered. "And if Sadie is an important ally, you don't want me poking her eyes out. Pool. Now."

His grin widened as he jumped in. Wolf took one look at Ava's face and followed him in. I couldn't help but think of when we'd been in this pool during her heat.

"Why are they undressed?" I asked, my voice gone still and quiet.

"Nobody has a lot of clean clothes here right now, and they were pulling out trees. They stripped to keep theirs clean," Ava said, as if the explanation was obvious. She moved over to me instinctively, at my obvious disquiet, and wrapped her arms around me. I let out a heavy breath, then breathed her scent in slowly. It had only been hours, but I'd missed her. I didn't know how I'd survived a decade without her. Looking back on it now, I think I'd become robotic, just solving each problem in front of me and moving onto the next. It hadn't been a life. This, our pack and the life we were building for her, or trying to, was everything to me.

"And you had no problem with Lexie seeing Wolf half naked?" She'd seemed so jealous the first night we'd arrived, especially around the other omegas. Her possessiveness, even though she wouldn't look me in the eye, had given me hope. It confused me that she seemed okay with it now.

"I would if it was anyone but Lexie or Maia. They're mated and our packs have become intertwined, which makes them my sisters," she answered.

"Hell yeah, we're your sisters," Lexie growled playfully, and Ava grinned at her. Those two together were trouble.

"Just so you're aware, that doesn't work in reverse. No stripping in front of other alphas. I don't care how close you think we are," I growled for real and pulled her hard into me. Her body trembled against me, setting off my predator instincts.

"Yes sir," she squeaked and her sweetened cherry scent washed me in a haze of desire.

Lexie laughed. "I think everyone needs a cool down."

"I'm good. You guys catch up," I growled. I grabbed Ava's hand and side stepped piles of greenery as I led her out of the ruins of the conservatory. As soon as we were outside, I pushed her up against the wall in the hallway and ran my hands up the back of her thighs until I felt her soft skin. I couldn't get enough skin contact with her. I felt starved.

"You're killing me, little bird," I growled before I kissed her senseless. Her soft lips parted and I dove in, needing her to feel what she did to me. I only pulled away when we heard a movement in the doorway and a pointed cough. I knew Wolf wouldn't care that I was kissing Ava, but I assumed Sam and Lexie were behind him.

"Coast is clear," Wolf said over his shoulder as I pulled back, but I couldn't take my eyes off Ava's lips. Seeing them swollen and red from kissing did something to me every damn time. He patted me on the shoulder as he passed, and I shook myself.

I pulled myself together as we headed into the formal living room. Cary, Nick, and Ryder were sitting on a couch together and each one tracked every movement Ava made with a hunger that matched my own. Only I couldn't handle letting her go yet. So I grabbed the chair next to them and pulled Ava into my lap. Wolf lounged against the back of the chair behind us.

Sam's face lit up as he approached his squad mates, Matt and Anders, and pulled them into a hug. The relief in his eyes was clear, and it was obvious he'd been worried about them. He'd expected them to be back within a day, but they'd been gone for three.

The third volunteer, Oliver, was hanging back, sticking close by Sadie's side. I watched him for a moment as he assessed everyone in the room, trying to figure out who the biggest threat was. He looked half a heartbeat away from yanking Sadie into his arms and dragging her out of the room.

Sadie was being much more subtle as she watched us with an air of studied casualness that would have hid her nervousness to a less experienced eye. But I wasn't fooled. She had dark blonde hair in a braid over one shoulder and a tough stance as she discreetly eyed everyone in the room. Her eyes lit up when she spotted Lexie's bright hair as she brought up the rear with Pala. Sadie pushed past the alphas, raising a few amused eyebrows, and strode straight over to her.

"Lexie," she called out confidently. Sadie ignored everyone else, even Oliver, who was hot on her heels.

"It is you, you sneaky shit," Lexie laughed, but she sobered up quickly as she gave Sadie a hug. "I'm sorry about Constance. She was an incredible woman."

Sadie nodded in agreement and pulled away quickly. She tried to step back but bumped into Oliver, Matt, and Anders, who had piled up behind her. She shot them a mock glare, but the affectionate smile that slipped free ruined it.

"Anyone care to explain the bite marks on the four of you?" Sam asked suddenly, his voice had gone lethally quiet.

Sadie just raised an eyebrow at him and put her hand on one cocked hip. She looked unimpressed to have someone up in her business.

"You're mated?" Lexie asked her, ignoring Sam for the moment.

"Yeah, it was obvious the moment these three showed up they were my mates. We got snowed in together in a small cabin, so things happened quickly."

"Was it consensual?" Sam asked, pulling the attention back to him again. I tensed, not sure what to expect, at the look on his team's faces.

"Sadie popped out from behind a tree and pulled a gun on us when we arrived, because we'd set off her alarms," Matt said, stepping between her and Sam. "Trust me, she's strong, capable, and smart as hell. She saved our lives up on the mountain. If she didn't want something to happen, it wouldn't. So while I appreciate you looking out for her, you can relax, Sam." I could see how much respect Matt had for Sam, but he wasn't letting anyone mess with his pack. Sam seemed a little thrown, but he quickly recovered.

"Yeah, and we'll try not to be offended by what you just asked," Anders growled. He was a darkly potent alpha, and his words felt like they held weight.

"Sorry, guys. I had to check. I'm happy for you," Sam said, in a voice that was still quiet, but had lost its coldness.

"Okay, let's bring it down a notch," Lexie said, then introduced everyone in the room that hadn't met yet and encouraged everyone to sit down. We'd taken to using this room to meet because there was plenty of comfortable seating.

"It's great to meet you, Sadie, but I'm guessing this is more than a social call? What do you need?" I asked her, getting straight to the point. Ryder rolled his eyes at me, but he was watching Sadie as closely as I was. So was Sam. She was getting increasingly fidgety. Which showed she was nervous about something more than meeting us.

"I came because I want to meet the omegas here and help them figure out what comes next. It was Constance's dream to free them from the Palace and I want to make sure where they end up is an improvement, despite the Crash. I have resources to help and can give them options."

"That sounds great. Lexie and Ava have already started on that, so we can get to that in a minute," I said. "What else?"

Sadie grinned at me, startling me. "I've heard about you. Gus, is a fan of yours. He says you're a straight shooter and highly observant. He wanted you and Ryder to work more closely with us, but it didn't fit your plans. I'm glad you found Ava."

Gus was my contact in the Network. It turned out he was also Sam's, but they had a much closer partnership. Gus was crotchety at times, but had a sharp mind and an agenda that mostly matched mine, so we'd worked together well.

"Thank you," I said, keeping it simple. If she thought her pretty speech would distract me, though, she was wrong.

She sighed when I didn't lose focus at her change of tack. "You're right, there is something else, but it's private. Is Maia here, Sam?"

Sam was instantly on alert, as were Lexie and Ava. "No, she's at the farm. What do you need with Maia?"

"I was hoping to talk to you both together, but it will have to be you. Can we go somewhere?"

Sam gave an amused chuckle. "If we go somewhere private, this lot will just listen at the door. I don't have any secrets. We can talk here."

I was suddenly intensely grateful for these pack dynamics and the way they seemed to be completely open with each other. Because Ava tensing up protectively at the mention of Maia had riled up my alpha.

"Okay," Sadie seemed surprised, but leaned down to pull something out of the backpack she'd dropped at her feet. "I have a letter for you."

Sam groaned as he reached over and took it from her outstretched hand.

"Is there a problem?" she asked.

"No. I love letters. But in the last one I found addressed to me, I lost a grandfather and a brother, and gained a half brother."

"I see," Sadie said, a frown marring her features.

"I take it you know who Maia and I really are?" Sam asked her, his bright blue gaze fixed on her, looking for signs of dishonesty. Ava had filled us in on Sam and Maia's history. Their abduction from Maven and how they'd been secretly adopted and hidden in plain sight amongst betas. They'd only recently found out they weren't related to their gramps who had raised them, or the mother who had abandoned them.

Sadie hesitated for a heartbeat, and I wasn't sure she'd answer. She swallowed hard. "Yes. I'm one of the few who knew who your parents really were. If you already know that, it may make this letter easier. I haven't read it, but I can guess what's in there."

My eyes stayed fixed on Sam, but I reached up behind me and patted Wolf's hand. He'd tensed up at the mention of Hunter. Ava was right. These packs were a giant, interwoven family.

"Who is it from?" Sam asked as he flipped the letter back and forth in his hand.

"Constance," Sadie said, her voice breaking a little on the name.

Sam sucked in a breath and opened it, as Lexie wrapped her arms around him. He angled it so she could read over his shoulder. I watched them closely and noticed Sam's hand shake as he read. Lexie took the letter from him and held it up between them while he rubbed his hands on his damp jeans. He was silent for a moment, as he seemed to focus on his breathing.

"Tell me," Pala begged him from beside Lexie. Lexie immediately passed him the letter.

"Sorry, Pala." Sam shook his head a little. "It turns out Constance was our aunt. Her sister was Maven's omega, our mother. When our mother died, she convinced our gramps to take us and hide us away. Constance was close with her sister and felt helpless when she couldn't save her. She said she started the Network to track the people responsible, trying to bring them down, and save as many other omegas as she could. She wanted to reach out to us, but knew Maven was hunting her and it would draw attention. She says we're the future of the Network. That its founding members are getting old and they need to think about succession and bringing in new blood. She wants Sadie, Maia, and me to be the next generation of the Network and lead it into the future."

Sam delivered the words matter-of-factly, as if he was slightly shell-shocked. Sadie looked sad, but not surprised, as she'd said. It struck me how the webs created by a pack nobody knew existed kept pulling us together.

"Wow," Pala said, as he reached behind Lexie and gripped the back of Sam's neck. They all had the same slightly dazed look, as if they'd been rolling with the punches for a while now.

"Maia is going to be gutted that she never got to meet her," Lexie said quietly.

I suddenly felt as if we were intruding on something intensely personal. "We'll leave you guys to talk and come back later."

"No, stay," Lexie said before I could lift Ava off my lap, and Sam nodded.

Sadie looked awkwardly at Sam. "Constance told me how much she wanted to meet you. She dreamed about it being possible one day. Your gramps sent her photos, and she kept them in a safe. But she knew having her in your life would put you in even more danger."

"Did she crochet?" Sam asked suddenly.

"Yeah, she found it relaxing. She used to make these bears she'd donate to charities for disadvantaged kids at Christmas."

"Maia and I both had one. Our gramps told us someone had made them with love but never said who. I always wondered why our brother, Ben, never had one." Sam blew out a heavy breath. "I have a million questions and I'd like to sit and talk with you about Constance later, if that's okay, Sadie. Maybe we could call Maia so she can talk to you, too? But right now, it changes nothing. It's just one more thing that Maven needs to pay for."

"We need to find them and end this," Lexie said, anger blazing from her eyes. "It's gone on for too long, and they've hurt too many people."

"We've been trying to do that for decades," Sadie said. "We know who they are. Individually, they're all public figures, but getting any proof that Maven as a pack exists and what they've been doing has proven impossible."

"We have it now," Lexie said.

"Yes," Sadie agreed, "but we have no way of making that information public and there's no-one left in any kind of authority to send it to, or do anything about it."

"If we could find them, we could capture and detain them ourselves," Ryder suggested. "We have the cells under the labs here. Let them see how it feels to live in them." Ryder wasn't usually a bitter person, but I could feel his anger roiling through him. He'd become protective of Wolf, and watched him for signs he was okay almost as much as he watched Ava.

"Do you want to spare the food to feed them when people are starving out there from their actions?" Sadie asked.

Ryder was silent, and Sadie's posture softened as she watched him. Watched us all. "Most of my guys in the Network would happily take them out if attacked, but none of us are murderers. It's a line we haven't yet crossed."

I noticed her use of the word "yet" and narrowed my eyes at her. She flicked her gaze at me and watched me quietly. Waiting for our next move.

"They've crossed it," I said. I kept my tone emotionless and my eyes on my brother. "They may not have pulled the trigger themselves, but through the military, they trained and ordered people to do it for them. A lot of the sanctioned hits the military undertook weren't in the national interest. They were in Maven's interest."

Ava shifted in her seat and wrapped her arms around my neck as she nuzzled into me, drawn in as she sensed my emotions spike and my scent turned slightly bitter. I wanted nothing more than to collapse into her softness and let her heal me, but I kept myself rigid. Now was not the time.

"It's the reason we left the military. We realized they would never let us claim Ava, no matter how far we rose through the ranks. Even if we'd become generals, it wouldn't have mattered. We'd planned to stay longer, collect as much information against them as we could from the inside. We left when we did because we couldn't stomach the things they ordered us to do."

Cary and Nick both put their hands on Ryder instinctively, as he visibly flinched at my words. I could feel his remorse and guilt pummeling me. "You mean I couldn't stomach them." It wasn't a question. He was wrong, though.

"No, I mean, we," I ground out. Wolf shifted and rested both his hands on my shoulders. The solid strength in those hands and the reassurance filtering through our bond grounded me. I needed it. I'd kept my emotions in check for so long, focused on our plan and trying to navigate Ryder's rage. Now I had six people's emotions pummeling me. I found I didn't want to tune them out, the way I'd thought I would. I found them strangely comforting, but I needed help to process them. Wolf's touch was a pillow between me and everything coming at me. It wouldn't stop it all, but it softened it.

"What happened?" Ava asked as she stroked my neck.

My gut churned as memories assaulted me. "They asked us to capture another soldier, then torture and kill him, on a made up accusation we knew was false. Our superior told us it was for the good of our country. That he was a traitor. They tried to use us to cover their own tracks. We tried to get him out but make it look as if we'd killed him. It backfired. They'd sent a second team in unknown to us. It had been a test. The soldier got badly injured and we couldn't get him out. We had to choose between taking him out, or leaving him behind, knowing they would torture him for whatever time he had left. He begged us to kill him, and I did. We barely made it out alive."

I could still feel the man's blood on my hands. Ryder hadn't been able to do it, so I had. I tried to pull my hands away from Ava, not wanting to sully her with my touch right now. She grabbed my hands and pulled them tight around her. The things we'd faced in the military had stoked the misplaced anger Ryder felt at Ava. He could never understand why I wasn't angry at Ava as well. The truth was, I hadn't been because I knew I would destroy myself to save someone I loved. It helped me realize that was exactly what she had done, too. To save us.

Ava looked up at me, and a tear rolled down her cheek, but her eyes shone with understanding. I couldn't feel any blame coming from her, or horror, just love. It was a soothing balm on my soul.

"And yet you harried them, even after you went AWOL. Discovered their next hits and got a lot of them out and to us. Some of them were our undercover guys, and you saved their lives," Sadie said. I could see why Constance wanted her to lead. She had an inner fire, but was also empathetic and supportive. It was a good combination for a leader.

I shrugged. We'd done it because we had the skills, and it was the right thing to do. It hadn't washed my hands clean, though. I could still see that man's face in my dreams. He'd known death was his best option, but it hadn't made it any easier when I'd cocked the trigger. There'd been so much regret in his eyes, for the life he hadn't yet lived, and now, never would.

"It's the same reason Damon and the guys left the military," Lexie said quietly from where she was sitting on Sam's lap. "Dave refused to give them an order he couldn't stomach. Damon blackmailed people and got his team out before the military forced Dave's hand. The military benched Dave after that. He ended up retiring early."

"Yeah," Oliver said with a deep sigh. He'd been a quiet presence at Sadie's side until now. "I've never heard of Maven before, but for the unit I was with here at the Palace, it was their classic M.O. I was in too deep before I realized how corrupt it was. By then, it was too late. I'd trusted my orders blindly for too long and I'd seen too much. They never would have let me out alive and I had no allies to turn to."

"You did what you could and helped when it counted," Pala said. He glanced at Ryder and me, as well as Oliver.

Oliver grunted, and I got it. The words were nice, but the blood remained. He looked up at Sadie and she reached out a hand to him, but didn't move into his lap, even though I sensed she wanted to. She seemed conflicted.

"Oh, for fuck's sake. Just hug him, Sadie. Nobody here will think any less of you. You can be an omega and the badass head of the Network at the same time," Lexie grumbled.

I worried for a moment that Sadie would get angry, but she grinned at Lexie and hopped straight onto Oliver's lap. She kissed him quickly, and he relaxed into her.

"I'm not looking for sympathy," Oliver said. "I'm just saying, Maven and whatever is left of the military hiding out with them won't hesitate to cross any lines. They don't have any. So if a line needs to be crossed to take them down, I'll do it. I'm not innocent anymore."

Ava glanced at me, feeling my determination. To keep her safe, I'd be at his side, taking whatever shot I needed to take.

"I would never ask you to do that," Sadie said. She gripped his face firmly and forced him to look at her when he tried to look away.

"You wouldn't have to. I'd do it in a heartbeat to keep you safe," he said, echoing my own thoughts.

Before Sadie could say anything, Wolf jumped in. "I think I know how to find them. Their fallback position was the manor, but I don't know an exact location. Can Max still do satellite surveillance? If I give him a general area and some landmarks, could he find a property?"

"I'm sure he could. He's brilliant at that stuff," Lexie said. "Give me the details and I'll get them to him."

I released a breath I'd been holding. Wolf had mentioned he thought he knew where they were the night after we met him. I'd wanted to know, and also dreaded knowing since then. Now that I had Ava back, I couldn't stand the thought of losing her again. Or her losing us. I wanted time with her. Yet the thought of Maven out there, potentially gunning for both Wolf and Ava, had kept me awake at night. Strategising. Without a destination though, I'd gone round in circles.

When Wolf finished giving the details to Lexie, he paused and looked around the room before his eyes landed on me. "If we do this, don't underestimate Maven, or think they've retreated and are off licking their wounds. I agree, they need to be taken out and for more reasons than you think, but we need to be prepared."

I could feel a tension through the bond that escalated sharply as Wolf glanced down at Ava. His hands tightened on my shoulders.

"What aren't you telling us, Wolf?" I asked. I tried not to let my frustration show in my voice, but I couldn't help if he wouldn't talk to me.

Wolf hesitated. He had no poker face, though. Our entire pack focused in on him.

"They watched her, Wolf. All the time," Cary said. "We need to know why. It's time." I felt my jaw clench hard, but I agreed. It was past time.

"He's right. I've gone through their servers," Nick said. "They have no records on Ava the way they do for you and Maia, Wolf. But there's a hell of a lot of footage of Ava. They were watching her closely, but they never pulled her into their programs. Why, Wolf? What don't we know?"

"Are you worried about scaring me, Wolf? Because I'm tougher than I look," Ava said, as she twisted and reached up over me to touch his arm. "I'd rather know what I'm facing."

"They would never have let you have a debut," Wolf ground out. "Maven left you alone because they planned on mating you themselves."

"What? Why would they want to mate me?" Ava asked. She sounded shocked, as if the idea was preposterous.

Understanding dawned. What Wolf hadn't wanted to say. "Because if they mated you, he'd join them and he'd never leave again. They'd have him with no cage."

Ava gasped as she searched Wolf's face. It had shuttered, though, preparing for a storm. I felt him emotionally brace himself, and it pulled at our bond.

"We're mated now, and we're already part of a pack. So their plan won't work anymore," Ava said.

"It won't stop them. Nothing will stop them, even our bonds. They'll just add their own bonds, then kill your other mates," Wolf growled. "They're not rational and they don't care about anything else. Not even the world going to hell. They're obsessed with power. Not influence, or business success, or even money. Real primal power."

I could feel Wolf's dominance rising with his emotions, as regret clouded his eyes for the briefest moment. Then it was gone, replaced by a feral wildness. His power churned through us as if to prove his point. He didn't have to bark, or even look at anyone, and everyone outside of our pack got up and shifted away from us instinctively.

"They want this, Ava, and they'll use you to get it."

Thirty-Three

Power, unlike anything I'd ever felt, swirled through me. It was instinctive, predatory and ancient. It was pure alpha dominance. I'd thought I knew what it meant to be in a pack with Wolf. My understanding hadn't even come close. The power that had swirled through us briefly when we'd mated, like a warm river, was nothing compared to this raging torrent. And I sensed he was still holding back.

Then suddenly, it was gone. As quickly as it had sprung up, it ebbed away. It left my senses reeling.

I didn't feel scared, though. His power lit me up inside, as if someone had turned a switch on within me and light had flooded me. I felt exhilarated. Yet there was an edge to it that had my instincts screaming a warning. The full force of his dominance was going to burn if it wasn't properly balanced, and that came with its own revelation. I couldn't filter it to the pack alone. *We need Cary.*

I looked back up at Wolf and my exhilaration faded, replaced by a sharp, all-consuming anger on the other side. Wolf wouldn't meet my gaze and I could feel a surge of negative emotions battering him. So I stood up and rounded the chair, backing him into the corner.

"Let me guess. You think you're going to push some dominance at us and I'm going to run and hide because you're a big, scary monster? Is that what you're freaking out about? Huh?"

Wolf's eyes were wide, and he kept his mouth shut as he backed up until he hit the wall. I slapped my hand beside his head.

"I told you Wolf. I'm not afraid of you. And we're stronger together. I've been hiding in the lion's den for a decade. I know what a monster looks like, and you're not one. You can't scare me off."

"I don't want you scared. I want you aware," he growled. "You need to know what's at stake. They'll burn what's left of the world if they get this level of dominance within their pack. I've fought to keep it out of their hands. But if it comes down to me handing it over to save you, I'll do it in a heartbeat. This power is a curse, and—"

"It's not a curse," I interrupted him, getting up on my tippy toes and in his face as much as I could. Needing him to know I could take anything he needed me to bear. My anger raged brightly, throbbing through my veins, thinking about what they'd tried to do to him and everything he'd shouldered on his own. It stopped now. This pack wasn't just about me. It was about us. "Your power is a gift and a responsibility. One nobody else can take. This power has always been *you*. Now it's *us*. I get it's a heavy burden, but you're not alone anymore. You have a pack now, and we're with you all the way. We figure it out *together*. Okay?"

Wolf wrapped his arms around me, lifted me up, and pulled me tight against him as he nodded brusquely. He looked too overcome for words, but I didn't mind. I could feel him. The words were just gift wrapping for me. I wrapped my legs around him and held on tight.

"You don't see how magnificent you are, Wolf, but I do. We do. Why haven't you let it out before? Even the first night, when you looked half wild, your dominance felt nothing like that."

He swallowed hard, then took a deep breath. "They'd drugged me that first night, and it affected my control. When I let it out in the humvee, it burst everywhere, and we ended up crashing. I didn't want to risk hurting you or Cary."

"You'd never hurt me." I knew without even having to think about it.

"How do you know that?" I could feel his genuine worry.

My anger fled as I cupped his face and stroked it gently. I rarely got angry, but when I did, it was a brief, passing flame. "You sat in a cage for me for years, Wolf. And I would do no less for you. Do you hear me?"

"I'll never let that happen," he growled.

"And I'll never let them have you back," I said, softly, right before I yanked his head to mine and kissed him. It was pure bliss. I ran my hands up into his hair and tugged roughly. He groaned and kissed me harder as he swallowed me up in his arms.

When we finally let each other go, I turned to see our pack had surrounded us, with their backs to us. They'd protected us from everyone in the room while we'd been distracted and vulnerable. Even Cary was standing shoulder to shoulder between Nick and Ryder. I could see Lexie's face peeking out from behind Sam and Pala in the corner they'd backed into.

"Holy shit, Ava. You're a little scary when you're mad. You didn't even flinch at his power, either. I almost wet myself," Lexie said, her eyes huge, and I laughed.

My body felt vibrantly alive, as if Wolf had zapped me with pure energy. I just hoped it didn't have a hangover effect if it wore off. Like caffeine.

"Okay, back to work, everyone. We have shit to sort out," Lexie added as she clapped her hands and motioned everyone back into their seats. She'd seen plenty of alpha tantrums before. Maybe not on that scale, but she was a pro at shaking things off.

"We need to get the omegas out of here, if you're a target, Wolf," Sadie said as she took her seat again, too. I could practically see the gears in her mind working. Her mates were still eyeing Wolf warily, especially Oliver, but they were following Sam's and Lexie's lead.

"And Ava, too," Lexie added. "We're too vulnerable here. We've stretched our resources thin, and it's Maven's turf. It hasn't been sitting well with me."

"I agree," Sam said. "I think we need to head back to the farm. Keep our packs in one place. Ava's right. We're stronger together, and that means all of us." Lexie looked giddy at the thought of having her pack together again.

"Is it defendable, if it's a farm?" River asked. He was frowning. "At least here we have sturdy walls and power."

"Oh, just wait until you see it. It's perfect," I reassured him. I couldn't wait to get back to the farm again. The warmth of the community there called to me and I'd missed it. I felt a little bad that we'd be bringing trouble with us, though.

"She's right. It's not what you're thinking, River," Nick said, backing me up. "Damon and his mates created a refuge and a base of operations for themselves. It's the safest place around."

"Will Damon be onboard?" River asked.

"I'm onboard and Maia will make sure Damon is, too," Lexie said, jumping in.

"Okay, but what about the omegas?" Ryder asked. "If having them around us right now means they're in danger, we can't take them with us. And we can't leave them here unprotected."

Sadie whistled to get our attention, and we immediately shut up. We'd been talking rapidly, almost over the top of each other. Like a family.

"I can take the omegas back with me. I have space. They'll be protected and comfortable."

"To the bunkhouse at the cabin?" Matt asked. "We'll have to find a hell of a lot of food to take with us. Foraging will be hard for that many people, especially with snow still on the ground."

"To the bunkhouse to start, for a few days until the snow clears," Sadie said, as she winked at him before turning back to us. "That's the other thing I wanted to talk to you guys about. The Network has a secret location we've been taking omegas to for years. We can fit the omegas you have here, and we have plenty of food. Both stockpiled and growing. We also have medical supplies and a doctor. I can't tell you where it is yet. That's not about trusting you, though. I just don't trust these walls."

"Have you been holding out on us, tiger?" Anders asked Sadie, as he tugged on her braid.

She shot him a wicked grin. "Not intentionally. We were just busy doing other things."

"You have a doctor?" Lexie butted in. "Maia is pregnant. It would be great if we could keep in contact. We only have a vet and some elders experienced in natural remedies at the farm."

"For an omega pregnancy, I'll move mountains. Consider it done," Sadie said, with a definitive head nod. Lexie and I both looked at each other and shared a sigh of relief. Sadie was proving to be a valuable ally. I also liked her tough, no-nonsense approach. I hoped we'd get some time to get to know her better. She'd fit in well with us.

"Can you transport the omegas?" Sam asked. "Or do you need help with that?"

Sadie thought for a moment, then nodded her head. "If you could help with transport, that would be great. It would take me a few days to get something here."

"We'll sort it out," Sam said. "The omegas will all need warm clothes if you're taking them to the mountains. I think we should get the omegas to pack what they need this afternoon, and work on getting everyone out of here in the morning. It's too late to move a big group today. Unless you think the danger is imminent, Wolf?"

He shook his head. "I don't think it's an immediate danger. The Palace techs seemed panicked when they left. I think it's going to take them a bit to get organized. Especially if we're together and they're going to take us all on."

"I think you might need to find space for a couple of alphas to come with you, Sadie," I said, trying not to smile. "Or we may need to bring another omega with us?"

"Oh, do tell," Lexie stage whispered.

"Um, Miles and Owen have become pretty attached to Emma. I think they may be her mates."

"Why am I only just hearing about this now?" Sam groaned. At this rate, most of his team would be in the mountains. I didn't think Matt, Anders, and Oliver had any plans for Sadie to go back on her own.

"If she's claimed them, I'm okay," Sadie said, but she was frowning. "But we don't let unmated alphas into the secret location with the omegas."

"I'll talk to them," Sam said.

"Okay. If we're all agreed to go in the morning, I think we should keep everyone together tonight. Including all of us," River said. "It will make it easier to organize a watch, just in case."

We voted and everyone agreed, but I noticed Nick blushing sweetly.

"I have an idea that may provide a good distraction tonight and help keep everyone calm."

"Let's hear it," River said, with an encouraging nod and a soft smile.

Thirty-Four

I stood alone in the library a few hours later. I'd come in hunting for the chocolate I knew Maia had stashed in here when she'd used it as her refuge. Most of the omegas had been so stoic since we'd arrived, doing whatever was needed without complaint. I figured they deserved a treat to go with the movie night Nick had sweetly suggested.

He'd found a projector and had planned to rig up a white sheet as a screen and set up a movie date for us outside tonight. Yet he'd gracefully offered to set it up in the ballroom instead, to keep everyone calm and entertained while we all slept in there tonight. It would be one giant pajama party. My heart had swelled as he'd talked about his idea. He was so perceptive of people's needs and so giving of himself.

I still pinched myself that he was my mate. If I was honest with myself, I was still a little nervous about pleasing them all, though. During my heat, I hadn't thought about anything but the next touch, the next lips. They'd opened my eyes to an entire world of sensation I hadn't known existed. My body felt different in a way I couldn't define. Even now that my heat had ended, I still craved them. Every brush of their hands on my skin, or the press of their lips on mine, had me on fire. I wanted to make them feel the same, feel them coming undone underneath my own hands. But I wasn't sure how to do that.

So I'd found myself in front of a row of shelves, feeling intensely embarrassed even though I was the only one here. This wasn't like a public library, with metallic racks that were dusted regularly. Somebody had hand carved the shelving in here out of timber, and it looked about a hundred years old. Most of the books in here were just as old, but I didn't care. It was dry in here, and a little musty, as the windows didn't open, but the smell of the old paper always put a smile on my face.

I put the box on the edge of a shelf and pulled a leather-bound book out that caught my eye. I read over the gold embossed title; A *sexual awakening for omegas*. It was a reference book on sex and what stimulated us. I hadn't known they had anything like it in here. I would have been browsing these shelves a lot sooner if I had. As I flicked through the pages, a drawing caught my eye of a woman going down on a guy. It reminded me of doing that to Cary while Ryder coached me.

A breath on my neck had me freezing. "I thought I'd find you in here," Cary whispered. I'd been so distracted I hadn't even heard him approach. "What are you reading?"

"Nothing," I snapped the book closed, but I wasn't fast enough. He jerked his hand out and caught it. It flopped back open to the page I'd been on. He looked at me with one raised eyebrow, and a slow smile spread across his face.

"Is this why you used to come hide out in here, Ava? To look at dirty pictures?"

"No, but I might have if I'd known they were here."

His grin widened at that, and he spun me around and crowded me into a shelf. "You need to look at a man's body, you come find one of your men, Ava. That's what we're here for."

"It's not all you're here for, Cary." He sobered at that as he traced my serious expression with his gaze. As much as I wanted to get lost in the feel of Cary pressed against me, we needed to talk more. I couldn't stand the distance that had sprung up between us since my heat started. He was here physically, but somewhere else emotionally. And after Wolf's explosion of dominance this morning, I knew it wasn't something I could let slide anymore. Yet, I didn't want to pressure him either by telling him about my revelation. I was stuck and hoped if I could get him to talk, he'd get there on his own.

"Ava, you're too good for me," he whispered as he wrapped his arms around me. It felt so right. Yet, him holding me this way just made me even more aware of the aching hole in my chest.

"No, I'm not. I'm entirely selfish," I whispered back.

He tilted his head. "You're the least selfish person I know, Ava. Why would you think that?"

I took a deep breath and let out what was in my heart. "Because I want to claim you and feel as bonded to you as I do the others, but you're holding back. You asked for time, and I get why. I'm trying to give it to you. But you always feel just out of my reach, even when you're with me. Not having a bond with you is leaving a ragged hole in my chest, Cary."

My instincts had pushed at me during my heat, sometimes painfully, to mate him, and we'd tried, but we couldn't. Not without an alpha.

"It's not you, Ava. You have to know that." I did, but it didn't help ease the ache. The pained look on his face said he knew that, too. "What does it feel like, the bond?" he asked.

"Safety, comfort, connection," I said. Even now, I could feel my mates sending me comfort at the feel of my shifting emotions. I could feel the aching sadness welling up the more I touched him, despite how hard I tried to stuff it down. It felt selfish, when I already had so much, to feel lost without him, too. Yet he felt so desperately essential to me, and to the pack.

He groaned as he stooped and picked me up. I wrapped my legs around his waist as he kissed me. He rocked against me in a smooth, rolling motion that had my blood heating in seconds.

"Ava, it's not selfish to tell me what you need. I want to feel that connection to you, too," Cary said as he sighed and pulled back slightly, stilling his hips. "But being back here, the sense of danger to you. It's messing with my head."

"Nobody is here but us, Cary. Nobody is getting to me now."

"It doesn't feel like it. There's a shadow following you I can almost feel. As if something is going to grab you whenever you're in these walls if we let you out of our sight. It's putting my instincts on edge."

"We've had no time since we ran to deal with everything we had to endure here, Cary. If being back in here is bringing it back up for you, do you need to get out of here? Maybe we could sleep outside again?" I was desperate to find a way past this for him.

"No, inside or outside isn't the problem. If I could, I'd take us far away from here, but we need to make sure the other omegas are safe. Especially Angel."

"Okay, but is that all? I don't see why that would hold you back from Wolf?" I hated pushing him, but I needed to know what we were dealing with before I could help him.

He groaned, but I wouldn't let this go. I was determined to reach him behind the walls he was trying to put up between us, and the pack, too. He pushed a strand of hair that had escaped my bun back behind my ear in a movement that was so gentle and caring, it almost broke me. He looked me straight in the eye with our bodies wrapped around each other. I could see his soul in his eyes as he begged me to understand something he struggled to find the words to express.

"I'm scared of an alpha bond," he finally whispered. The words felt as if they were bleeding out of him. "I've held the omega part of myself back for so long, I don't know what will happen when we start touching each other. I don't want to lose myself."

I could see the truth of his words. Those green eyes, so similar to mine, were hiding nothing from me now.

"I get it's scary for you. But they'd never hurt you, Cary. You know that, right?"

"What if I hurt them? What if I can't be what they need? I don't know how to be an omega for them and still feel like me."

"Oh, Cary, they don't need you to be anything but yourself. I can feel Wolf's emotions when he looks at you. He just wants you to be happy. I want that too."

Despite everything I had gone through, I loved being an omega. For me, an extra set of senses had opened up when I presented. One that helped me connect with the world on a deeper level. I felt stronger, more in touch with my surroundings and my instincts. I wanted Cary to feel that, too.

I put my hand up to his chest and felt his heart as it raced. I wanted to be so in tune with him I could feel it even when I wasn't touching him.

"You're so rare, Cary. Nobody knows what to expect from you. Your father made you feel as if that was a burden, because you made him question his prejudices. But have you ever thought that it actually sets you free? You get to decide who and what you want to be. All you have to do is look within your heart and figure out what that is. There is no rule book. None of us are saying you can't be strong and a fighter, because you're an omega. Do you see Lexie, or Maia holding back? Whatever feels right to you, we'll be on the sidelines, cheering you on. That's what it means to be a pack."

A range of emotions played across Cary's face so quickly it was hard to pick them all, but hope stood out.

"What if they try to keep me safe, protect me, if we're bonded? When what I really want is to be trusted to protect the people I care about," Cary asked me.

"They trust you now, Cary. Have the twins or Wolf ever tried to limit you? They've already started training you."

"I know, but what if that changes once we're bonded? They're alphas. What if they can't control it?"

"I don't think it will change. It's not who they are. But that comes down to *your* trust. Do not let anyone bite and claim you if you don't trust them, Cary. You just need to be clear about what you need, and decide who you trust to help you get there. Do you feel as if Wolf is your alpha? It felt pretty clear to me. If it doesn't for you, that's okay. Ryder would do it if you only wanted a pack bond, not a mate bond."

Cary tried to look away suddenly, but I grabbed his face and brought it back to me. I wasn't letting him hide from this, or me, anymore. I couldn't help him through this if he wasn't honest with me or himself.

"I get it's a hard question, Cary. But you can't run from it. It's hurting us all."

He bit his lip and stilled before he gave me a sharp nod in recognition of my words. His nod was a slice through this moment in time. The before and the after. His answer, either way, could change our future. He paused for a moment and the breath in my lungs vanished.

"Wolf feels like my alpha," he finally admitted in a quiet, shaky voice. "The moment he rounded that bend in the moonlight and started throwing alphas around, I felt a pull to him. I didn't have time to be scared then. It wasn't until later, when we were back here and memories hit me of all the alphas that have messed with me, that my head started questioning it. The pull is there, though, so it wouldn't feel right to let anyone else claim me. Wolf is mine, in the same way you are."

"Okay." I let out the breath I'd been holding, and Cary did too. I tried to keep my face neutral, but inside I was doing cartwheels. I could feel how hard that had been for him to say out loud. His body relaxed against me now, as his tension left him. "So, now you just need to decide if you trust him. Or at least give him a chance to earn it."

"I already told Wolf last night this wasn't about trust. He's wild, but he's also the most steadfast person I've ever met. So I guess I'm out of excuses," Cary murmured.

A small smile hovered at the edges of his lips before he kissed me lightly. I could feel a growing acceptance within Cary that made him feel lighter in our fragile bond. "How did you get to be so smart about this stuff?" he asked.

"I watch people a lot and I've learned a thing or two," I said, knowing Wolf and I were similar in that way.

My thoughts got muddled as Cary kissed a line along my jaw.

"So I'm mating Wolf then, I guess," Cary said with a studied casualness, but I could feel his heart beating against his ribs and I knew it wasn't all for me. I also knew I was okay with that. The thought of Wolf and Cary together had my heart skipping over itself in relief and excitement.

"Yeah, you are," I answered with a grin spreading across my face that I could no longer contain. I felt almost giddy. "At the next available opportunity. Not tonight, though. We probably need to wait until we're not in a room full of other omegas. It could start a riot."

Cary chuckled against my skin. "I love you, Ava. You know that, right?" he whispered as he teased his tongue along my neck, over Wolf's claiming bite.

The breath I'd just gotten back rapidly left my lungs. "I love you, too, Cary. I'm always going to love you. Sharing you won't change that. It will only make it better. You're enough, exactly as you are, for Wolf and for me."

He moaned as he grabbed my face and gave me a slow, drugging kiss full of heat and passion. I slipped my hand between us and unzipped his pants, then pulled out his hard cock and ground myself against it. I needed to feel him inside me, in any way I could, and I needed it now. The press of his hard heat through the lace of my underwear had me soaked.

"Anyone could walk in here and see us," he groaned, but he didn't stop me.

I laughed, a little breathlessly. "Nobody comes in here, you know that." I'd always thought it was such a shame, it was a beautiful library. Especially in the late afternoon, when the dappled light slanted in through the tall windows and the woodwork seemed to glow.

"I was supposed to come and find you, then bring you to the movie night," he protested weakly.

"But you haven't fulfilled the come part yet."

Cary groaned at my crude joke. "Just hearing you say the word come with that sweet mouth of yours does things to me," he said as he reached down and pulled my underwear aside. He teased his cock through my wet heat a few times, making me squirm against him.

"Have I mentioned how much I love this skirt?" he said, as he changed his angle and drove inside me.

I gasped and pressed my legs tighter around him. He made slow, shallow thrusts, each one edging deeper inside me. He didn't seem to be in any kind of hurry, despite his earlier objection.

He kept kissing me with long, slow, seductive kisses until I felt as if I was losing my mind. He pulled back slightly and watched me closely on his next slow thrust.

"Tell me again that you love me," he demanded, as his hands tightened on my ass.

"I love you, Cary," I whimpered on his next long slide. I looked deep into his eyes and felt the emotions spilling around us. The unhurried pace was destroying me. I could feel my insides melting. But it also eased the ache in my chest. He reached around and brushed his thumb lightly across my clit, causing liquid heat to pool inside me.

I cried out as his thumb pressed harder and he ran firmer circles over my clit as he ground up hard into me. The liquid heat rippled through me until a drawn out orgasm had me moaning and shaking in his arms. He lightly bit my neck as I felt him pulse inside me, dragged into his own orgasm as my pussy tightened and convulsed around him.

He held me close and kissed me until the last tremor finally subsided. Then helped rearrange my clothing after he dropped me back to the ground. I was about to walk into a packed ballroom with his scent coating me, but considering he was still marking my clothing, it wasn't much different from any other day. Plus, I knew it would drive Wolf wild to know I had Cary's cum leaking down my thigh.

I practically floated all the way there, as I clasped Cary's hand tightly. We may not have a bond yet, but I felt happier now, knowing that we were solid, and it was going to happen. Soon. I'd use my feminine wiles if I had to, to make sure it happened quickly. Now that I knew Cary was ready, I couldn't wait.

My happiness dimmed slightly though, as we walked the darkened hallways. I felt Cary's watchfulness slip back into place like a cloak. He seemed even more alert to danger tonight, as he analyzed every shadow. As if he could feel eyes following our every movement. The sooner we left this place, the better.

It felt almost as if fate, herself, was stalking us.

Thirty-Five

"Hey," I answered the satellite phone I was still carrying distractedly, as I cradled it against my shoulder while trying to hang fairy lights. We weren't on a call schedule for Ava anymore, but the team here had made me the liaison for Max at the farm. We'd only spoken a few hours ago, though.

"I have someone who wants to talk to you," Max said, the hint of a laugh coming through his too formal tone.

Before I could ask who it was, there was a rustling and a familiar voice came on the line. "Nick, is that you?"

I dropped the string of lights and scrambled to grab the phone properly, almost dropping it. "GG, hi. What's up?"

"Nothing much. What's up with you?" She asked tartly. I could almost feel her narrowing her eyes at me across the distance between us.

GG was the personification of love and light until you did something that crossed a line. She didn't have a lot of them. GG had raised enough kids to know we were going to learn the hard way and do stupid shit, despite her sage advice. She usually shrugged at our various scrapes and shenanigans. If it was serious in her eyes, though, you knew you'd really messed up. She never yelled, she only narrowed her eyes and waited until we confessed. Just that one look from her had you suddenly rethinking every choice you'd recently made.

Her biggest line involved family, and not keeping each other in the loop. And I'd disappeared for days without a word.

"Sorry, GG. I should have called to tell you I was okay." I'd asked Lexie to pass on a message to her, letting her know where I was when we'd first come to the Palace from town. But she'd probably worried when they all flew out here suddenly. Then only Maia and her guys had come back.

"Uh, huh," she said slowly. I could feel those narrowed eyes through her words.

I immediately started to sweat. But more than that, I felt bad. I hadn't meant to make her worry. Or make Max a partner in my crime. I could imagine the look he would have gotten when she cruised into the security office and demanded to speak with me. He loved GG, as everyone did.

I thought fast, trying to figure out how to make it up to her. GG was important to me and I didn't want her disappointed in me.

"GG, I-"

"Oh, stop worrying so hard," she said, even though I'd barely uttered a word. She knew me too well and knew I hated it when I felt as if I'd let people down. "You've given me the least trouble of any of my kids. I just wanted to make sure you were okay. They told me you were, but I needed to hear it for myself."

"Love you, GG." It covered everything I needed to say.

"Love you too, NikNik," she chuckled. NikNik was what she called me when I was little and started calling her GG while following her everywhere. She still pulled it out now and again. I didn't mind. "Now, tell me, have you met the rest of your pack and have you claimed your girl, Ava, yet?"

It was my turn to chuckle. GG knew about my dreams of joining a pack. It was why she'd told me the old stories about them. To help prepare me. Yet I hadn't mentioned my feelings about Ava to anyone. GG knew anyway. She always knew. I'd long since given up trying to figure out how. "Yeah. Ava went into heat quickly, so I didn't get to court her the way I hoped, but I'm so happy she chose me. Being part of a pack is more than I ever imagined."

"Well, she's a smart girl, and she saw your worth straight away. Like I knew she would. But making a woman feel special doesn't end when you mate her. You know better than that, Nick."

"I know, GG. She's just missed out on a lot in life and I wanted to give her a courtship. It won't stop me romancing her, though. I'm actually setting up our first date right now. We're having a movie night. It was going to be under the stars, because Ava enjoys being outdoors. But I've had to shift it to the ballroom and invite all the omegas along because we need to hunker down together tonight."

"Is everything alright?" she asked, sounding worried. "You said you were okay."

"Yeah, it's only a precaution. The people behind the Palace want Ava and Wolf back, but they can't have them. We're moving the omegas to a more secure location and heading back to the farm tomorrow."

"Good," GG sighed. "That's really why I'm calling. You need to trust in your pack because things are about to get bumpy, Nick. You know I rarely interfere, but there's a shadow following her. If your bonds aren't all in place, it could go badly and an innocent may get hurt. Your bonds are your strength, Nick, don't forget that."

My heart rate sped up. Nobody who knew GG dismissed it when she got a feeling about something and voiced it. Her instincts were usually spot on. She told me once that her gift of insight, and sometimes foresight, was also a burden. That nothing came without consequences in life and there had to be balance. GG didn't always speak up when her intuition flared because she didn't like to mess with fate. She believed people needed to make their own choices and live with them. So, she mostly nudged people, or planted an idea and left it at that. But sometimes she felt compelled to speak up, and it was usually when shit got real.

"All our bonds are in place, except one. And that one's complicated," I told her.

"Life is messy, and it never gets simpler. If you wait for that, you'll be waiting forever. Do what you can to make it happen, Nick. You'll know when the moment's right because you're their center, their balance. They need you."

"I will, GG."

"I know you will, Nick. It's your time. Know that no matter what happens, I'm proud of you. You always had a future bigger than this farm.

Now you get to go live it. Just make sure you bring your pack back when it's all done. I've been waiting a long time to meet them."

I felt choked up and needed to hug her in the worst way, but she was too far away. "Of course. Everything I am is because of you, GG. I don't know what I'd do without you."

"Oh, you'd do fine, NikNik. You got this. Now I'm going to put Max back on." And she was gone. She was always loving, but never one for lingering with emotions. She said what she needed and got on with her day.

"Hang on a second, Nick" Max said quickly into the phone, his humor gone. I walked to the arched windows at the far end of the room, listening to the sound of rustling and a door opening and closing, before he came back. "Wow. You told us you were bugging out tomorrow, but that there was no immediate threat. Do we need a change of plans?"

I looked out the window and noticed the sun was low in the sky and disappearing rapidly towards the horizon. "No. Sam was right. It would take us too long to pull everything together, and it's too risky to move the omegas at night unless we have no other option. We need to stay here tonight. Just be on alert."

"Roger," Max said, reverting to military lingo. "I'll stay in the security office tonight. I'll follow some loose ends I found in the Maven research. Call if you need anything at all. You be careful, you hear me? I'll see you tomorrow."

"Yeah. Thanks, Max." I appreciated him taking GG seriously, and I knew there was a reason she'd had this conversation with me while Max was listening. She was a wily one.

I continued to stare out the window, thinking hard, until a small arm snaked around my leg and clung on. I looked down to see Angel looking up at me with a serious expression. "Can I help?" she asked.

Her seriousness had me pausing for a moment. She could just want to play with the pretty lights, or she could be asking for something much deeper. She suddenly seemed far older than her years as she continued watching me solemnly.

"You sure can," I finally answered, deciding to take her at face value. Figuring my conversation with GG had spooked me.

"Are you making it pretty for Ava?" She asked as she looked around the room.

"I am. Do you like it so far?" I asked as I took her by the hand and walked back over to the lights I'd been stringing up.

"Yeah. Ava deserves pretty things."

"You like her a lot, don't you?"

Angel nodded. "Yeah. I like some of the other omegas, too. Emma and Rose are nice. But Ava always looks out for me and never gets cranky. I hated my handler. She never cuddled me the way Ava does and always yelled when other people weren't around. I didn't care when she left before the soldiers got here. Ava gives the best cuddles. Cary's and Wolf's are pretty good, too."

I felt floored. Angel was usually a mischievous bundle of energy, but she seemed quiet and introspective right now. When I looked back, I realized she'd been remarkably quiet today. Maybe it was because Ava had disappeared for a few days. If that was the case, we were going to have to do something about it. Omegas craved touch, and it seemed as if Ava was one of the few people in Angel's life who had given it to her willingly and openly. I hated that the Palace had deprived them both of such a simple thing, but I was glad they had found each other in this place.

"I like her too," I said softly.

"Duh, you're her mate," Angel replied. I tried not to laugh as she rolled her eyes at me. I wondered how much she knew about mates, though. *Surely the Palace hadn't started her on the same training as the older omegas yet? She needed to be climbing trees and splashing in puddles for as long as the world would let her.*

"Do you want to help me with the lights? You could reach if you hop up on my shoulders."

"Yeah, I wanna ride on your shoulders," she said, perking up.

Emma appeared in the doorway, but I waved her off when she offered to take Angel back to the kitchen. Angel had sought me out for a reason. I sensed her frequent disappearing acts weren't about being mischievous at heart. She was just searching for the connections she instinctively needed and she'd learned to be stealthy about it. She shouldn't have to be.

I crouched down so she could climb onto my shoulders, then passed her up the next string. I'd found fairy lights that were embedded in silk flowers. So I was in the middle of stringing them across the ceiling using discreet hooks I'd discovered in the ceiling cornice. I'd also rescued some of the greenery we'd pulled out of the conservatory and put into big urns around the room. Emma had helped me find it all earlier. She'd remembered they'd used a bunch of these lights for a debut ball once. Emma said she'd snuck in to see it before the guests had arrived and they had decked the room out with plants and lights to look like a fairy garden. She'd explored when the omegas had first been put in here to sleep, looking for anything useful, and found a store room up the back with the event decorations.

I asked Angel questions about what she liked to do, as she helped me string up the lights, and she happily answered me. It turned out she liked to draw and paint, and I made a mental note to find some art supplies for her. When we were done, she reached up to hold my hand while we surveyed our work, which made me melt.

Omegas had been coming and going throughout the afternoon while doing chores. But they'd all drifted back in here over the last few minutes. They were chattering excitedly and dragging mattresses into better viewing positions. Emma had even rustled up some popcorn.

I tried not to let my nerves get the better of me as I settled down to wait for Ava to arrive. She was late, but I knew she was with Cary, so I wasn't worried. I just wanted this to go well. I had the guitar I'd found earlier, so I played some songs for Angel to keep her amused. She happily cuddled up next to Wolf. But I kept glancing at the doorway.

Ryder patted me on the arm. "It looks great, Nick. Don't stress. She's going to love it."

Movement had my gaze snapping back to the door again. I wasn't the only one. The eyes of our pack tracked Ava and Cary as they made their way through the ballroom.

Ava stopped briefly to chat and hand over a bunch of chocolate bars to Emma, who was sitting on a mattress a few over from us. Ava winked at Miles and Owen, who were sitting on either side of Emma. Then she dropped off a few bars with Lexie. I heard her tell Lexie to keep them for Maia. It was a sweet gesture for her pregnant friend. I could feel the alphas behind me getting impatient with her slow progress, though. I didn't blame them. The few hours since I'd seen her last felt far too long.

When she finally made it to our mattress tucked up the back, she zeroed in on Angel and hugged her before handing her the final chocolate bar. Angel squealed in excitement and dove into it.

I patted the space between my legs when she made her way over to me. She settled in and leaned back against me while Cary sat down next to us. The guys had kindly kept the space around me clear, even though I knew they all wanted to snuggle with Ava right now. She looked up at the screen, only just seeming to realize we hadn't started the movie yet. No way was I starting it without her.

"Sorry I'm late. I was, just uh—"

"Yeah, we know what you were just doing. We could feel you in the bond," Ryder groaned, cutting her off, as he discreetly cupped the tent in his pants. He leaned over and whispered to her. "Do you know how hard it was to sit here with a straight face, feeling like we were going to cum in our pants while making polite conversation?"

"Oh," she squeaked, looking around the room, before shooting a look in Angel's direction, but Angel was busy enjoying her treat.

I hadn't thought those kinds of emotions would pass through a pack bond, but I'd been wrong. Knowing that we'd all felt her appeared to turn Ava on, as her scent spiked to a chorus of groans.

"We probably need to figure out a way to shield stuff from the bond. Lexie and her pack have been practising. I'll talk to her," she said, quickly. Honestly, I didn't want a shield between us. I said nothing, though. I didn't know how to without sounding stalkerish.

I nodded to River, and he leaned over to click start on the laptop connected to the projector I'd found in the lab. The opening music drowned out any further conversation.

I grabbed a soft blanket and pulled it around Ava. It was from our nest and smelled of our pack. She sniffed the blanket and sighed happily. She smiled up at me when I put the snacks I'd made for her on her lap. I'd cut up some fruit and made a mini platter with the last of the cheese for her. I knew she loved cheese. She looked it over before carefully choosing a few pieces. I could sense her feeling guilty, but not enough to knock it back.

"Thank you, Nick, this is my first date, and it's perfect," she whispered in my ear during a quieter scene in the movie. She put the plate down and turned around to snuggle right up in my lap. I felt like a god.

"You're worth it," I told her, and I meant it.

"It's a little crowded, though," Ryder said from behind us, as he shifted restlessly, trying to adjust himself again. "We could have so much more fun if we were alone."

Ava blew him a kiss over my shoulder before she turned her attention back to the movie. It was a PG movie, because we had a child and teenagers in the room, but she didn't seem to mind. Neither did anyone else. I stroked her hair absently and landed a few light kisses on her forehead every few minutes. She closed her eyes, as if she enjoyed the sensation, and I felt her go heavy against me.

I didn't know how I got this lucky. But I wasn't going to mess this up. This was only the start.

The Crash be dammed. I was going to make sure our girl got everything she deserved.

Thirty-Six

I must have dozed off. I only meant to close my eyes for a moment while I'd enjoyed Nick stroking my hair. But when I opened them again, a different movie was playing.

I shifted in my seat, suddenly uncomfortable, but not wanting to move. "Are you okay?" Nick whispered.

"Yeah, I just really have to pee," I said, and he chuckled.

"Do you want me to come with you?" he asked.

"No," I sighed. "Stay here. I'll be back in a minute."

I reluctantly worked my way out of the blanket cocoon Nick had built around us. I spied Angel still snuggled up with Wolf, wide awake. "Do you need to go to the bathroom, Angel?" I asked.

She nodded distractedly, still looking at the screen. "Come on, let's go," I urged, holding out my hand and trying not to dance on the spot. I really needed her to hurry.

We carefully maneuvered our way back out to the hallway, being careful to avoid stray hands and feet between the mattresses. Many of the omegas were still watching the movie, enjoying the rare treat, but plenty had already fallen asleep.

"Are you going to the bathroom?" Emma asked me as I passed, and I nodded. "Can I come too?"

I'd often seen in movies how women always went to the bathroom together, and I'd been curious about the phenomenon. At the Palace, we always used our own bathrooms and had handlers watching us when we were in groups or common areas. I don't think I'd ever had another woman in the bathroom with me, beside my handler.

"Sure. We can all go," I said easily. "Just hurry up, I'm busting." Emma laughed. It was such a simple thing, but it felt like doing something so mundane together made us both feel normal.

I brushed a hand over Angel's hair. She grabbed my hand, then Emma's, and walked happily between the two of us. There were men's and women's bathrooms in the hallway outside the ballroom, for when they held parties and we headed for them. I grinned as I came out to wash my hands and listened to Angel sing a song from the movie to herself in the stall next to me. She paused to yawn halfway through a lyric.

"So," I said to Emma, "Miles and Owen seem nice."

Emma blushed furiously. "They're just helping."

I nodded my head agreeably. "Uh, huh."

Her blush deepened and she suddenly blurted out, "They said they're my mates."

"Yeah, there seems to be a lot of that going around. Do you feel the same?"

She laughed nervously. "I feel pulled to them, but I haven't encouraged them. The pull seems to be getting stronger the more I resist it, though. I've been here since my early teens. I know nothing about alphas and I'm not really sure what I'm doing. Plus, I'm sharing a room with two dozen omegas."

She stumbled to a stop and put her hand over her mouth, as if she hadn't meant to say all of that. I didn't know Emma that well, but it seemed as if she really needed to talk. I also didn't know how I'd gone from the girl who hung back in the shadows to the one who people approached for advice.

"Uh, I don't know if Sam has spoken to Miles or Owen about it or not, but they don't let unmated alphas into the secret location with the omegas. If you want some time to figure it out, you could come to the farm with us instead? When we get there, we can sit down with Lexie and Maia to have a girl chat? They've both gone through it and really helped me. Cary can take Angel for a play with some of the farm animals," I said as I heard Angel's toilet flush.

"You don't think Lexie and Maia would mind if I came to the farm?" she asked.

"Not at all. They're a very welcoming community. Plus, I'm sure Sam would be relieved to have some of his team still with him, rather than Miles and Owen chasing you up the mountain," I laughed, as she blushed. I didn't want to tell her we'd already discussed that it might be a solution without talking to any of them first.

Emma looked relieved. "That would be great. Thank you so much, Ava."

"What's a mate?" Angel asked as she came out of her stall.

Emma and I both stared at each other. Another toilet flushing had me spinning around. I hadn't realized anyone else was in here. I'd been so busting to pee I hadn't even looked when we came in, I'd just dashed straight for a stall.

"A mate is someone who chooses an omega," Nicole said as she sashayed across to the taps and washed her hands alongside Angel. "It's a special bond, and an omega should feel privileged to be chosen. It's a little greedy to accept more than one, though."

Nicole shot both Emma and me a glare in the mirror, then plastered on a fake smile as she looked down at Angel. She held her hand out to her. "Want to come and get a treat?"

"Yes, yes, yes," Angel shouted, jumping up and down, proving she'd already had enough sugar. She threw herself at Nicole, who looked startled, but grabbed Angel's hand, anyway.

"I don't think that's a good idea," I said. "She's overtired and has already had chocolate."

"You're not her mother. Why are you being so mean?" Nicole said, as she turned and walked out the door with Angel. It was a low blow. None of us had seen our mothers in a long time. I didn't know how much Angel would even remember hers.

Emma and I shared a glance before we both hustled out the door after them. They turned down a different hallway to the one leading to the kitchen, though.

"Where are you going?" Emma asked her.

"I found a storeroom that had food stocked in it. I think it was for events. There's lots of yummy stuff in there," Nicole said, as we went down a flight of stairs and she flicked on a light in a dark hallway.

"Yay," Angel yelled and did a little happy dance as she walked. She was more jogging to keep up with Nicole, though. I wasn't sure why we were in such a hurry.

"Why didn't you tell us about it?" I asked her, trying not to let my annoyance peek through. "We're rationing and sharing food."

"I'm pretty sure I just did," Nicole said as she glared at me over her shoulder.

"Where exactly is this storeroom?" Emma asked as she looked around.

I followed her gaze and noticed we were heading past the doors to the secret labs.

"It's just up ahead," Nicole said as she picked up her pace and half dragged Angel with her.

My growing doubts suddenly flared into a feeling of imminent danger. The light at the end of the hallway didn't seem to work, and it wreathed the end wall in shadows. "I think we should go back."

"I agree," Emma said. "It's far too late to be wandering around down here."

Emma made to grab for Angel's other hand, but Nicole swung her around to her other side. "Don't be a spoilsport."

Suddenly, a panel opened up, and the end of the hallway disappeared into an abyss of darkness. A pale movement caught my eye, but before I could scream, someone yanked me forward and shoved a sharp smelling cloth over my face. I struggled, but my head was swimming and everything seemed to fade away. My legs wouldn't hold my weight and I crumpled as terror overtook me. I was being taken.

I'd thought when I'd first bonded with River and Ryder that it would never be dark again, with their bonds glowing in my chest. I tried to yank on their bonds now, but a fuzzy darkness cut me off from them before it swallowed me whole. I felt myself being lifted and carried deeper into the dank emptiness of a tunnel.

Then there was nothing.

Thirty-Seven

I watched the ballroom doors with a fixed determination, barely blinking. *How long did it take women to pee?*

I had no idea, but it felt as if Ava had been gone too long. River was shifting restlessly beside me and he kept glancing at the doorway, too.

A sense of annoyance throbbed in my chest. I told myself I was being irrational and that if I went storming into the women's bathroom, I'd embarrass her, or worse, piss her off. She was probably just talking to her friend. More than likely about us. I'd watched her with Lexie and Maia. My experience with friendships was nonexistent, but I could plainly see she got something from them she didn't get from us. I would never begrudge her that. After being alone for so long, I knew having people who cared about you was a good thing. My interactions with River, Ryder, and Nick brought me a simple joy, even if my interactions with Cary were complicated.

Yet she hadn't taken Lexie with her, and it seemed more likely she would talk to Lexie. She'd been a little reserved around Emma at times. I growled under my breath, as I felt the annoyance change into unease. River shot me a concerned glance.

"Did Ava say she was going anywhere else?" I asked Nick. He turned to look at me and shook his head. His eyes tightened with worry.

I took a deep breath, trying to quell my fears and paranoia. She was fine. She was just in the bathroom with a friend.

"She's fine," River said, as he echoed my thoughts. He sounded as if he was trying to convince himself, rather than me. His eyes stayed fixed on the doorway, too. I glanced at Ryder. His gaze was traveling over everyone in the room, as if he was trying to account for everyone and assess any threats. They always worked instinctively and seamlessly together.

"Should we go check on her?" Nick asked. But we all hesitated. None of us wanted to look like overbearing, possessive alphas, especially when our bond was so new.

"She could just be having a conversation with Emma that's making her uncomfortable. Or Nicole's being a bitch. She disappeared a while ago, too. None of them are back yet," River said, but tension was riding every line of his body in contrast to his words.

"What am I not getting?" Cary asked brusquely, as he turned to look at us all. He looked as tense as the rest of us.

"Ava's uneasy," Nick said, sounding more gruff than he normally did.

"You can feel that in the bond?" Cary guessed. His face went dark as he realized what was going on. That he couldn't feel her the way we could. "I can sense a slight uneasiness, but I thought it was just, nevermind."

I noticed Miles, a few blankets over, shoot us a worried glance, while Owen kept his eyes focused on the doorway. Which meant they were picking up on something from Emma, too, even though they hadn't claimed her yet.

"I should have said something earlier, but my great grandmother called to warn me a shadow was following Ava. She said we needed to trust our pack and be on alert because things were about to get bumpy. GG has a gift of insight, and occasionally foresight. Everyone in our family and at the farm listens to her. I told Max, and he immediately went on high alert. He's holed up in the security room at the farm tonight."

Cary went still. "I told Ava earlier tonight it felt as if a shadow was following her and it was putting me on edge. I've been picking up on it for days. It can't be a coincidence if GG said exactly the same thing."

I didn't know about foresight and such things. My knowledge of the world was so limited, but I believed that when we listened closely enough, our instincts ran deeper than most people realized. I felt a growl I couldn't contain rumble through my chest, as everyone tried to breathe through the sudden tension.

"I'm checking on her," I growled as I shifted onto my feet, unable to sit waiting a moment longer. I'd barely stood up when Ava's unease quickly spiked into full-blown panic. I was running instantly. "Move," I bellowed to people in my path, and omegas scrambled out of my way. River and Ryder flowed effortlessly around them, barely even looking at their surroundings, their entire focus on that door.

We burst through, Cary and Nick at the rear, followed by Miles and Owen.

My heart clenched as Ava's panic sharpened into fear. It felt as if she was struggling and tugging at us in the bond, trying to pull her to us.

"Ava," I roared. I tried to reach out to her through the bond.

"What the hell is going on?" Lexie yelled. I could hear omegas crying behind me. There wasn't time to feel bad. I was already running for the bathroom. I slammed the door open and barreled inside, but it was empty.

"Is there another bathroom near here?" I yelled out to Cary, fighting to keep the wildness from completely taking over.

"No," Cary said from right behind me.

It didn't matter, anyway. It was a wild hope. I could scent her. Omega scents saturated the room, but Ava's stood out. I knew she'd been in here recently, but now she was gone. I turned and pushed past everyone to follow her scent back out into the hallway.

I clutched at my chest as her panic and fear faded out until there was nothing. Just empty space at the end of the bond.

"Ava," I roared again, into the silence. *No, she can't be dead. She can't be.*

River grabbed my face, forcing it down to his. "She's not dead. The bond is still there. It's just muted. Focus, we need you." I calmed slightly as his touch centered me. His blue eyes were like ice and I could feel how cold he was in the bond. He had shut everything down and focused on only one thing. Her.

I nodded once, and he let me go. I turned right, away from the ballroom, and started running.

"He's got her scent. Follow him," he growled. Footsteps pounded behind me and I could feel my pack around me. I pushed my energy at them, so it wouldn't drown me, and I heard someone grunt behind me.

We ran through the secret door and down the stairs into the corridor that housed the secret labs, and my gut dropped. There was no reason for Ava to be down here. The lights were on, which meant someone had passed through recently. Yet there was a pool of darkness at the end, shrouded in shadows. My eyes zeroed in on a slumped mass on the floor, and I skidded to a halt alongside it.

I rolled the prone body over, pushing dark hair out of the way. It was Emma. Hands grabbed her, and I let Miles and Owen take over. "She's alive, thank Christ," Miles groaned, as he checked her pulse.

"Chloroform," Ryder said, as he sniffed the air.

Fuck. That wasn't good. I spun in place, knowing every second counted if someone was abducting Ava and Angel right now.

"What's going on?" Sam bellowed down the hallway as he tracked us down.

"Secure the omegas in the ballroom," River yelled back. "We have a breach. Ava and Angel are missing, possibly Nicole, too. They knocked out Emma. Miles and Owen will bring her back. Don't let anyone else in once you barricade the doors."

"Roger," Sam yelled and disappeared.

Owen nodded at River as he supported Emma's head, while Miles carefully lifted her into his arms. I knew it was dangerous to move an unconscious person without knowing their injuries, but River was right. We had no choice. They couldn't stay here if we had intruders.

My breathing was hard and erratic, and the wildness was pounding at me. The corridor was a dead end. But her scent led all the way to the end wall. Unless they had backtracked, I didn't think she was in any of the rooms behind us. But I couldn't be sure.

I bellowed in frustration. Panic threatened to pull me under as I tried to focus my energy, but it was a wild stallion resisting my every attempt at control. They had taken Ava, and Angel too. An innocent little girl who had wriggled her way into my heart, as well as my lap. She seemed to have an instinctive on-switch for my purr, the same as Ava. *Where the fuck were they?*

River grabbed my shoulder, focusing my attention back on him momentarily. "This is not the time to hold your instincts back. You're our best hope of finding them fast. Let that shit out. All of it. Now."

I roared in his face as I settled into the wildness, completely immersing myself. He didn't even flinch as my dominance flowed past him and my energy rushed through him.

"Good. Now hunt, Wolf."

I turned on my heel, zeroing in on her, knowing my instincts were right. She was on the other side of the wall. I punched at the drywall, not caring if I broke my hand. Then ripped and tore at the sheeting and framework until darkness loomed on the other side.

A beam of light shot past me, illuminating the darkness, as River and Ryder aimed torches through the wall. The beams of light highlighted a sloping roof and a set of stairs. More of the sheetrock tore under my hands. I shoved through the ruin of the wall, too full of rage and fear to keep tearing, and my momentum had me stumbling down the stairs. At the bottom, there was a dank tunnel, but it was wide and paved. I sniffed the air. Her scent was on this side, too. As well as the chloroform and an added smell of gasoline. I ran, following the path her scent had laid. Every beat of my blood called to her, but there was no answer.

"Someone had a vehicle in here," River yelled, as he came down the stairs silently and tracked along behind me. I could faintly hear the others coming through the wall behind us, too, but I couldn't wait. There was no sound of a vehicle, which meant they had too big a head start.

I ran. The beam from River's flashlight weaved erratically in the darkness as he ran behind me. Until it was joined by a second beam and Ryder's footsteps echoed alongside ours. We ran for about five minutes, and I knew from my wild run that first day that we were well out from underneath the Palace, way past the edge of the Palace grounds, too.

"Stop," River yelled, seconds before I would have collided with a hulking vehicle in the middle of the tunnel. I skidded to a halt, panting hard, as River flashed his light over it. It looked like an open golf cart with a tray on the back for moving goods. I sniffed it. It reeked of Ava's cherry scent, mingled with the stinging smell of chloroform. My roar echoed off the tunnel walls.

Ryder ran up the steps behind the cart to the wall at the end and found a lever he pulled. A door swung open, emptying into a building on the other side. He slipped through and I pushed through behind him with a growl I didn't even try to keep down. It was an empty garage. I ran through and yanked open the garage door, almost pulling it off its hinges. Moonlight bathed the yard beyond it, illuminating a decrepit old house and an empty yard.

Her scent had grown fainter, but it was still there. They'd put her in a vehicle, I was sure of it. I ran down the driveway until I reached the road, looking wildly in each direction for brake lights, tire tracks, anything. But there was nothing.

I vented my rage into the darkness, but it was no use. It didn't bring them back.

Ava and Angel were gone. And it was my fault.

Thirty-Eight

River

Ava was gone. Again.

I gave myself one moment. One breath to let emotions wash over me. Agony. Despair. Desperation. I felt them all as Wolf's rage battered the world. If anyone who wasn't pack was anywhere near us, he would have pinned them to the ground.

Ryder was suddenly in front of me.

"She's not gone," he said, as he gripped the back of my head and forced me to look into his eyes. Pure conviction shone in them. "We just got her back and I refuse to lose her again. Do you hear me?"

I reached up and clasped his shoulder, giving him a brusque nod as I pulled myself together. For years I had held it together for Ryder, and now here he was, pulling me back from the brink. This pack was good for him and I wouldn't let anyone tear it apart. We were getting her back. Again.

Ryder strode over to Wolf and hugged him without fear. "They can't have her, Wolf. She's ours. So I need you to channel that rage into getting her back. Can you do that?"

Wolf heaved several breaths as he stared down at Ryder until he grabbed him and hugged him back hard. He squeezed Ryder as if someone was trying to take his comfort teddy bear away. I could see Ryder wince, but he took it like a champ.

"Can you sense anyone in the area?" Ryder asked him. Wolf swiveled his head around before he shook it. I don't think he was capable of words right now.

Movement behind me had me spinning and crouching until I sighted Nick. He stumbled on the rocky ground as he ran out of the garage while talking into a satellite phone. "We've come out about half a mile east of the Palace. The tunnel seemed to run in a straight line, but it could have curved subtly."

"What's happening?" I asked as he approached, running as fast as he could on the uneven ground.

"I called Max. He found evidence of GPS tracking software for the Palace's vehicles when spying on their servers once before. When Lexie gave him Wolf's details for the manor house earlier today, he thought he found the location, but he wanted to be sure. So he turned on the GPS tracking software and was monitoring for any vehicles in that location. He found a bunch. I asked him to point the tracking software here."

His initiative impressed me. Nick was level-headed and a quick thinker in a crisis.

"Where's Cary?" I asked. My brain felt as if it was about to fracture. I wasn't used to having so many people to take care of. It had just been Ryder and me for so long.

"Following us in the tunnel," Nick answered quickly. "I couldn't get a phone signal down there. He told me to go, and he'd catch up."

Fuck. He'd be down there, alone, running blindly in the dark. Not able to feel what was happening with the rest of us.

I felt Ryder and Wolf move up behind me. "Check the house for any clues. Meet me back in the garage," I ordered Ryder. They both moved off. Wolf followed Ryder like a lost puppy.

A faint voice came from the satellite phone and a look of intense concentration passed over Nick's face. "White van heading North. That's the only vehicle in the area?" Nick asked.

"Tell him to stay on it," I said. "I'll find Cary," Nick nodded. He kept talking to Max, but kept pace with me as I took off back up the driveway. When I got to the door above the stairwell, I shone my flashlight down and called out to Cary. My voice echoed down the tunnel. A faint voice yelled back, and moments later, Cary appeared at the bottom of the stairs. He bent over double, looking as if he was about to vomit.

"Ava?" he demanded. I shook my head at him, and he slumped against the cart.

Ryder and Wolf came back through the garage and joined Nick behind me. "House is empty, has been for a long time," Ryder reported.

I breathed steadily and kept myself focused on the next step, refusing to think about anything beyond that. It was the way I'd coped for the last decade.

"We're heading back. Tell Max to call Lexie, she has the other satellite phone, and keep her updated. Your signal will drop out in the tunnel. We'll coordinate with her at the other end," I said to Nick. Then hustled down the stairs. We needed to marshall the troops.

"How the fuck did you run so fast?" Cary wheezed to Nick. He sounded frustrated. He was a fit guy, but he looked like he'd pushed himself to his limits. His face looked haunted, too.

"Wolf pushed energy at me through the bond," Nick said as he ended the call to Max and came down the stairs behind me. A look I couldn't discern flashed across Cary's face in the torchlight. The bond gave me no clues either. There were too many emotions pummeling me from the others, and his unformed bond was too faint. I didn't have time to stop and ask, either. I had to trust he would tell me if he needed something.

Luckily, we didn't have to run back. We got the cart turned around and used it to get back down the tunnel. Pala was waiting for us, guarding the destroyed entrance at the other end. His face was grim. He knew time was now a priority if we were going to get her back before they forced her to become Maven's omega. Apart from the worrying issue of them accessing Wolf's power, I could see a genuine concern for Ava in his eyes.

"We did a quick sweep of the Palace and there's no evidence of anyone else here. It seems like it was a snatch and grab," he informed me.

"Is there anyone else missing?" I asked him as we headed back into the main part of the Palace.

"No. Ava, Angel, and Nicole are the only ones missing," he answered quickly. I grit my teeth, picturing not just Ava, but Angel in their clutches as well. My heart clenched. "Inside job?" Pala asked, dropping his voice.

I nodded. Nicole had to have been in on it. I'd had a bad vibe about Nicole from the start, but I hadn't thought her capable of this. It was a mistake that Ava and Angel were now paying for. If they took Angel, it would likely be to use her as leverage against Ava. To make Ava compliant. And it would work. There was no way Ava would let any harm come to the young omega.

As soon as we walked into the main living area, Lexie dashed for us. "They're really gone?" she asked.

"Yes. What's our status?" I asked. She snapped straight into general mode.

"Sadie's got the Network on the line. They're waiting for confirmation of a location, but they've put everyone on alert. The van is still on the move, and Max is tracking it. He said it's moving towards where he believes the manor is located. Sam is already on his way to the farm to get the chopper prepped."

Dammit. Sam had flown Maia and her pack home in the chopper, then driven a dirt bike back here to reunite with Lexie and Pala while Ava was in heat. He hadn't wanted to waste fuel flying back again because we had a limited supply. But now the only two people who could fly it, Sam and Matt, were here, and the chopper was at the farm. It was a massive oversight that had me grinding my teeth again.

"Hey, I know," Lexie said, as she took a step closer to me, but didn't make the mistake of touching me right now. "But these are the cards we have, and we have to play them. I know the delay is going to kill you, but we should get there just after they do. It'll be tight, but we can do this."

I just nodded at her. As much as I hated it, she was right. There was no point wasting time wishing things were different. They weren't, so we'd deal with what we had.

I turned to Wolf. His entire body was vibrating, but he was watching every movement of my body like a hawk, waiting for his next orders. He was our prime alpha, but he had no interest in directing anyone or leading right now. I realized with sudden clarity that his wildness wasn't an anomaly, or something that would go away. It was a part of him he'd embraced a long time ago, but he needed a counterbalance. He needed me. I was a master at shutting everything down and focusing on the plan. I'd sometimes worried I acted too controlled to be an alpha, as they usually operated more on instinct, but I was what Wolf and this pack needed. Nick was right. Our pieces fit, as if we'd been made for each other.

So I focused on what was in front of me, and right now, keeping Wolf from tearing this whole place down was my priority.

I sent one more thought through the bond, desperately hoping Ava could somehow feel it.

"*Hold tight, little bird. We're coming.*"

Thirty-Nine

Rage, fear, and regret warred within me, like a seething confluence where powerful rivers met. Outside, my body was still with only the occasional ripple showing, but underneath, my emotions were churning.

They had taken Ava.

All this time, I had watched over her. I hadn't even known exactly what I was protecting her from, but I'd known instinctively she was in danger. I'd almost tasted it. The air of the Palace reeked with it. Even though we'd freed the Palace, it had gotten worse, not better, since we came back. Now my nightmares had sprung to life, and she was gone.

"Wolf. Outside. Now," I demanded. I'd always thought this ornate living room was ridiculously big, but right now, it felt too small to contain him. As tempted as I was to let him tear the place down, it wouldn't help us right now.

Wolf growled at me, but River and Ryder both gave me quick nods. Ryder turned Wolf around and pushed him towards the door. Not flinching when Wolf snarled. Nick looked at me with wide eyes, and I gestured for him to follow, too.

"We'll be back," I said to Lexie, before I stalked outside, past the wide stone steps of the entrance.

"Where do you want him?" Ryder asked.

I pointed to a section of darkened wall beyond the garden beds surrounding the entrance and the curved sweep of the driveway. Wolf turned at the wall and watched me approach with the eyes of a cornered animal.

I pulled my dark hoodie off, then my t-shirt, passing them to Nick. Wolf's eyes turned calculating before they narrowed on me. I pushed against his chest until I had him backed against the wall. I knew he let me. If Wolf didn't want to move, nothing would shift him.

"Bite me," I demanded as I got up in his face. His body heat seared me, even through his clothes. It wasn't how I had imagined doing this, but I had hesitated too long out of fear and now we were paying the price. Ava needed us. To get her back, we needed to be strong, and that meant having all our pack bonds in place. We couldn't afford any weakness right now. It was time.

"No," he snarled.

I felt my face twist with disbelief. I'd been so caught up in my own feelings I'd never imagined he would say no when I was ready. It had my head spinning. He couldn't do this to me now. The anger I had pushed down over the years, at the unfairness of being an omega, pushed against my skin. "You will not deny me, Wolf."

"You're not ready," he growled lowly. I cursed myself inwardly for my hesitation, and for thinking we had time. I'd known something was shadowing her. Omegas were highly instinctive, and I'd felt it, like an insistent pressure on my senses. If I hadn't been so busy ignoring my omega, I might have figured out what was going on sooner. Or at least the direction it was coming from. I had failed her in the most devastating way. This was my fault.

"They. Took. Her," I yelled in his face, pouring my emotions into the words, needing him to understand. He snarled and thrashed against me, wanting to chase her. Find her. I slapped the stone next to his head to get his attention.

"No," he said. A determined, set expression crossed his face, and a strangled noise I didn't know I could make tore from me. Part rage, part despair. I couldn't seem to find the words to make him understand.

"They took her and I can't feel her, Wolf. I *need* you to bite me."

"A forced bond you don't really want will destroy me," he growled, his face etched with pain in the moonlight, "and that won't help her."

I grabbed Wolf's face, pushed myself against him and kissed him, hard. He was unyielding against me, his lips firm, until he groaned and broke. The way he kissed me back, drenched with desperate heartbreak and need, had me breathless. He tasted of dark shadows, but he smelled like orchids and wild spaces. Everything in me yearned for her, and for him, and I let the emotion flood through me.

He growled possessively as I pulled away. "My fear held me back. I'll admit that. But Ava and I talked earlier. She made me dig deep and realize I'd already let it go, and all I had left were empty excuses. I've been letting my father and his friends dictate how I live my life, and I don't want that. You are my mate and I want your claim. I was just waiting for the right moment to tell you. Now I'm useless to her, to you both, when she needs us. Running alone down that tunnel in the dark, unable to feel either of you, wrecked me, Wolf. You said you would be anything I needed. I need this. I need you. Not only to connect me to Ava. I need *you*, too, and I need you *now*. Don't leave me in the dark."

The words felt raw, as if I was cutting myself and letting them bleed out. Wolf looked agonized but was still hesitating. Something bigger was holding him back.

"You need to listen to Cary, Wolf. Feel him. We're stronger together. If he says he's ready, you need to trust him," Nick said as he shifted into our peripheral vision. "I figured it out earlier today and I think Ava did too, which is why she went to talk to Cary. You can't use your full dominance without him, and you know it."

"What the hell?" I asked, whirling to face him. "Why can't he use his full dominance without me?"

"Our pieces fit, Cary. We're made for each other, and that includes you. His dominance is too much for one omega to channel. He needs two."

"Is Nick right?" I asked Wolf. "And did you know that?"

Wolf held my gaze as I whirled back to him. "I suspected, but I didn't know for sure. I wasn't willing to risk testing it any more than I did earlier today."

"Why didn't you say something? And why wouldn't Ava if she figured it out?" Wolf just looked at me.

"Neither of them would ever force you into something you weren't ready for," River said from behind me.

"They'd burn themselves out first," Ryder added.

I closed my eyes as a realization washed over me. "Holy shit," I whispered. "Ava trying to deny her heat wasn't only about Nick, was it? It was about me too."

"If it helps, I don't think she knew at the time. I think she just felt instinctively we weren't all ready," Nick said gently. "But I was watching her closely when Wolf's dominance washed through her. There was a moment of realization and I wondered at the time what it was. I didn't figure it out until GG called and warned me I needed to make sure all our bonds were in place for what was coming, or we'd fail."

"And now Ava needs us and we're not strong enough because I held back," I said, feeling like I was going to throw up as every second took Ava further away from us. I'd been a selfish fool. If I'd only opened myself to the pack sooner, I would have figured it out myself. I felt River and Ryder both laying hands on me in silent support, and it filled me with determination.

I didn't begrudge Nick stepping into this intense moment with Wolf. He was part of our pack, our center, and this was about all of us. I finally understood what that meant. We all had our role to play, and I needed to step into mine. They weren't complete without me. This was my pack, too.

Wolf's dark eyes glowed in the moonlight as they flicked to Nick and he nodded at our plucky beta before his eyes pinned me again. He cocked his head. A predator assessing his prey, knowing he had me now, and only waiting for the perfect moment to pounce.

"I'll bite you, claim you, but I won't mate you here. Not without Ava. And not when this place, those rooms upstairs, haunt you." His words shocked me. That he had picked up on the last source of my unease when I hadn't said a word. "I figured it out too late, too. We should have gone somewhere else for Ava's heat."

I could see the shrewd intelligence in Wolf's eyes, despite his wild aura. I could also feel his hardness pressing against my stomach. He wanted me, but he would hold back for me.

"Figured what out?" River asked, his voice a slide of dark ice in the night. He hated not knowing what was happening.

"The VIP suites are where his father's mates took him after the parties."

"Fuck, why didn't you say something, Cary?" Ryder asked. His voice was grim. I felt hands grasp me more firmly as my mates surrounded me. They centered and anchored me when Wolf's words had me spinning.

"There aren't a lot of places, except the library, where there aren't dark memories here," I bit out.

Nick's hand tightened on my arm. "I get why you need this now, Cary. We all need it. But if you're going to take a claiming bite without the mating, it's going to hurt."

"I don't care. I can take it."

"I don't know that I'll be able to hold back," River ground out. "I still don't feel attracted to you, but I need you claimed as a pack mate in the same way I did for Nick. My need to secure the pack and find Ava is riding me hard right now. If Wolf bites you, I may bite you, too."

"Me too," Ryder growled.

"I want to bite you, too," Nick said. "Even if it does nothing. Our pack needs to be strong to get her back. It's going to take everything we've got, and it's not complete without you."

It was so corny, but I felt like a cartoon character with the outline of a heart beating out of my chest. These men would never diminish me, only make me a better version of myself.

"I've let go of my fear of being claimed, and that goes for all of you. I trust each of you, and I trust this pack. You've earned it." I swiveled my head around to meet each of their eyes, needing them to know I meant it. Acknowledging the importance of the connection they were offering me. Before I swung my gaze back to Wolf. "Ava said accepting that I'm an omega would set me free. Now I know what she meant. I'm ready to let go of *everything* that's been holding me back. I'm ready, Wolf."

Wolf lifted his hands from where they'd lodged on my waist. I instantly missed their weight. He pulled his long sleeve t-shirt up and over his head, baring his chest to me and the frosty night air. Ava's bite shone like a beacon in the moonlight.

"The trust goes both ways, Cary. You have as much influence in this claim as we do, and as much power. You could break me," he said. His wild aura suddenly intensified, as if he was baring his soul to me as well. It didn't scare me. The vulnerability in his eyes destroyed me. I'd never thought about it that way. That he was trusting me, too. They all were. Making this decision outside of a heat or sex suddenly made it seem so much more purposeful. My teeth suddenly ached with the need to claim Wolf as mine.

"Do it," I begged.

He didn't hesitate. He lunged, grabbed my head, and swiftly turned it aside as he clamped down on my shoulder. A burst of searing pain blinded me as a cry forced itself past my clamped teeth. Three more bites followed quickly and the presence of my mates, along with Wolf's wild energy, flooded me. It was heat, comfort, friendship, and safety, exactly as Ava had said. It was agony and bliss mixed in a single sensation that had a tear tracking down my cheek. I opened my eyes and saw Ava's bite mark on Wolf's neck right in front of me. I moved on instinct, latching on alongside hers, so that our bites intertwined. Wolf groaned against my shoulder and his hips thrust against me as he pulled me harder against him.

A white light bloomed behind my eyes and washed through me as a feeling of peace settled over me. But a profound sense of loss chased it as I felt the muted space where Ava should be.

"Ava," I cried out as I released my teeth from Wolf's neck. That emptiness felt like death and tore at me.

Wolf wrapped his arms around me again as he held me close. My pack mates pushed in around me, seeking their own comfort from the contact. *Why had I been so afraid of this?*

"Whatever you need, I'll get it for you," Wolf whispered.

"I need her back with us," I groaned. She was our beating heart. Not me. And I was perfectly fine with that. It was a relief, knowing I didn't need to fulfill that role. I finally understood mine was to support her. It always had been. It was the thing I'd craved since the moment I'd met her. What I'd been born to do.

I felt the agreement of my pack mates, and the sensation was a little overwhelming. Each of their feelings crowded in alongside my own and I suddenly felt so much larger than myself. Every boundary between us fell away. It was a little overwhelming, but I felt lighter and more connected than I'd ever known. It was going to take some getting used to.

"We're getting her back," Wolf growled.

"Yeah, we are." Nick reached out and ran a hand over Wolf's hair, and I felt a deep appreciation for his steadiness. I suddenly realized what Hunter had meant when he talked about Max being their center. Ava was desire and heat, and a spark that drew us in and united us. Nick was the cool river that ensured we wouldn't burn out. He was a balm on my soul.

But right now, we had work to do and an omega to get back. My omega. I reached out to the space she should occupy through her bond with our mates, and there was only a fuzzy blankness.

River pulled back first. "We need a status update," he growled.

Wolf and I hastily pulled our shirts back on, and we hustled back inside. I felt a sense of unity I'd never known before, almost as if we were in sync, and I was one part of a whole. I could feel Wolf's energy stir through me, washing me with a potent force that made me feel as if I could take on an army. It had my dick hard. Ryder looked over at me and grinned, as if he knew exactly what I was feeling. *Asshole.*

His grin widened. He'd caught that.

Wolf suddenly reached out and grabbed my hand as we passed back through the Palace doors. I didn't mind. I could sense the wild need to get to Ava pulling at him, to run and smash the world until he found her. He needed me to ground him until he could get to her, and I was okay with that.

Lexie gave us a once over, but didn't comment beyond a raised eyebrow. She'd been busy while we were gone. She didn't even wait for us to ask. Just launched into an update while Pala talked to someone on the Network's communication device.

"Sadie is getting the omegas prepped to go in about ten minutes. She's not messing around. She's taking them to the mountains. We figured the risk of traveling at night is outweighed by the bigger risk of them staying here once we're all gone. They're taking the PMV for added protection.

We had a mechanic join us at the farm recently, and he's been in town repairing it. He managed to re-attach the gun turret after Wolf tore it off. One of Sam's team from town is driving it and will bring it back once everyone is secure on the mountain. We've sourced enough extra vehicles from town to transport them all. Matt, Anders, and Oliver are going with her. Miles and Owen are taking Emma, too, because Sadie has a doctor at her cabin. They'll meet us at the farm when we get back with Ava."

"Is that going to leave the farm unprotected? And town?" River asked, and Lexie frowned.

"Yes, but our community on the farm has emergency protocols in place to follow. Dave has been doing intensive training in defense measures with the farm workers to prepare for something like this. They're rookies but they know what to do and will defend their homes. There's honestly nothing much of value in town at the moment, so apart from some petty thievery, they should be okay until we get back. They're banding together. We've sent any vulnerable women and single mothers with kids to the farm for the next few days, just in case. Isobella and Sirena are looking after them all."

"How is Emma?" I asked.

"Emma is still unconscious. Miles and Owen will let us know when she wakes up. It should give us an indication when Ava will wake up too, as long as they used the same dosage. They're a similar body weight."

She deliberately didn't mention any other option, like Ava not waking up, and nobody called her on it.

"We should sense when Ava wakes up. We felt it as soon as she lost consciousness," River said.

"But a heads up will be great, too. Just in case," Ryder added.

Lexie grimaced and nodded. "The Network has sent out an alert for any teams in the area to assemble. They're going to gather at a rendezvous point and wait for our signal to approach. They'll time it to arrive as we do. We're going to land the helicopter right on their motherfucking lawn. Sam's just reached the farm. Damon and his pack are ready. They're all coming, including Maia. She insisted they were stronger together and refused to stay behind. They'll be here soon."

"Good. Let's get everyone on the move. It's time to make Maven and the Palace pay," River said, as he clapped his hands impatiently.

"I can help with that," came a deep voice I'd never heard before from behind us, and we all spun in place. I realized with a sinking gut that with everyone preparing to leave, nobody had locked the front door. Or was even watching it.

A tall, imposing man, clad in black and wearing a balaclava with a skull painted on it and a dark hood, stood in the entry foyer to the Palace. He had a rifle strapped to his back, but his hands were up. Heavy silver rings glinted on his fingers. One looked like a matching skull. River and Ryder immediately moved to flank him, but he let out a low warning growl and powerful dominance flooded the room. He didn't attack anyone with it, just warned them back.

"He's a prime alpha," River said stiffly, shooting a look at Wolf. Wolf didn't react immediately. He just took a deep breath as he scented the air before a slow, feral smile spread across his face.

"The sniper," he growled. "I remember your scent from that first night in town. I wondered when you were going to show up again."

The prime alpha reached up and slowly pushed the hood back, then peeled the skull balaclava off his head, revealing wavy brown hair mostly pulled back off his face, a dark beard, and surprisingly kind brown eyes.

"I've been waiting a long time to meet you, too. Wolf," he said with a thick accent I couldn't place, and Wolf tilted his head in sudden confusion. "Sorry, I couldn't introduce myself the last time. I wasn't ready to reveal my identity. I still had work to do."

"What kind of work?" River growled.

"The kind that requires a gun with a scope and a long barrel," he replied, perfectly calm. He could have been discussing the weather.

"You're the Ghost," Ryder breathed out with a sigh. "We've followed the chatter about you on the dark webs." All the alphas had tiptoed around River and Ryder when they showed up, including Sam and Damon. I didn't even want to know how lethal this alpha was if Ryder was fangirling over him. The prime alpha just grunted in acknowledgement.

"Welcome to the team," I said. Whoever he was, he'd taken out the Palace alphas during the attack on the town. He clearly wasn't a fan of theirs, which made him a potential ally of ours. At this stage, we'd take any help we could get. He nodded at me and gave me a curious once over. Both River and Ryder noticeably stiffened, but neither made a move to shift in front of me, although I saw River's hand twitch by his side. I appreciated their restraint. I knew their alpha instincts would have them feeling protective after just claiming me. Even if it was a platonic claim.

"What should we call you?"

"Ghost works fine, for now. We don't have time for more," he said.

"How can you help?" River asked him tersely, still tense. He didn't seem to trust easily, at least not anyone outside of his pack. It made his ready acceptance of Wolf, Nick, and me feel significant.

"I can get you in the house without setting off the alarms or activating the titanium barricade that would slam into place, sealing off the master rooms. Which is where they will take your omegas. I just need you to provide a distraction outside first."

"Oh, I think we can manage that. I'm very distracting," Lexie said. Pala reached out to put a hand on her, as Ghost's eyes danced with humor. She shook her head at herself when she realized what she'd said and how it sounded.

"Why would you help us?" River asked, not letting up on his blunt questions.

"I have my reasons. They're personal." His eyes shuttered suddenly, as if someone had closed the blinds behind them, and the humor disappeared.

"What else do you need, apart from a distraction?" Sadie asked as she stepped out from the hallway to his left, flanked by her mates. I could sense the rest of the omegas gathered behind her, but couldn't see them in the dim hallway.

Ghost stiffened and drew in a deep breath. He turned slowly in her direction as his nostrils flared and he let out a strangled groan.

She stilled under his gaze and her mates closed in around her. I knew that feeling. Intimately.

The sound of vehicles pulling into the driveway and the whir of a chopper in the distance broke the intensity that had settled over the room.

"The cars are here, and that's Sam on approach," Lexie said. "He's early. He must have flown like the devil was chasing him."

"We need to move," Wolf growled, as he shifted restlessly.

"I'm bringing the omegas out now," Sadie said. "We're ready to go." Ghost stayed riveted in place, as she stared at him for a heartbeat, then another. Before she closed her eyes briefly and pulled herself together.

"Let's go," she said over her shoulder. She only spared one laden glance at Ghost, who had focused his entire attention on her, as she passed him by. I could almost feel the magnetic pull between them. Then she was out the door and gone, as a stream of omegas followed her. Miles and Owen brought up the rear, with Miles carrying Emma. Ghost didn't look at a single one of them. His eyes tracked Sadie all the way to the PMV as everyone sprung into action around him. When Sadie finally disappeared into the vehicle, I walked up to his side, as Wolf tracked my own movements.

Ghost looked shell-shocked and seemed as if he needed a hug. I wanted to reach out to him, but I didn't want to rile Wolf any more than he already was right now.

"What's her name?" Ghost asked me quietly, but didn't acknowledge me beyond that. "And where's she going?"

"Sadie," I told him. "She's taking the omegas to a safer location." It's as much as I would tell him right now. We desperately needed an ally, but I wouldn't trust the safety of the omegas to anyone I wasn't one hundred percent sure about. River looked at me and nodded in approval at my discretion before he headed outside.

"So what's your plan, Ghost?" Lexie asked as she walked up beside me, shadowed by Pala.

"They've been gathering mercenaries and alphas from the city. There's going to be a wall of them between you and Ava." He grinned and finally pulled his attention away from the doorway Sadie had disappeared through, and looked at us. "Are you ready for a little crazy?"

"Oh hell, yeah."

Forty

A pounding against my skull had me stirring as I tried to reach my hand up to my head. My hand wouldn't do much more than twitch, though. I had a vague notion that the weighted feeling holding my body down should concern me, but I was too fuzzy to pay much attention. I tried to blink open my eyes, but they were heavy too.

Maybe I should sleep a little more. I gave up trying to move and focused on trying to breathe through the monotonous pounding. My pulse had turned into a loud drum and every beat rattled my brain. Nausea rose, and I tried to shift onto my side, but couldn't.

Other sensations were trying to fight their way through, but everything felt muffled. A sudden scent of passion fruit assaulted me, and I groaned. The scent wasn't bad; it was just overripe and overwhelming. It wasn't a smell I enjoyed, so I instinctively tried to pull away from it.

"There, there, sweetheart. This should help." The sudden cool of a damp cloth on my head helped soothe the drum beat and ease the pressure. I didn't recognize the voice, though. *Where was I?*

A confusing rush of panic and relief battered me, and made me sink further back into the soft surface I was lying on. The onslaught intensified until I could almost hear a gruff voice yelling my name.

"Wolf?" I croaked. The weighted feeling faded, but I didn't want to risk trying to move again yet.

"He'll be here soon, sweetheart," the voice from before replied from further away. But that wasn't the voice yelling in my head.

"*Wolf, is that you?*"

"*Oh thank god, Ava. Are you okay?*" Shock added to my confusion, as I heard Wolf's voice echo as if it was coming down a long tunnel.

"*How are you in my head?*"

"*I don't know. I've been pushing my energy at you, trying to wake you up. Can you tell me where you are?*"

That was a good question. I took a deep, shaky breath and nothing smelled familiar. But that passion fruit scent surrounded me.

"*I don't know. I can't move or open my eyes. All I can smell is passionfruit and I'm on something soft. A bed maybe?*"

"*Fuck. Ava, stay still and try not to move. You're with Maven at their Manor. Do they know you're awake?*" Wolf sounded panicked, which had my heart rate speeding up.

"*The passion fruit guy put something cold on my head and spoke to me a moment ago.*" A sense of wild rage barreled down the bond, and I whimpered as memories assaulted me. Hands pulling at me in the darkness and a cloth over my face. Nicole's self-satisfied smirk. "*Was I abducted?*"

"*Yes,*" his voice was the sound of icebergs breaking apart. "*We know where you are, my mate. Max tracked you and we're coming. You just need to hold on. We're five minutes away in the chopper.*"

I could suddenly feel my mates sending me love and reassurance down the bond, including Cary, which almost made me gasp. "*How can I feel Cary in the bond?*"

"*We claimed him to bring him into the bond and strengthen us. He insisted. But I haven't mated him yet.*"

Oh, Cary. I hated Maven had forced his hand, even though he'd been ready. It should have been a special occasion, something to celebrate. "*Is he okay?*"

"*He's fine. He loves you and he's coming for you.*" My heart swelled, and I shot love back to Cary in the bond. I could feel his relief. Their emotions channeling through me, and Wolf's power swirling through us, helped dispel the remaining effects of the drugs in my system. I instantly felt clearer and my body lightened.

My relief didn't last long. I panicked as the voice returned, much too close. "Can you sit up for me, Ava? I want to talk to you."

"*What's wrong, Ava? What's happening?*"

"He wants me to sit up."

"*Stay still. Pretend you're asleep. Can you open up to me more, so I can hear him, too?*"

"I don't know. I can try."

I tried to open my senses to Wolf completely. It felt like wading through dense water until a burst of Wolf's power had my senses sharpening. I didn't have time to marvel at the intoxicating thrum of power, though. The bed dipped beside me, and my panic spiked again.

"Ava, I know you're awake. I can hear how fast your heart is beating. I'm trying to be gentle with you, but I won't tolerate being disobeyed." The voice was practically purring in my ear, but the tone grew increasingly dark. My eyes flew open in my panic and I looked up into sharp gray eyes that bored into me.

Wolf's low growl vibrated through me and I tried not to react.

"*I'm going to kill him if he touches you.*" I figured that meant it worked and Wolf could hear him through my thoughts. It was a relief to know I wouldn't have to repeat everything and try to listen at the same time. "*You need to stall him and if that doesn't work, fight him off. Do not let him bite you, do you hear me? You are stronger than you know. You can do this.*"

I tried to curl inwards slightly and make myself look docile. This perfect, submissive omega act was almost second nature. "I feel sick," I whimpered as I looked up at him through my lashes.

He stroked a finger down the side of my face and I felt everything in me recoil. "I know, sweetheart. It's an effect of the chloroform. It will pass soon. Some cold water will help."

He lifted me up and carried me over to a chair in a living area. I was glad I wasn't on the bed anymore, but I couldn't stand having him touch me. It felt wrong and scraped at my bonds. My mates' rage echoed through me, and I found it oddly comforting. It helped dispel the unpleasant sensation of his touch.

I glanced around the room to get my bearings. We were in a luxurious bedroom suite, done in similar colors to the VIP suite at the Palace. The thought made the nausea flare again. Nicole was sitting on a chair next to me, that same smug smirk on her face. My captor released me and handed me a glass of cold water before retreating to the couch across from us. To my horror, Angel was lying unconscious on the couch next to him. I could see her chest rising and falling, so I knew she was alive, but she should have woken up by now. He gently stroked a strand of her golden curls and everything in me heated to a flash boil.

"How could you abduct a child?" I asked, my tone icy cold in contrast to the wild heat tearing through me.

"*Easy, Ava.*" Wolf's warning came too late, as my abductor turned his head and narrowed his eyes at me. I quickly ducked my eyes down and tried to hide the blazing anger I knew was within them.

"I didn't abduct anyone. I merely recovered my experiment, Ava. It wouldn't have been necessary if you hadn't run away, or encouraged your new friends to terrorize my employees."

"Sorry, I'm a little disoriented," I whispered as I kept looking down and dutifully sipped my water. I made sure I kept Angel in sight, though. My submissive omega act had always come easily. I had merely played up certain parts of my personality, but now I struggled to keep it in place. He nodded in approval and reclined against the couch, one arm propped casually along the back. I traced his features, but I didn't recognize him. He'd dressed in a tailored black business suit, with a crisp white shirt and a red tie. I briefly wondered why he bothered. *Who could he possibly be meeting during an apocalypse? Surely I didn't warrant a suit?*

"Since she's awake now and unharmed, let's discuss how you'll fulfill our deal," Nicole purred in a sugary voice. She twisted a curl of hair around her finger to draw attention to the long curve of her neck. It was a practised move designed to entice an alpha to bite. "You promised me an advantageous mating."

"Shut up, you stupid omega. If you can't recognize you were a pawn, I won't humor you after you've given up your only leverage. You'll do as I say, or I'll hand you over to my men as entertainment," he snapped.

Nicole blanched at his words, as her finger froze in her hair. She shot me a nervous look, as if she expected me to save her after she sold us out. I wouldn't let anything happen to her, but right now, it was only an idle threat to shut her up. So she was on her own. My focus was entirely on the only innocent person here. Angel.

"*You're doing great, Ava. Stay quiet and play the part for another few minutes. We're almost there, and we're bringing a surprise.*" Wolf's gruff, yet now familiar, voice was a solace, soothing me.

"Now, Ava," the alpha said as he turned to me. Arrogance was so thick in his manner, it dripped off him like too much honey on a slice of toast. "Do you know who we are?"

Movement caught my eye, and three more men moved into my field of vision. I hadn't noticed them before. They were dressed impeccably in suits, the uniform of corporate CEOs and rich men everywhere. I had no doubt I was looking at the rest of Maven, which was bad news for me. Only one looked vaguely familiar. He had auburn hair, and I guessed he was Wolf and Hunter's dad.

"*They're all here, Wolf.*"

"*Don't panic, stay calm,*" Wolf reassured me. "*It's a good thing. It means we don't have to hunt them down one-by-one.*"

The alpha on the couch narrowed his eyes at my silence, but my grip on the submissive omega act was tenuous. I didn't feel like the same person who had worn that cloak so easily before. I didn't trust myself to talk right now, so I just shook my head in answer to his question.

"My name is Phillip, and I'm the CEO of Alpha Tech. Beside the fireplace, looking bored, is Richard, the CEO of Integral Mining. On his left, drinking all our finest wine, is William, our State Governor. Over by the window is Arthur, who has an old-money wife and doesn't think he needs to contribute to society anymore." He pointed out each man, ending on Wolf's dad, but I barely glanced at them. None of their titles or status meant a thing since the Crash. While they were still dominant alphas, the apex predator in the room was Phillip. He was nowhere near as powerful as Wolf, though.

The first two men ignored me. Arthur briefly glanced at me, but seemed more worried about what was happening outside. "Do we really need to have all of our security surrounding the house outside? Shouldn't we have some in here with us?"

"Are you questioning my methods, Arty?" Arthur clenched his jaw. Either at the answer or the nickname, I wasn't sure.

Phillip glared at Arthur over his shoulder before he turned his attention back to me. "This manor is the most secure estate in the country. It's our escape from the world and it's not listed under any of our public assets, so nobody knows we're here. It also has every security feature my company has ever invented, as well as bulletproof glass in every window. The men outside are expendable, and merely a precaution. A show of strength, so to speak. Nobody is getting in here."

He paused to let his words sink in. A tactic that may have worked well in the boardroom, but had no effect on me. I figured he was trying to imply we weren't getting rescued. To me, it meant he severely underestimated my pack and our friends. I struggled to keep my face blank and politely interested.

"So, I have a proposition for you, sweet Ava. We're going to claim you as our omega. If you struggle or object, Angel will suffer the consequences. Which will be a pity. She's the youngest omega we've found through our testing. A process that is still being fine tuned. I was looking forward to studying her. But she serves a far better purpose now. Do you have any questions?" He raised an imperious eyebrow at me. There was no warmth or humanity behind his eyes, only a cold lust for power. There would be no reasoning with this deranged alpha.

Nicole sobbed quietly next to me, as she finally realized the mess she'd gotten herself into, but nobody paid her any attention.

I took slow, deliberate breaths, trying to keep my heart beating evenly, and blinked at him, as if I didn't understand. I only had one option. To stall him, keep him talking. *Didn't sociopaths always like to talk about their dastardly plans?*

"Who is Angel to you?" I asked.

"As I said, she's an experiment. The same as Maia and Sam. We tested mixing our genetics with different women and manipulating proteins within the body. We wanted to see if we could produce stronger alphas and omegas. Angel was our only success outside of using our omega. She's quite remarkable, but we haven't been able to replicate the results.

"Why do you need me?" I asked next, when he didn't appear interested in talking more about Angel. I kept my eyes downcast and my voice soft, as I put my glass down on the coffee table and folded my hands primly in my lap.

"Oh come now, Ava. Surely Wolf told you about us before he claimed you? I don't enjoy being played, especially by an omega." The way he sneered as he said the word omega clearly portrayed how he felt about us, if his treatment so far hadn't already clued us in.

I swallowed hard, and his eyes glinted at my perceived fear. "Did you think I wouldn't notice the bite marks on you? Or the way you reek of that delightful male omega. What was his name again, William?"

"Cary," William said from beside the fireplace, and he had the nerve to lick his lips creepily with a tongue stained dark red from too much wine. It was the first emotion he'd shown. Blind rage seethed within me and I battled to keep it off my face.

"They're taunting you, Ava. Phillip wants you to fight the claim. Pain gives him pleasure. We're almost there." Wolf's reassurance washed over me, but he sounded strained and his words were ground out. I latched onto my mates through the bond as I sank into the comfort the others were sending the both of us.

Phillip's eyes darkened and the veneer of civility he'd cultivated slid away. "We took care to keep you pure and gave you a comfortable life, Ava. Yet the moment our eyes turned away, you let not one, but multiple men sully and bite you."

I couldn't look away as a dark growl broke free and some of his dominance whipped around the room. He briefly pinned me in place, just to prove he could, before he released me. "But no matter, I don't intend for anyone else to see you or those marks ever again. You can keep pretending you're a princess in the tower we'll lock you in. We can still claim you and use you to control Wolf, then we'll kill your other mates."

Wolf's roar in the bond vibrated through me. I could feel his wild energy taking over and my protective instincts flared brightly. I would not let these spineless, wretched alphas hurt any of my mates. The growing sound of a chopper in the distance meant my pack was close.

Phillip's chilling smile was pure evil. Increasing his power was the only thing he cared about. He had no remorse for the destruction they had wrought on the world. He didn't even acknowledge it while lounging here in his luxurious manor. I was done with my submissive act. It did me no good here.

"So hundreds of years of power and influence have brought you what, exactly?" I asked him, as I dropped my facade and let him see the real me. "Four egotistical men hiding behind walls and technology, breaking their toys because they can't get their own way? You're pathetic. You're barely a man. Each of my mates is worth a thousand of you."

"*Ava, no,*" Wolf growled in the bond. He was suddenly frantic.

Phillip's icy smile grew, as if he'd won a prize. "There you are, sweetheart," he crooned. "We're going to have so much fun."

"Can you hear that?" Wolf's dad asked from where he was still standing by the window. "It's a helicopter."

Phillip didn't even register him. He focused solely on me. His prey.

"Where is Damon's abhorrent father?" I asked, as I tried to gather more intel on the people inside the manor for Wolf. "Isn't he an ally of yours?"

"Unfortunately, he won't be joining us. He has lost his privileges. I don't tolerate people not performing the simple tasks I give them, and we no longer need him, anyway. He's outside leading the unruly pack of misfits we hired, trying to get back into our good books. At the very least, he should distract Damon if he gets too close."

"I want Damon dead," William growled. "He killed Ronan, my only son, and is protecting Sirena, that traitorous daughter of mine."

"Yes, yes, all in good time," Phillip said, waving him off.

"*Did you get that?*" I asked Wolf, and he gave me an affirmative growl.

I shrugged at Phillip, as if Damon's father was of no consequence to me. "Damon's dad will get what's coming to him. So, what was the point of the government manipulation, the abuse of omegas, and messing with fertility rates?" I had to know, because I didn't expect these men were going to survive the night. Plus, I was still stalling. I was just using a fresh line of questions to distract him.

Phillip's smile turned indulgent. "It's all part of the same equation, Ava. It's simple science, really. The strength of alphas was weakening. We didn't kill off prime alphas. They were an evolutionary quirk that died out because we didn't need them anymore. The world was too safe. We actually wanted them back. We just didn't want too many, too quickly. The first step to getting them back was to create some instability and force a new evolutionary cycle. Once primes started presenting again a decade ago, we started working towards the second step. A balancing event that would reduce the numbers of betas and create an environment where the strongest, the alpha species, would thrive. If we made a few more billion dollars saving what was left of the world with my tech, that would be a bonus."

There were so many things wrong with that statement I didn't even know where to start. Yet, his eyes were the burning of a devout zealot who believed his own propaganda.

"But it didn't go according to plan, did it?" I argued, as I clenched my fists. "Your balancing event turned into an apocalypse, and the world went to hell. People are dying."

He shrugged, with a studied air of casual disdain, completely unconcerned. "I'll admit. It happened sooner than we were prepared for. We don't have the stockpiled technology we were planning. A few more people will die than projected, but people always die. It's no big deal. We have power and a secure base. We'll survive, and that's what matters. Other people will figure out a way to fix it and we'll manipulate that process, too. Power loves a vacuum."

Arthur yelling in the background as the sound of the chopper intensified distracted him, and he sighed. As if it was beneath him to deal with us all. "Arty, calm yourself. What is the problem?"

"They're here. A helicopter is landing on the front lawn."

"Yes, I can hear that," he growled. "We needed Wolf to follow her, and he has."

"But he wasn't supposed to get here so fast. We haven't claimed her yet," Richard argued as he moved to the window too.

"Which is why we have over a hundred alphas outside. They will capture them and bring Wolf to us. They can't fit more than fifteen alphas, maybe a few more if they don't have packs, in a Black Hawk helicopter. Our team will overpower them easily."

"There's people coming out of the trees, too. About twenty of them," Arthur said.

"So they brought some friends. It's not unexpected. If one or two make it to the house, they're not getting in unless they're brought in, anyway. If you're so worried, go out there and help," Phillip growled. He was starting to lose his patience with them, and his civilized act was slipping. The other three men stayed put, as expected. Cowards never fought their own battles.

"What are they doing behind the helicopter?" Richard asked.

"And why have all the men come around the front? What if someone else attacks from the forest behind the house?"

"Oh, for fuck's sake," Phillip said, as he stood up and moved over to a window.

"They're all at the window, watching you. Whatever you're doing, keep doing it," I said to Wolf.

"We're coordinating with the Network team. You're doing great, Ava. Can you see anything you could use as a weapon?"

I discreetly looked around the room. My eyes landed on scatter cushions and books. *Maybe if a book was heavy enough, I could whack him with it?*

I was kidding myself. I didn't have that kind of strength. My eye landed back on my water glass. It looked like heavy cut crystal. If I shattered it, I could turn it into a weapon. Or maybe smash it over his head. I grabbed it quickly and drank the rest of the water in it. Then tucked it down beside me between the chair cushions. Keeping half an eye on the alphas at the window, and the other on Nicole. I didn't trust her not to tattle on me, but she seemed to have gotten over her tears and was now too busy glaring at Phillip.

When I was sure they were still distracted at the window and hadn't noticed my movements, I took a moment to run my eyes over Angel. She still wasn't stirring, but I could see her chest rising and falling steadily. I didn't dare try to reach for her.

"Is Angel okay?" Wolf asked, guessing what I was looking at by my emotions.

"*She's still unconscious.*" If anything happened to her, I would burn this place to the ground, and everyone in it.

I flicked my eyes back to the group by the window and stilled when I noticed Phillip had turned and was now watching me.

"I wondered if one of you would try to escape while I had my back turned, but you're both such good little omegas. We'll just have to make things a little more interesting," Phillip said, as his eyes lit up with excitement. He pulled a switchblade out of his jacket pocket and snapped it open before he casually flipped it between his fingers.

The opportunity for stalling died as the light from the chandelier caught on the wickedly sharp blade.

We were out of time.

Forty-One

Sam white knuckled the helicopter controls as he brought it down on the manor lawn and we all let go of whatever we had found to hang on to. It wasn't the smoothest landing I'd ever experienced, but it wasn't the worst either. Especially considering the circumstances. Flying at night was incredibly dangerous. Flying at night with no light anywhere in the landscape to identify buildings or power lines, while overloaded with people as cargo, was suicidal. It was a testament to Sam's skill that we'd made it at all. But the danger was far from over. Sam hopped out before the rotors stopped turning and opened the cargo door from the outside. He'd angled the chopper so we could exit and use the metal body as cover while we got ourselves into some kind of formation.

Damon, Hunter, Leif, Max, Maia, Sam, Pala, Dio, Dave, Lexie, Ghost, and a couple of Sam's squad mates, who had been in town, had flown with us. To rescue Ava. Maia was wearing a bullet-proof vest that was a few sizes too big for her and covered her stomach. It was duct taped together at the sides.

I hadn't worked with any of these guys before, apart from the night they freed the town. River and I had mostly been on the fringes of that, our sole focus on Ava. Damon and Sam were warily eyeing Wolf now, not sure if he would take commands. His focus was on the manor, though, not on them.

Hunter was standing slightly between the two groups. He looked torn between needing to stick close to Maia and wanting to reach out to his long-lost brother. Wolf's body was straining to run, but Cary was standing in front of him with a hand on his chest. Cary had wasted no time settling into his instincts since we'd claimed him, and slotted right into our pack as if he'd always been a part of it. He was finally flowing with us, instead of fighting us, and I was intensely glad. We needed him.

River and Damon had tried to devise a loose plan during phone calls while Sam was traveling back and forth. It currently involved getting here as quickly as possible and assessing the situation on arrival. All while acting as a distraction by landing on the lawn. So it wasn't really much of a plan. Not knowing what was inside the manor, or what potential defenses it had, made anything beyond that impossible. Now we were standing outside a palatial house with over a hundred alphas between us and Ava.

I didn't know where they'd gotten so many alphas from, or what they'd bribed them with to get them here. They must have somehow put a call out in the city. I couldn't make out faces. The floodlights from the manor behind them were too strong. Yet, no-one was charging us. They seemed to be waiting for us to attack, and it made me wonder what lies they'd been told. *Had we been portrayed as the enemy?*

Movement at the fence behind us had each of the packs instinctively circling Maia and Lexie. No-one was happy having their omegas here, but each had refused to stay behind. It made me ache for Ava. My arms burned to hold her and pull her into the safety of our pack. At least she was awake now, and communicating with Wolf. The blank space that had bloomed in my chest when they knocked her out had gutted me. But she was still in immense danger and it had a growl hovering in my chest.

A voice called out to Sam, and he yelled, "Hurry up and get in here, Gus."

A beta with a full head of silver hair, who appeared to be in his mid seventies, appeared at the fence. At least twenty people appeared behind him, a mix of betas and alphas. "I'm going to need a boost," he said dryly as he looked at the chain-link fence in front of him.

"Hang on," I yelled as I twisted back towards the chopper. We'd put bolt cutters and other tools in a box shoved to the side earlier. So we could be prepared for anything. I grabbed them and hustled to the fence, quickly cutting a hole big enough for everyone to slip through. The noise of the slowing rotors finally faded enough that we could hear each other without yelling. It also potentially meant we were about to lose the only cover we had, if that was all the horde was waiting for.

"What's the plan now?" Gus asked, not bothering with pleasantries as he joined River looking around the side of the chopper, making sure no-one was advancing on us. They weren't, but the alphas that had been ringed around the building had joined the others in front. We were sitting ducks here, and we knew it. But that was the plan.

"What do you want to do, Wolf?" Damon asked. "Ava is your omega. We're happy to take your lead."

"He's talking to Ava," River said, over his shoulder. "I don't think they'll shoot. Especially while we're bundled together. They need Wolf alive, and they want their omegas back, too." Damon and Sam both growled low in their throats. Electricity crackled in the air, leaking from Damon. Having his pregnant mate in a hostile situation was making him incredibly volatile.

"They can come get us," Lexie said darkly. Sam looked like he was about to throw her over his shoulder and jump back into the chopper. So many alpha scents were saturating the air, including mine. It was nauseating.

"Hang on, talking to Ava?" Maia asked.

"Yeah, that's a conversation for later," I answered. Not wanting to get distracted right now.

"We meet them head on," Wolf growled. All eyes swiveled to him. His entire body shook with the strength needed to hold himself in place.

"There's over a hundred armed alphas out there. We're not taking our omegas into a close quarters fight," Damon growled, darkness riding him.

"We're not," Wolf growled back. He looked at me as he ground his jaw, and I nodded at him. Words were a struggle for him right now. I could sense what he wanted to do, and it just might work.

"Are you sure we can do it?" River asked, his focus swinging to Wolf, as Wolf nodded, before shifting back to watching the horde and the house.

"Anyone want to clue us in?" Lexie asked, sounding tense.

I answered for River, when I sensed he wasn't going to. He wasn't used to relaying instructions to other teams; we'd been operating alone too long, and he relied on me instinctively knowing what he was doing. So I was going to have to step up. "Sam, you held an entire room of people at the pub in town, just with your dominance. It seemed to get easier when your mates touched you, and Damon came to help, right?" I had watched the whole thing from a distance, fascinated.

"He did, and yes, it eased the strain when we made contact and Damon came," Lexie answered, putting her hand on his arm when Sam just narrowed his eyes at me. "Can you dominate that many people if you work together?"

Wolf, Sam, and Damon looked at each other. None of them seemed to have a lot of words right now, rage and fear for their omegas riding them hard.

"I guess we'll find out," I said.

"Can we offer them an out?" Maia asked. "When Oliver defected after the attack at the farm, half his unit came with him. I'm guessing a good chunk of those guys probably don't want to be here either. It would thin the crowd and give Ghost time to get in place, too."

That crazy motherfucking sniper, Ghost, had asked us to approach the manor from behind, flying low over the top. He'd jumped, free fallen and landed on the roof in the darkness, hopefully undetected over the noise of the chopper. He said he could take down their security system from inside. We just needed to give him a little time. Which was the only reason Wolf was vibrating in place and not charging the doors right now.

We'd taken a massive risk, trusting him. He could have us stalled out here while he double crossed us inside. But Wolf had approved him and I trusted Wolf's instincts. We were just waiting for his signal.

"I think we'd all rather turn them to our side than kill them," River said from beside me, finally speaking up. "But from what Ghost said, many of these men are hired mercenaries. Hopefully, there are a few decent men amongst them."

Everyone stilled as a woman's scream pierced the air and Ava's fear suddenly spiked in the bond. Wolf's wild energy smashed through us and he was moving instantly. He charged around the chopper, with Cary and Nick trailing behind him. The signal, a flashlight from an upper window, flared just in time, because we were done waiting.

"On Wolf," River yelled, as we raced after him, too. We ran in sync to catch up and each took a position at his shoulder, matching our strides to his and putting a hand on him. Nick and Cary were close behind us and they did the same, spurred on by Wolf's energy. I spared one glance behind them to see Sam and Damon close behind us on either side. Lexie and Maia were tucked in behind them, and their packs fanned out around them. They were laying hands on each other and their primes, the same as we were. The rest of Sam's team and the Network guys had taken flanking positions around our three packs.

I knew from the energy that had been in the room when we all hugged, that when our packs connected out here, with rage fueling us all, it was going to be explosive. I could already feel tendrils of it coursing over my skin.

The wall of alphas braced themselves in front of us, with no idea what was about to hit them. I almost pitied them.

The time for talking and stalling had ended. We were getting our omegas back. Now.

Forty-Two

Nicole screamed, and a flash of excitement crossed Phillip's face before he threw the knife at her. It lodged in her side, and she screamed again, as she frantically patted at the blood pooling around it.

"Ava," Wolf's roar echoed in my head, and rattled the windows. Phillip grinned the same way I imagined a shark would, if it could.

Arthur turned back to the window, uninterested in what was happening inside this room. Richard and William both wore looks of weary disdain, clearly used to Phillip's violent tendencies.

"They're charging," Arthur yelled suddenly. But Phillip ignored him, intent on the bloody scene in front of him.

I tried to jump out of my chair to help Nicole, but Phillip's bark had me pushed back in place. He got up and casually strolled over to her, in no hurry. He leaned over and stroked her face, examining her contorted features, as if he found beauty in them.

"I don't appreciate people glaring at me, Nicole. It's not polite. Now, be a good little omega and stay quiet for me," Phillip crooned, and she nodded. She clamped her hand over her mouth, leaving a bloody trail across her face, as he reached down and yanked out the knife. He carelessly wiped the knife on her ruined dress before he turned dismissively and sauntered back to the window.

"Grab the throw pillow behind you and push it onto the wound. Keep pressure on it," I hissed at Nicole, as Phillip's dominance released me and my gaze tracked his every movement. Wolf was a mess of growls in my head and rising, feral energy.

"*I'm okay*," I said to him quickly, but he was beyond replying, even in the bond.

"So sweet. Worrying about the woman who betrayed you," Phillip said. He used the same fake, polite tone from earlier, as he wiped a smear of blood off his finger with a handkerchief. It was the same tone I imagined he'd honed schmoozing other rich people at charity dinners. Only his eyes had changed. The scent of blood on the air had sharpened them.

I wanted to help Nicole, but Angel was lying on the couch between Phillip and me. Nicole whimpered under her breath as she did as I suggested, pushing a cushion into her side. "Help Angel," she mouthed at me when I glanced at her, and I nodded. It seemed she wasn't completely heartless.

"There's always been something different about you Ava, I just couldn't figure out what. And I like to know what my possessions can do. I would have put you down in the labs, but Wolf would have rioted and we barely had him contained as it was. I'm intrigued though. I thought you might have been able to deny a bark, the same as Maia, but you froze just now. So what is it?"

"I don't know what you're talking about," I said.

"I was hoping you'd be a good little omega and not fight me on this, but it seems you require some more persuasion." His eyes flicked to Angel, and we both noticed her stirring as her eyes fluttered open. My heart sank through the floor. She didn't need to see this.

"Ava?" she whimpered, sounding groggy and confused.

"I'm here, Angel. It's going to be okay," I tried to reassure her. Phillip just grinned wider, showing me his teeth.

I couldn't let him hurt her, not while I had any life in my body. Yet I also couldn't let him bite me. His vile emotions would taint me for the rest of his life, and I knew Angel still wouldn't be safe. So fight, it had to be.

I felt Wolf's energy cycle rapidly through our pack, building towards a colossal peak. It moved like a pure, wild energy in my veins and I could feel Cary channeling it alongside me. Yet the power was also tinged with that of our friends. I could feel Damon and Sam in there, too.

I didn't have time to dwell on it, though. Phillip's face lit up as he read the determination on mine. My calm, submissive façade had fled. What it left behind was pure, raw omega. A mama bear defending her cub.

I jumped up as Wolf flooded our bond with dominant energy. Phillip laughed as he lunged towards Angel, and the knife flashed wickedly in front of him. He vaulted over the back of the couch, dragged her still limp body up to his chest, and angled the knife towards her throat. Her eyes widened in fear as her gaze locked on mine, but I felt utter trust coming from her.

"*I need you*," I screamed at Wolf in the bond, shoving a sense of urgency at him as my adrenaline pounded. But I already knew they wouldn't make it up here in time. There was only me, Angel, and the knife as death slid towards her.

"*Now, Ava,*" Wolf screamed back in my head as he released his energy, and drove it towards the massing enemies outside. It spread out in a wave that reverberated with a sonic boom. I pulled at that energy with every ounce of inner strength I had, then flung out my hands and pushed it straight at Phillip. It forged its way through me and out of me through sheer force of will, burning a heated path through my veins as I roared my fury.

It was impossible. Yet, power poured from me, pushed by Wolf as my pack sensed what I was doing. They shored me up as Cary held the flow steady, taking as much of the strain as he could. It flowed around Angel and tore into Phillip, making him stagger backwards slightly before he froze. The knife halted, suspended in mid-air, centimeters from Angel's neck.

"Everyone's collapsed outside. All of them. They're either dead or out cold," Arthur shouted in disbelief as he stepped back from the window. He clutched his face in horror when he spun and saw Phillip frozen behind him.

Phillip's eyes blazed with rage as we became locked in an epic struggle. I could feel him fighting to break my hold. But I kept every ounce of my concentration fixed on holding him in place. I felt Lexie and Maia join Cary in holding me up and funneling power to me. My girls were here, and they were furious. I felt fierce as I let their fury join my own and I pushed it *all* at him.

"Did Wolf do that from outside?" Richard asked, his voice shaking as he looked from Phillip's frozen body to the window.

"No, she did," Arthur said, disbelief in his voice as he raised a shaky hand and pointed at me.

"She can't. She's an omega," William sputtered, but he had paled and his eyes were wide open in shock.

I growled low in my throat and felt a twisted smile cross my face, as I flung dominance over them, too. It wasn't a lot. I didn't want to lose my hold on Phillip, but it was enough to spook them. I sensed them shift away, trying to get as far from me as they could. They were alphas, yet not one of them tried to use their own dominance to stop me. They truly were cowards.

"Let. Angel. Go," I demanded, throwing sharp intention into every word. His arm relaxed just enough to loosen around Angel, and she wriggled free, carefully eyeing the hovering knife as she slid down. As soon as she hit the floor, she stumbled towards me on shaky legs. I grabbed her with one hand and pulled her behind me as I kept my other hand raised towards Phillip.

I wanted to tell her to run, but I didn't know who was outside the door. She was safer with me. I could feel Wolf getting closer, and it only fueled me further. Every step my pack took towards me was a drumbeat in my heart and added power in my veins. "Keep a hand on my back, Angel. So I know where you are. But don't look, okay?"

"Okay, Ava," she whispered, and I felt her small hand press into my back as she tucked into me. That tiny, trusting hand felt like a brand on my skin. It mirrored the one she'd already left on my heart. The one that had quietly melted me every time she sought me, or my pack, out.

I took a slow step towards Phillip, making sure my dominant hold stayed firm, before I took another one. It held like it was mine to mold. It didn't even drain me. The power buzzed through my veins as if it had come home. I reached out and pried the knife from his hands. He tried to hold on, but I growled and his fingers released the knife into my waiting palm.

"Kneel," I ordered, and he dropped to his knees even as his eyes blazed with the need to commit violence. I spun the knife around and pressed it against his neck, hard enough for drops of blood to trail down into his pristine white shirt. It didn't change his expression.

"You underestimated Wolf, and me, too, Phillip. I'm not your possession to do with as you please. I belong to me," I told him, feeling powerful and alive. I was tired of seeing omegas manipulated and mistreated by entitled alphas. Of pretending to be submissive just to stroke their egos. I didn't enjoy hurting people, unlike the man on his knees at my feet, but I wanted him to feel what it was like to be on the tip of someone's knife. Your life in their hands. "You want to play with knives, Phillip? What about people? You want to play with lives, too? Maybe I should play with yours?"

"Stab the arrogant fucker," Nicole grated out behind me. Words I don't think she'd ever uttered before.

The front doors of the manor smashed open. The crash reverberated in the marble entry and chased the sound of footsteps on the stairs. They rang closer every second. I smiled at Phillip. My mates and my family were here.

"Your fate is coming for you," I said with quiet conviction, and the words seemed to echo around the room.

Forty-Three

"They're inside. Why aren't the bars coming down?" Richard yelled frantically. Arthur dashed for a bookcase near him and tried flicking a hidden switch on the side, but nothing happened. William, a typical politician, stood and did nothing as his wine glass crashed to the floor.

A deafening crash behind me had my smile widening as I heard the bedroom door being ripped from its frame. More blood slid down Phillip's neck as his eyes blazed. Wolf's dark jungle scent, spiked with ginger, washed over me as he stormed into my space and wrapped an arm around me possessively. In the same motion, he picked Angel up and cradling her between us. She didn't seem bothered by the powerful dominance rolling off us both, as his touch sent another burst of power sliding through me.

"*Mine*," he growled in the bond. I got the feeling he didn't only mean me. He was an impenetrable wall at my back, supporting us both. He made no move to take the knife from me. Or convince me to back off. He was content to let me choose my path, as long as he could stand with me.

"I knew you'd come," Angel whispered to him and I felt a swell of satisfaction through him. Until his gaze settled on the alpha at my feet and a snarl ripped from him, aimed directly at Phillip.

"Having fun, little bird?" Ryder growled at my side as he stepped alongside us. He cocked his head and looked at the prone alpha. "I have to say, I was expecting someone a little more intimidating to be the head of Maven."

Phillip's eyes blazed, but he was powerless beneath me. Even if he wasn't, he was no match for Ryder.

The rest of my pack surrounded me as Cary grabbed my face and turned it to him. He kissed me hard and fast, uncaring that I had a knife to a man's throat. As soon as he pulled back, he shifted his focus to Angel. "Come here, chipmunk."

"Okay, squirrel," she replied. Her words sounded confident, but her voice wavered. She was a little kid, trying to be brave, when she shouldn't have to be. She should be wrapped up safely somewhere, playing with dolls and having tea parties. Not dealing with madmen.

I felt Cary pull her out from between us, and suddenly Nick was there, too. They squished her up in their arms and tucked her between them as they stepped back.

Wolf instantly wrapped his entire body around me and I sighed as I leaned back into him. I still had the knife firmly pressed to Phillip's neck, and my borrowed dominance holding him in place.

"What's the plan, little bird?" River asked as he stepped into my other side

"No plan, just teaching him how to submit," I replied. I was amazed at how calm I sounded. Wolf's wild energy seemed to center me, rather than batter me.

I felt the room fill up around us as our friends and family barged in behind my mates. So many emotions beat at me, but the biggest ones were love and relief. After spending a decade feeling so alone, I was grateful for each of them. I'd never imagined having so many people who cared for me and would put their life on the line for mine. It was a stark contrast to the four alphas in front of me. They had all the money in the world, but nobody was coming to save them. Not even the people they'd paid.

"Holy shit. You're a badass, Ava," I heard Maia whisper shout, and Lexie laughed, relief flooding through the sound. I couldn't help but shoot a grin over my shoulder at them. Maia gave me a big thumbs up.

"Have you got him?" I asked River and Ryder. They both nodded and Wolf stepped me back. I dropped my hand as I released my hold on Phillip, but held onto the knife. He surged forward instantly, his wrath focused entirely on me, but the twins grabbed him and pushed him down onto his knees again.

Letting the power go was harder than I thought it would be. It was a little addictive after feeling powerless for so long. My adrenaline crashed, and I was grateful for Wolf supporting me, as my legs suddenly turned to jelly.

"My power is yours whenever you want it," Wolf murmured in my ear, as he took more of my weight and let me lean completely against him. "It belongs to all of us now."

"It's not yours. It's mine," Phillip raged, spittle flying from his mouth as he struggled to rise against River and Ryder's hold.

"Just because you try to take something, doesn't make it yours," River growled, as he kicked at Phillip, landing a heavy blow to his legs that had him back on his knees.

"How's Nicole?" I asked, as I twisted, but I couldn't see her through the people crowding the room.

"Alive, but passed out," Pala called out. "She's lost blood, but she'll survive. It missed everything vital."

Nick pulled a first aid kit from his backpack before he tossed it to Pala. But I couldn't pay attention to what they were doing. Damon distracted me as he moved forward into my line of sight. He had a man slumped over his shoulder that he dropped carelessly at Maven's feet.

"Here's your henchman," Damon growled. "He deserves to share your fate, seeing as he was so loyal to you."

"Who's that?" I whispered to Maia, who had snuck up alongside me. Leif shadowed her closely.

"Damon's dad," she whispered back as she grabbed my hand and squeezed it. I felt Wolf flick a sharp spike of energy at him, waking Damon's dad up and showing extreme finesse in the control of his power.

"You little punk," the enraged man snarled as he blinked his eyes open and spotted Damon. He struggled to get to his feet. None of his friends helped him. "I'm going to-"

"You're going to what?" Damon snarled right back, getting in his face. "Beat me? Bark at me? I outgrew you a long time ago. You have no power over me anymore. You never really did. I just didn't realize it. We're done, old man. I have a new family now." It was a powerful moment for Damon, as he threw off the coercive control his father had held over him his entire life.

Hunter strolled up to Damon and gripped his shoulders, supporting him and anchoring him. "Hi Dad," he said to Arthur with fake politeness. "I'd say it's nice to see you, but it's really not. Thanks for not killing my brother, though. I'm enjoying getting to know Wolfgang finally. My half brother, Sam, too."

Damon turned his growl to Arthur, who blanched.

"You always gloated about having three highly dominant alpha sons. How's that working out for you now?" Richard laughed, before Damon turned his glare on him.

I realized suddenly that Maven had terrorized and abused each of their children. But had then hidden behind their henchmen, the military, and the Palace, once they'd reached maturity and their dominance developed.

"You really are the worst kind of cowards," I said to them, and they all flushed with rage at having an omega talk to them in that way. Only I was no longer the cowering little omega they were expecting. I never had been. I'd gripped the frayed edges of my bonds to me and used them as a shield against everything the Palace threw at me. Keeping to myself at my core. If omegas needed someone to stand up for them, and that had to be me right now, so be it.

"You little bitch," Richard hissed, seeming to have forgotten already that I'd just dominated one of them. Before he could draw another breath to add to his unimaginative and lackluster insult, power had him slammed against the wall. Wolf hadn't made a sound, but I'd felt the energy course through him. Richard shut up fast, but Wolf kept him pressed there.

As I watched them, another realization hit me. There was no rehabilitating these alphas. From birth, they'd been told they were invincible and gods amongst men, despite the waning alpha dominance in their family line. They had a lifetime of ingrained delusions they would never relinquish. I studied them one-by-one. Phillip was almost frothing at the mouth at our treatment of him, and was clearly unhinged. While Richard looked indignant, not used to being pushed around, even as I could see his hands shaking in fear. William and Arthur glanced at each other and I could almost see their minds working. They were figuring out how they could manipulate their way out of this situation, as they always did. They wore matching sneers as Wolf released Richard and he slid slowly down the wall.

"Okay, I think you've made your point, Wolfgang. Things have clearly gotten a little out of hand. Maybe now we can sit down as the civilized people we are and discuss how we move forward," William said. Condescension dripped from every word. He also had the audacity to step towards the couches and wave a hand graciously at the empty seats, as if we were indulging in a morning tea together.

"Shut the fuck up. Nobody here is interested in anything you have to say," Sam snarled at him. He shoved him back into the corner with a burst of dominance, before moving over to stand behind Damon and Hunter, supporting his found family.

I heard a small giggle and my heart melted a little more when I glanced over to see Nick had covered Angel's ears to block the cursing. He was making faces at her as she looked up at him adoringly. We really needed to get both her and Nicole out of here as soon as Pala had finished triaging Nicole.

"We're going to take Angel into the hallway and watch for anyone approaching," Cary said, as if he'd read my mind, and River nodded. Angel had the audacity to pout at me, but she went with Cary and Nick willingly. I was glad they both went with her. Watching Angel was definitely a two-person job. We did not want her sneaking away right now.

My pack was working in perfect sync together, each playing to their strengths. Wolf having my back, River and Ryder controlling the room, while Nick and Cary watched our six and took care of Angel.

"What do you want to do with Maven?" River asked me, bringing my attention to him.

"I don't think that's up to me," I said, surprised to find everyone watching me. I knew Maven had kidnapped and threatened me, but I had no relationship with these men. "Surely that's up to the people they're related to." I deliberately didn't call them family. It took more than giving birth to someone to earn that title.

"I know what to do with them," came a voice I didn't recognize from behind us, "and I'm related to them."

I twisted again to peek around Wolf. A scary looking alpha in dark clothing and a skeleton balaclava under a hood stood in the doorway.

"Okay, so who's the skeleton guy?" I asked Maia, surprised that nobody else seemed to be concerned. Wolf hadn't even tensed. "How much did I miss, exactly?"

"That's Ghost. Don't worry, he's an ally," Lexie answered instead, coming up alongside Maia. "We'll fill you in later."

Ghost pushed through the throng and walked up beside River. "Hi, Dad," he said to Phillip, tilting his head and looking at Phillip as if he was a strange creature in a science exhibit.

"Holy crap," Maia hissed. "How many kids do these assholes have?"

"Oh, there's a lot of us. Someone really should have taught these guys to keep it in their pants," Ghost drawled, as he pulled off his balaclava so Phillip could see his face.

"I'm not your father. I have no idea who you are," Phillip sputtered.

"Oh, sorry. You're right. You're just my sperm donor, and I'm your illegitimate bastard. Now I'm an orphan, since you killed my mother," Ghost growled as he towered over Phillip. "Or I soon will be."

"I don't know what you're talking about—"

River and Ryder stepped back instinctively as Ghost growled and kicked Phillip hard enough to sprawl him out on the floor. It was hard to watch, but watching Maia after she'd suffered at the hands of the Palace had been harder. Nobody made a move to stop Ghost.

"That was for Nellie," Ghost growled. "My mother, since you can't seem to remember having your men hunt her down and execute her. She didn't know any of your precious secrets. She was only trying to keep me safe. But I do. Ironically, it was the Crash you caused that finally led me right to you. It was easier to find you when the rest of the world got quiet and dark. Now I know all about what you and your pack have been up to. And it ends now."

Wolf flinched behind me, and Ghost looked up to meet his gaze. I remembered Wolf talking about his nanny, Nellie. The one that disappeared. Sadness flooded the bond, and I wrapped his arms around me tighter, pushing comfort into our bond.

"That's why you helped us that night, in town? When you shot the Palace alphas from the rooftop. For Nellie?" Wolf asked him.

"Yeah," Ghost growled and looked away. "She talked about you a lot."

"I'm sorry. Your mother was a good person. She was my world when I was little. She didn't deserve that," Wolf said with a quiet rumble, as his voice shook slightly.

Ghost nodded. "If I could have intervened to help you sooner, I would have. The Crash made it harder to move around."

"You were there when my mates were in danger, and you're here again now. That's all I care about. I owe you," Wolf said. He let me go before he moved over to Ghost and gave him a hug.

"You owe me nothing," Ghost said a little gruffly. He looked a little taken aback, but he returned Wolf's hug.

Damon and Sam both looked like they had a million questions, but now wasn't really the time. River jumped in before we could get off track, and brought us back to the problem at hand, the way he was good at.

"What's your plan, Ghost? I assume it's more than kicking him?" he asked dryly.

"The alphas outside are waking up from the mass knockout you guys delivered. I don't know how the hell you knocked a hundred alphas unconscious, but I'm impressed."

"Pack strength," Wolf said simply.

Ghost looked between us all, intrigued. "Huh," was all he said, though.

"How does the alphas waking up help us figure out what to do with these assholes, rather than create another problem?" Ryder asked, sounding frustrated.

Ghost grinned, and there was carnage in his eyes.

"Most of the hired mercenaries have left. I talked to them before the small team you have guarding the front entrance and the helicopter let them go. The mercenaries weren't interested in a second dance with you lot. The alphas that are left out front are mostly from abandoned military units or were lured from the city. Maven promised them food and safety for their families to come here and defend this place, but hasn't exactly been forthcoming with the goods.

"I explained to them the role Maven played in the Crash, and who they're really working for. Maven has screwed too many people, and crossed too many lines. Their payment is due. There's power here, and food stashed in the basements. Some of them want to stay and bring their families out of hiding nearby. After they've taken out the trash."

There were a lot of glances between everyone in the room. I understood where Ghost was coming from, but I didn't want more blood tainting River and Ryder's conscience if we could avoid it. They'd borne too much already.

"Wolf," Damon said, "technically, this is your house. Max found documents in his research naming you as the heir to Maven. What do you want to do?"

Wolf shrugged. "I want a home, and that's never going to be here. I don't plan on ever coming back. If families can use this place, or anything in it, they're welcome to it. I'd like knowing there are kids here, sliding down the staircase and drawing on the walls. The place needs it. As for Maven, whatever happens to them is no longer my concern, as long as they're not a threat to my pack. I have no loyalty to them. As a dynasty, Maven is done."

I moved back into Wolf's arms and caressed his face. "Let's go make a home," I said, and he smiled at me.

"Don't be rash, son. There are generations of tradition at stake here. Plus billions of dollars," Arthur started, and Hunter laughed.

"Nice try, Dad," he said as he shook his head. "You really don't get it. Money doesn't mean shit anymore. Not to us, and not to anyone out there. Family is what people care about, and their ability to provide for them. And you've taken both from far too many. Ghost is right, payment is due."

He turned his back on his dad and walked over to us, before he clapped Wolf on the back. "You both already have a home. With us. So let's get going," Hunter added.

Out of the corner of my eye, I noticed Phillip grab a small decorative box from inside his jacket while everyone's attention was diverted. He opened it and flicked a switch inside before I could call out. Instantly, a tone blared from hidden speakers.

"What the fuck did you do?" Damon's dad screamed. "We're not in the panic room. You'll kill us all."

"Everybody dies eventually. Nobody takes what's ours," Phillip screamed back at him before he started laughing. He'd completely lost the plot and slipped into mania.

"That's a detonation countdown," Max yelled, lunging forward and pressing Maia into Leif's waiting arms. They all turned and ran.

"Everyone out," Wolf roared as he picked me up. His energy drove through everyone, galvanizing us into action. Even our friends. They moved faster than I'd ever seen, as they practically flew out the door. I glanced briefly over his shoulder as we went through to see Damon's dad, trying to wrestle the device from Phillip. While the rest of Maven frantically tried to topple the bookcase and reach the panic room, believing their technology would save them.

Wolf charged down the stairs, with River keeping pace with us. Cary and Nick were already out the door with Angel, having had a head start, Ryder hot on their heels. My heart beat in my throat, half strangling me with fear, as Wolf's energy pushed them harder. I expected a boom at any moment as the tone sped up. We were halfway across the lawn when it finally came. It was deafening, and the ground vibrated beneath us.

We were thrown to the ground as glass and shrapnel flew past us. Wolf and River covered me with their bodies, pushing me into the ground as I screamed. I reached through the bond and felt my mates shaken, but alive. I couldn't feel Angel, though. We didn't have a bond.

"Angel," I yelled, as I twisted and tried to scrabble out from under Wolf, desperate to get to her. I couldn't stand the thought of anything happening to her after we'd just saved her. The world couldn't be so cruel. I spied a tangle of limbs a few metres in front of us.

"She's fine," Ryder called out, holding his head as he rolled off Cary and Nick, and I saw her clutched between them.

She reached her arms out towards me, and Wolf rolled off me so I could crawl to her. "You're okay. You're okay," I reassured her as she cried and snuggled into me. My pack settled in around us, arms twisting and gripping each other, needing the contact as we each tried to slow our breathing.

"Is everyone okay?" I asked, now that I had Angel back in my arms. They reassured me they were fine, with only minor scrapes, as hands stroked over Angel and me, checking us over. I looked at Ryder, who had blood trickling down his face.

River checked the shrapnel wound. "He's had much worse. He'll be fine."

"Lexie? Maia?" I called out. I heard two voices call back, but it was hard to make them out over the ringing in my ears.

"They're fine. So are their packs. Only Ghost is missing, but I saw him make it out the door and disappear into the darkness," River said as he scanned our surroundings and did a head count. He stilled for a moment as he pulled his attention back to us. "You saved us all, Wolf. I don't even know how you did that. Pushed us all. It felt as if we were flying, but it got us far enough away. We wouldn't have made it out without you."

Wolf just grunted. I pushed love at him in the bond, and he smiled tiredly at me. He was a giant, wild alpha, but even he had his limits. And he'd pushed them tonight, twice.

"Fuck. That was intense," Ryder groaned as he nuzzled my hair. It was the understatement of the century.

"How did you know she could bark?" River asked Wolf. He was frowning, and his need to solve the puzzle was riding him hard. "No other omega has ever done that."

Wolf closed his eyes, as if he was trying to pull enough energy together to talk. "I didn't. Not for sure. But I suspected. Ava pushed my dominance back at me when she got mad this morning. She didn't know she did it, though."

A gasp slipped out past my stunned lips. I hadn't realized; I thought he'd stepped back willingly.

"Why didn't you say something earlier?" Cary asked.

Wolf shrugged as he lay back on the ground. "I saw her. All of her. I knew you would too when she was ready to show you."

"If anyone could do it, it would be our Ava," Nick said with quiet pride shining in his eyes. My other mates agreed as they mirrored Nick's gaze.

I blushed and looked away, needing something else for everyone to focus on. What I did felt completely natural. I didn't want to be some secret sauce omega. I just wanted to be me. And I finally felt as if I was.

I looked past them to the burning building behind us. The entire center of the manor had collapsed inwards. Only the left and right wings remained, and as I watched, part of the left roof collapsed in on itself. Smoke billowed out the shattered windows as flames burned their way through the rooms left standing. The master bedroom was in the center, directly behind the grand staircase. There was no way anyone from Maven survived.

"Why the hell would he blow up his own home?" Nick asked, staring at the rubble now, too. It was such a waste. Purely because one man was incapable of sharing. All those families that could have sheltered here were now forced to fight for survival again. It broke my heart. I cuddled Angel to me, trying to comfort us both.

"He was the first head of Maven who wasn't a prime alpha. Take away their inherited wealth, and he had nothing. He wasn't even a particularly dominant alpha, not compared to River or Ryder. As hard as he tried, he couldn't become a prime. Maybe it pushed him over the edge," Cary answered.

"Never try to understand a psychopath," River replied. "They don't operate by our rules."

His eyes weren't on us though, as a handful of alphas started filtering out of the surrounding forest. I assumed they were the ones who had stayed, that Ghost had tried to help. A few were eyeing the helicopter.

"We need to move," Ryder said quietly. None of us wanted another fight on our hands.

I was suddenly over it all, as exhaustion washed over me. "Take us home," I begged. I wasn't even sure where I meant. I just knew I didn't want to be here anymore.

Anyone still in the area could scavenge over the building and salvage what they could.

There was nothing left for us here.

Forty-Four

The sounds of laughter and dogs barking in the distance, and the muted humming of insects nearby, had me blinking slowly awake. Pale light was filtering through an open window across from me and I could see trees beyond it. A fresh scent of growing things filtered in the window: pine trees and a hint of corn, alongside some citrus. I sniffed the sheets and got a hit of my mates' scents, too.

I knew beyond a doubt I was back in my bed at the farm. I'd missed this place. Even though I'd only been here a short time, it was the first place in a long time I'd felt any peace. I wasn't sure if it was our home, but it was a home that embraced us. That would always have a place for us. I looked back at the window and realized my perspective was off, though. The window was too high up, or I was too low down. I popped my head up to look around. Someone had taken out the big timber bed frame and there were now two mattresses lying squeezed together on the ground. They filled most of the floor space in the room. Someone had also piled them high with pillows and blankets. The guys must have wanted to sleep together last night, and the thought made me smile.

I remembered Angel sleeping with us for a while, but she was gone now. She had too much energy to sleep for long. I wasn't worried, though. I knew if she was here; she was safe. There were dozens of people on the farm who would look out for her. It would work for now, but she needed stability long term, and that was something I was going to have to talk to the guys about.

Right now, I was alone. I stretched and crawled across the enormous floor-bed to the window. There was a slight breeze wafting through the branches of the trees outside. They seemed to wave at me, so I waved back, and laughed at myself. A sudden urge to be out there washed over me. I wanted to let this place soothe the clinging ache wearing on my soul, and the lingering sadness that was waiting to well up and burst free. I didn't want it tainting my new life.

I grabbed the clothes I spied folded up in a corner. Some underwear and socks, a pair of soft, faded jeans, a t-shirt and a long, snuggly cardigan. There was a new pair of boots in a box as well, that were my size. I figured they came from Lexie and the treasure trove of wonders in her shipping container. I pulled off the oversized t-shirt I had on and got dressed. There wasn't a scrunchie or any hair pins, so I let my long hair hang free. It felt right. I was done with the prim buns.

I wondered briefly where my mates were. It was startling how quickly I'd gotten used to waking up surrounded by them. I vaguely remembered them washing me in a bath as I lay against Wolf and he purred for me last night. The gentle vibration alongside the feel of Ryder, Cary, and Nick soaping me up with sponges, while River washed my hair, had been heavenly. Afterward, I'd been bundled up and passed around until I was dry, clothed and felt like a limp, mindless noodle. None of them had tried to do anything more than soothe me as I fell asleep.

I thought I remembered them waking me up to eat something a few times, though. *Had I missed a day sleeping?*

A sense of need coiled within me, and I wondered if it was a residual feeling from my heat. I'd have to ask Lexie or Maia. I'd have to check how often heats happened too. With how quickly mine came on, I hoped to be better prepared next time.

I wandered downstairs but couldn't see anyone in the living area. I figured they were probably up at the dining hall. Either helping with breakfast or eating it. I knew they were nearby, I could feel it in the bond. It glowed with a sense of warmth and belonging, although Cary seemed agitated. I decided not to call out to them in the bond. I was happy to just be for the moment, and let the farm wash over me. Plus, I wanted a few minutes to settle myself.

I tipped my head up to the sky as I stepped outside. The low sun was shining in through the porch overhang and its warmth in the chill was an embrace. I'd finally broken free of the version of me I'd been for the last decade, the quiet mouse. Being an extrovert wasn't in my nature. I would never be the life of the party, and I was okay with that. I naturally gravitated to people who were, and I loved their energy, but it wasn't me. Watching and cheering them on was my jam. I was happy feeling as if I could stand up when I needed to, though, when it felt important to me. And that my mates and family saw me, and loved me for who I was.

I figured claiming my mates and then letting Wolf's power flow through me had a lot to do with the new connectedness I felt within myself. Yet, standing here on the porch, I felt so many emotions it was a little overwhelming. Hiding and shoving my emotions down had been my go-to for a decade, but now I had to face them. I couldn't live that way anymore. I had a pack that needed me and I wanted to be strong for them. *How could I hold them together if I couldn't even do it for myself?*

My steps halted as I came down the front steps. I could hear goats bleating somewhere and I suddenly needed a cuddle in the worst way. My mother's other favorite animal was goats. Baby goats, in particular. I felt an aching need to be close to something she'd loved, as memories of my early years and my mother hit me.

I followed the sounds and found a barn at the bottom of the hill. There was a young man inside who had just finished milking the goats. He had two giant pails of milk.

"Um, hi," I said awkwardly as I stepped inside the big barn door, not really sure if I should be there. "Is it okay if I hang out with the goats for a little while?"

He looked startled, but he recovered quickly. "Sure, just make sure you leave the barn door open when you go, so they have some fresh air until I come back and let them out. I need to take this milk up to the kitchen."

"Thank you," I said. He shrugged and blushed before he picked up the heavy pails and left quickly. He seemed shy.

I wandered around and pet the goats. I found a small tub of fruit cores near the milking pen. The young man had probably been intending to give them to the goats after milking as treats, but had forgotten about it when I arrived. I handed them out to a chorus of bleats. Then I found the baby goats in a pen up the back. I grabbed an old cushion off the railing and climbed right in there with them. As soon as I sat down, they immediately jumped all over me. One baby climbed up onto my chest and I pulled him into my arms for a snuggle.

That's when the heavy emotions hit me, sharp and sudden. A wash of grief for my mother and uncle, that I hadn't had a chance to really process yet. Chased by the residual fear of knowing I was being abducted and not being able to do anything about it as the drugs had set in. The shock of seeing Nicole stabbed and men shot in front of me. Silent tears tracked down my cheeks. I tried to dash the first few away, but soon there was a torrent falling into the soft fur of the baby goat in my arms.

A well of panic grew in my chest, but it wasn't mine.

"*Mate, where are you?*" Wolf asked in the bond, his voice anxious. It only made me cry harder, remembering their panic grasping at me as the world had faded to black. I tried to send him images, my thoughts chaotic. "*We're coming, okay? Sit tight.*"

A few minutes later, running footsteps skidded to a stop in front of the barn door and my mates piled inside. Wolf crouched down outside the pen and examined me carefully as River, Ryder, Nick, and Cary crowded behind him. I hid my face in damp fur.

"Talk to us, Ava," Ryder said quietly. I tried, but more sobs came out. They looked at each other with wide eyes.

"Is it something we did?" Cary asked. "I'm sorry I didn't realize you were awake. I could feel you unsettled, but I thought you were dreaming again. You must have gotten up when I went to the bathroom. I was reading in the living room while River and Ryder went for a run, and Wolf and Nick got breakfast. We only noticed you were gone when Wolf took some food up to you."

I shook my head.

"You can't do that to us, little bird," River said as he crouched down next to Wolf. "Disappear after just being abducted."

I looked up in shock, seeing their strained faces. River's hand twitched as if he wanted to reach for me, but wasn't sure if he should.

"I'm ssssoorry," I cried. Realizing I'd made them worry for no reason. I hadn't thought about that. "Went for a walk. But goats. Mom loved goats. Then this happened." I waved at my face and the goat in my arms. I was sobbing through my broken words and I wasn't sure how much they actually got, but their faces relaxed. They each pushed comfort at me.

"You've all been through a lot," Nick said in his usual calm, gentle tone. "It's going to take a while to process it all. Stuff's going to come up, but we'll be here for each other and work through it together, okay?"

I swallowed hard and nodded, trying to at least get my crying back down to a point I could talk properly. I wasn't used to having people to lean on. Figuring out stuff myself was how I operated, and that wasn't only because of the last decade. Growing up with a working single parent, I'd learned early on how to do things on my own. But he was right. We had each other now. It was just going to take a bit to get rid of old habits.

"Can you maybe let go of the goat, Ava?" Nick asked. I looked down at the baby goat and realized I had the poor thing in a headlock. He didn't seem to mind, though. He had woken up and was licking my arm. I tried to let him go, but my arms wouldn't work. I shook my head. He was my emotional support baby goat, so he was staying put.

Nick smiled at me and I figured he got some of that through the bond. "Can Wolf come in then? Maybe he can help settle your tears? I think he needs a hug, too."

I nodded vigorously and Wolf climbed straight over the pen, picked both me and the baby goat up, and plonked us down in his lap. The other baby goats started jumping around in excitement until Wolf started his purring vibration. My whole body relaxed into him and my tears slowed to a trickle as his warmth flowed into me. Wolf purring was like cuddling up with a super soft, snuggly lion.

I looked down after a minute and sleeping baby goats encircled us. They were pressed up as close to Wolf as they could get.

I smiled up at him. He hadn't said a word since he'd asked where I was through the bond earlier.

"Wolf's barely spoken since we got back," Cary said softly. Wolf flicked his gaze to Cary, but his eyes quickly returned to me.

I reached out to Wolf in the bond and realized his emotions were as messy as mine.

I ran my hand down his face. He'd been held captive for years, drugged, escaped, then found an entire pack and claimed us within days during an unexpected heat. Then had his omega abducted. It was a lot. We'd been bouncing from one crisis to another for days, weeks even. I wanted him to let me in, but that was a two-way street. *How could I expect him to open up to me if I didn't do the same?*

"Oh, Wolf," I whispered. "What do you need?"

"You," he ground out and his eyes darkened, sending need spiking through me.

"You have me, Wolf. I'm right here." He groaned as he leaned forward and kissed me as if I was his reason for living. I put the baby goat gently down on the hay and wrapped my arms around his neck, bringing myself as close as I could to him. His warmth melted my body and my heart. I shifted to straddle him, needing to feel him closer, and rubbed my body along the length of his. His hands wandered up and caressed the underside of my breasts through my t-shirt, making me ache instantly.

I mentally stroked our connection, begging him to open up to me fully. I wanted to feel him in every way possible, but I sensed he wasn't being completely transparent. He needed something he was trying to hide away, to suppress. Something that was pulling at him and wouldn't settle. Or someone. I put my forehead against his and breathed him in, before turning my gaze to meet Cary's. River, Ryder, and Nick had stepped away, but we had Cary transfixed. He watched us in a daze. I knew he could feel us in the bond, too.

Movement at the corner of my eye made me realize he wasn't our only audience, though. A row of adult goats had their heads over the edge of the pen and were intently watching us kissing.

"Oh," I gasped, startled.

"Don't worry, we'll get them therapy," River said.

Nick shook his head, but I couldn't help smiling. I'd missed the playful side of River and his dry sense of humor. Many people didn't get him, but I did.

I stood up carefully, trying not to step on any balls of cuteness, and pulled Wolf up alongside me.

"Let's get some breakfast," I said, but food wasn't what was really on my mind. I just wanted to be out of the barn for what happened next. We headed outside, making sure we propped the barn door open behind us. I angled us onto a less used path back to the cabin, hoping to avoid all the people on the main path at this time of day.

As we rounded a bend in the path, it surprised me to see GG striding purposefully towards us. She didn't seem surprised to see us, though. She was wearing a gorgeous purple velvet dress that was embroidered around the hems. It looked like something you'd wear for an important occasion, but she was just wandering around the farm in it, living her best life. She'd also wrapped her long white braid around her head in a crown and stuck some wildflowers in it. I was a little envious. She rocked the look.

"There you are, sweet girl," she said as she grabbed me and drew me into a hug. I went willingly. GG was irrepressible and slightly terrifying, but she gave incredible hugs. "Everyone's been worried about you, but I told you the day we met, you had a strong heart and would act when needed. I saw it in you. I bet that bark of yours took them by surprise. I wish I'd seen it. You're going to be a good mate for my grandson."

"I didn't do much," I answered quietly. "It was mostly the guys."

"Oh, you did more than you know. Things are going to change now. Omegas needed reminding they're tigers, not lambs. Your story will be told for generations." I was at a loss for words, but she didn't need a reply.

"Now," she said, as she released me and faced Nick, "introduce me to the newest members of my family. I've been chasing you and your pack all over the farm."

She sounded stern, but there was a definite twinkle in her eye. GG didn't chase anyone. She just appeared when people needed her, whether or not they knew it, like some kind of fairy godmother.

"Uh, GG, this is River, Ryder, and Wolf. You've met Cary already," Nick said as he pointed everyone out. "Guys, this is my great grandmother, or GG to everyone on the farm."

She looked at the twins and held her arms open wide. "You've traveled a long, dark road, you two, but you persevered. Glad you finally made it. Welcome to the family." They flicked confused glances at Nick, who just grinned and nodded at them. Honestly, I felt like they'd gotten off easy. They both leaned down to hug her. River was a little formal, patting her gently as if she might break, but Ryder gave her a big squeeze and she laughed in delight.

She turned to Wolf next. She had to tilt her head way back to look up at him. He immediately kneeled down in front of her so she could look at him easier. "Hello, earth mother," he said.

"Oh, you're a smooth one for a beast of a prime alpha. Those poor little omegas had no chance. No wonder you needed two," she said with a wicked grin. Wolf blushed, but she carried on mercilessly. "You're not alone anymore, wild one. Take care of them, because the worst is over, but the world still needs you all."

"I will," he said, as if he knew exactly what she was talking about. She nodded decisively, as if it was done, and hugged him gently, as if he was precious. Which he was.

She turned to Cary next and gave him a quick, fierce hug, before she pulled back and grabbed his face. She pulled it right down to her, so he had no option but to look her in the eye.

"You stopped watching and started acting for the people you care about, but you have to do it for you, too. Fate doesn't like it when you try to cheat her. Holding back will not stop nature, child." Cary's eyes widened, and he blinked rapidly as he stared back at her. She leaned forward and kissed him on the forehead, as if he was one of her grandbabies and he had a boo boo. He looked a little shell-shocked. I got it. It was confronting how she could see right to the heart of you with a glance. But she did it with an immense love for her family and her community.

"Alright, GG, stop scaring Cary," Nick said as he drew her back and wrapped her up in his own hug. "We've got him, I promise."

She smiled while she patted him on the cheek. There was so much love for Nick in the simple gesture. "I know you do. You waited so patiently for them. You did good, my boy."

She kissed him on the other cheek, still smiling at him with joy lighting up her wizened face. It was clear he held a special place in her heart.

"Now, I have sitting to do and gossip to catch up on. So you lot go have some fun," she waved over her shoulder at us as she turned tail and left, back the way she'd come. Her work done.

We stood and looked at each other for a moment, taking each other in and processing what had just happened. I always needed it after an encounter with GG. "I love your great grandma," Ryder finally said, and Nick chuckled.

"Yeah, she's easy to love."

We were quiet after that as we headed back to the cabin. Especially Cary. He seemed focused within, barely watching where he was walking.

The noises of the farm seemed to fade away until there was only us. I could feel a building intensity within our bond, a need for connection, and a heat that was primed to explode.

Only it wasn't mine.

Forty-Five

"We're going to have a quick shower while you guys get Ava some food," River said, as he and Ryder rushed upstairs to the bathroom. They were both wearing only loose fitting shorts and joggers, and the sweat sliding down their bodies had Ava transfixed. She watched them as they left, hypnotized by the play of muscles along their backs as they moved. I resolutely looked away. I did not need to be lusting after my pack mates right now.

"Breakfast?" Nick asked Ava as he waved a plate of jam covered toast in Ava's face. He had a glass of orange juice in his other hand and a cheeky grin on his face as he blocked her view.

I heard her stomach growl, and she snatched the plate from him as he laughed. "Did I sleep one night or two?" she asked.

"Two," Nick answered as he grabbed another plate off a tray and sat down next to her. There were some eggs and a little bacon, too. But I knew we were rationing stuff like that now. We were sending a lot of food to town every day until we could get them better established with their own food supply.

Ava seemed happy eating just the toast. She lived with five tall, fit guys, and Wolf had serious bulk. They needed the protein, and she'd know that. Besides, I knew she didn't enjoy having a heavy breakfast, something Nick had clearly noticed as well. I'm sure he would have piled her plate with eggs and he would have gone without if he'd thought she wanted some. It was just the type of guy he was. They all were.

When I'd first heard about packs, I'd wondered if there were enough decent alphas in the world to make the risk of meeting your mates worthwhile. What if you ended up mated with an asshole? The world was full of them. Now I knew there were a lot more good alphas out there than I'd known.

I gazed at Ava and Nick as I munched my toast. Nick watched her carefully, making sure she ate enough. They were cute together. But I also noticed the way his eyes kept running over the hair cascading down her shoulders and chest. He couldn't take his eyes off it. She usually had it piled high on her head, but today it was all loose flowing waves and it was gorgeous. He brushed a strand away from her face and she smiled at him.

Ava was pretending not to watch Wolf and me, but she kept shooting us surreptitious glances.

We were sitting on the adjacent couch together and the space between us felt filled with a potent mix of awkward tension and electricity. Sparks were firing all over me. I tried hard not to look at him, but it felt as if every molecule in my body was straining towards him. His energy had felt muted since we got back, but now it felt even more pronounced. He didn't touch his breakfast, and he was holding himself impossibly still. He hardly even seemed to be breathing. I couldn't deny that I was in heat and it was influencing both of us.

I didn't like feeling him so muted. I'd watched him charge across the lawn at the manor, a pure unleashed beast. Then felt the surge of power he'd channeled from the three packs, as he'd knocked out a hundred alphas. It had been exhilarating and humbling to know he was mine.

Now, a growing ache I'd felt since yesterday afternoon, that had built slowly at first, had reached a fever pitch that made my bite marks burn. I'd slept restlessly last night and this morning I'd been driven to the bathroom to relieve the pressure of my dick straining against my pants. The guys had made excuses and left, trying to give me some privacy. It had been useless anyway. No matter how much I stroked myself, it wasn't what I needed. My body was demanding an alpha. The drumbeat of building need in my veins, and the desperate tension in my body as I tried to make myself come, was why I hadn't noticed Ava up and about.

I'd been trying to hold off for her. I needed her here for this, but I hadn't wanted to wake her after what she'd been through. It had felt selfish, and her welfare was more important to me than my own.

Yet now that we'd found her and were back in the cabin, I wasn't sure how to broach the mechanics of it. Wolf and I were both waiting for the other to make a move. I wanted the mating desperately. I could feel how much Wolf did, too. *But who would take the lead? Would Wolf be okay if I did? Would he like what I wanted to do to him? What if our needs weren't compatible? He was a prime alpha. What if he needed to be in control?*

I tried to eat some more, knowing I'd need energy for my heat once it took hold. But the food got stuck around the lump in my throat. I coughed and choked a little. Out of nowhere, Ryder was there, patting me on the back forcefully. He must have had the world's quickest shower. I looked up at him to nod in thanks and almost groaned when I noticed he hadn't gotten fully dressed. He'd just thrown on a pair of sweats, and beads of water were still rolling down his chest and dripping from his damp hair.

"What's this?" Ryder asked as he waved my leather-bound journal in his hand.

Shit, I must have left it lying on the side table earlier. I tried to lunge and grab it, but he easily held me off with one hand. He plonked himself on the arm of the couch, forcing me to shift closer to Wolf. We were inches apart and I could almost feel his body heat searing me.

"Is this a diary?"

"No, it's a writing journal," I told him, as I shot him a sideways glance. I'd given up trying to grab it from him. There was no way I'd win. He was way too agile, and much too fast. Plus, his six-pack abs were in my eyeline, distracting me.

I didn't know why Ryder turned me on when River didn't. They were identical, but there was just something about Ryder that intrigued me. There was a curiosity there, a feeling of something that could be fun and lighthearted. Maybe it was just the way he wore his heart on his sleeve that drew me to him. River had warmed up, especially towards Nick. There was a bromance blooming there. But he still had a cool, reserved demeanor about him. He was always thinking ten steps ahead and strategizing. Wolf may be the most dominant alpha out of the three, but even he deferred to River.

"For writing stories?" Ryder asked, jolting me back to the moment. "Can I read them? I love reading and I don't have any books with me."

"Oh, uh. I've never shown them to anyone before. I don't think they'll be your thing. They're kind of smutty." I couldn't look him in the eye.

"Even better, I love smut. Paranormal and fantasy romance are my favorites," he said easily, as he slipped off the leather thong that held it closed and flicked through some pages. "Let me find a steamy bit."

"It's true," River said. "He has them stuffed everywhere and usually travels with a few in his go bag."

"I love epic fantasy, but I've read everything we have here at the farm," Nick piped in. "I've never read fantasy romance before. Do you have any with you I could read?"

"Not with me," Ryder said, only half paying attention as he skimmed stories.

"We had to bug out in the dark last time and he couldn't reach his stash," River answered for him. "You should have heard him bitching about it. I don't think he's read anything in weeks. When Ryder and I head out to gather supplies from our other nearby bunkers in a few days, I'll grab some."

I could feel my mouth hanging open at their casual conversation while Ryder read my journal. A stifled noise had me glancing at Ava, who was trying to smother a laugh at my predicament. I shot her a glare, but the warm smile and the wink she shot back at me eased my nerves. I could feel her subtly sending me encouragement. Knowing she wanted this, however it happened, had me relaxing.

"Oooh, here's a spicy bit," Ryder said, as his voice roughened. "*She trailed her hands down his chest, lightly tracing the ridges of his hard muscles until she reached the gathered fabric at his waist. His wings flared behind him as he prepared to take flight. He knew staying would only put them both in unimaginable danger, but every illicit touch made it so much harder to leave. She was a princess, and he was a guardsman in the king's army. They couldn't be together. Yet he wavered a moment too long and forgot how to breathe as she reached a hand up and traced the edge of a sensitive wing with a finger. Only mates touched the wings of a warrior. His eyes stuttered closed as ecstasy pulsed through him and his resolve disappeared like mist in the light of day. Her other hand slipped beneath the fabric of his loincloth, and her breath hitched as she stroked the hard length of him. She trembled in his arms-"*

"Stop," I groaned as I flung my head onto the back of the couch and my hand instinctively reached out to clutch at Wolf's thigh. I desperately tried to anchor myself against the sound of my written words spoken in Ryder's dark, sexy voice. They had my whole body alight. Each word was a lash of white-hot need.

"Oh, I don't think I will. It's just getting interesting," Ryder said. "Don't you agree, Wolf?" It was typical of Ryder to try to save me from myself. He always seemed so in tune with how I was feeling and seemed to recognize when I was overthinking. It disarmed me.

Wolf was as still as a statue underneath my hand, his hard thigh like a rock as his body tensed. Yet, with my eyes closed, I could hear him breathing hard in the sudden silence. I felt how much he wanted me, as the wall I'd put up between us cracked at my touch.

"What do you need, Cary?" Wolf asked on a pained breath. He stayed perfectly motionless as his need leaked through the bond and wrapped around me. I could sense the amount of control it was taking him to hold back, and he wasn't a creature of control. He was a bright, wild energy that stirred the blood in my veins. Yet, what I needed was for him to submit to me. The thought thrilled me and woke up something dark within me.

"Look at Ava," River demanded roughly. My eyes shot open to see him standing behind her. He had his hand around her throat and she was panting heavily. "She wants this as much as you do. Whatever you need, and however you need it, it won't break us. You won't break us, Cary. You make us stronger."

River stripped me bare with his words, as he saw through to the core of me. He was showing me they were strong enough to handle my needs, as well as hers. To handle all our needs.

"Please, Cary. Tell Wolf what you need. Let him see you. All of you."

Ava had her eyes fixed on my hand on Wolf's thigh and her desire wrapped around me in the bond. I loved watching her letting go of her constraints and exploring her sexuality. She gave breathy little moans and whimpers that drove me wild. Her enthusiasm to learn and explore us as well was addictive. The press of her need had my hand instinctively inching further up Wolf's thigh. She moaned, and the last of my restraint shattered. I stopped overthinking this as her desire overrode everything else.

"You, Wolf," I groaned, answering his question. "I need to fuck you."

"Now we're talking," Ryder growled as I turned to Wolf and pressed him hard up against the corner of the couch. My kiss was rough and unyielding, not letting either of us escape this. He more than matched me, letting his pent up desire wash over me.

"You can fuck me any way you want," Wolf rasped as I bit a line down his neck. His voice was raw as his need for me blasted through the bond. It was different to the all-consuming way we both felt about Ava, but we needed each other too. "Tell me I'm yours."

"You're mine, Wolf. Just as we're both Ava's and the pack's," I reassured him, in a raspy voice I barely recognized. I belonged to all of them, in whatever way worked for us. That was pack.

I embraced everything Ava and I wanted, as I felt the heat I'd been barely holding back burn through my veins.

Forty-Six

Need overtook me, as I felt Cary give in to his heat. My world focussed on the enticing show of hands and tongues playing out like a movie just for me. Cary bit a line down Wolf's throat, leaving a trail of red marks as he rapidly unbuttoned Wolf's shirt, exposing his hard chest.

Cary kept his eyes on Wolf as he leaned back and pulled off his hoodie. He hadn't bothered with a t-shirt, as if he'd hated the feel of too many scratchy clothes on his skin this morning. I remembered that feeling. His sweatpants disappeared just as quickly. He hadn't bothered with briefs either. The sight of Cary's hard dick straining towards Wolf, and his heat pheromones saturating the air, had slick wetting my thighs.

"Can I taste you?" Wolf asked. His words coming out rough.

Cary's eyes glinted darkly as he nodded and sat back, spreading his legs wide. Wolf kneeled in front of him and kissed a line down his chest and across his stomach, making Cary's abs tighten as he hissed. They fixed their eyes on each other as Wolf reached Cary's straining cock. He licked over the tip, and I groaned as I remembered the feel of that wet heat on my skin. Hands moved down my legs and pulled my jeans with them as Nick moved in front of me. He trailed wet kisses back up my legs, before he spread them wide and tasted me in long licking motions. The sensation, teased in unison with the show, had me flying high.

"Can I join in and help you through your heat?" Ryder asked Cary. His bright blue eyes had darkened, too, and there was a mix of curiosity and hunger in the way they roved over Cary's body.

"Please say yes," I whimpered. I hadn't meant to say that out loud, but watching the three of them together would be a fantasy come to life.

"Yes," Cary answered, eyes still fixed on Wolf.

"You have me so intrigued, Cary," Ryder admitted. "I've been dying to have some fun with you, and make Ava moan while I touch you."

"Fuck-" Cary's words bit off as Ryder slid closer and ran his hands down over Cary's chest. Cary tightened his hands in Wolf's hair in response.

"Look at him, Ava. He's so fucking beautiful," Ryder moaned. Cary broke Wolf's gaze and glanced up at him. Ryder was oblivious as he looked down at Cary's body, his eyes following the trail of his hands. Cary's lips parted as if he was about to object until he saw the sincerity on Ryder's face, and he relaxed. Cary almost glowed under Ryder's gaze as he pushed his body up into his hands. Hungry for more touch and finally allowing himself to have it.

Cary's hips thrust up into Wolf's mouth, too, and Wolf grunted as he took more of Cary. He sucked hard, too needy to be gentle, as he reached down and cupped Cary's balls. Cary groaned as his heat set in and his scent turned syrupy. His muscles went rigid, as if the heat had his body in a grip of iron. It was the opposite of the way my body had gone limp.

I felt like a voyeur as my desire spiked, and I thrust into Nick's mouth. I was trying to be quiet and not distract Cary, but a moan slipped free as I felt River's hands move down my body. He quickly removed my cardigan and t-shirt so he could fondle my breasts before pinching my aching nipples. It set me on fire. I wouldn't last long with the combined stimulation of hands, mouths, and an erotic show. This was going to be over embarrassingly fast for me if they didn't let up. I could already feel sparks spiraling deep in my core.

Cary suddenly grabbed Wolf by the hair and yanked his head back. Wolf's eyes looked wild as he pulled off Cary's cock.

"I'm close, and so is Ava. I can feel how much she's loving watching us. But I want her to come while I'm fucking you."

Oh god. I almost came on the spot, but Nick eased back and switched to kissing the inside of my thigh, while River shifted his hands so they were resting below my breasts. It seemed they were both on board with Cary's request.

"Bend over the end of the couch, Wolf," Ryder demanded. Both he and River liked to play the role of ringmaster, it seemed. Cary didn't object.

"Oh god, yes," I moaned. Cary glanced over at me as Wolf moved out of the way. He grabbed his dick around the base and gave it a hard tug, with his eyes firmly on Nick's head moving between my thighs. "Please, Cary. I need to watch you fuck him."

I knew how much Cary loved dirty words coming out of my mouth. He groaned and shot me a dark look, before he turned his attention back to the prime alpha who stood at the end of the couch next to him, waiting patiently. I could feel Wolf aching for Cary in the bond, and his cock wept with pre-cum. Cary licked his lips. He looked hungry, but there was too much wild, heated need riding him right now.

Cary stood up and walked around behind Wolf. He ran his hand lightly down Wolf's back, and Wolf trembled at the touch. Cary applied pressure as his hand traveled back up and Wolf obediently bent over the couch. He rested his face over his hands, trapping them beneath him. There was no resistance or reluctance coming from him. He seemed genuinely happy to let Cary take charge.

"Is this okay?" Cary asked Wolf, a new confidence coming over him at Wolf's submission. I marveled at such a dominant prime alpha submitting to an omega, because his omega needed it. My heart bloomed with love for him. For them both.

Wolf looked up at me, and his eyes flared hot and bright as he answered Cary, "I'm okay with anything you and Ava need. I'm yours."

I watched as Wolf relaxed his whole body and submitted to Cary completely, both physically and in our bond. He seemed almost at peace. Despite the wildfire of need I could feel raging within him. As if he needed this, too. To fully give himself over to someone he cared for deeply and just drop into the sensations as they washed over him. To let go completely.

Letting instinct overtake him was a big part of who Wolf was and the way he navigated the world. It seemed to wake him up but also center him.

Wolf sighed as he closed his eyes. A surge of dominant, primal power burst through us all, making me gasp before it seemed to settle within Cary. I remembered what it had felt like when Wolf had pushed his power at me, to use however I needed. Cary moaned, as if Wolf had injected him with a drug, and I figured he was going to use it very differently. I reached up and grabbed River's arm, needing him to anchor me, and he wrapped both arms around me. Wolf's power was a ghostly finger stroking me intimately.

"Holy shit, that's intense," Nick hissed as he turned to watch Wolf and Cary. I noticed Ryder strip off his pants and grab his cock roughly, pumping it hard as he breathed heavily. His eyes stayed fixated on the two men in front of him. An ice cream addict in a gelato store, eyeing up his next sugar fix.

"Oh fuck, yeah." Cary's breathing sped up, and his dick wept, as slick coated the shaft. He lined himself up, his eyes glazed with need, and rammed into Wolf. Wolf grunted and Cary paused, looking like it took everything in him to hold still.

"Too much?" Cary asked through gritted teeth. Cary was not a small guy, but then again, neither was Wolf.

"No," Wolf moaned. "Keep going, I can take it. I need you to own me."

"You feel so good," Cary moaned as he pumped harder. He leaned down and wrapped his fist in Wolf's hair, making Wolf's eyes roll back in his head as he grabbed onto the couch cushions.

I bit my lip while watching them, as I built a wish list in my head of the things I wanted to do with them, and for them to do with each other. The view and the power still thrumming within Cary had me burning with need. I thrashed around on the couch, held in place by Nick and River, as molten desire coursed through me. Cary's heat was an electric charge running through us all. It was exhilarating feeling the energy without being so mindlessly lost to my own heat haze.

Nick and River had worked me to the edge, and now they were devilishly holding me there. Nick lightly stroked me while River rubbed circles around my nipples. I was so close but couldn't get myself over the cliff, no matter how hard I thrashed against them. I needed it so badly, but I also wanted to wait and come with Cary and Wolf.

I closed my eyes briefly, trying to lessen the onslaught. But when I opened them again, both Cary and Wolf were looking at me, as if they could feel me and burned for me as much as I did for them all.

"I need you all," Cary begged. He didn't need to ask me twice. River released me and in a flash, I was off the couch and dropping to my knees in front of them. Cary used his upper body strength to pull Wolf upwards. It brought his cock in line with my face as Cary continued to slam into him, Wolf's borrowed dominance riding him hard. I licked my lips and bent forward. I had my mouth wrapped around Wolf's dick and my hand running possessively along Cary's ass before he could say another word. They both groaned loudly at my touch.

It seemed we'd all only been waiting for an invitation, because Nick was there too. He'd lost his clothes at lighting speed and was naked beside me. He wrapped my hair around his fist to keep it out of the way and directed my movements over Wolf's cock, as I grabbed his own cock in my fist. Wolf grabbed Nick's shoulder to anchor himself, as his eyes locked on my mouth. Nick didn't seem to mind. I felt River drop to his knees behind me as he ran his hand over my ass before he slipped two fingers inside my pussy, giving me something to grind against.

"Ryder, Cary needs more," Wolf growled, sounding almost delirious. "He needs to be knotted while still feeling in control."

"No, it should be you first," Ryder insisted.

"Ryder, please. He needs you," Wolf begged, "and I want him full of your cum when I take him."

Cary moaned loudly. I'd almost forgotten about Wolf's fixation with breeding and his pleasure in going after another of his pack. I hadn't thought it would apply to Cary, but I was wrong.

"Cary, it's your call. What do you need?" Ryder asked, but he was grabbing his cock so hard as he asked he looked in danger of squeezing it off. His knot was already swelling.

"Please," Cary begged. His head was shaking from side to side. He looked blissed out and tortured at the same time as his heat gripped him in torment. "Wolf's right. My heat is demanding a knot, but I need to take Wolf right now."

Ryder jumped over the back of the couch and moved behind Cary at lightning speed. He licked over his bite mark on Cary's shoulder as he pressed up close behind him, supporting him even as he pushed into him. "Oh fuck, you have slick too. He feels like heaven, Ava," Ryder moaned.

Cary almost lost it. His movements became jerky, and he slammed himself harder between the two men. Ryder and Wolf met him thrust for thrust, and within moments, Ryder's knot was jammed and locked inside him. Cary threw back his head and leaned on Ryder's shoulder as he roared.

The sight of the three hard male bodies moving together, and their pleasure seeping through the bond, had me in ecstasy. We were finally together, with nothing held back. Our shared desire, wrapped up and mixed in the bond. The added taste of Wolf in my mouth, the feel of Nick in my hand and River pumping his fingers into me mercilessly had me exploding. I yanked my head back and latched onto Cary's hip, biting hard.

I felt Nick yank my hand off his cock and up towards Cary's mouth. Cary bit into my wrist as he went over the edge with me, on a shout. Wolf grabbed my other hand and bit into it too, gifting me a second bite as he came all over his stomach. The white light of our bond rippled through us and the circle closed around us, as the bond I had with Cary connected fully through Wolf. Our pack bonds became almost a solid feeling in my chest. River was right, having two omegas in our pack took nothing away and only strengthened us.

I felt utterly blissed out, and complete in a way I'd never imagined possible.

"Thank you, Wolf," I murmured, as I shifted back to kiss him lightly on his hip. He smiled lovingly down at me.

A moment later, Wolf pulled away gently with a quick squeeze of the hand Cary had clutched possessively to his abs. Cary slumped back fully against Ryder, grinding against him through the aftershocks of his orgasm with a euphoric smile on his face. Ryder maneuvered and slid them both onto the arm of the couch, keeping a careful hold on Cary.

I leaned into Nick for support as he slid back to his knees beside me. My body still felt taut with need despite the intense orgasm I'd just had. A moan ripped free as River continued to thrust his fingers into me. Cary and Ryder both watched those fingers intently. The sight had them grinding against Ryder's knot, still locked inside Cary, who was hard again instantly.

Nick had let go of my hair as I'd lunged to bite Cary, which I was grateful for, or he may have yanked my hair out. Most of it had draped across his chest now. Cary's eyes flashed, as if he'd had a cheeky idea.

"Ava, push Nick back up against the couch and run your hair down his body."

I looked at Nick and his eyes widened, so I did as Cary asked. This was so new to me, but I wanted to explore all these feelings and sensations. I trusted they would guide me safely as I gave myself up to them.

I pulled my hair to one side and shook it lightly, so it trailed down Nick's body, then shifted my head slightly so it slid in soft waves down to his hard dick. I was curious to see what his reaction would be.

"Oh god, oh fuck, oh shit," Nick mumbled incoherently as he stared down at his dick disappearing into the waves of my hair, and River chuckled.

"I think you just unlocked his kink," River said, as he maneuvered to a better angle to give me more room to torment Nick. "Is it all hair or only Ava's?"

"Only Ava's," Nick groaned. "Every part of her turns me on."

I smiled, feeling desired and alive.

"Hurry up and breed her," Wolf growled at River. River growled back, but obeyed as he slid his dick inside me in a rough push. I was so wet my slick was dripping down my thighs. I moaned at the fullness I'd been craving since I'd gotten the first whiff of Cary's heat scent. My hair swished back and forth over Nick as River pumped into me, slowly at first. Nick shuddered as his hips jerked. At Nick's matching moan, River set a faster pace, slapping into me, making me writhe. Cary started grinding down on Ryder harder, making him moan, too. They both came again, quickly, while watching River slide into me. Cary splashing his come over his own stomach.

"Holy shit, how are you still hard? You just came twice," Ryder asked Cary as he looked down. He shifted Cary onto his lap, as his knot deflated and he slipped free. He reached over onto the side table. There were some damp clothes there he must have brought down earlier after his shower. Trust the twins to be prepared. He grabbed one and started cleaning Cary up, as if it was no big deal.

Cary's eyes widened in surprise. I don't think anyone had ever taken care of him during sex before. Ryder did it instinctively and didn't seem to notice Cary stilling. Or maybe he did, and chose not to comment on it. Cary was going to have to get used to being taken care of in all the small ways around these guys. It didn't change how they saw or treated him about the things that mattered to Cary, like trusting him to help protect the pack. This was something our alphas needed just as much. This was about Ryder. I saw the moment Cary realized it, and he relaxed again.

"Perk of being a male omega," Cary finally answered, a little distractedly. I knew how warm and strong Ryder's hands felt on my body and I could feel the pleasure it brought Cary to be cared for and touched.

"Lucky bastard. I can only stay hard when I'm knotted. I take a good fifteen minutes to get going again after my knot deflates," Ryder grumbled, as he threw a cloth to Wolf, too.

"Don't clean him up too much," Wolf grunted impatiently, as he wiped over his stomach before he hauled Cary off Ryder's lap, into his own. Only he spun him so that Cary was straddling his legs while facing him. "I need you to ride my knot now."

Cary's surprise filtered through to me and I grinned at him through the curtain of my hair, as he glanced down at me. "What? You thought he'd turn into beast mode and get all dominating afterwards? It's not Wolf's style," I said as I panted, feeling another orgasm building already as River upped his pace.

"Not until he asks for it," Wolf growled.

"Holy shit, you're a switch," Ryder said to Wolf.

"What's a switch?" Cary asked, confused.

"It means he can switch from dominant to submissive based on how he feels in the moment while having sex. He can be either and gets pleasure from both," Ryder explained.

"Is that true?" Cary asked Wolf.

Wolf shrugged. "I don't know the words for kink stuff, but I can be whatever you need and it feels good for me either way."

"Huh," I vaguely heard Cary mumble. I could feel his mind working. I knew him well enough to know he was wondering if that might be true of himself, too. As if the word had given him permission to seek both, and be whatever he needed in the moment. It was only a label, but for him, it was a possibility he'd never considered.

Oh yes, please. I wanted a turn with either of them in beast mode. Or maybe both. It was going on my list of things to ask for. Just the idea had me slamming back into River.

"Oh, you like that idea, little bird," River said, as he smacked me lightly on the ass, bringing my attention back to him. It started those sparks back up, whirling around inside me. I was so close again. "You want to be dominated?"

"Yes," I moaned. I wanted it all. Everything they had to offer.

"Yes, who?" he asked with a growl, as he stopped his thrusts and held himself still inside me.

"Yes, sir," I moaned as River tightened his hold on me possessively.

"Stop thinking Cary, and fuck Wolf already, before he explodes. You're distracting Ava," River demanded, continuing to hold still inside me. His control was tremendous.

"Please, River," I begged, needing him to move. His bossy tone as he ordered Cary about doing all kinds of tingly things to me. River relented and started fiercely thrusting into me again as he gripped me harder. It had my hair swishing over Nick in a frenzy. He looked possessed as he watched his cock sliding through my hair, his hips jerking erratically underneath me.

"Uh, you all need to hurry, or I'm going to come in her hair," Nick moaned.

Wolf was hard as a rock again and looked pained by how badly he needed Cary. Cary held Wolf's stare as he slid down onto him and rocked over him a few times. I watched as Wolf grabbed him by the waist, gently supporting him rather than directing him. I could feel the trust between them, as Cary finally accepted that he was enough and Wolf would never take more than he could give. They almost seemed to get lost in each other's eyes, and my heart swelled again.

This was what I had been wanting since the night we all met, but hadn't known how to make it happen on my own. It turned out I hadn't needed to, because we'd made it happen together. River, Ryder, Nick, and Wolf had worked just as hard as me to bring Cary into our pack. To give him a home.

Nick tried to shuffle away from me suddenly, as if the pleasure was too intense. But Ryder shifted forward and slipped his arm around him, holding him trapped in place for me with a wink. Our earlier boundaries with each other during my heat seemed to have completely disappeared. It made my heart expand until it felt as if it was going to burst, watching my mates touching each other.

Cary seemed to have completely settled into our pack bonds and finally left his hesitation behind. Wolf had subtly pulled his dominance back into himself, so it was all Cary, now. He was freely chasing his pleasure in this moment. Wolf was giving it to him just as readily, making his own pleasure so much more intense. As I'd known he would. I watched them hungrily from beneath the curtain of my hair as I felt River's cock pulse and thicken inside me. My imagination was in overdrive, and I couldn't wait to get in between Cary and one of our other mates. The idea had me moaning loudly. Wolf growled as he shot me a dark, dangerous look. Oops, I must have sent him a visual through our bond.

I looked back through my hair at Nick. He was panting heavily as he clutched the lifeline of Ryder's arm across his chest. He looked almost pained as all of our pleasure hit him in the bond. I noticed Ryder was hard again and stroking himself as he watched. Despite his earlier words, Cary's heat seemed to have ramped up his need. I reached out, and Ryder slipped onto the floor next to Nick, before he placed my hand under his own on his cock. He tightened his grip around mine and used my hand to pleasure himself.

"Cary," I begged helplessly as my need peaked.

"Wolf, I need you to fuck me so hard I scream," Cary panted, his need matching my own. Wolf roared as his beast came out to play. He flipped Cary over onto his stomach and grabbed him possessively around the throat as he slammed into him, completely letting go. Cary's moan was guttural and desperate as he lost himself in the heat haze. He writhed underneath Wolf, and when Wolf slammed his knot inside Cary, I felt both their ecstasy reverberate through our bond.

It amplified each of our needs. River started completely dominating me in a pounding rhythm that felt like it re-arranged my insides. He shifted slightly and hit a spot that had me seeing stars. I yelled something nonsensical, completely beyond coherent thought now, barely hearing Cary screaming Wolf's name. River groaned as he jerked roughly and slammed his knot inside me. I flicked my hair out of the way and slid my mouth over Nick's straining cock. He spilled instantly and took me over the edge with him. Cary and Wolf came too, Wolf biting into his claim mark on Cary's shoulder with a growl and holding Cary tight to him. Even Ryder followed us, man-handling his cock with my hand roughly and as he spilled ropes of cum over the floor. He even managed to get some on the couch.

"Dibs not cleaning that up," Nick joked weakly as Ryder groaned.

"We need some of those plastic picnic mats," Ryder said, as he slumped and rested his head next to Nick on the edge of the couch.

"Or we move to the nest," River said dryly, but with an affectionate humor, as he settled me into his lap and cuddled me. I loved it when he dropped the fierce leader mode and relaxed with us, just as much as I loved him growly and demanding.

"Yeah, I second that," Nick said with a laugh in his voice as he leaned forward and kissed me. It made me smile against his lips.

Cary's heat had banked slightly, giving us a reprieve. But it was still simmering below the surface as it waited for it to spring back to life and demand its due. For the moment, he had openly snuggled up to Wolf and was breathing in his scent, while Wolf's knot had him locked against him. Wolf had closed his eyes while he stroked Cary's stomach lightly and purred for him. I could feel the vibration of it through the bond. My mind was a blissed out stream, flowing aimlessly, as somebody stroked my hair. I wasn't sure if it was Nick or River, and it didn't matter to me either way. I craved both their touches.

Now that Cary had embraced our pack, I knew I was the luckiest omega in the world. I could feel in our bond that he felt exactly the same way as he grinned down at me.

Forty-Seven

"What are you thinking about?" Wolf asked me as we wandered up a path, holding hands. Cary's heat had only lasted a day. We'd all crashed, exhausted, at about midnight. I'd taken Wolf on a quick morning stroll to show him some of the farm while Cary slept in and Nick watched over him. The twins had disappeared early somewhere. We were working our way back up to our cabin now.

I couldn't wipe the smile off my face, but I really wasn't thinking about anything in particular. For once I was just happy enjoying the moment. It was so easy to spend quiet time with Wolf. His wildness was still there, but now it was a sweetly flowing mountain stream. One you could grab an inner tube, jump in, and float along on happily for miles, watching the jungle as it passed.

I shrugged. "Cary recently asked me what I used to think about when I stared out the windows at the Palace. I told him it was being free to run and climb, just to be outside with nature. But also to touch the people I loved whenever I wanted. Now here I am doing both and I feel content. I'm just happy walking with you and not really thinking."

Wolf stopped in his tracks and tugged on my arm to bring me closer to him. A light breeze was playing with his hair and the morning was chilly under the shadow of the trees, so I happily stepped into his heat.

"You love me?" He asked. That wide-eyed, vulnerable look that broke my heart crossed his face. I wanted to wipe it away forever.

"You doubt that?" I asked him, concerned.

"I can sense that you have deep feelings for me in the bond, but you've never said the words."

I thought I'd told Wolf how I felt, but maybe just not using those words in particular. I fiddled with a strand of his hair and wrapped it around my finger. "Growing up, my mother and uncle were both tough, hard working people. Neither had a lot of time for the soft stuff in life. I knew they loved me, they showed me in little ways every day, but they didn't always express their feelings with words. I guess I've picked up the habit if I've never said them to you."

I looked up, wanting to hold his attention for what came next. "Have no doubt, though, Wolf. I love you."

His eyes blazed, yet he didn't smile. His face became intensely serious instead as he cupped my cheek. "No-one has ever said those words to me before. You're the first, Ava. I wasn't sure I'd ever recognize this feeling, but you make it so easy. I love you too."

He slipped his hand around the back of my head and pulled me in for a kiss that was as tender and sweet as my gentle giant. I sighed into him.

"*Love you,*" he repeated in my head as he kissed me, just in case I hadn't heard it. Or maybe he just wanted to say it again.

"*Love you, too, Wolf,*" I said as I smiled against his lips.

I'd been happy to find we could still speak to each other through the bond when I'd woken up yesterday. Part of me had wondered if I'd been hallucinating. It appeared it was here to stay, though. Our mates had tried to do it too, it just hadn't worked for them. Hopefully, time would change that because I loved it.

"We should get back," Wolf said, a little reluctantly, as he broke our kiss. "River wants to talk to us before we meet the other packs in the dining hall."

I grabbed his hand and dragged him along behind me. A sudden urge to be surrounded by my mates drove me. My footsteps rattled the porch stairs as I dashed up them. River and Ryder were right behind the door, as if they'd been about to open it.

"What happened? Why are you anxious?" Ryder asked, as River scanned the path behind us.

I pulled them both into me, as I wrapped my arms around their necks and surrounded myself with their salted caramel and dark chocolate scents. "You guys know I love you both, right? I mean, I've always loved you, but I don't think I've ever said it and it should be said. I'll say it every day if you need to hear it."

"What brought this on?" River asked, shooting a glance at Wolf.

"I told her nobody had ever said they loved me before today," Wolf explained.

"Little bird, we know you love us. You don't need to say the words if it makes you uncomfortable," Ryder said as he stroked my hair.

"I'm not uncomfortable. I watch and I feel, I just don't always say what needs to be said," I mumbled into their necks, "but I'm working on it."

"We've loved you since before we even knew what the words meant, little bird," River whispered into my ear. "I don't remember a time we didn't love you."

"Our hearts spoke in ways other than words," Ryder added, "but we always heard each other."

I breathed deep and blinked rapidly, not wanting to cry right now. My heart felt so full. *Who knew my childhood sweethearts were hiding such romantic souls?*

I pulled back with a watery smile and a gentle kiss for each of them, then looked for Nick.

I spied him standing awkwardly at the bottom of the stairs, so I slipped away from the twins and strode over to him. I passed Cary on the couch, and he winked at me. It brought back the memory of our conversation in the library when he'd made me repeat the words. So I mouthed "I love you," at him now and he grinned as he made a love heart with his fingers.

Nick opened his arms to me as I got closer and nuzzled into my hair. It made me blush thinking of the things I had done to him with it and the way he'd responded. "It's okay, Ava," he whispered. "I don't mind waiting until-"

I kissed him gently, cutting off his words. "Love you, Nick," I said against his lips. "You're the sweetest, kindest, bravest guy I've ever met. I've loved you since the moment you tried to take on an army of alphas with a broom. Don't think for a moment I love you any less than our other mates."

He groaned, but his grin could rival the sun. "You know I ran into that fight for you, right? I mean, my other friends too. But I've loved you since the first moment you smiled at me." My heart bloomed. Everything about Nick was so easy. He made everything seem playful and fun, but it didn't make it any less meaningful. He was my person.

"The broom move sounds smooth, Nick," Ryder teased. "I need you to teach it to me at our next training session."

I laughed as I stepped back from Nick, squeezing his hand lightly as I let him go. Everyone was settling in the living area, so I moved back across the room to Wolf. He'd sat down next to Cary and thrown his arm over the back of the couch behind him. I noticed him discreetly brush a few fingers across Cary's neck, and Cary instinctively leaned into it. Like a cat wanting a head rub. Wolf had that effect.

I plopped myself on Wolf's lap and his purr helped settle my emotions as I snuggled into him. Cary reached down and grabbed my legs. He pulled them into his lap, yanked off my boots and kneaded his thumbs into the arches of my feet. I was instantly a limp puddle of bliss.

"Where did you get this sweater from, Wolf?" I'd noticed it earlier. It was a cable-knit sweater in a light, creamy brown color that fit him beautifully. It was incredibly soft under my cheek. I couldn't help running my hands over it.

"Nick's great grandmother knitted it for me. She left it on the porch for me with a note while we were busy with Cary's heat. Nobody's ever made anything just for me before. I love it."

His words were heartfelt. I got the impression we were going to have a hard time getting him to wear anything else. I blushed as I realized what she may have overheard if she'd made it onto the porch, though. Hopefully, it was after we'd migrated upstairs.

"Apparently, GG and her friends kept watch outside during the day yesterday and made sure nobody came near us," River added with a grin. He'd settled on the other couch with Ryder, while Nick took the occasional chair between us. "She's pretty feisty with a broom, too. I see where Nick gets it from."

Nick just shook his head and took the ribbing good-naturedly. "She wants to spend time with you, Ava. She's going to treat you all as her grandkids now, fair warning."

My grin felt like it split my face as I nodded. "I'm good with that." GG was a little terrifying in how direct she could be, and how deep she saw when she looked at you. Yet she was also fiercely protective of this community and the people she loved. Something else Nick got from her. I counted myself lucky to be considered family.

"What did you want to talk about, River?" Cary asked, changing the subject.

River sobered up and sat forward in his seat as he clasped his hands together over his knees. He shot a look at his twin, who nodded at him.

"Damon wants to meet in a few minutes and talk about where we go from here. We figured there's something you should know first, Ava."

"Oh?" My throat tightened. He seemed anxious, which made me nervous because River was usually so calm.

He cleared his throat and unclasped his hands to rub them on his jeans, as if they were suddenly sweaty.

"You're making her nervous, Riv," Ryder chided. "Just say it, man."

"We own your uncle's farm," he blurted out.

"What? How?" That wasn't what I had expected.

"Your uncle didn't have any kids of his own. He planned to leave everything to you. But he changed his will the night he died and left everything to us. He knew presenting as an omega meant you lost your rights to hold any assets in your name. Your mom witnessed his new will, and he mailed a copy to us and his lawyer before he and your mom left the city that night. Our parents got it a few days later. We were still underage, and we'd already left for military school, so they became trustees until we were old enough to claim it."

"Oh, wow." I was speechless, and my mind was whirling. I was grateful for Wolf's steady purr. It was the only thing keeping my head from exploding.

"We wanted to have a safe space for you when we got you back. We finally figured out living on the run forever wasn't a healthy life for you," Ryder added. "So we bought up the land surrounding your uncle's place, mainly other small hobby farms, and turned it into a larger farming compound. Then we made it a family trust with our parents, combined with their land, while we were still in the military. We didn't want anyone to take it when we went AWOL and technically became criminals."

"We actually own all the land that runs right up to the edge of Damon's farm, finishing just over the ridge behind us," Ryder said. "Ours doesn't extend into the forest the way Damon's property does. He owns that, but we own everything between the road, the river, and our parents' house when you head north from here."

"We borrowed a truck and went and checked on our parents this morning while you were out touring the farm with Wolf," River said. "We wanted to make sure everything was okay before we take you there. Our farming setup isn't as innovative as Damon's. But our dad came and visited his grandfather a few times and they talked a lot about sustainable farming being the future. We weren't completely off grid, but it seems they've been doing alright since the Crash."

"Our parents helped us build a cabin away from the main farm. We were going to bring you to live there eventually, after we got you out. Kind of hide you in plain sight once everything died down," Ryder added. "It's actually closer to here than to your uncle's farmhouse. So if you want to stay here we can, but we also have a home we built within walking distance of here that we could move to. There are tunnels in the caves that connect to here. Few people know about them. Riv and I stayed in them sometimes. We could also move to your uncle's farmhouse if you don't like the one we built. We know you have wonderful memories there."

"We just want you to know, as a pack, we have options," Ryder finished in a rush. Then they were both silent as they watched me.

"You built me a home?" The words came out choked and those tears I'd swallowed earlier came rushing out with them.

They both watched me nervously as they nodded. I flung myself out of Wolf's lap and onto the other couch with them. All those years of silence and the whole time they had been single-mindedly working to secure our future.

"You were so mad at me, yet you still built me a home?" I asked Ryder.

He groaned and shook his head as he tucked me more snuggly between them. "I was more scared than mad," he admitted. "I wanted our future so badly, but there always seemed to be so much against us."

"Not anymore," I said. "I want to see it."

"We can go after the meeting. But if we don't hurry, they're going to send someone to drag us there."

"Too late," came a sassy voice and a flash of pink hair from the front door we'd left flung open. "And where the hell do you think you're going?"

Forty-Eight

I jumped up from the twins, clambered over the back of the couch, and launched myself at Lexie next. She grabbed me with a surprised "Oof," as I wrapped her in a bear hug that almost knocked her off her feet. I felt like the tiny metal ball in a pinball machine, spinning and getting pushed around by my emotions today, but it was heaven to have so many people to love on.

"Missed you, too," she whispered in my ear. "Don't go getting yourself kidnapped again anytime soon. I couldn't take it."

An elbow in my side, a blonde head pushing up between our arms, and a shaggy one pushing in between our legs had me giggling.

"Let me in, too," Maia complained. We opened our arms and Maia happily snuggled into my side, as Lexie's giant dog, Bear, pushed into our circle with a happy whuff. I could see Hunter and Sam standing behind them.

"Thanks for coming for me," I said to them. They both nodded solemnly. There were no words for what had gone down that night.

"Where's Angel?" I asked, looking around and feeling anxious about her continued absence. Maia had left notes during Cary's heat to say Angel was with her, but she wasn't here now.

"She's fine. Angel was with us until this morning. She's been keeping my guys on their toes, but I figure it's good practice for when this little one comes," Maia said, as she rubbed her stomach. "She's with GG now, baking cookies."

"Okay, thank you," I breathed, trying to shake off my sudden anxiety. I trusted my friends, but I needed to see her for myself and make sure she was okay.

"So, what's this talk about leaving? Are they trying to talk you into it? Because I'm going to have a big problem with that," Maia asked while shooting daggers over my shoulder at my mates. "This baby needs both her aunts."

"I'd have a problem too. I just got my brother back," Hunter said, with a frown marring his face as he looked through the door towards Wolf.

"Relax, guys," I said, as I gave Maia a squeeze. "If we go anywhere, it won't be far."

I explained to them what the twins had told me as my mates filtered out onto the porch behind us. Wolf immediately ambled over to Hunter and hugged him, making Hunter grin. Wolf was incredibly tactile, but Hunter seemed to eat it up. Sam seemed surprised when Wolf hugged him too, but relaxed into the hug after a moment.

I let the girls go as Cary handed me my boots, and Bear sniffed each of my guys in turn. Wolf gave him a friendly pat, while River watched him with a raised eyebrow. Ryder got down on the ground and gave him scratches behind his ears, letting Bear get up in his face.

"Hey, boy," Ryder said. "Do we pass your sniff test?" Bear whuffed in approval before he turned back to Lexie. I'd been nervous around Bear at first, due to his size, but he was just a big, protective fluff ball once you were in his pack.

"How the hell did you guys afford to buy all that land? Weren't you on the run for the last few years?" Sam asked as he leaned up against the porch railing with his arms crossed and a confused frown.

"We worked some lucrative black market jobs. We rescued a wealthy CEO's daughter, stuff like that," River said, completely unfazed by Sam's sometimes gruff exterior.

"Is that where you guys went this morning?" Hunter asked, and the twins nodded in unison. "When Damon took over the farm, he tried to buy the land on the other side of the ridge, knowing one of the cave tunnels came out there. But it was owned by a family trust under the name Ford and they wouldn't sell. Which is why we didn't know the name Fischer when Maia arrived, asking about Ava's uncle."

"So if you leave, we'll still be neighbors?" Maia asked as she bounced on her feet like an eager puppy, making Bear circle her protectively.

"You're never getting rid of me, you know that, right?" I teased her, and she grinned back at me.

A flashback hit me of the first time I'd come across her in the library at the Palace. I'd heard the handlers gossiping about her ability to deny an alpha, and I'd felt drawn to her strength. Yet that day she'd looked so worn down and lonely. I'd been so hesitant, and probably awkward as hell, but she'd lit up when I'd approached her and asked her what she'd been reading. Our stolen moments together got me through when I'd started to despair of ever getting out. She taught me to be strong just by being around her. She never gave up, no matter what they threw at her. Watching her thrive within her pack now gave me hope everything was going to be okay for both of us.

"We need to find you an electric dirt bike so you can come visit easily," Lexie said, and my eyes widened. *Oh, hell yeah.*

Lexie was going to be a bad influence on me in the best kind of way, and I looked forward to seeing where our friendship led.

"Ava used to have a kid's one. She was a menace on that thing," Ryder said affectionately. "She's also a great rider, and mom has horses. We'll figure it out."

"I always wanted to learn how to ride. We didn't have horses on our farm growing up. Could you teach me?"

"Sure, but can we wait until you're not pregnant?" I didn't want to be responsible for anything happening to the precious little bun in her oven or incur the wrath of her mates. She just laughed and agreed.

"That may take a while. I plan on knocking her up again straight away," Hunter said with a smirk. Maia whirled and smacked him on the arm, but she was grinning.

"I haven't ridden in so long. I can't wait to get back on a horse again," I said.

"I've gotta say, your perfect princess routine was one hell of an act if you grew up a tomboy farmer's niece," Lexie said.

"Not really," River replied.

"She was always sweet, and kind of quiet," Ryder said, finishing River's sentence as he leaned over and ruffled my hair the same way he used to do. It made my heart happy to see them back in sync. "She just didn't mind getting her hands dirty either, and couldn't stand being left behind whenever we were getting up to mischief."

"Would you be willing to barter or trade if your family is growing things over there we aren't?" Lexie asked them.

"Of course," River said quickly, as if he didn't even have to think about it. "Mum's taking an inventory of what they have stored and can spare to send to people in town after I told her what's been happening. But she can put stuff aside if there's something you need here. She wanted to help before, but they weren't willing to venture far since the Crash. Their electric fences are down and they don't have any security. They weren't part of the Network, but my dad buried something in the backyard when Ava's uncle called from the city the night she disappeared. I confirmed with dad it was his comms device. Dad's going to dig it up so we can communicate."

"Our parents are pretty limited at the moment, though," Ryder added. "They only have a couple of buildings with solar power, and it's not enough to keep the place going, let alone the fences. We could do with some advice on setting up wind or turbine power off the river like you have here, as well. I'd love to see the two farms become a working cooperative if you're open to it. We've only farmed a part of our land, so we have plenty of space to expand and help people who are struggling out there."

"Helping your family get secure is a given. We'll work on that straight away," Hunter said. He came across as cheeky and lighthearted, but I'd noticed he was always the first one to jump in and help anyone who needed it. Maia shot him a soft smile as she leaned over to grab his hand and squeezed it.

"We'll help any way we can," Lexie said. "I think a cooperative is a great idea, too, but everybody gets a vote here. We'll have to bring it up at the family meeting." I could almost see Lexie's brain working, though, and I didn't see anyone here having a problem helping their neighbors. It was the foundation they built this place on.

"I think we should move our family meeting until this afternoon, or maybe even tomorrow. It can wait a day," Maia said. "You should go reunite with River and Ryder's family, and see your house now."

"Really? Are you sure?" I asked, almost bouncing on my feet. I desperately wanted to go. River and Ryder's mom had been a second mother to me growing up. I could almost feel the hug she had waiting for me. And I was insanely curious about the house they had built.

"Of course," Lexie said. "Maia's right. Family is important. Everything we need to talk about can wait another day."

"We have to grab Angel first, though. If we're seeing our home for the first time, we need the whole pack there," Wolf said.

I froze, hardly daring to breathe. "You want Angel there, too? As part of our pack?"

"Of course," Wolf said, looking at me with a frown. I could feel his confusion. "She's ours. Why wouldn't I?"

"Because you can't just claim someone else's child. We really should look for her parents," Ryder said. He felt conflicted in the bond, and I wasn't sure he wanted to. It was the right thing to do, though. As hard as it would be to see her leave.

"You really think if Maven were experimenting on her, they would have left her parents alive?" Wolf asked softly.

"He's right," Nick said as he pulled me into his arms. I went willingly, needing him to anchor me in the spinning. "I found files on Angel on the Palace servers. So much has happened, I haven't had time to talk to you all about it. Phillip was her father, her mother didn't survive their brutal testing regime."

"He held a knife to his own daughter's throat?" River growled, fury making his dark chocolate scent deepen with a charred edge. "If he wasn't dead, I'd kill him."

I could feel each of my mates vibrating with a similar fury, and their protective instincts were flaring brightly. Matching mine. Growls broke out around me, including from Sam and Hunter. Lexie and Maia both looked livid, too.

"He called her an experiment when I asked him about her. He treated her as if she wasn't a person," I said, that rage I'd felt in the moment flaring back to life.

"He treated most people that way," Wolf said, as Nick stroked my arms, trying to calm me. "Philip had developed a very good mask to get by in society, but he had no empathy or remorse that I ever saw. He was a true psychopath."

A psychopath that had been destroying the world from the shadows. I couldn't help but be glad he, and Maven, were gone.

"So you're adopting Angel?" Lexie asked. Never one to hold back.

"You can't ask that," Maia hissed as she pinched her. Lexie just swatted her hand away.

"I can, because I'm family, and taking on a five-year-old as a newly bonded pack is a big deal. I want to make sure they know what they're doing, and the impact it's going to have on their dynamic now. But not just that, they're going to blink and she'll be a teenager yelling 'you're not my dad,' five times over. It's a commitment they need to make for the rest of their lives." She watched us closely. Lexie didn't mess around when it came to protecting people in need, even from people she loved.

I felt my heart rate speed up as I glanced at my mates.

River, Ryder, Nick, Cary, and Wolf just looked at each other over my head and grinned before they said, "Yes," in unison. They didn't need to discuss it. They were all in. It was clear in our bond how much love they had for her.

"We know exactly what we're doing," River added. "As long as Ava is on board, too."

All eyes turned to me, but it no longer bothered me. None of my guys looked worried about my answer. They could sense how I felt.

"Yes," I said, as I breathed out heavily. I couldn't think of anything more perfect. "Besides, I think she adopted us already, with the way she seeks us out."

My mates surrounded me in a hug and I felt joy wash through me as happy tears ran down my face. I hadn't dared to hope my guys would agree to bring a child into our pack so soon, but I shouldn't have underestimated them. Their capacity for love was endless, and they'd already proven that by how quickly they had accepted and bonded each other.

"I'm still breeding you, though," Wolf growled, and the guys laughed.

"Of course," Cary added. "Angel's going to need an entire tribe of brothers and sisters."

I rolled my eyes at them, but I was secretly over the moon. It was fine by me. Being an only child, I'd always wanted a big family.

"Get in here, Maia. I know you want to," I called out.

"I'm such a sucker for hugs," Maia laughed, as she squeezed in. Lexie, Hunter, and Sam quickly joined her.

"We're going to be the best uncles," Hunter said.

"She may hate us when she's a teenager, and some guy wants to take her out on a date, though," Sam chuckled. "He's going to have to get through a wall of us."

"She's going to be an amazing big cousin to your baby, Maia," Lexie added, and Maia agreed. I melted all over again at how willing our found family were to embrace us all.

"Okay then," Maia said, reluctantly pulling away. "Let's go get your girl and get you guys on the road. You can borrow Damon's truck."

River grabbed my hand as everyone else stepped back, before he led me down the stairs. When we got to the dining hall, people surrounded us, everyone wanting to check I was okay after the kidnapping and exclaim over what I had done. Apparently, word had spread that I'd barked an alpha into submission.

Having people worried about me, and interested in me, was nice, but also a little bewildering. I didn't think I'd done anything special. My instincts had taken over, and I'd protected what was mine. I wasn't the first person to do that, or even the only person to do it that night. My mates had been much more impressive in my mind. I got that what I'd done was unheard of, but I didn't feel like I was anything extraordinary. I was just me.

The crowd made my mates nervous, though. They huddled around me, and their protectiveness flared, causing dominance to spill into the room.

GG stepped into the fray and clapped her hands loudly before things could get out of hand a moment before Lexie was about to do the same.

"Give the girl room to breathe, people. She's newly mated. Do you all have a death wish? We're going to have a bonfire to celebrate tonight and you can talk to her one-on-one then. For now, you all have work to do to get it ready, so get on with it."

It had my heart melting to watch them immediately capitulate out of respect for the tiny elder.

"Thank you for my sweater, GG," Wolf said to her quietly, before she could turn away.

"You're very welcome, son," she answered with a grin and a pat on his arm.

Suddenly a small body threw itself at my legs, and I looked down to see Angel. I immediately picked her up and smushed her into me, not caring about the cookie dough on her hands. Everyone had assured me she was fine, but it wasn't the same as seeing her myself. She wrapped her arms tightly around my neck. She prattled to me for a minute about everything she'd seen and done on the farm until she slowly quietened.

"I'm glad you're done resting, finally," Angel whispered as she beamed up at me. I guessed that's what Maia had told her I was doing.

A shadow loomed over us, and she switched her attention to Wolf. As soon as she saw him, she reached her little arms out and half launched herself out of mine. He caught her like he was born to do it. She grabbed him around the neck and tangled her fingers up in his hair. Squeezing him tightly. She then did the same to each of my mates, demanding hugs they were only too happy to give.

"Do you want to go see our new home?" Cary asked her while she was cuddled up in Ryder's arms.

"Isn't this your home?" She asked.

"No," River answered. "We built a house next door for Ava, but we made it big enough for our pack before we even knew we had one."

"Okay," she said, quieter than I'd ever seen her.

Forty-Nine

Ava

I sat in the car, feeling overwhelmed. We'd just spent an hour with River and Ryder's parents, Helen and Alexander. The hugs had been amazing, as I knew they would. They'd been surrogate parents to me growing up, and they'd embraced me like a long-lost daughter. They'd embraced our pack, and Angel, too, in the same generous way. Their mother had been best friends with mine as teenagers and their close friendship had continued into adulthood, even after we had moved to the city. It had been a home-coming.

I'd seen my uncle's farmhouse, too. While it had been nice, it hadn't felt as much like home as I'd thought it would. The building was the same, but they'd been using it to house farm workers, so a lot of the furniture had been different. They had boxed everything in my old room up and there were practical twin bunk beds in it now. I hadn't minded, despite everyone worrying that I would. I was glad the house was being used. Without my uncle in it, it was just that. A house. It would have made me sadder to see it sitting empty and abandoned.

After leaving my uncle's place, we'd driven down a long forest trail alongside the river. We were now parked out the front of the house River and Ryder had built together. For me.

"Are you going to get out?" River asked me nervously from the driver's seat. "We can come back another day if you don't want to do it right now. I know today has been a lot already."

"No, I want to see it now," I said, taking off my seat belt and hopping out.

I rounded the front of the car, but I stopped again a few yards away from the bottom of the stairs, trying to take in everything in front of me.

"It's beautiful," I whispered.

They'd built it in a black, modern A-frame style, with lots of enormous picture windows and a full length deck out the front. It had two main wings with peaked roofs, connected by a flat roofed area in the middle. It was all dark lines and weathered timber decking, surrounded by tall trees. At night, without the lights on, it would disappear into the shadows in the darkness.

The land fell away, down towards the river in the front. I couldn't see the river from here. They had built the house further up the slope, to avoid anyone traveling on the river from seeing it, I assumed. But I could hear it. I leaned forward and looked above the tall trees to see a rocky outcropping behind it. We really were just on the other side of Maia and Lexie's farm. I hoped there was a hot spring on this side too. It was a slice of heaven in the wilderness. Private and quiet, yet our loved ones were so close, on both sides. I loved it. I was in complete awe. It looked like something out of a movie that a reclusive, rich superhero would live in.

"How did you manage to build this?" I'd been picturing a little rough-hewn log cabin. This was an architectural marvel.

"We, uh, had help," Ryder said with a chuckle. "River and I hired a contractor and paid him and his entire team enough to retire early, to build it and keep it off the books, as well as the public records. We gave them a hand when we were here, though. And we built a lot of the furniture inside ourselves."

"Do you want to see inside?" River asked.

I nodded, lost for words. They each grabbed one of my hands and led me up the stairs. Inside, it was even more spectacular. It had exposed timber vaulted ceilings with black beams. The walls were cream colored, while the fixtures were black and timber. Yet there were accents of blue and blush pink everywhere, in varying shades, my favorite colors.

As they led me through every room, our mates trailing behind, I got even quieter. They'd filled the inside with custom timber furniture in a pale oak wood to match the ceiling. It was simple and modern, with clean lines, but it had been built with love. You could almost feel it in the timber. There were comfy couches, lots of soft rugs, and creamy sheer curtains that would stir gently in the breeze when the windows and doors were open. Sprinkled around were also loving touches their mom had helped add. Including some framed photos of my mom and uncle. She'd put them up for me this morning as a surprise, along with photos of the three of us as kids. She'd had them waiting for me, but had been keeping them close until now.

If I could have made a mood board for my dream home, it would have been exactly this. There was even a study at the back, with a full-length window looking straight out into the trees, and shelves filled with books. I could imagine snuggling up in there on a rainy day, maybe reading a book with one of my mates.

"What do you think?" Ryder asked when we got back to the main living area again.

I grabbed his hand, feeling choked up. "I can't believe you built this for me. It's perfect. I love it." It was too easy to picture our whole pack living here and making it a home.

Both Ryder and River blew out deep breaths and grinned at me, before I pulled them both to me.

"What do you guys think?" I asked my other mates. "Could you all live here?"

"Oh hell yeah, it's amazing," Nick said. Cary and Wolf readily agreed, too. Their eyes were wide, and they looked as awed as I felt.

"I love all the light inside, and the views of the trees everywhere," Wolf said simply. River and Ryder may have built this house for me, but it was so expansive and airy, it was perfect for Wolf too. Even the doorframes were taller and wider than normal. It made me wonder, not for the first time, just how deep our instincts went. *Had River and Ryder somehow known, on a deeper level, what our pack would need?*

"Is it completely off-grid? Does it still have water and power?" Cary asked. I'd seen him eyeing off the huge open shower in the bathroom. It looked like there was plenty of room in it for two or three people, and I couldn't wait to test it out.

"Yeah," River answered. "There were no utility connections out here, so it had to be, to keep it secret. Most of Mom and Dad's new farm workers don't even know it's here."

"Looks like it's in an easily defensible position, but with good escape routes too," Wolf noted.

Ryder just chuckled. "Yeah, that was deliberate, too. We didn't know how much heat would be on us once we freed Ava. There's a hidden panic room underneath the house, too. It doubles as a fireproof bunker. We'll show you later."

"Nick, I was thinking we could do a supply run and see if we can find some gear and set you up with a security office in one of the spare bedrooms," River said. "It would be good if we could get you connected to the satellites that are still working, the same way Max is, but also with cameras and security feeds for the farm. We need some kind of connection to our parents too, in case of an attack, seeing as how we're so spread apart."

"That sounds great," Nick said, as his face lit up. It meant a lot that River trusted him to run our security. He didn't trust easily, but Nick had more than earned it.

"You'll need to figure out which room you want first, Angel," I said, kneeling down in front of her. She'd been holding Cary's hand and following us around, but she wasn't her usual perky self and it had me worried.

"My room?" She asked, and her brow crinkled in confusion.

"Yeah, your room," I confirmed.

"You want me to live here, too?" She asked. Her voice lifted at the end in hope, but her posture was tense, as if she was wary. *Had she been worrying we'd leave her at the farm?*

"Not just live here," Cary said, as he kneeled down too. "We want you to be part of our pack."

"You want me to be part of your pack?" Angel asked, repeating his words. She seemed to be taken by surprise. Her eyes looked suddenly huge in her face as she turned to me. "Would that make you my mom, and Cary my dad? Would River, Ryder, Wolf, and Nick be my dads, too? Forever?"

I was too overcome with emotion to speak for a moment. Cary jumped in and rescued me.

"If you can handle a mom, and five dads, that's what we all want. But only if you want it too, chipmunk," Cary said to her.

"It's okay if you don't, or you need to think about it for a while. We're not going anywhere either way," I added, finding my voice. I needed her to know she had a say in this. She'd had so little, like every omega. But we'd been allowed childhoods. She hadn't. I was determined to make sure she was taken care of, no matter what, and that she had a childhood filled with all the hugs and cookies she deserved.

"Yes, please. I want to be in your pack," she cried and nodded vigorously. Big fat tears streaked down her face as she sobbed silently, overcome with emotion. I hated that she'd learned to be quiet while crying. I grabbed her and held her tight as my mates surrounded us. Hers weren't the only tears. My face was wet too, and there were plenty of glazed eyes surrounding us. Our bond glowed brightly, despite the tears.

"Does that mean GG is my family now, too?" she asked Nick when her crying subsided. She'd already figured out where the cookies were going to be coming from. She was a smart kid.

"She sure is," he answered as he stroked her cheek lightly, brushing away her tears. "You'll also have an entire farm full of aunts and uncles, including Maia and Lexie. River and Ryder's family, who we just met, will be yours now, too."

A huge grin split her face. "I always wanted a family."

"Me too," Wolf said to her, his voice sounding haunted.

"We can share," Angel whispered as she reached out for him, and he hugged her to him. His purr started up, and she sighed in happiness as it eased them both. She squeezed him tight, and I could see the bond between them already. Two people with so much aching loneliness, who'd found a home together. "I wish I'd kept looking for you."

He shook his head. "You found me when the time was right, my Angel."

She snuggled into him, and we just watched them for a moment, as I rested my head on Nick's shoulder.

"I want to live here, but can we go back for the big bonfire tonight, Daddy River?" she asked, perking up quickly as she turned to him. The use of the word daddy slipped out so quickly, I figured she'd been waiting to use it for a long time.

He swallowed hard as he nodded. Ryder looked like he was choking back a sob.

"Sure thing, baby bird," River said. And my heart exploded.

Epilogue
Lexie - one day later

I brought a new carafe of chicory coffee out to the big dining room. Breakfast this morning was a strictly serve yourself affair. Yesterday afternoon we'd made an enormous batch of creamy overnight oats and cut up fruit to go with it. It was all in the big kitchen fridge, ready for when people trickled in throughout the morning.

The bonfire last night had been a massive celebration. We'd ended up inviting River and Ryder's parents, and their farm workers, too. I figured if we were going to be working closely together in the future, it was a good way to start. There had been singing and dancing, with Nick and a few of the farm guys playing guitars and bongo drums. We'd also emptied the bar from the function center, but nobody had cared. It had been worth it. The end of Maven was worth celebrating. There were a few sore heads around the farm this morning, though. So the chicory was essential.

Arms came around me from behind, and I smiled as Dio's lips met my neck. My guys loved to kiss over my bite marks, and not just their own, they kissed each other's too. I'd taken to putting my hair up in a ponytail to give them easy access. I loved it as much as they did. Both Dio and Dave had been extra attentive since we'd gotten back the other night. Heading into a battle with me after not having seen me for days, so soon after my heat, had been rough on both of them. Me too.

As if I'd conjured him, Dave's mouth met the other side of my neck.

"What can we do to help?" Dave mumbled against my skin.

"I'm pretty sure you're doing it," I answered, feeling those butterflies in my stomach I still got whenever one of my mates touched me.

A loud cough and light laughter had them stepping away, as Dio groaned playfully. I spied Ava and Nick standing at a nearby table. "We came to help set-up, but the others will be here in a few minutes, too."

"Thanks, but we're all set," I said with a grin.

It didn't take long for the rest of her pack, and mine, to arrive. Her guys had dropped Angel off at the daycare cabin so she could play with some of her new friends. I remembered the first night I'd met Ava. The night Leif and his mates had rescued her and Cary from the Palace. Ava had seemed shy at first, but I'd sensed she had a quiet inner strength even then. She'd proved it quickly when she'd run into the attack on the farm, chasing down Bear with me. Although, if anyone had told me that first night she could bark down an alpha, I'm not sure I would have believed them.

Ava was the talk of the town now, but she seemed genuinely perplexed by the attention. At least she wasn't hiding in the shadows anymore. She was sporting a new confidence that was subtle, but looked good on her. She'd handled everyone wanting to talk to her last night like a champ. Once she'd gotten her mates to relax and let people get closer without growling at them.

Her pack was moving to their new home this afternoon, but they'd stayed here after the bonfire last night. I'd make sure they knew they always had a place here. Ava was a kindred spirit, for both Maia and me, just in quieter packaging.

I whistled to get everyone's attention. "Maia and her pack won't be joining us this morning. She's been vomiting all night. We're pretty sure it's morning sickness, as she's been feeling increasingly nauseous the last few days, but her guys are a little freaked out. Damon said he's happy for me to make any decisions that are needed on their behalf. Does anyone have any issues with that, because we can postpone again if you'd prefer."

"We're good," Ava said, as she smiled that sweet smile of hers.

I let out a subtle breath. I was used to making plans for myself and barging my way into things, but nobody had ever given me the reins on something this big before. Damon had always been our lead. But he'd sat Maia and me down yesterday and said he wanted to take more of a back seat and just look after the farm operation here. He asked us if we'd be happy to take more of a lead with figuring out how we move forward in the world and working with our allies. He'd said the world was changing, and it was important that people saw how capable omegas really were. I was more than happy to step up.

I'd talked to my pack about it and they'd immediately agreed to help me take on more responsibility. Maia had been keen, too. It was bad timing that she was so sick this morning. She'd told me to go ahead with the meeting today, then pop in later and give her an update.

It boosted my confidence that Damon trusted me to do more. Not that I really needed the boost. I was ballsy, and I knew it. But I had so much respect for Damon that his trust meant a lot to me. He didn't hand it out lightly. The letter Sam had left for me in our mailbox this morning, telling me how proud he was of me, put a little more pep in my step, too. I cherished every letter he sent me, and I hoped he never stopped.

"Okay then. Sadie's going to join us on the comms device. If we're brainstorming about where we go from here, she needs to be a part of the discussion," I said, and everyone readily agreed.

In this new world, our allies were proving our most important resource. None of our packs could have taken down Maven on our own, but we all probably would have died trying. Even now, with Maven gone, we could build homes and grow food, but it could get torn down in an instant without the support of a village and a new way of thinking. So we didn't repeat the mistakes of the past.

"There's a lot we need to talk about, but we don't have time for idle hands," Isabella said as she came through the kitchen door, closely followed by Sirena. "We're feeding a lot of people and the pea harvest came in. So we're shelling peas at the same time."

Nobody complained. This was a working farm. Everyone had willingly chipped in when it was a business venture. Now the food we grew was our means of survival. I directed the guys to drag a couple of tables together so we could fit, then grab two big bins by the kitchen door. Dio put a tablecloth down and emptied one straight into the middle of the tables, then put the empty bin to the side for the husks, while Pala handed out large bowls.

"Oh, I asked Isabella and Sirena to sit in today, too. We need to talk about the kids and local refugees they're looking after as well. Is everyone okay with that?" Everyone nodded again. I was lucky we were such an easy going bunch.

We still had the single moms and kids from town with us here since the battle with Maven. We'd also found quite a few orphaned and abandoned kids that Sirena and Isabella were looking after in a family cabin at the moment. They'd have a good understanding of what they needed. Plus, I valued and trusted Isabella's input. She'd helped me so much with the secret refuge I'd set up here at the farm. She deeply understood the effects of trauma on people.

"I'm sorry about your dad, Sirena," Wolf said, surprising her. "I heard him talking about you sometimes. So, I get he wasn't nice to you, but I'm sorry, anyway."

Sirena seemed more reflective than sad as she looked at Wolf. She shrugged nonchalantly, but there was tension around her eyes. "He was a shitty person and an even shittier father. He would have killed me if he ever got his hands on me again after I betrayed him. I'm safer with him dead. But thank you."

"Okay, anyone who doesn't know how to shell peas, pair up with a buddy who can show you. The husks will go back in the bins and we're going to use some in a stock, then compost the lot," Isabella instructed. Nothing in our world went to waste anymore.

Wolf, Dio, and Pala were the only three who didn't know. So Ava sat next to Wolf and showed him how it was done. While I sat with Dio and Sam sat with Pala. Wolf was a little clumsy at first with his enormous hands, but he quickly got the hang of it. So did Dio and Pala. I actually enjoyed shelling peas. I found the repetition calming. Doing a monotonous task seemed to focus my brain.

"Where's the comms device?" I asked, so we could get started once we were settled.

Sam looked around, then jumped up and picked the communication device up from the breakfast buffet where it was sitting amongst the coffee cups. Someone had casually dumped it there as if it wasn't the most valuable piece of technology we had at the moment. He set it up at the end of the table. Sadie and her guys came on the line quickly, and everyone talked over each other, saying hello. It was cute. It struck me that the Network operated more as an extended family than anything else. Or maybe only our group did. Sadie didn't seem to mind, and it made me like her even more.

"How are the omegas?" I asked when there was a brief pause. I was dying to know. Most of them were only teenagers. They'd been vulnerable in the old world. The new world was even scarier, but I wanted that to change. Everyone here did.

"They're holding up. Most of them seem to have bonded over the last few weeks since the Crash and are happy together in the bunkhouse for now. The Palace lies that omegas don't get along was such hogwash. I think they were scared about what we could achieve when we worked together."

"What about Nicole? How's she doing?" Ava asked. We'd sent Nicole up the mountain to Sadie, knowing she had a doctor up there. Gus from the Network had taken her. He'd wanted to visit Sadie, anyway.

"Good, she's stable. She'll stay here with us until I decide if we can trust her with the location of the sanctuary," Sadie said. It was a smart move. Nicole seemed contrite, but nobody was ready to move past what she'd done yet. And Damon wasn't comfortable having her at the farm. She was going to have to earn our trust. "We'll be moving everyone else to the sanctuary in a few days, but I have Emma here and she's talking about going back to the Palace. We won't stop her. Emma's a free woman and can do what she likes, but I think we need to talk about how we'll back her up. Emma, do you want to hop on and explain?"

"Uh." Emma's voice was shaky, and she sounded incredibly nervous to suddenly be in the spotlight. "Maybe you could explain what we were talking about, Lexie. You said it so much better."

I was all for people standing up and speaking loud, but I would never force someone to do it. Pushing someone forward who wasn't comfortable or ready could be as damaging as holding someone else back. So I quickly stepped in.

"Emma had a great idea she talked about to Ava and me. I was thinking of something similar for the farm. But Emma's version solved the problem of letting strangers in here while Maia is pregnant," I said, making sure I wasn't taking the credit. Emma deserved to be acknowledged, even if she hadn't found her voice yet. I explained our idea of replicating what we had done at the farm, then turning the Omega Palace into a teaching center where people could come and learn. With the expectation, they would then take the knowledge back to their own communities. It would get change happening faster.

"That is a great idea," Dio said. "It would be a waste having an empty building with power and nobody using it when so many people are suffering."

"I think so, too," Isabella added. "Sirena and I were thinking that moving the local refugees to the Palace might be a good move. We could finish the vegetable garden you started in the conservatory. Then get started on crops. We could set up some goat and chicken pens, too. It would take the pressure off the farm. We're kind of bursting at the seams at the moment, unless we build more housing. I'm sure they'd be willing to help set up Emma's idea. They've all said they're not afraid of hard work if it means security for their kids. And the place is enormous from what I understand, it's going to take a lot of work."

"I like it. Expanding the farm isn't a problem if it's needed and we can find the resources. But it's a good idea not to have all our food resources in one location," Sam mused. "It makes us vulnerable to losing everything in an attack, but not only that, crop disease or an infestation could decimate us. River and Ryder's family can help with that, too. We were just talking about starting a farming cooperative yesterday and Hunter was on board."

At Sam's urging, River quickly updated everyone on their farm next door.

"I agree. An interconnected network of properties and a system to back each other up quickly will be good for all our futures," Dio jumped in when they'd finished. I could see his brain spinning as he looked at it from every angle. If he couldn't find a downside, there probably wasn't one.

"Chatter from the Network shows people are abandoning cities around the country," Sadie added. "Food is running out and gangs fighting turf wars in heavily populated areas are leading to a lot of deaths. Which means we're likely to see people shifting to rural areas."

"It's what needs to happen, though, isn't it?" Dave asked, and everyone looked at him. He'd been swinging on his chair while shelling a pea, but he quickly dropped his chair back to the floor and put his hands up quickly. "I don't mean the gang fighting and death. I mean, people moving out of the city. There's no way to grow enough food to keep cities functional right now. Things need to go back to an older way of life. Smaller communities that can sustain themselves. If we can figure out how to make the power sources we're using more accessible, it will help. But it's going to take time and the scale will still be small because our only building resources now are timber or scavenging. I don't see a way to make cities sustainable in the next few decades."

"Cary pointed out when Ava, Emma, and I were originally talking that our biggest problem will be security for the Palace," I said, and Cary nodded. It surprised me he hadn't brought it up again himself. He seemed to be deep in thought and only half listening. "So I was thinking about the alphas that Ghost was talking about. The ones that stayed behind at the manor because they had families to feed and were looking for shelter. What if we offered to let their families be our first students, as long as they stay and provide security?"

"That's a great idea," Pala said, always backing me up. I blew him a kiss. "We could send a team to approach them and check them out. We should probably have some of our own guys at the Palace too, though. At least to start. Until we know for sure we can trust them."

"Could we also get the town set up as an example of what can be done, so people can see it in action, and then use it as a trading hub? We could make it known the pub is the point of contact for the Palace. Hopefully that would stop people randomly turning up and keep it more secure," River added.

"Now, that's a great idea, too," I said. I loved how our found family collaborated so well. We made an awesome team and I couldn't wait to see what we got up to in the future. With Maven out of the way, the world was going to need strong people who could stand up and make sure the new world was a better place for everyone.

"Okay. Does anyone have anything else they want to add?" I asked, focusing back on the table of people looking at me expectantly. I was happy we'd covered a lot, really quickly and excited about the ideas. Once I updated her, I knew Maia would agree with everything, as would her pack.

"I have one tiny thing," Sadie said. "We've always operated via a handful of comms devices held by our most trusted members. Sam and Maia's gramps built them in secret and he never made any more. But I now have the blueprints for them, as well as instructions on how to scale them for bigger projects. It was in a pack Constance left me, but I only just received it. She said they weren't to be used until we took down Maven. It was too risky otherwise."

I drew in a sharp breath, along with the rest of the table. "That will change everything," I said in a hushed voice.

"Yeah. Our only problem is, we no longer have the expertise to understand them. Matt and Anders think Max and Nick working together are our best shot at building more and getting the scaling right for bigger projects. If we can figure it out, and simplify it, it's one more thing we can teach people at the Palace."

Nick looked stunned. I wasn't sure he was even breathing.

"Can you guys do it, Nick?" Ava asked, leaning over and touching him to anchor him. The rest of their pack reached out to him, too.

Nick nodded, and he started drumming his fingers on the table rapidly as his brain went into overdrive. "We couldn't figure it out without taking one of them apart, but we didn't want to risk that because we only had one device and the badly scaled model at the Palace. Having blueprints changes everything. Would you be willing to help us build the new prototypes River? You're good with mechanics and seeing synergies with things. We could set up a workshop at the new house. It's away from everyone and we'd be able to keep what we're doing quieter."

Ryder laughed. "You just activated Riv's geek mode."

"Absolutely," River said, ignoring his twin. He'd sat forward, and he looked excited by the chance to work on a new project. "I've never had any training in this sort of thing, but if I can help, I will."

"None of us have," Nick said. "This is completely new."

"If we can start producing more devices, it will help open the world back up," Ryder added, more serious now. "I imagine it's going to take time, though, and we don't want to make the first people we hand them out to a target. Maven wasn't the only risk. Since the Crash, people could just as easily fall prey to their neighbors."

Everyone was quiet for a moment.

"There's a lot to unpack here," I said, thinking it through. "I think we need Nick, River, and Max to get eyes on the blueprints and make sure you can do it before we get too far ahead of ourselves. I don't doubt you guys, but Ryder's right. It's going to take time so we can't put all our hopes on it. People need help now."

"I agree with Lexie," Sadie said. "I'll get Gus to bring the blueprints to you when he comes to pick up the explosives. Then we'll go from there when we know more."

We'd found the explosives that had been attached to Winson's detonator the night we freed the town. He'd been trying to blow up their food supplies in the storage room Pala and I had found, to create a diversion and so the townsfolk couldn't have them. We'd dismantled his bomb, but we weren't comfortable keeping explosives on the farm with so many kids around. The Network were going to take them and store them safely.

"Anything else?" I asked, as everyone went quiet again.

"There's another thing I think we need to discuss," Cary said. His frown was still there, but he straightened his shoulders as he met everyone's eyes. "If we do everything we just talked about, we need to make it clear that we respect omegas and we will defend their rights if necessary. It needs to underpin everything we do from here on out. Other omegas may want to look for their mates now that they're free. We'll need safe spaces for them to do that, and I think the Palace could be that, too. Kind of like a gateway to the sanctuary. There's no better way to destroy the history of the Omega Palace than to give it a makeover and turn it into the complete opposite. A place where omegas have all the power."

Ava and I both nodded, and I noticed Ava grab Cary's hand. He'd always seemed so protective of the omegas around him. He was their champion, but he wasn't operating in the shadows anymore. I knew he would fight to make this happen. As would Ava and I. Maia, too.

"That. Exactly that. I want to see it happen, Cary, and I'll help in any way I can," Emma said. It seemed she'd finally found her voice, which meant we'd already started on the right path. It made me smile.

"Once it's filled with families, it's going to feel a lot different," Ava said quietly. "I don't think the omegas from the Palace will have a problem coming back then."

"I'll back you in any way you need to see that happen," Sadie added, with a quiet note of respect in her voice. "A safe place for omegas to go when they want to venture out into the world is something I've been thinking about as well. Especially for the ones that have been hiding for a long time. I'll talk to them about it, but I think they'll be happy with that."

"I think safe spaces for omegas is something we will all support, and as alphas, we need to hold other alphas accountable. It's the only way we'll get genuine change, because omegas have never been the problem," Sam said, he looked incredibly grave suddenly. "But we need to be realistic in the short term. Ryder is right. We need to be careful. There's too many people hurting out there and we can't help everyone at once. We won't survive ourselves if we try. It's going to have to be baby steps."

The twins had been out in the world more than any of us, so we listened when they said it was bad out there. Ryder seemed to be an easygoing guy, but his eyes looked haunted at times. I knew Sam, Dio and Pala had seen stuff when the Crash happened that had stayed with them too.

"Ryder and Sam are right," River said, as he looked at his twin. "Things are likely to be unstable for a while. With Maven gone, there's going to be a power vacuum when the world opens back up. We need to watch for who's going to step into it. Some alphas may need convincing about the new status quo. The Network will need to step up, and they'll need us to back them up."

"The Network is mostly made up of older retired betas," Sadie said. "They'll help, but while their minds are willing, their bodies aren't. You read Constance's letter, Sam. It was her hope for you, Sam, knowing that you were a prime alpha, that you'd help fill that role and work alongside me."

"It would be an honor," Sam said simply, and I couldn't have been more proud of him.

"I'm with you," Wolf growled. He'd been quiet until now, happily listening and watching. "If prime alphas are needed, I'll back you up, Sam. I want a better world for Angel."

"Thank you, Wolf," Sam said. "If we need to become enforcers to keep omegas safe and alphas in line, so be it. We have three prime alphas at this farm right now who would step up and fight that battle if needed. For our sons and daughters, those that are here and the ones who aren't born yet."

I knew Damon well enough to know Sam spoke the truth. He would be right back in the mix of things if the world needed the power of our prime alphas again. No matter what, with this family we'd found surrounding us, and walking alongside us, we were going to be okay. We'd make sure our new world was okay, too. We had the power to do it.

"Four prime alphas," Ghost said quietly, and everyone jumped to their feet. He came in through the kitchen door, munching on a carrot like a cat with a stolen prize. He didn't have his skeleton mask or hood on today, though.

"What the hell? How did you get in here unnoticed?" Sam growled. He took a step forward until I put a hand on his arm.

"I noticed," Wolf said quietly. "I sensed his arrival a few minutes ago, but he had no ill intent."

"He's an ally," I said to Sam. "Calm down."

"Allies still need to knock on the front door," Sam growled.

Ghost shrugged and winked at Sam. "Maybe you guys should stop leaving the door open."

I burst out laughing. I liked the cocky prime alpha. As far as I was concerned, by adding himself to the list, he'd marked his place in this village. Like a handprint in wet cement.

"What can we do for you, Ghost?" Dio asked, as he walked over and shook Ghost's hand. Smoothing things over with his gorgeous smile, as he always did.

"I'm looking for Sadie," he answered with a friendly, answering smile.

We turned as one and looked at the comms device on the table.

"Sorry, Sadie's not here right now. Please leave a message after the tone," came the sassy reply from the device.

I couldn't help the grin that split my face. This was going to be fun.

Epilogue
Maia - one month later

"Are you ready?" Lexie said, as she stood with her hands over my eyes.

"Yes, let me see already," I groaned, as I reached around to poke Lexie, but she shifted out of my way.

I'd started vomiting about a month ago, and while I wasn't as bad as those first few days, I'd been nauseous on and off ever since. Standing with my eyes closed was making me a little woozy.

Ava, Lexie, Ryder, and Pala had accompanied my pack into town to check out the new medical exam room Damon had pulled together. He'd taken over the old clinic in town. Sirena had met us here, too. She'd moved to the Palace with Isabella and I missed them both. So I was glad she was here.

Damon had lured a doctor to come live here with the offer of shelter, food, and protection for his family. It was going to double as a birthing suite for me and any other mums in the area. It would save us hiking up the mountain to get to the doctor living up there. He'd already made a few special trips down for me, but it wasn't a long-term solution.

"Okay, here goes," Lexie said, excitement lacing her voice. I wasn't sure what she was so excited about. I'd seen the room when we'd dropped off the ultrasound machine Damon had scavenged. It had been painted all white, with white tiles on the floor too. There'd been some other basic equipment in the room and a mattress on an old stainless steel gurney. The room had given me chills, and not in a good way.

When she pulled her hands away, I blinked rapidly before my mouth fell open.

"What the hell?" Was the first thing that slipped out of my mouth. It sounded ungracious, even to my ears, but I was genuinely shocked.

The only thing in the room that was the same were the practical tiles on the floor. Someone had painted the walls and ceiling the bright blue of a summer sky. They'd then painted white clouds floating up above and big tall flowers on long stalks around the room. There was a new hospital bed, too, and a bright blue wooden screen on wheels with the same flowers printed on it. When I stepped forward and looked behind it, the equipment had been hidden back there on rolling trolleys.

I looked at Lexie and Damon. Lexie looked nervous suddenly, but Damon could feel me in our bond, and he had a smile on his face.

"What do you think?" Lexie asked.

I burst into tears. Huge, happy, wet tears. Before I ran to them and pulled both of them into a hug. The rest of my mates and our friends piled in around us.

Lexie's eyes were huge in her face, and she still looked worried.

"Don't worry, she's happy," Damon said, as he elbowed her.

"Really? Because we can change it if you don't like anything," Lexie asked.

"I love it," I said, my emotions spilling over. My hormones were already making me feel erratic on a good day. "Is this what you've both been disappearing to do?"

I knew they'd both been mysteriously absconding over the last week. But I'd been pushing myself to still help around the farm every day, despite my guys' protests. It had left me too tired to wonder more than vaguely what they were up to.

"Yeah, we saw your face when you were here the last time. We knew you'd never say, but we figured it looked too similar to the lab they kept you in at the Palace, with the white walls and equipment," Lexie said. "So we changed it."

They'd done more than that. They'd realized a fear of mine and taken it away without me having to say a word. I loved them both for it. I knew

Sirena had also had the labs at the Palace gutted, and those spaces were used for food storage now.

"Thanks, Sis," I said to Lexie. Now she looked as if she was about to cry.

"And thank you, Damon. You didn't need to go to so much trouble."

"It was no trouble," he growled, glaring at me. "I need to know we have all the equipment we could need if something goes wrong, but I want you to be comfortable when you bring our baby into the world. I want it to feel special for you and you can't feel that if the room is giving you flashbacks."

It was typical Damon, taking care of everyone, even when they didn't know they needed it.

"Sirena helped, too. She found the painting supplies and met us here to get it done," Lexie said. Always making sure people were acknowledged for their work.

I smiled at her and repeated the words I'd said to Lexie, "Thanks, Sis." It wasn't something we'd openly called each other yet. We were still feeling our way through getting to know each other. But it was something we were both working on, and both wanted. She seemed choked up and just nodded her head.

The room wasn't the only thing that was bothering me lately, though. Damon narrowed his eyes at me, then jerked his head towards my friends.

"We've got a few things to set up. Why don't you go have a catch-up with Sirena at the pub while we get things sorted?"

"What thing—" Hunter started to say, but he shut up when Damon elbowed him. "Oh yeah, the things."

Lexie looked at me with concern, as did Ava and Sirena. I shook my head at my mates. But Damon was right in giving me a nudge. I needed some girl time. I knew I had a habit of doing things on my own and not asking for help. But I had a village now.

"Let's go," I said with a reassuring smile at them.

The pub didn't have alcohol anymore, but it was a familiar space and people naturally gathered there when they wanted some company. Or when new people first arrived in town. We'd given them a kinetic energy device, so they'd have power. Whenever people had leftover food that was going to spoil, or they were feeling generous, they dropped it off there. The pub owner distributed it to anyone who needed it. We had a few crates of fruit and vegetables in the truck for him. The guys would bring them in before we left.

We were the only ones in the pub right now. The pub owner had brought us some cold glasses of water with lemon slices in it and put on some background music for us. It was nice. It was the sort of thing I'd missed out on doing in my life. Going to the pub with some friends. Only my drink was a yellowy brown color, instead of clear.

"Um, thank you. But, what's this?" I asked him. My guys would kill me if I drank something, not knowing what it was.

"Homemade ginger tea," he said, looking a little nervous. "I heard you were coming into town today and you'd been suffering morning sickness. I put the word out to see if anyone had any ginger. A few people brought some in. I made a bottle for you to take home, too, and bagged up the extra ginger. There's enough there to last a few months, and you can plant more from it if it helps, although it takes about ten months to mature enough to harvest."

I was shocked. GG had mentioned ginger would help, but we didn't grow it at the farm and the guys hadn't been able to find any when doing supply runs. "That's so sweet, thank you. Tell the others thank you, too."

"It's the least we can do. Your packs have been so good to this town. Even before the Crash, you helped a lot of people around here," he flicked his eyes to Lexie. "Anything you guys need, just ask."

Lexie leaned over and took a sip, like my own personal taste tester. "Oh, that's actually yum."

"I added some lemon and honey for flavor. It's my wife's recipe. She used to swear by it when she was pregnant. I found the recipe in her old cook book and copied it for you. But you can use whatever works for you," he said.

I got up and hugged him. Merely thanking him didn't seem quite enough. He gave me a quick hug and backed away, eyeing the door. "It's all good, lass. Feel better."

"Thanks," I called out as he retreated, embarrassed.

I took a long sip of the cool ginger tea, and Lexie was right. It was yummy. The sweetness offset the bitter ginger.

"So what's going on?" Lexie asked as soon as I put my glass down.

"I'm scared," I blurted.

"About what?" Ava asked quietly, reaching out and squeezing my hand briefly. Her eyes bounced away quickly, then zoomed back to me. I knew she was talking to Wolf in her head, she always glanced away when she did it. Not many people noticed, but I did. He'd probably checked in when he felt her getting worried all of a sudden. I hoped I'd have a connection to Damon like that one day.

"Is it about giving birth?" Sirena asked when I didn't add more.

"No. I'm worried about being a good mom," I said, feeling embarrassed. The actual birth didn't worry me, I'd faced enough pain in my life to know I could take it. It was the rest of it. The stuff that came afterward.

"Oh, Maia, you're going to be an amazing mom," Lexie said, jumping right in.

I fiddled with my glass, not meeting their eyes. "Am I? I mean, I didn't have a great example growing up and I'm worried I'm going to mess this up. Facing down a raging alpha, that I can do no problem, but this has got me spooked. I didn't think motherhood was in the cards for me, with the fertility rate so low and living in hiding. Even when I got to the Palace, I honestly thought I'd never make it out of there alive. I was so happy when I found out I was pregnant, but as soon as I started getting sick, I started worrying about the baby. Then it kind of spiraled, I guess."

"You should have come talked to us sooner. Or to the guys, at least," Sirena said.

"I know. I already talked to the guys, and they said this baby was all of our responsibility, not just mine, and we'd figure it out together. They're right, I *know* that, but there's this niggling worry in the back of my mind I can't seem to banish."

"I get it. I never had a mother and I think it's a big part of me not feeling ready. But Ava had a good example, and she'd never let either of us mess it up. And look at Sirena. Her mother was crappy from what I've gathered." She paused and looked at Sirena, who nodded with a wry grin. "Yet, Sirena's a natural. You've seen her with the orphaned kids. Who needs a mom as a positive role model when you've got Ava and Sirena? They'll have your back. Not that you're going to need it."

"I get it. I'm scared too, and I had a great mom," Ava said quietly.

"But you're terrific with Angel," Sirena said.

Ava scrunched her nose, and I noticed Lexie narrowing her eyes.

"It's time, fess up," Lexie said to Ava.

My mouth fell open, suddenly seeing what was right in front of me. "You're pregnant?"

"Uh, huh," I pulled her half out of her chair to hug her and she laughed.

"Why didn't you say, and why does Lexie know and not me?"

Ava shook her head as she looked across the table at a grinning Lexie. "I didn't tell Lexie, but nobody can keep anything from her. She sees too much. I wasn't trying to hide it, though. We just didn't want to tell Angel until she'd settled in. We wanted her to be the focus for a while."

"That makes sense. Transitioning into a new family can be tough. There's a lot of unexpected emotions," Sirena said, nodding her head.

I let Ava go so she could breathe. I was so excited for her. Sirena was right, Ava was a natural with Angel. She needed a whole brood of kids. "So, why are you scared?" I asked her, feeling curious.

"Maybe scared isn't the right word. I'm nervous, maybe? I think it's normal. It's a big thing to be totally responsible for a life. Angel is school aged already. I've never even held a baby. But knowing we're going to be doing it together makes me feel better. I just keep picturing our little ones running around the farms the way I used to with the twins, getting up to mischief. Plus, we've also got GG, and River and Ryder's mom. She's dying to mother you, if you'll let her."

I shook my head and took a deep breath, not wanting to cry again already. Picturing our kids running around our two farms together had me welling up. "That actually makes me feel better, knowing we'll be doing it together."

Ava reached out and grabbed my hand again, and I held on tight this time. The same way I'd done when we'd found ourselves alone in the library at the Palace. She was my quiet rock, always sharing her strength.

"I think the exhaustion from the constant nausea is wearing you down," Lexie said gently. "We know you're a badass. You don't need to do every job around the farm yourself."

Lexie had focused on working with Sirena, Isabella, and Sadie, in setting up the new operations at the Palace, as well as the new work we were doing with the town. So I had taken over a lot of what she and Isabella had done around the farm. It was where I wanted to be. My overdoing it had been stressing everyone out, though. I knew that. "I just really want to be part of the community on the farm. The guys are always so hands on, I don't want to be seen as some protected princess."

Ava laughed. "I think it's pretty clear you've never been that."

"Yeah, everybody on the farm loves you as much as we do," Lexie said. "They appreciate you wanting to help, but maybe you can focus on one thing, or find some stuff for you to do sitting down for a while. At least until your nausea settles. Being exhausted isn't good for you or the baby."

I nodded, feeling so much better. "Thanks Lexie. I'll pull back a little, but only for a bit, until I feel better."

"Don't make me come sit on you," she said, and I laughed. Because I knew she'd do it.

"You know what your biggest problem will be? Getting your guys to stop spoiling the baby and put the little rugrat down," Sirena added with a grin, teasing me out of my mood. It made me laugh.

"Our rugrat will never even know what the ground is," Hunter said as he came up behind me and kissed the top of my head. He looked relieved when I looked up at him and smiled.

Damon, Leif, and Ryder were close on his heels, bringing in crates for the publican. Pala and Max followed behind. "You ready to go?" Hunter asked.

"Yup," I nodded. My stomach was actually feeling better, too. I thanked the pub owner again, as he handed over a box with the ginger tea and extras to Damon.

I gave the girls massive hugs goodbye. Lexie and Pala were driving back with us, but Ava, Ryder, and Sirena were going their own ways.

"You got this, Sis," Sirena whispered to me, before she let me go.

Sirena was so different from the persona she'd worn most of her life. Her armor still went up sometimes, especially when she felt threatened. But we all did that. Meeting Isabella had been wonderful for her. She was such a calming influence. They both looked so happy together, even with their rapidly growing family.

When we got back to our house, Leif plopped down onto the sunken couch and tapped his lap. I didn't need to be asked twice. I snuggled up into my giant teddy bear and felt my whole body relax. The guys had only finished building the new extension upstairs yesterday, with the nest for us and the nursery next to it. So it was finally quiet. I loved the new space, though.

I smoothed the frown lines between Leif's eyes with my finger. I knew the guys were worried about me, especially considering I'd lost some weight over the last few weeks.

"Do you need anything?" Max asked me, hovering.

"Maybe something to eat? That ginger tea settled my stomach really well." It was the first time I hadn't felt nauseous in weeks.

Max beamed and dashed off to the kitchen. They'd taken to stashing some food here so they could tempt me whenever I felt like I could keep something down. He was back with an apple he'd lovingly cut up for me. "Eat this for now. I'm going to run up to the kitchen and make you a sandwich."

He was out the door before I could stop him. Leif just chuckled as he fed me a piece of apple. "Let him do it. We've all been worried, sunshine."

Damon sat down next to us, and took off my shoes to rub my feet, as Hunter brought over another cup of the delicious tea. "I'll make you some more tonight. I'm pretty sure we have some lemons and honey left. If not, we'll find more."

I smiled at them, grateful to have such loving mates. Not to mention amazing friends, a few new sisters, and an entire community surrounding us. I could be strong when I needed to be. I'd proved that. But it was nice not needing to be. I had people willing to share the load now. I'd forgotten that for a moment, but I knew they'd gently remind me whenever I needed it again.

"You're going to put the baby down at some point, right?" I asked them, knowing how much they loved carrying me around on the rare occasion I let them. Especially Leif.

"Nah," Leif said with a cheeky grin. "Walking's overrated."

Epilogue
Ava – one year later

"Stop hogging the popcorn," Lexie laughed as she snatched the bowl from where Maia was resting it on her lap.

"But Lexie, I'm hungry," Maia whined and fake pouted when she unsuccessfully tried to snatch the bowl back from Lexie.

"That doesn't work on me, babe," Lexie said. I could see her trying not to smile, though. "I'm not one of your mates."

"Fine," Maia shrugged with a cheeky grin. "It was worth a try."

"Do you want some popcorn, Ava?" Lexie asked me, trying to bypass Maia and pass me the bowl. I laughed as Maia whacked her on the arm, making Lexie spill some of her precious popcorn. She picked it off her sweater and threw it at Maia, who happily caught it and ate it. I still loved the dynamic between those two. They ribbed each other a lot, like the sisters we'd become, yet there was a lot of love there. They had so much more spirit than I did, but I loved to sit and watch them interact and eventually get dragged into their shenanigans. I still didn't know what had made them adopt me into their inner circle initially, but I was eternally grateful they did. We were family now.

I tucked my feet up under me as my attention went back to the private show that was being enacted in my tree-lined yard, just for us. The reason for the popcorn.

Max was leading Leif, Hunter, Wolf, Cary, Pala, Sam, and Dio through an advanced yoga session. The guys had really taken to it, and the energy of the group yoga had proven great at helping Sam calm and channel his temper. He was much less volatile and more in tune with himself now.

Wolf had helped too. They'd talked a lot about Wolf's wildness and how he embraced it. Sam had gradually let go of his fear of becoming feral and settled into himself. His dominance no longer leaked all over the place, now that he wasn't fighting it. The more time they spent together, the more cohesive a unit they became. They'd barely known each other as a group when we'd battled Maven, yet they'd been formidable. They were a powerhouse now. A brotherhood. Their trust in each other ran deep.

We still got along with Sadie and her pack, too, but we didn't see them as much now that the Palace was up and running as a learning center. Emma, Isabella, and Sirena were running it together now, with help from Cary. While a few other omegas had moved there, most had stayed in the sanctuary for now. Between running the Network and the Sanctuary, life kept Sadie pretty busy. Sam and Lexie saw her the most, because they dealt with the Network stuff as our liaisons.

We could be intimidating for other people, though, when we ventured outside our compounds. The people in town and the Palace were used to us, but elsewhere we got a lot of nervous looks if we all traveled together. So we tried to do it in smaller groups, unless we needed everyone. I remember the day an alpha had surprised Maia and me while our guys were in another room, while visiting a potential new ally. He'd tried to bark at Maia. She'd slapped him on the nose like a naughty puppy, before pointing her finger in his face and saying, "No. Bad boy." I'd yanked on Wolf's power and barked right back at him. His shock as his body had frozen had turned to terror as Damon and Wolf had come charging into the room. The memory made me smile. Poor little alpha.

I fanned myself as I watched Wolf and Cary now. They kept sneaking glances at each other, too. They had removed their shirts in the sunshine and a light sheen of sweat coated their muscled bodies. It was a sight to behold. The guys had invited us to join in. Max had even promised to adapt his vigorous routine for us, but we'd declined. We were perfectly happy enjoying the show and having some well-deserved time out.

"Ugh. We need to ban the girls from watching us," Dio called out playfully to Max. "Your yoga routine is hard enough without a hard-on."

I glanced at Maia and Lexie. Their mates had them as transfixed as mine did, and our scents were flaring. We sniggered, knowing our horniness was filtering through our bonds.

As I watched my mates, I wished River and Ryder were back and Nick would come outside. I was loving having girl time, but I'd gone almost an hour without a cuddle. I needed contact with one of my mates to settle me.

Nick was in his tech room. He had so much equipment now the room rivaled Max's. The guys had scavenged a lot of equipment from abandoned public buildings for him over the last year. He also had a shed we'd built where he and River made kinetic energy devices. After figuring out how the blueprints worked, we'd set up a production facility in town that grew bigger every month. The Palace was also teaching people with existing technical know-how, how to build them. We'd hoped just to hand out instructions, but it had turned out to be too difficult for the average person, and a little dangerous. He and River still made custom pieces here, though, for bigger, more complicated projects. Max often helped, too. Nick was working on the plans for one right now.

"*You okay?*" Wolf asked me in the bond.

I heard Nick moving through the house towards me, as if I'd called out to him. No matter how much the guys had worked with him, he found it impossible to be stealthy.

"Yeah," I answered. "*Do not break that warrior pose. It's really doing it for me. Nick's coming.*"

I felt his chuckle vibrate through me.

"You need a hug?" Nick asked, looking hopeful, as he popped his head out the door. The guys still couldn't talk in my head the way Wolf could, but our bond had gotten stronger to the point we could send more specific emotions or needs.

"Yeah. I do," I said. He darted over to me, and I hopped up out of my chair so he could sit down and I promptly settled myself in his lap. As soon as he had his arms around me, I felt better. Maia's book said it was normal for packs to be touchy feely in the first few years after bonding. I hoped the feeling never faded. I loved how much they needed it as much as I did.

Damon immediately stomped up the stairs, his face full of thunder and the scent of lightning trailing in his wake. We'd banished him to sit under a tree with Bear so we could chat. Not that he'd sat. He'd been standing guard and glaring at the trees surrounding us as if he expected them to pounce on us at any second. I couldn't wait to see what he'd be like when he had a giggling toddler determined to escape his clutches.

"If Nick's allowed to be up here, so am I," he growled.

"Calm your farm, daddy," Lexie said as she promptly vacated her spot with a grin so Damon could snuggle up with Maia. Bear curled up at Lexie's feet as she settled into another chair. He immediately started purring and Maia's whole body softened against him. It helped him relax, too. He was more chill than he used to be, but he always got growly when his daughter was out of sight.

"The kids will be back soon," I reassured him, and he nodded at me, but his frown remained.

Right on time, Helen and Alexander came around the bend in an electric golf cart. We'd scavenged a bunch of carts from an upmarket golf course we'd come across and used them to get around. Each grandparent was wearing a sling with a baby snuggled in it. Angel was strapped into the back seat.

Damon shifted Maia aside and was up and off the deck before they'd even come to a stop. Maia just laughed, not at all put out to be dumped.

"Sorry, Maia," he called out over his shoulder when he realized what he'd done. She just waved him off. He grabbed baby Frankie out of the sling as soon as Alexander got out with her, and brought her up to the deck to snuggle back up with her and Maia. Frankie fluttered her baby-blue eyes open, but promptly closed them again when she spotted her dad. She happily went right back to sleep, knowing she was safe, as Damon nuzzled her and cooed nonsense to her. He was an amazing father. All our guys were.

I loved the name they'd chosen, a unisex variation of Frank, Maia's beloved gramps. She'd made her peace with knowing he'd adopted her and Sam when his omega died. Sam hadn't quite gotten there yet, having a different relationship with the man who was a brilliant enigma to the rest of us. But we wouldn't be here today without the decades of work he and Constance put into the Network. It had brought us all together, and Sam acknowledged that.

Helen brought Lucas up to me, while Alexander got Angel out of her seatbelt. Angel came flying up the stairs after her baby brother. He had her absolutely besotted, which was incredibly sweet. She snuggled up next to us and stroked his chubby cheek lightly while he slept, as Nick brushed her hair away from her face lovingly. He'd put it in a braid for her this morning, but it had gotten messy and some had fallen out. Lucas stirred and grabbed Angel's finger. He was a heavy sleeper, but he always knew when Angel was close. He loved her just as much. They were inseparable.

We'd named Lucas after my Uncle Luke. Maia and I had both wanted to use family names for our babies, to connect them to our histories. We'd both lost so much in the Crash, and in our lives, it felt like an important part of us to keep.

"Stay for a bit," I said to Helen, and she agreed. She and Alexander had not only embraced our pack, but all three packs. They'd spent so long apart from River and Ryder, they'd been overjoyed to have them back. When they'd learned that many of us were parentless, they'd swooped in. They were now ecstatic to be grandparents, and treated Frankie as much as their own, as Lucas and Angel.

They'd claimed they wanted to give Maia and me a break for an hour this morning, and I'm sure they did, but I knew they also wanted time with the grandkids. We were lucky. Our kids would never want for love in the way many of our pack had. Between our three packs, Helen, Alexander, and GG, we sometimes had to fight for a cuddle. We had no need for prams because there were always so many people around wanting to carry them. We needed more kids to keep everyone busy.

Nick's hand unconsciously slid down and rubbed over my belly, and Lexie narrowed her eyes at me with that sixth sense she always had. She was becoming too much like GG, or maybe just enough like GG. There were worse people to grow into. GG liked to pop up unexpectedly at our house. I'd walk into the kitchen and find her baking with Angel, or we'd open the door in the morning and find a knitted present on the porch for one of us, but I didn't mind. She had an open invitation, and she was never intrusive.

I just smiled at Lexie, and she winked at me. She wouldn't out me until I was ready. I wasn't hiding my pregnancy, but I wanted to tell Angel first and my scent had only just changed. An unexpected heat had hit me a week ago. It seemed my body liked to spring them on me. My guys had been ecstatic. Especially Wolf. He'd been enthusiastic in his attempts to breed me, again.

A wistful expression crossed Lexie's face as she watched us, though. She'd been overjoyed to find out her birth control implant had held up through the two heats she'd had, about six months apart, but I wondered if that had changed. She'd been a force to be reckoned with over the last year, getting people onside with our vision for the world and making the impossible happen. Maia and I, and even Sadie, had just followed in her wake. In complete awe of her.

Sadie was also pregnant at the moment, but she hadn't let it slow her down at all. Much like Maia and I hadn't. It turned out all omegas needed to be incredibly fertile was a true mate, or four, and a heat. No genetic manipulations or barking required.

"You all make it look so easy," Lexie said to me. "You and Maia have gotten so much done while pregnant and now carrying around babies. It hasn't slowed Sadie down, either. You've helped set up this farm and the Palace, taught sessions there, helped with the town trading hub, and held the hands of the returning omegas. You amaze me."

I shook my head. "Helped, being the key word there. We couldn't have done any of it without you leading the way, Lexie. You're our captain."

She'd inspired so many of the omegas coming back into the world. Not just us. And she'd powered through every obstacle in their way to help them.

"What she said," Maia added, with a head nod in my direction and a wink at Lexie.

"Women were giving birth in fields, and getting on with their lives, for a long time before modern conveniences came along," Helen said. She had a gentle expression on her face as she watched Lexie. I knew she'd find her later and talk to her about whatever was on her mind.

"I guess," Lexie said, looking thoughtful. I noticed Sam, Dio, and Pala pause in their stretches and turn to watch her carefully, but she was oblivious to all our attention for the moment.

"Plus, we've had a lot of help," I said, reaching out and giving Helen's hand a squeeze. She'd propped herself on the edge of a chair next to me.

It was one benefit of pack life. Our guys treasured us and were always willing to share the load. I'd only ever had to wince and one mate was drawing a bath while another gave me a foot rub. Yet, Helen had also been a big help to me. We'd spent a lot of time around the farm together, and she'd talked a lot about my mother and uncle. It had helped ease my grief. It was still there, but it no longer hit me like a raw punch when I wasn't expecting it. I could remember them now, and smile at Helen's stories.

The guys finished up their cool down routine and headed up onto the deck. Sam picked Lexie up and popped her back onto his lap. She stroked his chest lightly, not seeming to mind that he was sweaty.

"Do you want to stay for lunch?" I asked.

"Thank you, but we'll head off," Maia said, as she grinned at Damon, who nodded.

"Us too," Lexie said, eyeing off the bare chests of Pala and Dio. I figured I knew how they'd all be spending their Sunday afternoon.

"We'll head off too. We'll go take over from River and Ryder so they can enjoy some downtime," Helen said to me with a wink, and I blushed. River and Ryder were checking fences after one had gone down in high winds last night. I figured it wasn't anything to worry about, or Nick wouldn't be out here with us. He'd be back in the security office.

"Tell Hunter we're on for chess tomorrow night," Wolf said to Damon. Wolf and Hunter had made it a priority to spend time together after we'd moved next door, and they'd bonded over board games, of all things. They both loved them. Hunter was currently teaching Wolf how to play chess. But Hungry, Hungry Hippos was their favorite. I think they were reliving the childhoods they'd missed out on together. Hunter and Dave hadn't come today because they were running a training session for Dave's expanded cadet program. The guys took turns going into town twice a week with Dave to teach a group of teenagers self defense and close combat skills.

"Will do," Damon answered, as they quickly got themselves sorted and headed down the steps towards their own golf carts.

"Bye, love you," Maia called out to me, as she climbed right onto Max's lap in the golf cart rather than finding her own seat. Damon and Leif trailed after them, waving at us distractedly as they crowded in, too. Damon had Frankie securely strapped to him in the sling.

"Love you too," I called back.

Lexie, Pala, Sam, and Dio hopped in the cart behind theirs, followed by River's parents, and in seconds, they were gone.

I eyed Wolf, who had leaned against the railing to wipe himself down with a damp towel he'd grabbed from inside. We had hot water but we were always mindful of wasting it.

"Not going to shower?" I asked him.

"No," he said, as he looked at me with heat in his eyes. "I want to take a bath with you and Cary later."

I groaned and buried my face in Nick's neck.

"You've been ogling them both for an hour and getting everyone riled up in the bond. Did you really think there wouldn't be repercussions?" Nick asked, forgetting Angel was sitting next to us. He covered his grin with a hand as I dug my elbow into him.

"I have no problem with a bath," I said. "Later just sounds too far away."

"What's happening later?" Cary asked, as he came back outside with a damp towel as well. Nick just laughed at me as I groaned again.

"Wolf and Ava are having a bath with you," Angel piped up.

"Lucky me," Cary said with a matching grin.

"I'm going to have one with Lucas so I can splash him the way he likes," Angel added, and I smiled down at her.

Wolf took pity on me and pulled a lavender button-up shirt on, but left it open at the front. He'd changed out of his sweatpants and thrown a pair of pale blue jeans on when I wasn't looking. The total effect was ridiculously sexy and didn't help at all.

The guys had found a specialist menswear store for alphas on one of their supply runs that no-one had ransacked. It had a range of bigger sizes and we'd taken Wolf back. He'd never picked out his own clothes before and he'd put on a whole fashion show for us, trying to figure out what he liked. It turned out pastel colors were his thing. He'd also taken a shine to the jewelry and now sported a bunch of braided leather bracelets.

Even the pale pink nail polish he was sporting failed to ruin the effect. It was courtesy of a manicure from Angel. Lexie had given her a rare bottle as a treat and shown her how to use it. I smiled at the memory.

Cary picked up Maia's discarded popcorn and started munching on it, waving Angel over. She went willingly, climbing up into his lap. She still followed the treats. We knew it was because she'd been denied them when she was young. So we rarely denied her now. There weren't enough treats floating around in this new world for it to be an issue. Wolf joined them, and we sat in companionable silence for a few minutes. Nick absentmindedly stroked my belly again as he stared down at Lucas, completely enraptured with our son, and it made me glow inside.

I looked out to the forest, loving how peaceful it was here. It was getting better out in the world, but traveling, or even existing really, still wasn't without risk.

There was still suffering, but not on the scale it could have been. There was a lot of respect for the Network now, and they had stepped in to resolve a lot of disputes in local communities. Some alphas had objected to a group of betas wielding so much influence and had tried to throw their weight around. Mostly those from the upper echelons of our old society. The ones who had not only lost their wealth, but their power and influence, too. Our prime alphas stepped in, though, including Ghost, and we quickly stamped out any attempted alpha uprisings.

Other packs had sprung up as well. Most without prime alphas, but a few more of those had turned up, too. It amazed me how quickly it had happened, and how easily most people accepted the change in status for omegas. Nobody seemed to care or object. Packs could now meet omegas open to courting at the Omega Palace. It was heavily supervised, but the omegas had all the power. A few omegas had even found their packs already.

We'd even had a few omegas flee forced matings and turn up at the Palace, seeking the Sanctuary. Sadie had taken them all in, and provided protection, backed by our packs. It was humbling that the Palace, the place omegas had hid from, was where they now ran for help. Cary had been right. Turning the Palace into a beacon of hope had helped dismantle everything it had previously embodied.

I didn't know what was going to happen in the future, but for now, what we were doing was working. Not always, but enough of the time for things to balance out.

A crunch of tires had me looking up as River and Ryder came around the bend in the golf cart their parents had been using. I jumped up, passed Lucas to Wolf as he held his arms out, and launched myself at them as soon as they got out.

"Everything okay?" I asked, as they wrapped me up in a twin sandwich.

"Everything is great now," Ryder said as he breathed in my scent, and his body relaxed into me.

"Everything is better when you're with us, little bird," River added.

Yeah. I felt the same.

Want to know more about Sadie and her growing pack? Knot Your Present is currently available as a novella in the Knotty Holiday Nights anthology. It shares the story of how Sadie, Matt, Anders, and Oliver came together while stuck in her cabin in the mountains during the snowstorm. It's a side-story in the pack origins world.

Author Stuff

Thanks for visiting the Pack Origins world. I hope you enjoyed reading Knot Your Possession as much as I loved writing it. If you liked the story, please, please, please consider giving it a review (cue shameless author begging). I'm a new writer, and this is my first series, so I need your help to get the word out. If you're shy, even a star rating helps.

Would you like a **free bonus scene** for the first book in the series, Knot Your Princess? Do you want to find out what went on when Damon and the guys were renovating the cabin? Or read about Damon letting his beast out to play a little more, and two of Maia's fantasies getting fulfilled?

If so, subscribe to my newsletter through my website at www.laclyne.com. I promise not to spam you, I'm busy writing so I'll only be sending out newsletters every other month or so, when I have something to tell about upcoming books.

If you're keen to find out how I see characters and settings in my head, check out my Pinterestmood boards. I have a mood board for all the books in the Pack Origins series, including Sadie's novella.

You can also stalk me on Facebook and Instagram, or join the private Facebook group L.A. Clyne's Tribe. The tribe is where I plan on giving sneak peaks into the next books, and will happily chat about spoilers, books, and share home library porn. Anyone looking for a reading tribe is welcome.

Acknowledgements

A huge thank you to Cassandra, Nadine, Carla, and Tracy, my incredible beta readers. This series would not have been the same without you. Those aren't just empty words. Every suggestion you made, and all your insights, made this book so much better. I hope you enjoy the final version. It's got your fingerprints all over it.

I also need to thank all the family and friends who have supported my during this crazy ride to becoming an author, Pete, Lachlan, Angus, Amber, Mum, Dad, Adam, Eve, Sienna, Catherine, Donna, Kerry, Monica, and Lyndall, you all mean so much to me.

Want to read more of the Pack Origins series?

Knotty Holiday Nights – An omegaverse holiday anthology
Knot Your Present – A pack origins novella
Out Until 10 Feb 2024
When a snowstorm hits, and three mysterious alphas turn up at Sadie's mountain hideout, heat ensues.

Knot Your Princess – Pack Origins Book 1
Out Now
Maia's story begins with the start of the Crash, when she escapes the Omega Palace. She's happy to save herself, but is looking for a place to belong. She takes refuge on a farm that is more than it appears to be.

Knot Your Problem – Pack Origins Book 2
Out Now
All it takes is one moment, one breath, and everything changes for Lexie. Yet she won't take threats to her safe haven lightly. She's willing to cause all kinds of trouble to keep the people she loves safe.

You can find out more by visiting my website at www.laclyne.com. You can also head to my author page or the series page on Amazon.

Printed in France by Amazon
Brétigny-sur-Orge, FR